THIS BOOK SHOULD BE RETURNED ON OR BEFORE THE LATEST
DATE SHOWN TO THE LIBRARY FROM WHICH IT WAS BORROWED

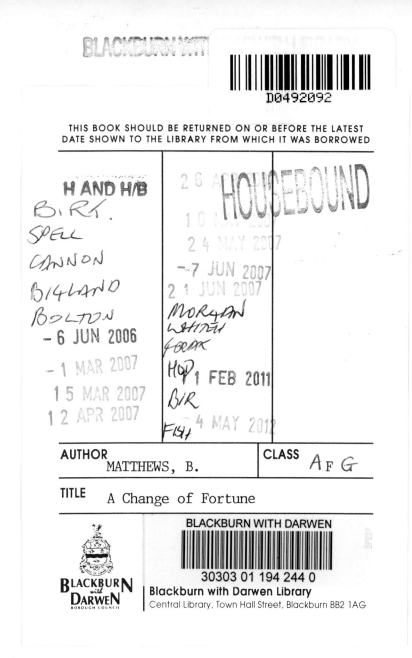

H AND H/B

Bi.R.f.
SPELL
CANNON
BIGLAND
BOLTON
- 6 JUN 2006
- 1 MAR 2007
15 MAR 2007
12 APR 2007

26
10
24 MAY 2007
-7 JUN 2007
21 JUN 2007
MORGAN
WHITEY
CROAK
HOP 1 FEB 2011
BIR
FISH 4 MAY 2012

HOUSEBOUND

AUTHOR MATTHEWS, B.	CLASS A F G

TITLE   A Change of Fortune

A CHANGE OF FORTUNE

Can a girl hide from her destiny?

Eugenie Winford is devastated when her beloved father commits suicide, having lost his fortune in the Wall Street Crash, leaving Eugenie and her proud spoilt mother ruined. Eugenie changes her name and becomes a housemaid for the Stannard family – anything is better than what her mother has planned for her. When her identity is revealed she flees again and finds a poor but good family in Lambeth, but she is being pursued both by her greedy, manipulative blood family and by the son of the kindly Stannards. Who will find her first?

A CHANGE OF FORTUNE

A CHANGE OF FORTUNE

by

Beryl Matthews

Magna Large Print Books
Long Preston, North Yorkshire,
BD23 4ND, England.

British Library Cataloguing in Publication Data.

Matthews, Beryl
    A change of fortune.

    A catalogue record of this book is
    available from the British Library

    ISBN   0-7505-2446-4

First published in Great Britain in 2004 by Penguin Books

Copyright © Beryl Matthews, 2004

Cover illustration © Richard Jones by arrangement with
Artist Partners Ltd.

The moral right of the author has been asserted

Published in Large Print 2005 by arrangement with
Penguin Books Ltd.

Magna Large Print is an imprint of Library Magna Books Ltd.

Printed and bound in Great Britain by
T.J. (International) Ltd., Cornwall, PL28 8RW

194244

1

November 1929

It was a beautiful crisp day with hardly a cloud in the sky. Eugenie Elizabeth Winford glanced up from the essay she was attempting to write about her namesake: Eugénie de Montijo, French empress from Spain and the consort of Napoleon III. Worry gnawed at her, destroying her concentration. Why had her parents made her stay here during the entire summer holiday? Surely she could have gone home for a week or two. It had been her sixteenth birthday on 28 August, and her father usually made a point of being home at that time each year, but in July the head, Miss Patterson-Hay, had told her that she was to remain at school. No reason had been given. You were discouraged from asking questions and had to accept what your elders told you. She found the edict frustrating and had the utmost difficulty in holding her tongue. One brief explanation would have saved her weeks of wondering and worry. Even her father's last letter had been unusually short: all he'd said was that he was very sorry but would come as soon as he could. His business was in America, so she understood that he couldn't always be here.

Her smile was wistful. Perhaps he would take her to the seaside again. They always had such fun together visiting museums, old houses and churches, walking along country lanes and stopping for tea in quaint village tea rooms.

She gazed out of the window and watched the gold and red leaves floating down to form a colourful carpet beneath the ancient oak trees. The Templeton School for Young Ladies was a lovely place, set in the heart of the Kent countryside. She was happy here, but after weeks spent in this tranquil setting Eugenie found the thought of London exciting, and she longed to see her father again.

'Miss Winford,' Miss Staples said sharply, 'that's quite enough daydreaming.'

Eugenie put her head down and tried to marshal her thoughts, chewing the end of her pen in concentration. The classroom was silent except for the scratch of nibs as the pupils set about their allotted task. When was it the empress had died? What was it the history book said? She tried to picture the words on the pages she'd been reading yesterday... Ah, yes, she remembered now. After Napoleon III was overthrown and captured in 1870, his empress fled to England and died at Farnborough.

After putting in the final full stop, she grimaced at the page. Miss Staples wasn't going to be very impressed with this effort. It was too short, and even the fact that she'd made her writing larger and spread the words out to cover more space couldn't disguise the puny effort. Well, it would just have to do; she really couldn't think of anything else to say. Now, if they'd asked her to write about the Pankhursts, then she would have had plenty to say. She admired the way they had

8

fought, and even been imprisoned for their passionate belief that women should be given the vote. Last year the voting age had been lowered to twenty-one, and that had been a tremendous achievement for all those women who had struggled for so many years.

A quick look at the clock on the wall told her that there was still nearly an hour of the lesson left, so she put her head down as if working on her essay and returned to her musing.

Would she be able to go home for Christmas? How she hoped so. The lovely house they had in Russell Square was always so festive, with a huge brightly decorated tree and crackling wood fires burning in the grates. Her mother made a great show, trying to outdo her friends. That was important to Elizabeth Winford: the social round and making an impression seemed to be the only things driving her mother's life. Her daughter came very low on her list of priorities. Eugenie accepted that. She really didn't know her mother all that well, as she'd had a nurse from the time she'd been born and then off to boarding school at the age of six. Her father loved her, though, and she adored him. He was from New York and still spent most of the year there. She didn't know much about his business, but Cyrus D. Winford was obviously a wealthy man. She had asked him many times to explain his work, but she found it hard to understand. It was all very confusing. Still, she'd ask him again when he came home. He was very patient.

'Miss Winford.' Miss Staples was standing beside her. 'You are to go to see Miss Patterson-

Hay at once.'

The head's office was up a flight of stairs, at the end of a long corridor lined with portraits of past dignitaries who had either run the school or made some important mark in life. Eugenie was sure she'd never be one of them! She was bright enough but not academically brilliant. Not that that mattered too much at this school. The girls were taught all the social graces – how to run a large household, make polite conversation and generally fit into the upper echelons of society. She walked briskly, for it was not the done thing to keep Miss Patterson-Hay waiting. When she issued a command, it had to be obeyed with alacrity.

On reaching the door, she paused to catch her breath, wondering what on earth she had done now. It wasn't unusual for her to be hauled in front of the head for some misdemeanour, but she couldn't think what this urgent summons was for. To be taken away from a lesson – something quite unheard of – was worrying.

She knocked firmly and waited.

'Come.'

Turning the ornate brass doorknob, Eugenie stepped inside the room.

'Ah, Eugenie.' Miss Patterson-Hay studied her carefully for a moment and then sighed. 'Sit down.'

What? Now she really was worried. The girls were never called by their Christian names at the school, and certainly *never* told to sit in the presence of this lofty personage. She obeyed by perching nervously on the edge of the delicate regency chair, hands clasped in her lap.

'You are to return home immediately. Pack a small bag. The maid will see to your trunk, and it will be sent on later.' The head looked at her with something very close to sadness in her eyes.

Eugenie was alarmed. 'But why, Miss Patterson-Hay? Am I not coming back? Have I done something wrong? Am I being expelled?'

Miss Patterson-Hay held up her hand to stop her. 'You are not being expelled. Your family have sent for you. That is all I can tell you. Your father's chauffeur is waiting outside the main entrance for you.'

Forgetting her manners, Eugenie rushed to the window. The Rolls-Royce was parked on the sweeping driveway, with Edwards standing beside it.

'You have been a bright student, if somewhat wilful at times, Eugenie, and we shall be sorry to lose you.' The severe lady actually smiled. 'Apart from the academic studies, we have tried to teach you self-discipline and strength of character. Those qualities will stand you in good stead in the future.'

Her senses were reeling as she focused on the woman behind the desk. One thing was clear: she wouldn't be coming back here, and that was upsetting. The thought of leaving her friends... She fought back the emotion that was trying to burst out, along with a torrent of questions. Now she was sixteen she'd known that she would have to leave soon and maybe go to a finishing school. Her mother was extremely old-fashioned in her outlook. But not walk out like this – not like this!

11

'May I have the time to see my friends?'

'You must leave immediately. You may write to them. Goodbye, Miss Winford.' The dismissal was abrupt, as if the head wanted to be rid of this unpleasant task.

'Goodbye.' Eugenie's voice shook and she left the room quickly, before she made a fool of herself. Self-control was a prized quality in this school and much encouraged. She closed the solid oak door behind her and ran. Tears clouded her vision, but she didn't need to see where she was going: she'd attended this school for the last five years and knew every inch of the building. Although she'd wanted to go home for a visit, leaving Templeton was not something she'd thought of doing for a while yet. The regime was strict, but she had been happy here. A gulping sob escaped as she ran. *What was going on?*

After packing a few necessities, she hurried to the waiting car.

'Ah, there you are, miss.' Without smiling Edwards took her bag and held open the rear door of the car. When she scrambled in, he closed it and put her bag in the boot. The trunk, her father always called it in his lovely American accent. Had her father come home unexpectedly and sent for her? But no, he'd have come for her himself if that had been the case. Her insides were turning somersaults with anxiety.

Edwards got in, started the car and drove slowly down the long oak-lined drive. Her throat closed with distress as she swivelled round and gazed at the beautiful limestone mansion until it disappeared from sight.

'What's happened?' she asked the silent driver, turning round to face the back of his head as they left the school gates. He was usually quite talkative, but today he'd hardly uttered a word.

'Can't say, miss.' He closed the glass partition, making further conversation impossible.

There was nothing for it but to wait until she arrived home, and she felt like crying in frustration. Why all the secrecy? She was so bewildered that it was impossible to stop all manner of disasters running through her fertile mind. Yet she couldn't come up with one reason that could wrench her so abruptly out of the school. Fifteen minutes ago she had been struggling with an essay... She wiped away a tear as it trickled down her cheek. She'd never know what Miss Staples thought of it now.

There was a strange hush about the house when Eugenie rushed into the drawing room. As soon as she saw the scene, she knew that some great disaster had befallen them. Her mother was prostrate on the couch, moaning, with her personal maid, Gladys, trying to comfort her. As Eugenie rushed to her mother, she was stopped as someone caught her arm in a fierce grip.

'Leave her!'

Eugenie looked into the harsh face of her mother's sister: her Aunt Gertrude. How she disliked this woman. She was sharp, unkind and never had a good word to say about her father. Wrenching free, she knelt in front of her mother. 'Where's Papa?' She used that term of address because it always made him laugh.

Aunt Gertrude hauled her to her feet. 'He's dead. Lost all his money and shot himself, the coward.'

Eugenie almost fainted as the callous announcement stunned her. She held on to the back of a chair to steady herself. The word that raged through her mind was not one Miss Patterson-Hay would have approved of. The bitch! The lying bitch!

'Don't look so shocked. I always knew he would end up in trouble.' Aunt Gertrude's expression was smug.

Incensed, Eugenie lashed out at the considerable bulk of her aunt. 'He wouldn't do that!'

'Well, he has,' her aunt sneered, 'but at least he had the decency to do it in America. That saves us the expense of a funeral.'

A red mist gathered in front of Eugenie's eyes and she launched herself at the taunting woman but was caught from behind and lifted off her feet by the only man in the room. And if she disliked her aunt, she loathed him. He was supposed to be a good friend of the family, but she knew that her father had never liked him. And she tried to stay out of his way, because he was always trying to touch her. She kicked back with her foot and caught his shin, making him grunt in pain. He dropped her and laughed. He actually laughed.

She spun round to face him, fists clenched ready for a fight. 'You're lying! How could he lose all his money? And if he did, he wouldn't kill himself. He isn't a coward! He isn't!'

'Your aunt's right.' He still had a smirk on his

14

florid face. 'Your father lost all his money in the stock-market crash last month and didn't have the guts to face the consequences.'

A loud moan came from her mother, who hadn't opened her eyes or bothered to acknowledge her daughter's arrival.

The fight drained out of Eugenie. It must be true. She was finding it hard to accept. Her dear father was so kind, with a ready smile and soft rolling American accent. Her mother had hated it and tried to make him sound more English, but she'd loved it. She wouldn't have cared if they didn't have money. They'd have managed somehow. He shouldn't have left her. How could you leave someone you love? He had loved her, hadn't he? He had been the only one in her life who had shown he cared for her. Her mother's one interest was in attaining a high position and moving in the right circles. Her Aunt Gertrude couldn't stand the sight of her niece ... and what the blazes was Albert Greaves doing here? He wasn't family.

'Now that you've calmed down, perhaps we can sort out this unholy mess,' her aunt snapped. 'We have only three days before the bank confiscates the house and its entire contents.'

There was a strangled scream from her mother and Gertrude glanced over her shoulder. 'Be quiet, Elizabeth!' She turned her attention back to the girl standing in front of her. 'At least you've got more fire than either of your parents. Your mother will be coming to live with me. I will not, however, be burdened with you as well. Albert will take you in.'

Eugenie ground her teeth but remained silent.

15

They could forget that plan right away, for nothing on this earth would make her move into *his* house.

'How old are you now?' her aunt demanded.

'Sixteen.'

'Damn. That's a bit too young, Albert. It will cause gossip. You'll have to wait at least a year before marrying her.'

'That's all right, Gerti, she can still live with me.'

Eugenie's stomach heaved as her gaze swept from one to the other in disbelief. She was in the middle of a terrible nightmare. *Marry him?* He was at least fifty, bloated from too much food and drink – and she'd never liked the way he looked at her.

'Of course she can. You can get your sister to look after her.'

Her aunt appeared satisfied with the arrangement as Eugenie fought back the bile. What they were planning for her – without her consent – was too dreadful to contemplate.

'Splendid, that's you settled, then, Eugenie. You'll still live in luxury, for Albert is wealthy. That ridiculous school you've been attending has made you unfit for any other kind of life.'

'Mother!' She rushed over to the couch. 'You must pull yourself together. You can't let this happen.' She whispered, not wishing to let the others hear her pleading so desperately. They were arranging her life as if she had no say in the matter! But she did. It was nearly 1930, for heaven's sake, and she was old enough to make her own decisions. Her father would never have allowed this to happen. The pain that thought

16

caused was almost unbearable. But he wasn't here any more.

Mrs Winford moaned and pushed her away. 'Do as you are told.'

It was clear there wasn't going to be any help from her mother; she was too distraught to think straight, and anyway, she was well aware that her mother had no great affection for her. She didn't know why, because, as far as she knew, she'd never done anything to upset her mother.

Eugenie was shaking so badly it was difficult to stand up. With sheer determination she found the strength from the anger now raging through her. So her aunt thought she wasn't fit for anything but a life of ease. Well, she was wrong about that! All her life she'd had a determined nature, and if she wanted to learn something or to do something differently, then she never allowed herself to be beaten until the task had been mastered. She would do anything – except marry that odious man!

'You're wasting your time appealing to your mother.' Aunt Gertrude had a look of contempt on her face for her sister. 'She's lost the only thing in life she cared about. Money.'

'I want to know what happened!' Eugenie stubbornly stood her ground. 'How could father lose all his money?'

Albert Greaves stood in front of her with a sneer on his face. 'Your father was one of the elite brokers, a member of Wall Street. He was always so sure of his position and wealth, but the crash wiped him out.'

'I always told him what he was doing was too

risky, but he wouldn't listen to me.' Aunt Gertrude looked superior. 'He should have invested some of his money in property and gold like all sensible people, but he gambled and lost. You're lucky to have someone like Albert to take you in because you're now destitute, Eugenie. You'll be moving out of here in three days. Go to your room and start packing. You may remove only your personal things from this house. Everything else has to remain.'

Eugenie ran from the room, anxious to get away. She needed time to think. Once in her own bedroom she flung herself on to the bed and allowed her grief and fear to overflow. She would mourn her father in private, and then she must decide what to do. One thing was certain, though: she would not go to that horrible man.

There was so much to grieve for: the loss of her father, her home, her school and her friends. She sobbed freely and remembered the game they played in the dormitory at lights-out with the aid of a torch. There were four of them: Alice, Paula, Mary and herself. They drew a circle on a large sheet of cardboard and divided it into four sections, one for each of them, then they had spun a coin and if it fell tails up in your space, you had to do a forfeit. They'd got up to all sorts of innocent things, like creeping up to the head's door and leaving finger marks on the highly polished brass handle, or squeezing through a window at night to bring back a flower or leaf. Leaving the dorm at night was strictly forbidden, and they'd had great fun carrying out the forfeits.

She dried her tears and sat up, hugging her

18

knees. The coin had spun into her space and fallen as tails. Everything stable and secure in her life had been forfeit. She was so frightened!

2

An hour later Eugenie was still sitting in the same position, no nearer to deciding what to do and fearful for her future. If only she were a few years older it might be easier, but at sixteen she was still considered a child by her family and society in general. She stood up and turned round to face the mirror. She was quite tall and could probably pass for nineteen – well, seventeen at least – but what could she do? Her aunt was right about one thing: as lovely as the school had been, it had taught nothing that might be useful in the outside world. You had money if you attended the Templeton School, so you were expected to move in the circles of the wealthy. But she no longer belonged to that section of society. She'd better start trying to sort herself out, because there were only three days and she would have to decide quickly.

She washed her face and combed her long dark hair, all the time fighting to clear her mind. If she panicked, she would end up with that dreadful man. She couldn't let that happen.

The tears welled up again, but she brushed them away. She had to think. Her father was dead, and, painful though it was, that was something she had to accept. They were also penniless.

Her mother was too upset to help, and that left Aunt Gertrude, their only relative, in charge. Her aunt was, with obvious reluctance, going to take her sister in and give her a home, but she'd never had any time for Eugenie. That left Albert Greaves. Because he was immensely rich, her aunt and mother had always fawned over him, but there was something about him that made her stomach churn when she was near him.

She began to pace the room, anger rising once again through her distress. How dare they give her to him! Oh, Father, she cried silently, I loved you so much. How could you kill yourself? I wouldn't have minded if we didn't have money. You were so clever – you would soon have found some way to earn a living. You could have taken me to America to live with you. I wouldn't have been any trouble. I would have helped and looked after you. I loved you so much. I don't understand why you did this!

Her fists clenched and hammered on the dressing table, making the array of trinkets and boxes jump up and down. They were all presents from her father. Every time he'd arrived from America he'd brought her a gift. He would hug her and laugh at her delight in the small piece of jewellery or fancy box. He'd been such a gentle man, in sharp contrast to her cold mother.

She caught her breath. He must have relatives in New York. Perhaps she could go there. She'd always begged him to take her with him, and he'd promised he would when she was older...

Rushing down the stairs, she found the drawing room empty. 'Jessop,' she called.

The butler appeared at once. 'Yes, Miss Winford?'

'Where is everyone?'

'Mrs Osborne and her guest have left.' The butler always showed his dislike of Albert Greaves in small ways by never calling him by name. 'Your mother has retired.'

'Thank you.' She sped upstairs, knocked on her mother's bedroom door and entered the room.

Her mother was propped up in bed, only opening her eyes as her daughter entered. It was like stepping back into an earlier period. The huge four-poster bed was swathed in rose-coloured floating silk curtains that could be pulled around to hide the occupant of the bed. They were pulled right back now, though, so that anyone coming in could have full view of the distressed woman. Playing for sympathy, Eugenie thought uncharitably. The rest of the room was just as hideous, crammed with ornate furniture, which now all belonged to the bank.

'Go away, Eugenie.' She lifted the smelling salts to her nose and moaned.

Something inside Eugenie snapped. She didn't believe her mother had loved her husband. 'We have to talk, Mother. I will not go to live with that awful man – and I refuse to marry him. The whole arrangement is cruel and distasteful.'

Mrs Winford opened her eyes wide at this defiance. 'You will do as you are told, my girl. At least you'll have a future. Your father has left me with nothing! *Nothing!*' She slumped back against the pillows and moaned. 'Oh, the disgrace.'

This was hard to believe. All her mother seemed

21

to be concerned about was her own personal loss of position. 'Mother,' she snapped, 'Father must have relatives in America. Why can't I go there?'

Mrs Winford sat up then, glaring at her daughter. 'He had a mistress and two boys by her, and they certainly won't want you. Had the nerve to call herself Mrs Winford! I'll bet the beast hasn't left *them* penniless!'

The shock nearly knocked Eugenie off her feet as the room swam before her eyes. She was learning new things about her father. It was hard to believe this was the same person she'd adored. 'You knew? Didn't you mind?'

'Of course I didn't. I refused to have any more children after you; this other woman kept him out of my bed.'

'You only wanted his money.' It wasn't a question but something that Eugenie had long suspected. She'd never heard her mother speak so openly, but they'd had biology lessons at school and she knew what her mother was talking about. They'd also learnt about sex from the gossip of other girls. Some of them seemed remarkably well informed, Eugenie remembered.

'What else do you think I married him for?' Mrs Winford's expression was as hard as her sister Gertrude's. 'I did my duty having one child. I wasn't prepared to have another squalling baby.'

The last illusion that she held about her parents' marriage shattered. She knew her mother had engaged a nurse as soon as Eugenie had been born, so when had she ever had to get up in the night to deal with a crying baby? Their marriage had obviously been a sham. No wonder her father had spent so little time in this country. The visits and gifts had been for appearances only. All respect she'd had for her mother drained away. Although she was shocked by what she'd just heard, the love she had for her father couldn't be destroyed.

She turned slowly and walked out of the room, knowing that she was going to have to grow up quickly. She was on her own. Time to find out more details if possible, and the people who would know were the staff. They were, after all, about to lose their jobs and would have been told the reason.

The talk stopped immediately when she walked into the kitchen, and the warmth and smell of freshly baked bread wrapped itself around her like a blanket. It was so comforting, so normal. Her bottom lip trembled as she came close to losing control again. She mustn't do that. There was so little time.

'Come in, miss,' the cook, Mrs Dobson, urged. 'We're so sad to hear about your poor father.'

Eugenie breathed in deeply, wiped a hand across her eyes and said, 'Do you know what really happened? I didn't understand what I was told.'

'Ah, Gerry's your man.' Mrs Dobson sent the kitchen maid to fetch him. 'He's got a good head on him. Understands these things, he does.'

Gerry, the footman, arrived almost immediately. He was a tall man, around twenty-two, quite good-looking, with large intelligent blue eyes.

'Tell Miss Winford what's happened in America.' The cook made a fresh pot of tea as all but the scullery maid sat around the large well-scrubbed table.

Eugenie gazed at them with troubled eyes. Here were the butler, gardener, cook, chauffeur and footman. How must they be feeling at this moment? 'I'm sorry you've all lost your jobs.'

'Don't you worry about us. There're jobs around for good staff.' The cook patted her hand and pushed a plate of freshly baked apple tarts towards her. 'Now, you ask your questions and we'll tell you what we know.'

'What was so bad that my father' – she gulped – 'felt he couldn't go on living?'

'It's like this, miss.' Gerry pitched in with the explanation. 'There's a place in New York called the Wall Street stock exchange. It's where shares in businesses are traded. On 29 October the prices on the stock market collapsed completely. Many people have lost fortunes, including Mr Winford.' The footman gave her a sympathetic look. 'Some have lost everything, and your father is not the only one to have committed suicide.'

'But if that's happening in America, why are we losing our house?' Eugenie was confused; she didn't understand this talk about shares. Her father had tried so hard to explain it to her, but to her mind it just didn't seem to make sense. All they seemed to do was deal with numbers on bits of paper. Tickertape, her father had explained.

'The effects of such a disaster will be felt everywhere. Mr Winford must have had great debts. Everyone's panicking and the banks will take what's owed them any way they can.'

She gazed at the young man in wonder. 'You are very knowledgeable – why are you working as a footman?'

Gerry shrugged. 'It was the only job I could get. I don't intend to stay a servant all my life, though.'

'I suppose you'll be living with Mrs Osborne when the house goes.' Mrs Dobson's look was inquiring.

'I expect so.' Eugenie didn't know why she'd lied. They obviously didn't know about the plan to eventually marry her off to Albert Greaves, so she'd keep that bit of news to herself. Gossip was rife among servants, and she didn't want them talking about this when they took up new places. She stood up. 'Thank you for explaining. I hope you all soon find employment.'

'All the best for the future, miss.' The butler smiled and held the door open for her.

By the time she had reached her bedroom and closed the door behind her, Eugenie had made up her mind. There really was only one thing she could do, and that was to find a job. It would have to be something with accommodation, and she had only three days.

The panic sweeping through her was so over-whelming that she leant against the wall and sank down until she was sitting on the red Persian carpet. Even if she could find something in such a short time, what could she do that would put a roof over her head and food in her stomach? What skills or talents did she have? Very few was the honest answer. She'd been taught how to arrange flowers, set a table for a dinner party, how a meal should be served...

She leapt to her feet. Of course she didn't have

any business skills, but she could go into service. What was it Gerry had said? He was a footman because that was the only job he could get. If she could find a place in a large household, it would be a start. Perhaps a governess?

The sight of herself in the mirror, still wearing the light grey and maroon school uniform, was enough to convince her that she was too young. They would want someone more mature. However, she was fired up with the idea now. It would be a solution to her immediate problem and would keep her away from that awful man. Even scrubbing floors would be better than that!

Eugenie had always had a methodical mind – everything in its place, and a place for everything – so she began to lay her plans. It wasn't going to be easy, she knew that, but all she had to do if she became discouraged was to think of Albert Greaves. That would stiffen anyone's resolve.

She was going to have to make herself look like a servant. Holding her long hair up and away from her face made her look plainer and a little older, so it would have to be cut short. She would need different clothes and that would take money – something she didn't have. Her aunt had said that nothing could be removed from the house; she would have to sell her own things. How she longed to have someone she could go to for help, but this had to be kept a secret. When she walked out of the house in three days' time – and she was determined to do that – no one must know what she was doing or where she was going otherwise her aunt would find her. And however hard her life was going to be, that mustn't happen.

Tremors rippled through her as she thought of what she was planning to do. If she failed, years of belonging to that man faced her; if she succeeded, a life of what? Drudgery, hard work and loneliness, but that would be preferable to the alternative. Her mother didn't care what happened to her and would be glad to be rid of her. It was a bitter realization, and something she had shied away from admitting before.

The boom of the dinner gong made her jump. A quick glance at the clock on her mantelshelf told her that it was eight thirty. She hadn't even noticed it getting dark; she'd been preoccupied with her planning. Her mother would be cross about her still being in her school uniform, but there wasn't time to change now. To arrive late was an even greater crime.

She quickly straightened the grey woollen stockings, made sure the sensible lace-up shoes were clean, put on the maroon jacket and hurried down the stairs just as the second gong sounded. The last thing she felt like doing was eating; yet she must make the effort.

The dining room was empty expect for the butler. 'Mrs Winford will be dining in her room,' he informed her solemnly, while holding out her chair at the long table set for only one.

'If I'd known I would have done the same and saved you from going to all this trouble for me.'

'It's no trouble, miss.'

She sat down and made a pretence of eating, as each course was set before her. She was hurting too much, and it was an effort even to swallow. To lose her father was a terrible disaster; to find that

27

they were penniless and that she was expected to go to Greaves was terrifying. The tears gathered again and she stared down at her plate, not knowing or caring what was on it. If she put too much inside her, it would refuse to stay there.

At the end of the meal she said, 'Please apologize to Mrs Dobson for me. The meal was excellent, as always, but I'm not at all hungry.'

'Cook will understand.' He poured her a cup of coffee.

'Do you have somewhere to go when you leave here?' she asked.

'Mrs Dobson and myself have already obtained new places with Lord and Lady Buckheart. They have a fine house in Surrey, and we're looking forward to working in the country for a change.'

'Oh, that's wonderful.' She really was pleased for them. 'What about the others?'

'They all have interviews within the next two days. I expect they will soon be suited.' He lifted his head proudly. 'Superior servants are always in demand.'

'Er...' She hesitated for only a moment as she schooled her expression and tone of voice to sound casual. 'How do you go about finding domestic work?'

'There are advertisements in the newspapers and a very good agency in Tottenham Court Road. And' – he allowed himself a small smile – 'word gets around.' She returned the smile and stood up, relieved to have found out where to start on her quest for a job. She would visit this place as soon as possible.

After returning to her room the next couple of

hours were spent in trying to create a new identity. Her hair was cut with a small pair of scissors from her workbox – not an easy job to do herself. It was passable when finished and did make her look a little older. Short hair was all the rage now, so it was unlikely to be commented on. A rummage through her wardrobe showed that even her oldest clothes were too good. She'd heard about pawnbrokers' shops where they gave you money for almost anything. She'd take some things to one of them in the morning, and also see if she could buy more suitable working clothes from there. Then she collected together all the pieces of jewellery and the trinkets her father had brought back from America for her. They would have to go as well. It was no good being sentimental about them; the past had to be put behind her.

The final part of her plan was her name. The girls at school had called her Jenny. That would be more suitable than Eugenie. Her surname would have to be changed as well; otherwise her aunt would be able to find her too easily. What could she call herself? Something ordinary like Baker? Yes, that would do. The other thing she would have to watch carefully would be her accent. The polished speech taught at the Templeton School for Young Ladies would have to go.

It was nearly midnight when she finally settled down to sleep. The tears soaked the pillow, and then, as exhaustion overcame her, the new Jenny Baker slept.

3

The only people moving around the next morning were the servants. The housekeeper, Mrs Charlton – who Jenny had never liked – was holding a list in her hand and pointing out what could be packed and removed from the house. There was very little on the list, and it was obvious that the bank was claiming almost the entire contents.

Breakfast had been prepared and Jenny forced herself to eat, although it was an effort. There was a tense day ahead of her and she would need all of her strength. She was so anxious that her insides churned most alarmingly, making her hesitate before swallowing a mouthful of scrambled egg in case she was sick.

After about fifteen minutes she gave up, leaving a plate of crumbs where she'd crushed the toast in agitation. After casting an apologetic glance at the butler, she opened the door and nearly bumped into the housekeeper.

'Ah, Miss Winford, I shall ask one of the maids to help you pack.'

'There's no need for that. I won't be taking much.' The last thing she wanted was someone looking over her shoulder as she sorted out what to take with her.

Mrs Charlton looked doubtful. 'You must remove only your own personal belongings. I shall be checking the room to make sure you haven't taken anything that doesn't belong to you.'

Jenny bristled at her tone. 'I'm not a thief, Mrs Charlton!'

She turned and ran up to her room, closing the door with a satisfying thump. That woman had always had a snooty air about her. It was clear she was enjoying seeing the Winfords' downfall. Wandering over to the window, she gazed out at the garden, now dressed in the last of the autumn shades as it prepared for the long winter ahead. A dry sob shook her slender body. What trials and hardships would this winter hold for her? Did she have the courage to go ahead with the plans she'd made? Would it be wiser to go to live with Albert Greaves for a while in order to give herself more time to plan her escape? But if she did come under his control there might not be a chance to get away in the future. Did she even have a hope of succeeding with this crazy plan of turning herself into a servant?

With hands clenched she spun away from the window. What choice did she have? It was either make a life for herself or go to live with Albert Greaves. No! That was impossible. She hadn't known that he had a sister, but if she was anything like him, Jenny wanted nothing to do with her.

She scrambled on her hands and knees to reach to the back of her wardrobe and, after much tugging, pulled out an old battered suitcase. This would be perfect to take with her when she left. Her father had given her this when she'd been ten. He'd taken her to the seaside for two days: a rare treat and it had been so wonderful. The two had walked along Brighton seafront, explored the shops in the small alleys, and eaten fish and chips out of newspaper.

She ran her hands over the case and wiped a tear away as it splashed on the worn leather. That had been such a wonderful time, and she would always cherish the memory... Jenny shook herself out of her reminiscences. She had to get on. Her mother wouldn't appear today – she'd never been able to face anything unpleasant– and it was a safe bet that she would keep to her room. Aunt Gertrude wouldn't show her face until after lunch. Her plans must be put into action this morning while she had the chance to slip out unnoticed. If Aunt Gertrude discovered what she was doing, then she'd be locked in her room, and her fate would be sealed.

Leaping up, she began to search through her clothes, choosing the plainest and oldest garments. The case was only small and soon full, but there was room for one more item. The dress her father had bought her for her fourteenth birthday. It was most unsuitable, of course, and there wouldn't be an occasion to wear it in the life she was planning for herself, but she had to keep some small memory of the way things had been, and of the father she had loved so much.

After wrapping the white lace and beaded dress in tissue paper, Jenny tucked it underneath her other clothes. Now she had to find a way to raise some money. She would have to try one of those pawnbrokers she'd heard about because she didn't know any other way.

It wouldn't be wise to leave the house with a large package, so, after choosing a couple of good frocks, she tipped out the trinket boxes. There wasn't much jewellery, but it was all gold and must be worth something. There was a bracelet, a heart-shaped locket on a chain, a couple of brooches, and this: she held up a fine gold chain with a small pendant, a diamond surrounded by emeralds. It was the most valuable gift her father had ever given her. After gazing at it for a few moments she made up her mind to keep it and fastened it around her neck, tucking it out of sight under her blouse. It would be wise to keep that as insurance, because she didn't know when she might need money in a hurry.

Gathering everything together, she crammed it into a leather handbag. That could be offered to the pawnbroker as well.

With heart hammering, she crept down the stairs, hoping no one would see her, and slipped out of the front door with a sigh of relief. They'd all been too busy to take any notice of her. Now, where would be the best place to go? Somewhere she wasn't known, she thought, as she hurried towards the bus stop.

A bus was pulling up with the destination LAMBETH on the front. She'd never been there and was sure that none of her family had either. She jumped on and made her way upstairs. All she had in her pocket were two shillings and sixpence, but that would be enough for the moment.

When she got off the bus and started to walk along the high street, Jenny felt as if she was in another world. No tall elegant houses here with smart cars waiting outside for well-dressed passengers. The contrast was startling. There were women towing along scruffy children, and groups of men standing around with cigarettes hanging out of their mouths. The snatches of conversation that drifted her way made her flinch; they cussed freely, and the general air of poverty made her want to cry. How sheltered her life had been.

'Hello, darling.' A tall youth blocked her path as he eyed her from head to toe. 'What you doing down 'ere?'

As frightened as she was, some instinct told her not to show fear and her head came up. 'Minding my own business. Why don't you do the same?' Where the courage came from to utter those words she couldn't imagine.

He tipped his head back and roared. 'Oh, la di da.' He grinned at his friend who had come to join in the fun. 'Did you 'ear that posh voice?'

'Yeah, sounds like one of those bloody blokes on the wireless.'

Every time she moved to get around them they blocked her way. She was breathless with panic, feeling very small, very young and very vulnerable. It had been foolish to answer back.

The tallest of the boys made a grab for her bag, and she swung it behind her back out of his way. She mustn't lose this because it contained everything she owned of value. The other boy made to dart for the bag when a loud voice stopped them both. They turned to look at a burly man coming towards them.

'Leave the kid alone!'

Her first tormentor glared at him. 'We ain't doing no harm, Fred, was just having a bit of fun.'

'Well, bugger off and stop pestering decent people.' Fred watched them with narrowed eyes until they were well down the street; then he turned his attention to Jenny, who was now trembling in reaction. 'You shouldn't be here on your own, miss. Those kids don't mean no 'arm, but they can be frightening if you don't know them.'

'Thank you for helping me, Mr...?'

The man's stern features broke into a smile. 'Just call me Fred. Now, where are you heading?'

She didn't know why, but she felt she could trust him. He might be shabby, but there was something about him. He was about forty-five years old, she guessed. He looked clean, and his pale blue eyes had a glint of kindness in them. 'I'm looking for a pawnbroker's.'

'Ah, well, you've come to the right place, then.' His fierce frown was back again. 'Need money, do you?'

She nodded in embarrassment.

'You'd better do something about your accent, 'cos they'll know you're new to this and take you for a ride.'

'A ride?' Why would they want to do that?'

Fred laughed at her puzzled expression. 'They'll cheat you.'

She blushed at her ignorance, feeling helpless to deal with this terrible crisis in her life. It'd seemed so easy in the comfort of her bedroom, but now all she wanted to do was to run away and hide. It was all too much. She gathered the tattered shreds of her courage around her and said, 'Oh.'

'Hit 'ard times, have you?'

Her eyes clouded and she gulped. 'Yes.'

'What's the trouble, Fred?' A woman of around the same age came up to them.

'Hello, Glad. The Preston boys was pestering this young girl. I sent them off with a flea in their ear.'

Jenny was in a strange land, where they were speaking a different language. Did they have fleas in their ears?

'Good for you. Bloody menace, those kids.' She opened her shopping bag for Fred to see inside. 'Got you a nice pair of almond rocks in the market.'

Jenny gaped as she looked from one to the other. What?

'Oh, you shouldn't 'ave done that, Glad. We can't afford luxuries like that.'

'Luxuries!' The woman shook her head. 'Those you're wearing can't be darned any more, and you know it. I know they're rubbing your poor old plates of meat. They must be damned uncomfortable.'

Jenny knew what darning was. You did that to things with holes in, like stockings or socks. She glanced down at Fred's shoes as realization dawned. Almond rocks – socks. Plates of meat – feet. It rhymed! She giggled, her earlier fear forgotten. She looked back at her companions, so obviously husband and wife.

'Never heard cockney rhyming slang before?' Fred's eyes sparkled.

'No. Are there many words like that?'

'Bless you, ducky,' Glad chuckled, 'you can 'ave a whole conversation with them.'

Jenny giggled again. 'Please don't do that, I'll

never understand a thing you say.'

'So what you doing down here on your own?' Glad studied her intently.

'She's looking for a pawnbroker. In bad need of some money,' Fred explained.

'Ah, then old Uncle Bob's your best bet – 'e's reasonably honest.' Glad frowned at her husband. 'But she can't go to him sounding like that. We'd better do the business for her.'

'Be best. That's if it's all right with you, miss. You'll get a better deal with us there, 'cos we know the crafty old devil.'

'Umm, is he a relative of yours?'

'Gawd 'elp us,' Glad gasped through her laughter. 'We all call him uncle. When anyone says they're going to see uncle, we know they're going to pop something.'

'Pop?' Jenny was becoming more confused by the minute.

'Pawn something,' Fred explained with a twinkle in his eyes. 'You come with us and we'll see you all right.'

Relief swept through Jenny. She'd been dreading doing this on her own and these seemed nice people. 'I really would appreciate it.'

'Come on, then, let's see what we can squeeze out of the mean old sod.' Glad took Jenny's arm and steered her in the right direction.

They'd been walking for only about five minutes when Jenny spotted the three brass balls hanging outside the shop. Once inside she gazed around in wonder. It was dingy and packed to the ceiling with goods of every description. There was a short, rotund man behind the counter,

37

almost bald with a few strands of grey hair smoothed across his shining head.

'Hello, Fred, Glad. What can I do for you today?'

'Not us. It's our young friend here. She's got some things to pawn.' Fred turned his back on the man and whispered in Jenny's ear, 'You leave this to us.'

'Let's see what you've got.' The shopkeeper sounded impatient.

She emptied the contents of her bag on the counter. The man went for the jewellery immediately; a magnifying glass appeared rapidly from his waistcoat pocket and he clamped it to his eye. It seemed to take him ages as he examined each item carefully, uttering only a grunt now and again. Suddenly he looked up, dropping the eyeglass into his hand.

'Where'd you get these things? I ain't taking nothing what's been pinched.'

'Stolen,' Fred muttered for her benefit.

'They're mine!' In her panic Jenny forgot about not speaking. She just had to have some money! She gazed imploringly at Fred and Glad. 'They are mine. Honest!'

Glad patted her arm. 'Don't you take no notice of Uncle, ducky, he's as bent as a four-penny piece. All he's trying to do is get your nice things for as little money as he can.'

Jenny was relieved they were here because it was so difficult to understand these strange ways; if she'd been on her own, she'd have run out of the shop in horror.

'Stop playing games,' Fred growled. 'The kid's

desperate enough to bring her to Lambeth, so what're you going to give her?'

'Two quid for the lot.'

'What?' Jenny was horrified. That wouldn't last her very long. 'But the dresses cost a lot and the jewellery is real gold!'

'I don't have much call for posh frocks round here, and–'

'I'll go somewhere else, then.' She didn't give him a chance to finish speaking and reached out to gather up her precious things. There must be other pawnbrokers around. If she didn't get more than that, her plan to run away would come to nothing. And that frightened her more than this peculiar man standing in front of her.

The pawnbroker slapped his hands over the jewellery before she could remove it from the counter. 'Let's not be 'asty.'

Fred chuckled. 'She's got more savvy than you thought, hasn't she?'

'Another ten bob, that's all I can go to.'

Jenny pushed his grubby hands out of the way and shoved the things back in her bag.

'How much do you want, then?' He had come from behind the counter now, obviously not wanting her to leave.

She could see the look in his eyes and knew he wanted the jewellery. She relaxed a little. 'Five pounds.'

'What?' He mopped his brow in mock distress. 'That's bleeding robbery!'

'Don't foul mouth her,' Glad scolded. 'She ain't used to our rough ways.'

The scruffy man looked her over very carefully,

clearly pricing everything she was wearing. 'What kind of trouble you in?'

These people didn't know her, and if she didn't mention any names ... well, she might get a better price. 'My father lost all his money in the Wall Street crash' – her bottom lip trembled as she whispered –'and he killed himself.'

Glad dragged an old chair from a heap of furniture and made her sit down, standing beside her with her hand on Jenny's shoulder. 'Ah, I'm sorry, ducky.'

Uncle's gaze became calculating. 'You must have lots of nice things at home to sell.'

She shook her head. 'The bank's taking everything. This is all I've got.'

'You must have family who'd look after you, though.' Fred stooped down in front of her.

She looked into his kindly face and felt a single tear trail down her cheek. 'My aunt is going to give my mother a home, but she doesn't want me.'

Glad looked scandalized. 'And what does your ma think about that?'

'She's so upset I don't think she knows what's going on, or cares. They've arranged for me to live with–' She stopped. 'To live with a man and when I'm old enough he's going to marry me.'

'And you don't want to do that?' Glad asked.

'Oh, no, he must be fifty and he's awful,' she wailed in anguish. 'I'm only sixteen...'

'My God!' Fred exploded. 'I didn't know this kind of thing still went on, did you, Glad?'

'Disgraceful the way some of these high-and-mighty people carry on.'

Jenny gazed up at the husband and wife who had befriended her, giving a violent shudder. 'I can't go to him!'

'Of course you can't. Give her the fiver, Uncle, or I'll break your mean old neck.' Fred glowered at the pawnbroker. 'You know the stuff's worth that and more.'

'Throw in the leather bag and it's a deal.' He didn't appear too upset about the agreement.

After she'd handed over the bag with its contents, he counted out four pound notes, a ten shilling note and another ten shillings in small coins. Then he wrote several tickets and handed them over to her as well. She tried to read the scribble on them.

'They're in case you wants to buy anything back,' Glad explained.

'I'll only give you three months, though,' Uncle said hastily. 'If you don't come back by then, I'll sell the goods.'

Jenny doubted she'd ever be able to get them back, and she wasn't sure she would want to. Nevertheless she put the slips and money in her pocket. 'Er ... can I buy a coat and dress from you?'

'What on earth for?' Fred rubbed his chin in puzzlement. 'Them you've got on are real good.'

'They're too good.' Jenny grimaced and felt she ought to explain. 'I've got to get a job quickly and need to look like someone who would seek employment as a servant.'

Fred muttered fiercely under his breath, 'Find her something, Glad.'

It didn't take long to sort out a couple of

garments that fitted her, or almost. The coat was on the big side but Glad assured her she would grow into it. Jenny was staggered by the amount of clothing in the back of the shop. The dress they finally settled on was dark blue, a little faded but in reasonable condition and it looked clean. The coat was navy blue and a bit frayed around the cuffs. Glad said that after a trim up with a pair of scissors no one would notice. After much fierce haggling, Fred managed to get both items for two and sixpence.

Jenny was well pleased and left the shop clutching her parcel of working clothes. That was the first part of her plan completed, though how she would have managed without her new friends was hard to imagine.

There was a café next door, and Glad urged her through the door. 'Let's have a nice cuppa, shall we?'

That would be welcome, Jenny thought. She realized she was shaken by the whole experience in the pawnbroker's, and would like a sit-down before the worry of getting back into the house without being seen. She took some coins out of her pocket. 'You must let me pay.'

Husband and wife both shook their heads. Glad smiled kindly.

'Bless you, my ducky, but we can afford a cup of tea. You're going to need that money by the sound of things. We're used to having a struggle to make ends meet, but you ain't never had to do that, have you?'

'No, but you must let me repay you for helping me.'

'Just saying thanks is enough.' Fred sat opposite her and three mugs of piping hot tea were immediately put in front of them.

'We comes in here whenever we can,' Glad explained. 'The tea's hot and cheap.'

Jenny examined the mug in front of her and was amazed at how thick the china was – it didn't look like any china she'd ever seen. The crockery at home was so thin that you could see the liquid through it.

Fred sipped his tea and studied Jenny over the rim of his mug. 'That there Wall Street crash thing was in America, wasn't it?'

'Yes, my father is ... was American.' She took a drink of her tea and nearly scalded her mouth.

'Well, he must have family,' Glad said. 'Can't you go to them?'

'I don't know any of them ... and my mother said they wouldn't want me anyway.' She looked away and worried her bottom lip, feeling very lonely.

'Dear God!' Fred looked furious. 'We ain't got much, but we'd never see one of our own in want.'

'What you gonna do?' Glad asked.

'I must get a job with accommodation.' Jenny turned her mug round and round in agitation. 'And I've only got another two days to find a place. If I'm lucky, I might be able to find something as a lady's maid. I know what a lady's maid does,' she assured them quickly. 'My mother has one.'

'A servant?' Glad shook her head in disbelief. 'That don't seem right for the likes of you.'

'There isn't any choice. It's either that or go to that horrible man.'

'I can see how you'd not want to do that, but being a servant's hard graft,' Glad told her. 'I know 'cos I've done it. But of course that was some time ago. From what I've heard, things are a bit easier going now. It still won't be easy, though.'

'I'll manage.' Jenny dredged up a smile. It wasn't right to burden these kind people with her problems, but it was such a relief to have someone to talk to about the disaster. When she'd got off the bus, a feeling of loneliness had engulfed her, but having someone to talk to had helped. She was able to give a genuine smile. 'It will be quite an experience.'

Fred whispered to his wife, who nodded. Glad found a scrap of paper in her capacious bag and wrote something down, then handed it to Jenny.

'That's where we live. Now, you keep it safe because if you finds yourself in trouble any time, you're to come to us and we'll give you a roof over your head. We ain't got much, but you'll be welcome.'

As Jenny took the paper from Glad, her hand shook. She was quite overcome by the kindness of these strangers. Fred and Glad were obviously poor in worldly goods, but they had given her the one thing they had in abundance: kindness and understanding, without thought of reward.

4

The morning excursion to Lambeth had taken longer than anticipated, and it was one o'clock before Jenny ran up the stairs to her room. The first thing she did was to put the clothes she'd bought at the pawnbroker's in the old suitcase and place it at the back of her wardrobe again. Then she had to sit down for a moment, because she was trembling with a sense of triumph and fear. What an adventure! The forfeits they'd played at school had been nothing like this. Thank goodness no one had seen her coming back into the house with her bundle of clothes. If her aunt had spotted her, she would certainly have demanded to know what was in the parcel. Then she'd have been in trouble.

She saw her trunk had arrived from the school and the servants had put it at the bottom of her bed. With a sense of urgency bordering on panic, she rushed and knelt in front of it. Her aunt was bound to arrive at any moment, and it was imperative that she believed Jenny was falling in with her plans. She must try to fool her by packing her best clothes in the trunk. This would be left behind, but Aunt Gertrude mustn't have the slightest suspicion that she was intending to run away – if she could, of course. This morning had been a step towards that, but another two days was not enough.

If only she had more time. She was desperate to go out again and find a job, but if she left the house once more today it might arouse suspicion, and she mustn't risk that.

When she opened the lid there was a note from her friends saying, 'Write to us.' She clutched it to her and bowed her head as sorrow flooded through her. That was something she couldn't do, for no one must know where she was going or what she was doing. Secrecy was of the utmost importance. Also trying to keep in touch would only add to the pain. They wouldn't want anything to do with her now, and she would never see them again. They were nice enough girls and had been fun at school, but they were all from very wealthy families and inclined to look down on people not in the same class as their own. A clean break was the only way.

For a moment she remembered the ballroom-dancing lessons they'd had to prepare them for their 'coming out' parties. She had loved the music of the dance bands, and they had all sighed over the lovely crooner Al Bowlly. But none of that would happen now.

Pushing away the unhappiness, Jenny tossed the note on to the bed and began to empty the trunk. The school things wouldn't be needed, so they could be left behind. She piled these in the corner of the room, and, without wasting any more time, she grabbed her good clothes from the wardrobe and shoved them in the trunk, not bothering to fold them properly. It didn't matter if they got creased, because she wouldn't be wearing them again. If her aunt saw that she was

46

packing, she might not watch her too closely over the next couple of days. The trunk was nearly full when the door burst open and her aunt strode in.

'I'm glad to see you're getting on with the packing. Whatever have you done with your hair?' she exploded.

Jenny looked up from her task, her expression carefully schooled to show little emotion. But it was difficult because her heart was fluttering badly. 'I've cut it in the latest style,' she answered innocently, changing the subject quickly. 'I've nearly finished packing, Aunt Gertrude. I'm taking only my best clothes.'

'Your hair was past your waist and I don't think Albert will like it short! Now, where's your jewellery?' Her aunt was pulling open drawers in the dressing table.

'I'm wearing the diamond pendant; everything else is at the bottom of the trunk.' Jenny didn't even blink as she lied, praying that her aunt believed her and wouldn't insist on seeing them. And she wasn't the slightest bit interested in what Greaves thought of her hair!

'It will be safe enough there,' her aunt said briskly. 'None of it is of much value, but you may as well take it with you. As Albert's wife you will have only the finest gems.'

Jenny breathed a silent sigh of relief when she knew she'd got away with the deception. However, she couldn't understand why Greaves wanted someone as young as her, and the question was out of her mouth before she could stop it. 'Why doesn't he marry my mother? She's

47

still quite lovely.'

Aunt Gertrude snorted in disgust. 'He doesn't want a neurotic woman who would refuse to give him an heir. He needs someone young and biddable.' She narrowed her eyes and glared at her niece. 'You *are* going to be biddable, aren't you?'

'Yes, Aunt.' Jenny had been considered quite an actress in the school plays. She used that talent now with a demure downward cast of her eyes. 'He's offering me a home and a secure future. What else could I do?'

'Exactly! I'm relieved to see that one member of the Winford family has some sense.'

The rest of the day was agony for Jenny. She had to endure not only lunch but also dinner alone with her aunt and Albert Greaves. Her mother was still refusing to leave her room. She spoke when she was spoken to and listened with feigned interest as they discussed their plans for her. She even managed a shy smile or two, and wondered if she was overdoing the play-acting, but Greaves seemed highly pleased with her conduct – apart from expressing his disapproval of her short hair and ordering her to grow it again.

It was nine o'clock before she could get away from them, and, after receiving a kiss on the cheek from the repulsive man, she raced up to her room. After shutting the door firmly behind her, she locked it just to be on the safe side, in case they were staying the night. She hoped they weren't, because she was due to move into Greaves's house the day after tomorrow. So little time!

She paced the room, questions and doubts

running through her head. Suppose she couldn't find a job that quickly – what was she to do? She was certain that as soon as she was under Greaves's roof, she would be watched all the time. Her freedom would be gone. She wrapped her arms around her in desperation. A floorboard creaked under her foot and she froze in case her aunt heard her pacing around, but it was difficult to keep still. She must have somewhere to stay – somewhere they wouldn't find her.

Fred and Glad! She scrabbled in her purse and took out the address they'd given her. They'd seemed sincere when they'd told her she could go to them if needed. She chewed her bottom lip. She wouldn't want to bother them, of course, as they could ill afford another mouth to feed. Still, having the address was a comfort but she'd use it only as a last resort. She put it back in a separate compartment of her purse. She mustn't lose that.

Kneeling beside the bed, she bowed her head and prayed as she had never prayed in her life. 'Dear God, give me the strength to do what I have to. And let me find a job tomorrow... I'll take anything – but please help and guide me. Oh, and by the way, Lord, from now on I'm going to be known as Jenny.'

The next morning Jenny was up at seven, before it was light. She had passed a long sleepless night worrying about the day to come. As each minute had dragged by, she'd convinced herself that her plan didn't stand a chance. How was she going to get a job? She didn't have any experience or

49

references. What if an employer looked into her background and found that someone called Jenny Baker didn't exist? In the dark of the small hours it had all seemed hopeless. But she *had* to try.

The dining room was set for breakfast with silver dishes full of hot food on the sideboard, just as normal, but the smell of bacon nearly made her heave. She was relieved no one was around because her eyes were red from crying. The loneliness and fear she felt were awful, but she made a great effort to appear outwardly composed. Whatever the future held for her would have to be faced. She was about to spin the coin again, and fervently hoped it would fall as heads this time.

An hour later she was creeping along the hallway, her hair pinned back to make her look older, wearing one of her own dresses, with the old coat thrown over her arm. She didn't dare to put it on in the house in case she was seen. If that happened, then questions would be asked. Her hand was on the latch of the front door when a voice called from the top of the stairs.

'Eugenie! Where do you think you are going at this unearthly hour?'

Jenny stopped as if she'd walked into a wall. Aunt Gertrude! She turned slowly, holding the coat behind her, and gave what she hoped was an innocent smile. 'I'm going to post a letter to my friends at school,' she lied.

'The servants will do that for you.'

'I'll enjoy the walk, Aunt. We always had a long

walk before breakfast at Templeton.'

'Disgusting habit,' Gertrude snorted. 'Well, if you must, then put on your coat. Albert won't want a sickly house guest.'

'Of course Aunt Gertrude,' she replied meekly. Then she shot out the door, slamming it shut in her haste, and ran down the street, not stopping until she was out of sight of the house. Only then did she pause long enough to put on the coat, as she leant against a wall and waited for her heartbeat to stop pounding in her ears. What a fright! On the rare occasions her aunt had stayed over, she'd never left her bed before noon.

Jenny drew in several gulps of air, welcoming the reviving coldness that filled her lungs, then headed up the road. If her aunt were staying, she'd have to sneak in the servants' entrance when she got back.

A bus for Tottenham Court Road arrived and she ran up the stairs. After paying her fare she gazed out of the window as doubt assailed her again. This was crazy! She was crazy. She had been offered a good home, comfort and security. With head bowed she picked away at the frayed cuff of the coat with shaking fingers. But the price was too high.

Lost in misery, she jumped when the conductor called her stop. After getting off the bus, she stood and stared up and down the long road. Where to start? Jessop had said that the domestic agency was in this road.

By the time she'd walked up one side and started down the other, it was nearly nine thirty. At last she found a notice nailed on to a side door saying that this was Mrs Dearing's Domestic Agency. The door was locked and there was nothing to indicate when it would be open.

She hurried into the haberdashery shop next door to ask the assistant if she knew when Mrs Dearing would be there.

'Any minute now,' she was told. 'She's usually arrived by now.'

'Thank you so much.' Jenny smiled in relief, and then noticed the shop lady studying her with a frown on her face. She left the shop quickly. Her accent didn't go with the tatty coat she was wearing. It was time to act again; she would have to be careful not to slip back into her usual way of speaking. She tried to fix Fred and Glad's voice in her head. She would have to try to sound something like them – without the cockney rhyming slang, of course. There was no way she'd get away with that.

A smartly dressed woman of middle years walked up to the door and put a key in the lock.

'Mrs Dearing?'

'Yes.'

'I'm looking for work. The servants I'm with said you might be able to help.'

'Come in.' She held the door open and walked up a flight of narrow stairs.

The room at the top was small, clean and bright. It contained a desk, two chairs, a large wooden cupboard, holding crockery and a biscuit tin, and a table. In the corner she could see an ancient gas stove and a tiny sink. Everything was so clean it sparkled.

'Sit down,' Mrs Dearing said, as she removed

her coat and hat.

Jenny sat down and waited, feeling sick with apprehension.

'Now what kind of work are you looking for?'

'Anything, ma'am. I know 'ow to be a lady's maid.' When Mrs Dearing looked up sharply, Jenny thought she might have overdone the accent.

'I haven't any vacancies in that line at the moment. If you'd like to come back next week...'

'Oh, I can't do that,' she blurted out. 'I've got to find a job today so I can start tomorrow.'

'It is most unlikely that I can find you a place that quickly. Have you tried applying for a job in a factory, or a shop? That's where most of the young girls want to go these days.'

Jenny shook her head, shoulders drooping in disappointment. 'I must find employment with accommodation provided.' Her attempt at a cockney accent had all but disappeared.

The woman sat back, looking puzzled. 'Where have you been working?'

'I've been with Mrs Patterson-Hay.' It was the first name that came into her head.

'I don't think I know the household.' Mrs Dearing was obviously suspicious now.

'You wouldn't.' Jenny's mind was working like a steam train. 'She lives in Kent. They're shutting up the house and moving to Scotland.'

'I see. Do you have any references?'

'The mistress isn't there. She didn't give us none before she left. The servants are packing up the house.'

'No references? Most irregular. I certainly

wouldn't send anyone there for a job.' Mrs Dearing stood up, filled the kettle with water and put it on the stove to boil.

'I'm sure you wouldn't want to; it was very hard work.' Jenny was getting into the swing of this now. 'Not that I'm afraid of hard work; I'll do anything.'

Mrs Dearing glanced back at her as she made the tea. 'Tell me what this is all about. You are clearly well educated and trying to hide it.'

Oh, help! As soon as she'd become anxious, the pretence had slipped. This was going to take a lot of explaining. Then an idea shot into her head. 'My dad was a great one for reading and he tried to bring me up properly. But he's dead now.'

'Recently?' She handed Jenny a cup of tea.

'Yes.' At least that was the truth.

'What about your mother?'

'She's dead too, and after tomorrow I won't have a job no more.' Don't ask me any more questions, she pleaded silently. I'm running out of lies!

'I understand your need for a job, then. What is your name and home address?'

'Jenny Baker.' She had remembered that, thank goodness. Then she gave Mrs Dearing what she hoped was a forlorn, pleading look, which wasn't too difficult because that was just how she felt. 'I lived in Lambeth, but with Mum and Dad dead that ain't my home no more. When I leave Mrs Patterson-Hay, I won't have nowhere to go.'

The agency owner stirred her tea, lost in thought, leaving Jenny to struggle with doubt. If she couldn't convince this woman that she was suitable as a servant, what chance did she have? Tears burnt the back of her eyes, but she refused to let them spill over. She blew her nose on a delicate handkerchief, tucking it quickly out of sight before it was seen, not sure if this was the kind of thing a servant would own.

'Drink your tea.' Mrs Dearing's voice was gentle. 'You are obviously in desperate trouble, so I'll see what I can do for you. The lack of references might not be a barrier these days. Servants are hard to come by, and families make allowances in order to keep them. Since the war ended not many girls want to go into service, and most now prefer the freedom of the factory or shop.'

Jenny sipped her tea, watching Mrs Dearing going through the files. That sounded hopeful for her. After about five minutes the woman sat down again, studying a letter, then she looked up.

'The only thing I've got is for an under housemaid with the Stannard household. They need someone right away.'

'I'll do it.' Jenny put her cup down and sat forward eagerly.

'You'll have to buy your own uniform. Can you afford to do that?'

Jenny was stunned by that piece of information. Just when she thought things were going to work out, this came up. 'How much?'

'Four pounds.'

That wasn't going to leave her much. Jenny chewed her lip in worry. Thank goodness Fred and Glad had made the pawnbroker give her five pounds. She smiled. 'I can manage that.'

'Good. The lack of references is not in your favour, but I'll write a letter to Mrs Stannard explaining your situation. She might agree to take you on for a trial period to see how you work out.'

'I'll work hard. I won't let you down, Mrs Dearing.' She sounded too eager, even to her own ears.

'You'd better go immediately in case there are other applicants.' She wrote the letter, sealed it in an envelope, then put the address on the front. 'It's in Bruton Street, Mayfair. Can you find your way there?'

'Yes, Mrs Dearing.' Jenny took the envelope and smiled again, but in relief this time. Perhaps things were going to work out after all.

The house in Mayfair was really elegant. It had three floors and a basement. A beautiful tiled path led up to a sparkling clean step and solid wooden door, with a brass letterbox and doorknocker polished to such a shine you could see your face in it. But Jenny knew servants didn't go in the front, so she hurried round to the back entrance. After knocking on the door, she waited, head bowed, praying that the place hadn't been filled already.

'Yes?'

Her head shot up at the sound of a man's voice. He was no more than twenty-five, she guessed, and his dark green and gold livery marked him as a footman. 'I've come from Mrs Dearing's agency about the job of under housemaid.'

He stepped aside. 'Come with me.' He led her through an enormous kitchen, which was lovely and warm after the cold wind outside. She received curious glances, but the cook and her staff were too busy to stop what they were doing. The footman led her along a dark passage and rapped on a door at the end.

'Young kid here about the job, Mrs Douglas.'

The door opened to reveal a small, comfortable sitting room, and a woman who was not so small. She was wearing a black dress with a chatelaine at her waist from which hung a large bunch of keys and various useful items. She gave Jenny a quick head-to-toe appraisal, then without a word turned and walked back into the room. The footman winked as he pushed Jenny over the threshold before closing the door behind her.

The housekeeper held her hand out for the letter Jenny was clutching to her as if it were a good-luck talisman. She fought to stop her hand trembling as she handed it over, though it was so difficult. She was shaking from her feet upwards; it wouldn't take much for her teeth to start chattering. The words Miss Patterson-Hay had drummed into them at the school echoed in her mind: 'Remain serene and composed at all times. Never show fear or anger.'

Remain serene! She could feel a hysterical laugh bubbling up inside her. That was impossible. She was so terrified that her legs wouldn't hold her much longer.

'No references.'

The housekeeper's voice made her jump, and

with a sense of desperation she gathered her scattered thoughts together. 'No, Mrs Douglas, but I'm a hard worker.'

'You had better be,' she snapped. 'I don't tolerate slackness in this household.'

Jenny couldn't help comparing the Winford housekeeper with this one. She didn't seem quite so severe, but there was little to choose between them. Were they all like this?

'Come with me. I'll find out if madam will see you.'

The housekeeper sailed out of the room, heading for a flight of stairs, drawing Jenny along in her wake. At least she hadn't been sent away as soon as she'd arrived, so perhaps there was hope. She had to get this job or she didn't know what she was going to do. If she went to anyone she knew, they would only go straight to her mother. Anything like that was doomed to failure and would bring the wrath of her aunt down on her. She gave an involuntary shudder; that was too awful to think about.

The door at the top of the stairs opened to another world. There was a long passage, and the walls were covered with delicate gold and pale lemon wallpaper. Portraits and paintings by famous artists lined the long hall. Most of the furniture was the work of famous designers and very expensive. One of the aims of the Templeton School had been to teach them to identify and appreciate things of quality. The floor was highly polished wood with the most beautiful carpet runner she had ever seen, in the same colours as the wallpaper. Add to that breathtaking Venetian chandeliers and you had a house furnished to the highest standard. Her mother would be impressed and very jealous if she could see this.

The housekeeper stopped outside a door, knocked and waited. As soon as a female voice called to enter, she disappeared inside, leaving Jenny to gaze around her in appreciation.

It was only a couple of minutes before the door opened again.

'Madam will see you. And watch your manners,' the housekeeper said, her voice stern.

The woman sitting by the window with a book open on her lap was around forty-five and beautifully groomed, her blonde hair cut short in the latest bob. Jenny dipped a good curtsy in front of her. Her first emotion was one of profound relief that she had never met the lady at some social function her mother had dragged her to during the school holidays. Though it was doubtful if anyone would recognize the shabby Jenny Baker as being Eugenie Winford. She kept her eyes lowered as Mrs Stannard read the letter.

Mrs Stannard looked up after a few moments. 'You are in urgent need of employment?'

'Yes, madam.' She was trying hard not to speak any more than was necessary, knowing how difficult she found it to stick to a working-class accent.

'What do you think, Mrs Douglas? I do prefer to have someone with good references.'

'Mrs Dearing always sends us good staff, madam. And we are in great need of an under housemaid, so perhaps a three-month trial?'

The mistress turned her attention back to Jenny. 'We are prepared to take you on and see how you work out. The uniform will cost you four pounds, but for that you will be outfitted with a complete wardrobe of working clothes.'

Jenny pulled the pound notes out of her pocket and held them out. 'I've got enough for that.'

Mrs Stannard nodded and glanced at the letter again. 'Very well, Jenny, give the money to Mrs Douglas.'

The housekeeper took the money and tucked it in her dress pocket, then caught hold of her arm and ushered her from the room.

Once back in the kitchen Mrs Douglas called a young girl over. 'Edna, this is Jenny; she's to be the new under housemaid. You will be sharing a room with her.'

The two girls gave each other a hesitant smile. The housekeeper continued speaking, not giving the girls a chance to say anything to one another. 'You will start at six o'clock tomorrow morning. You had better move in this evening. Be here by ten o'clock and Edna will show you your room.'

After issuing those crisp instructions, she sailed out of the kitchen.

'Don't be late.' Edna smiled. 'She can be fierce if you don't do as she says, but if you don't give her no trouble, then she's not bad. I hopes you don't snore.'

'I don't.' After sleeping in a dorm with lots of other girls Jenny knew that was true because they'd have soon told her if she did.

'Good. It'll be nice to 'ave someone to gossip with.'

Feeling buoyant with hope, Jenny made her way back to her house for the last time. She was stunned, not being able to believe that her crazy scheme had succeeded. She'd actually got a job!

Now all she had to do this evening was get out of the house without being seen.

5

Dinner that evening was agony for Jenny. Her aunt had forced her mother to come to the table, and the only time she showed a spark of interest was when Greaves was talking. It was clear that her mother was not displeased with the prospect of having him as a relative. Jenny was disgusted by the attitude. How shallow her mother's life must be.

'Have you packed all your belongings, Eugenie?' he asked.

She smiled brightly. 'I'm all ready.'

'Good, good.'

He looked smug and Jenny swallowed silently, hoping her performance was good enough to convince everyone that the arrangement made her happy. Her mother was nodding in approval.

'It will be for the best, Eugenie. You will have social standing as the wife of a wealthy man.' A momentary flash of doubt crossed her mother's face, and then it was gone. 'I will be only ten minutes away. You can visit – now and again.'

Jenny couldn't help but feel pity for her mother, who was once again looking confused. They had never been close, but perhaps she should stay to help her mother through this disaster. That thought was instantly dismissed. She couldn't stay. She just couldn't! And really, by the way her mother was acting, she had her doubts if she would even be missed.

'I shall collect you at twelve tomorrow. You will like my house, but it does require a woman's touch.' Albert Greaves laughed as if that were a huge joke. 'At least that school taught you how to manage a large household.'

'Yes, I've been well trained.' Her smile was wide as she glanced at each person around the table. She hoped they didn't look at her eyes, for she was sure that her distaste would be showing in them. She lowered them quickly, just to be on the safe side.

Greaves leant across and ran a hand over her short hair. 'You'll make a splendid wife – when you're older, of course. And you must let your hair grow again. I like long hair.'

The laugh he gave made her shiver. There was something not quite right about this man. She watched him drain his glass and hold it out to be refilled. The butler carefully poured until it was full to the rim with red wine. Before walking away, Jessop frowned at Jenny, obviously shocked by what he'd heard. She gave no indication that she was anything but pleased. They would all know by morning that she had run away.

She fixed her gaze on her mother, then a pain raged through her. She had never been an affec-

tionate mother, but nor had she been unkind –
until now. She was prepared to give her daughter
to this awful man. That was hard to forgive or
understand.

Jenny's lip trembled as the enormity of what
she was planning swept through her. A secure
comfortable life was all she had known. Now that
was finished, and she was about to become a servant. It was a terrifying prospect. She bowed her
head to concentrate on stirring her coffee until
she could force a smile back on to her face. She
mustn't weaken. She was too close to success.

It was a relief when the meal ended and she
could escape to her room. Half an hour later she
heard her aunt and Greaves leave. She already
had on her coat, and, giving one last, sad glance
around her pretty bedroom, picked up her case
and crept down the stairs. To her horror Jessop
appeared just as she reached the front door. The
look she gave him was full of pleading. Don't give
me away!

He took in her shabby coat and battered
suitcase, and then, with a look of utter sadness on
his face, opened the door for her, bowing her out.
She knew he understood because he'd heard the
talk at dinner.

'Good luck, Miss Winford,' he whispered as he
closed the door silently behind her.

Her mind was in turmoil as she caught the bus
to her new life. Was she doing the right thing?
Would she fit in as a servant without being discovered? She sat with her small case on her lap,
her knuckles white as they gripped the handle.

She arrived at the Bruton Street house and was

taken straight to the housekeeper.

'Just in time,' Mrs Douglas said, heading for the kitchen.

The staff obviously had their dinner after serving the upstairs meal. I certainly won't go hungry, Jenny thought as she saw the quality and quantity of the food they were enjoying.

The housekeeper then introduced her to everyone. She tried to force their names into her mind. There was the butler, Mr Green, the cook, Mrs Peters, the footman, Ron Stokes, the scullery maid, Milly, and of course Edna Jenks, the housemaid. She was so agitated at that moment that it would have been difficult to remember even her own name – her new name!

'Sit yourself down,' the cook said.

Although she'd already dined she hadn't eaten much, and, as her plate was piled with succulent roast beef and the lightest Yorkshire pudding she'd ever seen, she realized just how hungry she was. There was laughter and friendly banter around the table, making her relax a little. This seemed like a happy household. However, she must remain alert. No one must guess at her background.

When they'd finished eating, Edna picked up Jenny's suitcase. 'Come on, I'll show you where we sleep.'

It was right at the top of the house, under the eaves. The room was small with a sloping ceiling; there were two beds, a cupboard – and it was freezing cold. After the warmth of the kitchen it came as a shock. Edna didn't seem to notice it, though. On one bed were her uniform and other garments, including underclothes. Quite a lot for four pounds, Jenny thought.

'Pack your things in the cupboard and shove your case under the bed,' Edna said.

When that was done they got ready for bed. It was so cold that Jenny gasped as she dived into the icy sheets.

Her roommate laughed. 'Bloody perishing, ain't it? You'll soon get used to it.'

As she curled into a tight ball with her teeth chattering, Jenny wasn't sure about that.

'Cook will start making the Christmas puds and cakes soon. The house will be crammed to the ceiling then.' Edna chatted happily. 'All the family will be home, so I'd better warn you. Madam's got three sons. John's the eldest at twenty-four. He's right snooty and won't lower himself to talk to the likes of us. The next is Luke and he's twenty. Watch him. He's always after the girls and don't care who they are. A servant is fair game to him. The youngest is Matthew. He's eighteen and a real gent; always got a ready smile for everyone. Don't be fooled, though; they might all have names from the Holy Book, but they ain't no angels.'

'What are Mr and Mrs Stannard like?' Jenny asked.

'Not bad. They're a rich banking family. We don't see much of them. They leave the running of the household to Mrs Douglas. Don't get on the wrong side of her or you'll know it. The last girl was chucked out for being lazy and not doing her cleaning properly.'

'Oh, dear.' Jenny shivered even more. This all

sounded very frightening.

'Don't worry.' Edna laughed. 'Do your job and it's not a bad place to be. I knows a lot worse. Get some sleep and I'll make sure to wake you at five. Mustn't be late on your first day.'

When she'd been sitting in the warm kitchen she'd felt quite hopeful; that disappeared as she listened to Edna. She prayed she was going to be able to do this.

Burying her head in the pillow to muffle the sound, Jenny Baker, the new under housemaid, cried herself to sleep.

'Jenny! Wake up.'

Someone was shaking her roughly. She opened one eye. It was dark, very cold and for a moment she couldn't think where she was. Then Edna whipped the covers off her and she leapt to her feet as she remembered. She was now the under housemaid in the Stannard household.

'Get washed and dressed quickly. Put on the striped frock and pinafore. Hurry, hurry!' Edna urged.

Jenny had never been this rushed before but within ten minutes her roommate was inspecting her and nodding approval. They ran downstairs and presented themselves to the housekeeper.

Mrs Douglas handed Jenny a sheet of instructions. Every job was listed with the time beside it and she couldn't help wondering how anyone could get through so much in one day.

'These will be your duties. You must keep strictly to the times. Edna will show you today. Watch her carefully because you'll be on your own from tomorrow. Is that understood?'

'Yes, Mrs Douglas.'

'Off you go, then.'

Jenny followed Edna as the housemaid hurried from room to room, cleaning out the fireplaces and laying them ready for the footman to light. After watching her do three, she asked if she could have a go, and received a smile from Edna when she'd finished.

'The next job,' Edna told her after they'd dealt with five fireplaces, 'is to scrub the front step. You can do that while I take up the early-morning tea. You've only got ten minutes, then we've got to get the day rooms ready before the family have finished their breakfast.'

As Edna hurried away, Jenny tumbled down the stairs to collect a bucket of water, scrubbing brush and cloth. She was puffing by the time she reached the front door. The biting wind was blowing straight at her and it felt as if her hands were frozen around the scrubbing brush. She gritted her teeth and scrubbed with all of her might, determined to do a good job – and on time. The step was gleaming and her hands red and sore when Edna reappeared.

'That's good, Jen. Now take the water out the back, clean the bucket and come up here again. I'll be in the blue sitting room.'

'Where's that?'

'Third door on the right. Hurry now.'

Picking up the cleaning things, Jenny hurried down the servants' stairs, rushed out the back to tip the water away, cleaned the bucket and put it back with the others in the large cupboard. She was just hurtling towards the stairs again when she was called.

'Jenny, no running.'

She slithered to a halt. 'Sorry, Mrs Douglas, I didn't want to keep Edna waiting.'

'Very commendable of you. Walk quickly, don't run.' By the time the servants had their breakfast at eight o'clock, Jenny was already exhausted. The rest of the day was equally hectic. The list of things to be done was never ending. Dusting, polishing, making beds, cleaning bathrooms, laying meals in the servants' hall, washing up, cleaning brasses – the tasks went on and on.

Ten o'clock that evening and bedtime found her numb with fatigue and close to tears. Her hands were so painful she could hardly move them.

'Let me look at your hands.'

Jenny held them out and Edna tutted when she saw them. 'Oh, dear, I can see you're not used to hard work. I've got something to help.' She fished out a jar and an old pair of gloves from the bottom of the cupboard.

'What's that?'

'Cook's special remedy. It's got butter in it, but I'm not sure what else. It works, though.'

Jenny gasped in pain as Edna began to smooth the thick cream over her raw and cut hands. Her nose wrinkled at the smell, making her roommate laugh.

'Shocking, ain't it, but you'll be glad in the morning.' Edna eased the gloves on her, giving a sympathetic smile. 'There, keep those on all night. You'll soon get used to the hard graft. You did well today.'

'Thanks.' She jumped in bed and yelped when she hit something hard ... but warm.

'I put a hot brick in your bed for you. You're going to need a good night's kip if you're to survive another day.' Edna chuckled. 'We've got all the beds to change tomorrow as well.'

'I'm glad I was the fastest runner in my school.'

Edna laughed again. 'Yeah, you can't hang about in this job. What school did you go to?'

'One in Lambeth. You wouldn't know it.' Jenny's heart raced. That was careless of her.

'You come from Lambeth?'

'Yes.'

'You don't sound as if you do.'

Jenny's mind was working like mad. One unguarded remark and the questions came. 'Blame that on my dad; he was a stickler for talking proper.'

Edna's ready laugh erupted again. 'I'm glad you came, Jen. The last girl was a right misery, but you're nice. You come to me if you need help. I'll see you're all right.'

Jenny turned her head and smiled at Edna in the gloom. 'Thanks. I'm glad I came too. Can we be friends?'

'Sure, I'd like that. We can go out together on our time off.'

'That would be nice.'

'Yeah, night, Jen.'

'Goodnight, Edna.'

Once again the silent tears began to flow, but the new under housemaid was determined to make this the last time.

The weeks passed and Jenny grew in confidence. For the first couple of weeks she'd been on edge waiting for her Aunt Gertrude to storm in and drag her back. But when nothing happened, she began to relax. They had probably given up looking for her, and anyway they would never think that she was working as a servant.

The work was harder than she could ever have imagined, but with Edna's help she soon fell into the routine. Her hands had toughened up and were not giving her as much trouble now – cook's special cream was good stuff. Mrs Douglas was so pleased with her willingness to work without complaint that she had been made a permanent member of the staff already. She didn't dare look too far into the future because the outlook was bleak. But for the moment she was housed, clothed, fed, paid and her aunt hadn't found her. That was enough for now.

6

There was a good fire burning in the grate; the curtains were drawn across the windows to keep out the cold December weather; a mother and father were reading peacefully with their three sons around them. An idyllic family scene, but Matt Stannard was about to disturb the calm.

He laid his book aside, drew in a deep breath

and said, 'I'm not going back to university, Father.'

His father looked up from his newspaper, seemingly unperturbed by his youngest son's announcement. 'Having difficulty managing on your allowance, are you? I'll see what I can do in the New Year.'

'It hasn't anything to do with money.' Matt stood up. His father was a reasonable man, but he wasn't going to like this. 'I mean it. I'm not studying any more. I've finished with Oxford. I'm going out to work.'

Now he had everyone's complete attention: John was on his feet and frowning fiercely; Luke was grinning as usual; and his mother had set aside her book, calm as ever.

'But why?' his father asked. 'You have a good brain, better than the rest of us, if the truth be told. You could end up as a professor.'

'I don't want to be a professor.'

'Where did this sudden idea come from, Matt?' His father looked perplexed.

'It isn't sudden,' he explained. 'I've thought about it very carefully. I want to leave university.'

'If your mind's made up, then I suppose we could find you a position with the bank.'

Matt sighed quietly. They had all been given freedom to choose their own careers, but, nevertheless, they were going to find this hard to understand. 'No, thank you, Father.'

'Well, what do you want to do?'

'I intend to be a car mechanic.'

'Don't be ridiculous!' John exploded. 'What kind of a career is that?'

71

'A very good one. Cars are the future. There will come a time when almost every family will own one.'

'Haven't you been listening to the news lately?' John was now pacing up and down. 'The Wall Street stock market has crashed and it's being felt everywhere. There's going to be a depression. The signs are all there. Who's going to buy cars then?'

'John!' Their mother spoke firmly. 'Raising your voice won't solve anything.'

He threw himself back into his chair, looking thoroughly disgruntled. 'He's a blasted idiot, giving up the chance of an academic career for some ludicrous whim. Matt's damned clever.'

'I must agree with John,' their father said. 'This doesn't appear to be a very sound notion, Matt.'

'Maybe, but I'd like to give it a try. Give me two years, Father. If at the end of that time I can't earn a living at it, I'll go back to Oxford and pick up where I left off.' It was a concession he didn't want to make, but he had to be fair to his parents, and this would make them feel more at ease.

'You're determined to do this?'

He nodded to his father, and then glanced at his mother, who smiled her support.

'I see.' His father was now leaning on the mantelpiece with a glass of brandy in his hand. 'I'll buy you a garage to start you up.'

'Father!' John was up again. 'You can't do that. Our bank has weathered the crash better than most, but we've still lost money and must be careful.'

'We've suffered some losses, but it's nothing we can't handle.' He looked at his eldest son with pride. 'It was your insistence that we spread our investments and not be swept up in the euphoria of the stock market chase for fast money.'

John appeared mollified by the praise. 'We still need to be cautious.'

Matt watched the exchange with interest. John might be young, but when it came to banking he was a master. Their father turned to him more and more for advice, and Matt didn't think he'd ever been wrong in his predictions. In this instance the family had cause to be very grateful to John, for he had undoubtedly saved their bank from collapse. Although his elder brother could be a touch volatile at times, he knew what he was doing. Underneath his stern and serious nature lurked a kind man. There wasn't anything he wouldn't do for his family.

'Don't worry, John,' Matt said. 'I don't want a garage. I'm going to take an apprenticeship and learn the trade that way – from the bottom up.'

John's mouth opened in disbelief. 'You mean you're going to work in dirty overalls and get grease all over your hands?'

A chuckle of mirth came from Luke, who was keeping out of the conversation. As a future lawyer he already knew the wisdom of listening to both sides of a story.

'I couldn't strip down engines without getting greasy, could I?' Matt said, laughing.

His father appeared stunned and turned to his wife. 'What do you think about all this, my dear?'

'I think we should let Matt do as he wishes.

He's promised to return to his studies if it doesn't work out and you know he always keeps his promises.'

'Hmm. Yes, you're quite right. Many young men take time out from studying to travel, so Matt might as well get this out of his system.' The worry faded from his expression. 'Where do you have to go to get this apprenticeship?'

'I've already spoken to Mr Porter of Mayfair Automobiles. He's the best in the business and is prepared to take me on after the Christmas holiday.'

'Ah, I know the man. He's the owner of a very prestigious garage. Only works on the best cars.' He drained his glass and smiled broadly at his youngest son. 'Very well, you may get your hands dirty for two years with my permission.'

'Thank you.' Matt went over and shook his father's hand. He was aware that they all thought this was something he would grow out of; he knew differently. This was a desire he'd nursed for a very long time.

'You're mad,' John said. 'There are going to be tough years ahead. Some people have lost entire fortunes in this disaster.'

'Yes, it's truly dreadful,' their mother said. 'I've heard some men have killed themselves because they've lost everything. Is that so, John?'

'I'm afraid it is. Peter Tarrant killed himself and at least two Americans I've heard about.'

'Poor souls.' Her eyes were full of sadness.

'Do you remember that American gentleman we met at the Stock Brokers' Gala Ball last Easter, my dear? We spent most of the evening

74

with him.'

'Yes, I remember him. He seemed a pleasant man. Unusual colouring, if I recall. He had dark hair and eyes of such a pale brown they looked almost gold.'

'My word, the things you ladies notice,' her husband remarked. 'As I was saying, I heard a couple of weeks ago that he was dead. Don't know the details, though.'

'How terrible.' Mrs Stannard was clearly shocked. 'Didn't he have a young daughter?'

'He did and was very proud of her. He told anyone who would listen what a charming girl she was.'

'Oh, poor child.' Their mother stared at the fire.

Christmas Day and Matt was excited about the future. He had always loved working with anything mechanical and couldn't wait to start his apprenticeship. He now had two years to do something he was really interested in. He didn't intend to fail because going back to the academic life was the last thing in the world he wanted to do. He found it too easy. While the other boys were spending hours studying, he had only to read something through twice and he retained the information. Quite frankly he soon became bored, longing for a challenge. Now he would have one.

'Put your jackets on, boys.' Their mother swept into the drawing room. 'And stand up. It's time to give the staff their gifts.'

Her husband groaned. 'Do we have to go through this performance every year?'

'We most certainly do.' She chivvied him out of his chair and herded her sons into line. 'We must show our appreciation. They work well for us all year. We hardly know they're around.'

'You're right as usual, my dear. Are those the presents?' He indicated a pile of brightly wrapped packages on a side table.

'Yes, they have the names on them. When Mrs Douglas introduces each one, you will give them the gift.'

'I know the routine.' He sighed again. 'We do it every year, but couldn't you hand them out this time?'

'You are the head of this house, Gilbert. It's your job.' She smiled encouragingly. 'It will only take a few minutes.'

He kissed her cheek. 'Of course, Louise. I don't know how you put up with a grumpy old devil like me.'

There was a tap on the door and the house-keeper came in.

'We're all ready, Mrs Douglas,' Louise said. 'Send them in.'

Matt watched the staff file in. Most of them had been with them for a long time, except for the young girl last but one in the line. She had her head bowed and was obviously uneasy about being in the presence of the entire family.

'Who is that?' Luke whispered in his ear.

'From her position in the line I would say she's the under housemaid.'

'Hmm. She'd be quite pretty with a touch of rouge and better clothes.'

Matt was about to tell his brother to keep his

76

eyes off her, but didn't have a chance, because the servants were walking along the line and bowing to each of them before leaving the room. He was well aware of Luke's tendency to chase any pretty girl he saw. He would have to keep an eye on him, because this girl was too young and shy. She hadn't looked up once. She curtsied gracefully in front of his parents and accepted her gift with a hesitant smile. Still she kept her eyes lowered. Why? They weren't that frightening as a family, surely? For some strange reason he didn't think it was because she was shy. There was something else. It was almost as if she didn't want to be seen.

She reached Luke and he said, 'I haven't seen you before.'

'No, sir, I only started two months ago.'

'I hope you are happy here?' Luke persisted in trying to gain her attention, without success. She still had her gaze lowered.

'Yes, thank you, sir.'

She moved along to Matt and the words he spoke surprised him as much as her. 'I wish you a happy and safe New Year.'

Her head came up and what he saw made him draw in a deep breath of appreciation. What beautiful eyes; she was going to be a real beauty in a couple of years.

'What have you got, Jen?' Edna asked.

She unwrapped her parcel, trying to stop her hands from shaking. That had been an ordeal. She felt safe down here with the servants, but was terrified she would meet someone upstairs who might guess who she really was. The deception was a constant worry in case she slipped and said something revealing. In a way the hard schedule of work she had to do every day was helping to push the fear to the back of her mind, but at times like this it came rushing back.

'Oh, that's lovely,' the cook said as Jenny held out a bright red scarf and matching gloves.

They all showed their gifts, smiling with pleasure as they inspected each one. All were things servants would not have been able to buy for themselves. Jenny couldn't help wondering if her mother had been this kind...

'Back to work,' the housekeeper ordered. But there was a smile on her face for once. 'Edna, Jenny, cook will need your help today.'

The time flew as they hurried from one job to another. It was nearly eleven that night before the final clearing up had been done. It was then they had a party of their own in the servants' hall. They had a wind-up gramophone and some records, and this was played after they had eaten their fill of the Christmas food. They danced to and sang the popular tunes of the day. Tomorrow was still a working day for them, so at midnight they began to bring the party to an end. The footman put on a record by Jenny's favourite singer, Al Bowlly. He told them that it had only been recorded the month before, and he'd bought it last week. It was called 'S'posin I Should Fall in Love with You'. It was a sentimental song and touched Jenny's heart, as she listened to his lovely voice. It brought back such happy memories of their dancing lessons at

Templeton. Her friends would all be enjoying a family Christmas now. For a moment sadness tried to overwhelm her, but she fought against it. She was doing well on her own, and mustn't dwell on the past.

Jenny joined in the laughter as they washed their plates and glasses, feeling much more relaxed. It had been silly to get in a panic about meeting the family upstairs. No one would see her as anything but a lowly under housemaid. She was safe here.

7

They were even busier on New Year's Eve, when they prepared the house for a lavish dinner party in the evening. Mrs Douglas didn't scold as Edna, Jenny and the footman, Ron Stokes, ran up and down the servants' stairs.

The family had a late breakfast at ten o'clock, which was a blessing, and by the time they'd finished eating, the fires were burning, floors cleaned, guest rooms prepared and everything was gleaming without a speck of dust to be seen.

Edna leant on the banister at the bottom of their stairs and mopped her brow, still grinning broadly. 'We made it.'

Jenny was beginning to wonder if anything put her friend in a bad mood. No matter how hard the work, she seemed to sail through it with a smile on her lips and a joke or two.

The footman, Ron, slithered down the stairs. 'Is that all you've got to do?' he joked.

'Just catching our breath. Look at poor old Jen, she's gasping for air.'

Jenny giggled, enjoying the friendly banter. There was a strict order of rank among servants and, being very low in the order of things, she hadn't expected it to be this friendly. But it was. It never ceased to amaze her and she couldn't help wondering if this household was unique in that way. If it was, then she had been very lucky to get this job. She didn't always feel like that of course. Many nights, as she crawled into bed absolutely exhausted, she felt anything but grateful.

'Well, make sure you recover by tonight because while the Stannard family are enjoying themselves we're going to have a knees-up of our own.' Then he was off as Mrs Douglas appeared at the top of the stairs.

'Jenny, collect the tea tray from the library. The family have just retired to the drawing room.'

'Yes, Mrs Douglas.' She waited for the house-keeper to come down and then sped up to carry out her task.

Finding the library empty, she stood in the middle of the room and gazed at the shelves of books, breathing in the lovely smell of leather. This was something she missed so much. She walked over to a small table, picked up a leather bound book and ran her fingers over it, her eyes dreamy. She'd always loved reading, but now there wasn't time for such things. When she reached her bed at night she was too tired to do anything but sleep. Again her thoughts turned to her friends at school, remembering how they had read at night using their torches. They'd had such fun.

She was angry with herself. It was pointless to yearn for those days. They were gone for ever. And she shouldn't be moping for the past; she should be proud of herself. She'd had the courage to make a new life, and she had done pretty well. It had all come as a terrible shock at first, but she had adjusted and fitted in with the other servants, working hard. Mrs Douglas never had cause to complain. After finding out about her father, Jenny had felt unloved and unwanted; now she was a part of this household, accepted by them all.

She was about to put the book down when a voice said, 'Do you like reading?'

She jumped violently, not realizing that anyone had come into the room. The thick carpet must have muffled his footsteps.

One of the Stannard sons took the book from her hands and put it on the shelf. 'I didn't mean to startle you. You were looking at that book with such longing. Why don't you borrow it?'

'I couldn't do that, sir.' She edged away from him.

'Of course you could. No one would mind.'

'No, sir.' She reached to pick up the tray, but he blocked her path.

'What's your name?'

'Jenny Baker, sir. I must get on with my work.'

He laughed. 'I'm sure you can spare ten

81

minutes to talk to me.'

Trying to remain calm, she edged past him, but he moved in front of her again.

'Please, sir, I'll lose my job if I don't go back downstairs at once.'

'Luke! Let her go.'

He stepped aside, hands in the air and a wide grin on his face. 'Ah, the voice of reason. I'm only talking to her, Matt.'

'Don't you realize that with over twenty guests arriving tonight, the staff are rushed trying to get everything ready in time?'

Still smiling and in obvious good humour, Luke said to her, 'Sorry, it was thoughtless of me.'

She grabbed the tray and fled, giving the other brother a grateful glance as she rushed past him.

'What took you so long?' the housekeeper scolded.

'Sorry, Mrs Douglas, I was detained.'

'By whom?'

'Mr Luke.'

'You want to watch that boy,' Mr Green, the butler, said. 'Full of devilment and too fond of the young ladies.'

'Did he take liberties?' Mrs Douglas didn't look at all pleased.

Jenny shook her head. 'He said he only wanted to talk...'

The cook snorted in disbelief.

'His brother came in and made him let me leave. The tallest one of the three.'

'That was Matthew.' Edna breezed in. 'I've just passed the library and he's really having a go at his brother now.'

'Don't be so familiar,' the housekeeper scolded. 'It's Mr Matthew to you.'

'Sorry, Mrs Douglas, I meant Mr Matthew. Just a slip of the tongue.' Edna gave Jenny a sly wink.

The housekeeper accepted the apology, but didn't look as if she believed it was sincere. She glanced at the watch pinned to her dress. 'Jenny, you are to come to me at once if you have any trouble with the young gentlemen. Now everyone back to work. All must be perfect for this evening.'

The dinner party was under way and it was bedlam in the kitchen. Jenny was amazed that they didn't keep colliding with one another, but each person seemed to know what they were doing – except her. This was her first experience of a large house party from below stairs. She had never realized just how hard the staff had to work to make the serving of food and drink go without a hitch.

'Jenny.' Even the housekeeper appeared flustered as she sailed into the kitchen. 'You'll have to take this dish of vegetables up. Hurry now.'

She lifted the heavy silver dish and climbed the stairs as quickly as possible. Then only two steps into the dining room and it seemed as if her heart stopped beating for a moment. From the hub of chatter coming from the guests one voice stood out. Suddenly she was running from the room, still clutching the dish, without even knowing that she was doing so.

'Jen!' Edna caught her arm. 'Stop. Where are

you going?'

'I can't go in there,' she gasped, thrusting the dish at her friend. 'You take it. Please!'

'What's going on here?'

'I don't think Jenny's well, Mrs Douglas.'

The housekeeper placed her hand on Jenny's forehead. 'Feels like she's running a fever. Go and ask cook for a drink of water and one of her remedies. She'll have you right in no time. Edna, you take the vegetables in. Quickly now.'

Jenny struggled down to the kitchen on legs so weak they would hardly hold her. Once there, she sat on a stool in the corner out of everyone's way, and bowed over as if in pain. Dear God, that was her worst nightmare come true. She'd been feeling safe, but she wasn't. Discovery could come at any time. Gloria Tremain was upstairs. She had been the head girl at the school for two years and knew Jenny well. Even her disguise as a servant wouldn't have fooled Gloria. Had she seen her?

At that moment someone pushed her head down between her knees and held her there. When she sat up again, cook thrust a glass of pale green liquid into her hand.

'Drink that. It'll bring some colour back to your face.' Jenny was so disorientated with shock that she emptied the glass without even noticing what it tasted like.

'There now, you sit quiet for a few minutes.' The cook smiled kindly.

'Thank you, Mrs Peters.'

Slowly she became aware of her surroundings and her heart slowed to a more normal rate. She was dismayed to see everyone rushing around while she did nothing. This wasn't right; they were frantically busy. She forced herself to stand.

Mrs Douglas was working as hard as everyone else in an effort to keep the dinner party running smoothly. With so many guests, each of them needed to pitch in and do whatever was necessary. 'Stay where you are, Jenny, until you feel well again.'

'I'm all right now. Please let me do something down here. I'm sorry, Mrs Douglas, I don't know what came over me.'

'You can't help being taken ill,' she said. 'But if you feel well enough, ask cook what she wants doing.'

'Take the cakes out of the oven, then help Milly with the washing up.' Cook mopped her brow. 'I hope they're eating all this food, Mrs Douglas.'

'It's disappearing as fast as we can serve it,' the housekeeper said, before rushing off again.

Cook gave a satisfied nod, and then glanced at Jenny. 'You sure you're all right, Jen?'

'I'm fine, thank you, Mrs Peters. Your remedy worked wonders.' Jenny arranged small cakes on a large dish. There were fruit ones, some covered in lashings of cream; others were chocolate and coffee. They looked delicious.

'You've made a real professional job of that.' The cook gave Jenny a sly wink. 'I've got a few of those put aside for our little party tonight.'

The presentation of food was something she had been taught at the Templeton School. Jenny's nerves steadied. If she made herself useful here, they might not ask her to go back upstairs again.

There was at least one person in the room who had witnessed Jenny's flight of panic. Matthew had seen her come in and stop suddenly, the colour draining from her face. For a moment he thought that she was going to drop the large dish she was carrying. He was almost on his feet when she turned and fled. There wasn't a sound of a crash, so she must have held on to the serving dish. For some strange reason he felt concerned for the young girl, wanting to protect her. That was why he had been unusually harsh with Luke for playing his games with her. It was that instinct that kept him in his seat. Was there something or someone here she didn't want to see? Someone who was a threat to her?

He glanced around the long table, studying each guest carefully. It was unlikely that an under housemaid would know any of these distinguished people – unless she'd worked for them of course. That idea was quickly dismissed. She was far too young. This was probably her first job. Nevertheless there was something about the girl... He silently cursed his overactive imagination.

The older housemaid had come into the room carrying the same dish. He watched her whisper something to the butler. When Green came round to refill the wine glasses and bent over near Matthew, he said quietly, 'Is the young girl all right?'

'Yes, sir. She felt unwell and is being taken care of.'

Matt nodded, satisfied, turning his attention

86

back to the guests. His mother expected all her sons to play their part in keeping the conversation going.

'Matthew!'

He looked across the table to Gloria Tremain, a polite smile on his face. She always called him Matthew, not Matt like everyone else.

'Your father told me you are going to learn about engines.'

'That's right. Car engines.'

'What a strange profession.' Her expression said that she disapproved. 'But I suppose that as the third son you are allowed to do much as you please.'

'It has its advantages.' Gloria always spoke as if the Stannards were a titled family. Her pretentious ideas irritated him. Not wishing to talk to her any longer, he turned to listen to something the person next to him was saying. That should get rid of her, he thought, as a chuckle of amusement rose inside him. It had been obvious for some time that Gloria was trying to attach herself to him. John was too serious; Luke too fond of chasing the girls – any girls; and that left him as her way into the Stannard family. She was wasting her time, though. He couldn't stand her. She was a snob, and, having been educated at the Templeton School for Young Ladies, useless except as a hostess. He preferred girls who had depth to them, some conversation and knowledge of what was going on in the world. Living with someone as shallow as Gloria would be purgatory for him.

Through the chatter he heard the Wall Street

crash mentioned and the suffering it was causing some families. He strained to hear what was being said further down the table.

'Terrible business,' Lady Arlington was saying. 'They can't find a trace of the Winford daughter. One dreads to think what might have become of her. Only sixteen years of age, I'm told.'

'That's right,' Gloria announced. 'I knew her. She was at my school. Always was on the wilful side, though I cannot understand why she wanted to run away when Albert Greaves would have married her. I never thought she was lacking in good sense. The stupid girl – she could have had a life of luxury.'

Matt bristled at her scornful tone. 'I don't know the man, but perhaps she didn't want to marry him.'

Gloria gave him a withering look that said quite plainly that he didn't know what he was talking about. 'He is said to be immensely wealthy.'

Matt ignored her; he didn't know the girl they were talking about anyway. His mind kept going back to their under housemaid. He hoped she was feeling better. He couldn't understand why he felt so concerned about her; she was little more than a schoolgirl and he hardly knew her. Still, he'd had the impression that she was frightened about something. He gave a wry grimace. His father always said that he had a romantic nature and a too-vivid imagination. He was beginning to think his father was right.

The master had sent down beer, wine, lemonade and even a bottle of whisky for the staff to welcome in the New Year. There was also plenty of good food – cook had seen to that – and everyone was determined to have a boisterous party to see in 1930.

They were all laughing, but the fright earlier was still haunting Jenny. When midnight arrived, they toasted the New Year and she smiled, sipping her lemonade. Being so young they wouldn't allow her anything stronger and she couldn't tell them that she had been allowed a little wine at home. They treated her kindly and she hated deceiving them. There had been many times over the last few weeks when she'd wanted to confide in Edna, but she didn't dare risk it. Gossip spread at an alarming rate from household to household.

'Don't look so serious, Jenny.' Mrs Peters held up her glass. 'Are you still feeling rough?'

'I'm fine, thank you.' She gazed at the smiling faces and wanted to weep. They cared about her, yet she was lying to them. It made her most uncomfortable to have to watch what she said all the time. With practice the London accent had improved, coming more naturally, though she still found the work very hard. It was only the thought of Greaves that kept her gritting her teeth and getting on with it.

After a vigorous dance to 'Knees Up, Mother Brown', they cleared up and went to their beds at twelve thirty. There would still be an early start. That never changed.

Jenny sat on the bed to kick off her shoes, then saw Edna looking at her with a strange expression on her face.

'What was that all about, Jen?'

'Sorry?'

'You know what I'm talking about. You wasn't ill. Something or someone in the dining room sent you into a panic.'

When Jenny opened her mouth to deny it, Edna held up her hand to stop her. 'It's no good you trying to fool me. I've known from the start that you're not what you seem. I only had to see the state of your hands that first week to know you wasn't used to hard work.'

Oh, Lord, and she thought she'd been doing quite well. She shook her head and looked pleadingly at her friend. 'I can't tell you, Edna. I wish I could.'

'It's all right, we all have secrets. But will you answer a couple of questions?'

'If I can.'

'Was there someone upstairs who would have known you?'

Jenny nodded.

'That means you're hiding from someone.'

She nodded again.

'Are you running from the law?'

'No!' Jenny was on her feet in alarm, the lino on the floor feeling like ice on her bare feet. 'I haven't done anything wrong. Honest.'

'I believe you. So what happens if they find you?'

She sat down again on the edge of the bed, wrapping her arms around herself and moaned, 'They mustn't!'

'Last question. Is it family trouble?'

'Yes. I wish I could tell you, but I can't.'

Edna sat beside her and took hold of her hand. 'Many of us run away for some reason or other. I did myself. Five years ago my dad took off and my mum had a lot of *friends*, if you know what I mean.'

Jenny gripped her hand and nodded. Edna was some years older than her and much more worldly-wise. Her sound common sense and cheerful nature often helped Jenny through a difficult day. She liked her very much. 'What happened?'

'One bloke she came home with moved in. He was a right bastard and I had to pile furniture against my bedroom door to keep him out. I wasn't going to put up with that, so I scarpered.' Edna smiled at her. 'They'll stop looking for you eventually, Jen, so stick it out.'

'Oh, I hope so. I get very frightened at times.'

'Don't you worry. You let me know if they get too close and I'll swear blind that I've known you, Jenny Baker, for more than three years. That ain't your real name, I take it?'

'No.'

Her friend stood up and started getting ready for bed. 'When you feel like you wants to talk, you can trust me. I won't breathe a word to anyone about this. You must 'ave been desperate to throw yourself into a life you know nothing about. 'Cos from what I've seen of you these past weeks, I reckon you're more used to having servants than being one. I can guess what you're going through.'

Jenny sighed in relief. One day she would tell her friend the whole story, and it was a comforting feeling to know she had an ally at last. 'I'll tell you when I feel safe again.'

'I know you will.'

8

September 1930

'Okay, you're on your own. Let's see you strip that engine down, then put it back together. I'll count the parts you have left over.'

Matt tipped his head back and laughed at his boss. 'You don't think I can do it, do you?'

'You've learnt a lot in nine months and I know you've been itching to have a go, but I think it's unlikely you can do it yet without help.' Mr Porter tossed him a spanner. 'Don't shout for help because from now on I'm deaf.'

'I'm going to prove you wrong.'

'Can't hear a word you're saying.' Jake Porter wandered away, shaking his head in mock bewilderment.

Chuckling to himself, Matt watched him for a few moments, then tucked the spanner into one of his overall pockets, propped up the bonnet of the car and rubbed his hands in anticipation. This was going to be a real challenge, but he was confident he could do it. He didn't regret leaving university. There was nothing like the pleasure of getting his hands covered in grease as he worked on the engines. He'd never been so happy. The only worry he had was watching the depression take a grip on the country. The stock market crash in America last year was having an impact on most countries now. Britain's shipbuilding, textiles, coal and things like steel were suffering because of a slump in world trade. Unemployment in Britain was at something like two million, causing hardship for many families. All seemed well with the garage at the moment, but he was watching carefully. The economic signs indicated that things were going to get worse, and, if they did, he would see if he could help the business ride out the storm. He hadn't mentioned any of this to his boss, of course, as he was just an apprentice. He would wait and watch.

Pushing aside the concern, he turned his full attention to the engine. He removed each part, nut and bolt, placing them in order on the concrete floor; then it should be simple to put them back the same way. That was the theory anyway. He was determined not to have so much as a washer left over. The crucial test would come when he tried to restart the engine.

He whistled happily to himself as he set about his task.

The train to Brighton wasn't too crowded when Edna and Jenny got on. They found themselves seats in a carriage with only two people in it. Sitting opposite each other, they grinned. A whole day off together was a rare treat. This had only been possible because four weeks ago the Stannards had employed another housemaid, Pat.

'Hope the weather stays warm,' Edna said. 'I'm going to have a paddle first, then we'll have fish and chips, and buy a stick of rock to suck on the way back.'

They'd been planning this from the day Pat arrived, carefully saving enough money for the fare and a little to spend. Jenny gazed out as the train chugged along. It had taken weeks for her to get over the fright of seeing Gloria at the New Year dinner party. But nothing had happened and she'd gradually begun to relax as winter had turned to spring and spring to summer. Edna was a stalwart friend and hadn't asked any more questions. She felt secure after all these months. Aunt Gertrude must have stopped looking for her by now.

As they got away from London and the countryside took the place of buildings, Jenny's thoughts went back to the lovely school in Kent. Her friends would be preparing for the start of the autumn term. Did they miss her? Did they understand why she had run away? She missed them and the fun they used to have together. If it hadn't been for Edna, she would have been desperately unhappy during these last ten months.

'Don't look so sad, Jen,' Edna said. 'We're going to have a smashing time today.'

'Yes, we are.' She smiled brightly, pushing the painful memories away. She constantly told herself not to dwell on the past, but the thoughts had a habit of sneaking past her guard. She still grieved for her father and was desperately upset that he'd felt he had to take his own life.

Although the appearance of a happy family life had been a sham, she had loved him and he'd been kind to her. Her mother hadn't seemed to care what happened to her, but Jenny couldn't help but wonder how she was. Living with her sister, Gertrude, couldn't be a happy experience. At times doubts assailed her. Should she have stayed and tried to help her mother? But the answer was always the same. If she had, she would have been facing the prospect of marriage to Greaves, and that was more than she could have dealt with. It had been her seventeenth birthday last month, and she doubted he would consider that too young! There certainly wouldn't have been any family opposition. A shudder rippled through her. She'd had to think of her own future, hadn't she?

The couple in their carriage got out at the station before Brighton, leaving behind their London newspaper. Jenny picked it up, and as she flicked through the pages something caught her attention. She gasped in dismay as she read the announcement: 'Missing from home since November 1929. Eugenie Elizabeth Winford. Now seventeen years of age; dark hair and brown eyes. Well educated. A reward of £100 is offered for information of her whereabouts. Contact Mr Albert Greaves through the police.'

Jenny dropped the paper as if it were on fire. Oh, dear God!

'What's the matter?' Edna asked, alarmed. 'You've gone white. Are you feeling ill?'

'They're still looking for me,' she whispered in horror.

Edna picked up the paper from the floor. 'How do you know? Is it in here?'

'Yes.' She took the paper away from her friend. Edna knew she had a secret, but she didn't want her, or anyone, to know who she really was. One hundred pounds was a fortune to most people; it would be a very great temptation. Not that she believed her friend would turn her in, but it was better not to put temptation in her way.

'You must be someone important if they put it in the papers.'

'I'm not at all important, but this person wants me back, and it looks as if he will do anything to track me down.'

'He?' Edna sat up straight, frowning fiercely. 'Some man's after you?'

Jenny nodded, clasping her shaking hands together and screwing up the paper. 'He's around fifty, fat and not a pleasant person. The way he looks at me is frightening.'

'One of those.' Edna was clearly disgusted. 'Well, don't you worry. No one knows who you are – not even me – so I don't think there's much chance of him finding you after all this time. He must be desperate to put it in the newspapers.'

One hundred pounds' worth of desperate! The fear that Jenny thought had left her came rushing back. Thank goodness they hadn't put a photograph of her in there, but she doubted if they had one; she'd tucked them all in the bottom of her case before leaving, along with her other treasures. 'I do hope you're right.' She leant out of the window and tossed the paper as far away as she could. It made her feel better to watch the

96

wind catch the pages and send them tumbling and twisting over a field.

'You mustn't let it spoil our day, Jen. He'll never find you. My family don't know where I am to this day, and it's been three years since I left home.'

'Of course he won't.' She took a deep breath to steady her racing heart. 'It gave me a fright, that's all.'

'This is Brighton, so let's forget everything and just enjoy ourselves, shall we?' Edna gave her an encouraging smile.

'You're right. I'm being silly to let it bother me after all this time.'

Once out of the station they made for the beach, eager to get to the sea.

'Oh, isn't that lovely!' Edna gazed out to sea with a rapt expression on her face. 'Just smell that. Come on, let's have a paddle.'

They sat down and removed their shoes and stockings, and, clutching them in their hands, walked gingerly over the pebbles to the water's edge. They gave a little squeal as the cold water splashed over their bare feet.

Jenny closed her eyes and lifted her face to the sun, enjoying its warmth, and listening to the soothing sound of gentle waves as they tumbled on to the beach. The tension she was feeling after seeing the newspaper seeped away. A larger wave hit her and she opened her eyes, looking down at her wet legs. Sand and tiny pebbles were swirling around her toes, tickling her and making her laugh. As the wave rushed back, the undertow sucked the silt from under her feet, throwing her

97

off balance.

'Whoops!' Edna caught her, laughing. 'Let's get some fish and chips. I'm starving. We can have another paddle before we have to go back to London.'

The rest of the day was fun. After lunch they walked along the pier, hanging over the rails at the very end to gaze out to sea. Just before they had to catch their train they paddled again. Their feet were still wet when they put their stockings and shoes back on, but they didn't care. They'd had a really lovely day.

They arrived back at six o'clock, flushed with a day in the open air and very happy. However, as soon as they walked in the kitchen Jenny knew by the grim expressions that something had happened.

'What's wrong?' Edna asked.

Cook checked on her roast in the oven, then said, 'We've had a dreadful day. Madam found that two of her snuffboxes were missing from the collection. All our rooms were searched and they were found under the new housemaid's mattress. She's been dismissed.'

Jenny's heart hammered.

'We was all searched.' Mrs Peters looked very put out. 'In all my years of service I've never been so humiliated.'

'Jenny!' The housekeeper appeared in the doorway. 'You are to go up to see Mr and Mrs Stannard immediately.'

'Why, what have I done?' She gripped the edge of the table to steady herself. If they'd searched her case...

'The master will tell you. Quickly, take off your hat and coat.'

Jenny thrust them at Edna and then ran to catch up with Mrs Douglas, who was making for the library.

As soon as she stepped through the door Jenny knew that her security had vanished. Spread across a small table were the beautiful lace and beaded dress and the diamond and emerald pendant that her father had given to her. Not the kind of things a maid would own. She had been foolish to bring the dress, and she should have kept the pendant round her neck, but she'd been afraid of losing it by the seaside.

'You have heard about the thefts?' Mr Stannard didn't waste any time.

'Yes, sir.' She clasped her hands tightly to stop them shaking.

'A thorough search was made for the missing items and these were found in your suitcase. We want to know how you came by such expensive items.'

'They are mine. I didn't steal them.' She knew that was not an acceptable answer, but she couldn't explain. Her eyes filled with tears as she reached out to touch the beautiful dress. It held such lovely memories. 'I didn't steal them, sir,' she whispered. 'They *do* belong to me.'

'I think that most unlikely!'

'My dear.' His wife stood up and walked towards her husband. 'Perhaps someone gave them to Jenny as a gift.'

'Nonsense.' He glared at the frightened girl in

front of him. 'Well, I require an explanation.'

Jenny didn't answer, as large tears began to course down her face at the memories the dress evoked. Her father's smile as he'd told her how beautiful she was, and her mother's nod of approval. They'd taken her to Covent Garden that evening. Such happy memories.

'And how did you come by the diamond and emerald pendant? That cannot have been a gift!'

Jenny remained mute. She had gone through hardship to get away, and if she spoke now it would all have been in vain. They would go straight to her mother. He believed her to be a thief – his mind was made up. And there wasn't a thing she could do about it.

'Your silence condemns you,' he snapped. 'As you are not prepared to give a satisfactory reason why these items were in your possession, then you are dismissed with immediate effect.'

His wife tried to intervene, but he held up his hand. 'I'll deal with this. I won't have staff who can't be trusted.'

'But I haven't done anything wrong,' Jenny protested, terrified at being thrown out. 'My father gave them to me–'

'It's no good trying to explain now. You've had your chance. You may leave at once and thank your lucky stars that I don't hand you over to the law.'

She reached out to pick up the dress and pendant.

'Leave those. They will be given to the police to see if they can trace their rightful owner.'

It was over. Her aunt was bound to have

searched her things to find out what she had taken, and then told the police to be on the lookout for them. Terror surged through her. The pendant was her only means of raising money. That was necessary because she was going to have to run again.

With a moan of despair she lunged for her precious things, hugging them to her as she rounded on Mr Stannard, fear and anger loosening her tongue. There was little point in pretence now. 'They are mine. My father did give them to me, but now he's dead.'

There was a stunned silence in the room. Mrs Douglas, who was still standing by the door, had turned quite pale. Jenny was frantic and spun round to face Mrs Stannard, the words tumbling out without thought. 'I've worked hard for you, never complaining about the long hours, yet you are going to let your husband dismiss me without proof of wrongdoing. I am *not* a thief!'

In her anguish she had quite forgotten her cockney accent, and the words gushed out in her best Templeton School accent.

'Who are you?' Mr Stannard demanded, surprised.

'My dear,' his wife said, as she took her husband's arm, 'something is very wrong here.'

'I know that,' he said sharply. 'She doesn't sound like a servant now.'

'Jenny.' Madam glanced at the dress again. 'You appear to be a well-educated young lady. Will you explain why you are masquerading as a servant?'

'I can't tell you. All I can say is that these are

my things and you have no right to take them from me.' Jenny knew that if the Stannards found out who she really was, Aunt Gertrude would take over her life again.

Mr Stannard had obviously lost patience. 'As you refuse to say how you came by these things, then you must leave. I will not have someone under my roof of doubtful reputation.'

Jenny heard his wife whisper, 'Do not be so hasty.'

'My mind is made up. This girl is lying.'

Jenny knew that this was the end of her time here. Still holding tightly on to her things, she ran past Mrs Douglas and up to her room, where she shoved everything into her case. The uniform was left on top of the bed. It didn't take her more than a minute. Edna had left her hat and coat over a chair, so she put them on, grabbed her case and ran down the servants' stairs, reaching the door just as Mrs Douglas came rushing after her.

'Jenny, madam is asking for you.'

She sidestepped the housekeeper and tore through the door towards the street.

'Jenny! Wait.'

She kept running.

There was a bus at the stop and Jenny jumped on, standing by the door for a moment as it pulled away, watching Mrs Douglas waving frantically at her until she was out of sight. Finding a seat near the door, she sat down and bowed her head, too frightened even to cry. Over the months she had begun to feel safe, but in one day her world had collapsed again. It had been a day of complete contrasts: happiness at the seaside, and dismay on her return. Now she was completely homeless.

'Are you all right, miss?'

'Erm...' The conductor was standing in front of her. 'Where is this bus going?'

'Marble Arch, miss.'

It took a great deal of control to stop herself from laughing hysterically. What did it matter? She didn't have anywhere to go!

Fishing in her purse, she found a penny and gave it to the conductor.

'Where are you going?' he wanted to know.

'The next stop but one.' That would take her far enough away from the Stannard house. Then she must decide what to do. She had to find lodgings before it was dark. There was one pound note in her purse and a few coppers. She immediately regretted the money she'd spent on the trip to Brighton. But how could she have known this was going to happen? It was then she realized that she was owed a week's wages, and in panic she had run away without asking for the money. Fool, she berated herself. All she'd thought about was getting away before they found out she was Eugenie Winford.

A quiet moan of despair escaped through her lips. What was she going to do? Resting her forehead on the window, she gazed out, trying to still the panic rushing through her. But what she saw only increased her anxiety. The light was fading. It would soon be dark and she had nowhere to go, no shelter for the night. She thought of the room she shared with Edna and wished fervently that she were back there, safe and secure.

The conductor came along to take the fares of two people who had just got on, so Jenny fished in her pocket and held out a sixpence when he stopped near her. 'I've decided to go to Marble Arch,' she told him.

He gave her another ticket and frowned when he took the money from her trembling hand. 'Are you sure you're all right, miss?'

'Yes, thank you.' Slipping the change back in her pocket, she tried a smile, but without much success. 'Will you tell me when we're there, please?'

He nodded and went back to his job.

Jenny knew there was an underground station at Marble Arch, so perhaps she could find shelter there.

9

Matthew was buoyant after his success with the engine, but, returning home that evening, he found the house in uproar. His mother was furious about something and arguing fiercely with her husband. Gilbert was standing there with a stunned expression on his face, not able to believe that his usually calm and pleasant wife could explode like this.

Matt went over to his brothers, who were standing by the window looking equally surprised.

'What's going on?' he asked. 'Our parents never argue.'

Luke pulled a face. 'They are now. Father's handled the situation badly, and he's not going to be allowed to get away with it this time.'

'What situation?'

John then explained about the theft, the new housemaid who had been dismissed, and the expensive items found in the under housemaid's case. 'She ran up to her room, grabbed her case and left the house while Mother and Father were still arguing about it. Mrs Douglas tried to catch up with her, but it was too late.'

'She stole them?' Matt was appalled. He'd rather liked the quiet young girl.

'No.' Luke shook his head. 'She insisted that they belonged to her, but Father dismissed her as a thief without any proof. Mother tried to stop him. He wouldn't listen, though; you know what he's like when his mind is made up. When he tried to send her away without the dress and the necklace, she grabbed them off the table and held on to them tightly. The girl was determined to keep the things she declared were hers.'

John looked across at their parents and shook his head. 'This is a very strange business. She was frightened, and in her agitation her accent changed to that of a very well-educated girl.'

'I always felt she was hiding something.' Matt was furious with himself for not following his instinct about her.

John rounded on his younger brother. 'If you had some doubts about her, then why the hell didn't you tell us, Matt? It would have saved all this trouble.'

Matt shrugged. 'What could I say? It was only a feeling I had. You'd have thought me mad if I'd said that we should look into her background.'

'Well, Gilbert, what are you going to do about it?' Louise Stannard had by no means finished with her husband. 'The girl is obviously in terrible trouble, and you have just turned her out on to the street.'

He looked thoroughly disgruntled. 'We've paid her a fair wage–'

'Gilbert!' His wife raised her voice in exasperation. 'Haven't you heard a word I've said?'

'It isn't our responsibility.'

Matt flinched when he saw his mother's face change. She normally had a placid nature, but he knew that she could erupt on the rare occasion. And this was obviously one of those times. If his father had overruled her in the matter of hiring and firing of staff then he was really in trouble.

'Oh, isn't it? You accuse an obviously well-bred young girl of being a thief and then turn her out.'

'How was I to know? For God's sake, Louise, she's been scrubbing our floors.'

'Exactly! So how desperate do you think that makes her?' Louise wiped a hand over her eyes and sighed. 'This is terrible, Gilbert. I didn't expect her to flee from this house so quickly. I thought I would have time to see her on her own and put the matter right. We've got to find her before anyone else does. She might not have anywhere else to go.'

106

Finally his parents became quiet, and Matt could almost taste the tension and worry in the room. The sense of triumph he'd felt, when the engine had roared into life after he'd put it back together, evaporated. What was going to happen to that poor girl now?

The door opened and Mrs Douglas hurried in, very out of breath. 'I'm so sorry, madam, but she's gone. There was a bus at the stop and she jumped on just as it was pulling away.'

'Which bus?' Matt asked. There was no way he was going to keep out of this.

'I couldn't see, Mr Matthew.' The housekeeper was clearly upset. 'She glanced back at me as the bus went up the road, and she looked so young and frightened. I don't believe she knew or cared which bus she was on. All she wanted to do was get away.'

His parents now had an air of hopelessness about them, and his brothers were not contributing anything to help with the crisis, so Matt took over. 'Who among the servants knew her the best?'

'That would be Edna. They shared a room,' the housekeeper told him.

'Bring her here, please, Mrs Douglas.'

The housekeeper returned with Edna, who was red-eyed with weeping.

Matt left the questioning to his mother, who now seemed in control again.

'Edna, do you know where Jenny might have gone?'

'No.' Another tear trickled down her face. 'I'm that worried, madam. She ain't fit to be out there on her own.'

'Do you know who she is?' Gilbert asked.

'She never talked about herself – not even to me, and we was friends. But I know she wasn't used to hard work. You should have seen her poor hands at first. There was never a complaint, though; just got on with the jobs, she did.' Edna's eyes were brimming over. 'She isn't a thief. Mrs Douglas said she'd told you she owned those things. If she said that, then it was the truth. She ain't a liar neither.'

Louise handed the housemaid a handkerchief.

The maid mopped up her tears. 'I did know she was hiding from someone. Real frightened of him, she was.'

'We've got to find her, Edna.' Matt didn't like this situation at all. The thought of a defenceless girl like that running scared worried him. There was no telling what might happen to her. 'Didn't she tell you anything about friends she might have – someone she could go to?'

Edna chewed her lip. 'As I said, she didn't say nothing about herself. Except...'

'Yes?' Matt prompted, when the girl stopped what she was saying.

'She did say she came from Lambeth and went to school there.'

'We know that isn't true.' Matt's father was now pacing the room with an empty glass in his hand as if he'd forgotten to fill it with brandy. 'She's probably seen sense and gone home.'

'Oh, no, sir!' Edna was clearly horrified. 'That's the last thing she'd do. Too frightened, she is. This man what's after her is not nice.

When we was on the train today she saw something in a newspaper. Went white, she did – I thought she was going to faint. No! She won't go home.'

'Which newspaper?' Louise sat down as if drained of all strength and began to scan the papers on the table.

'I don't know. She threw it out the window before I could see it.' Edna hesitated, then gave Matt a pleading look. 'You got to find her. She ain't got no one. On her own, she is.'

He nodded grimly. 'I'll do my best.'

But where did he start?

'Keep a sharp lookout, Luke,' Matt ordered as he drove slowly up the road.

'This is hopeless, you know that,' his brother complained. 'She could be anywhere by now. And why the hell are you bothering?'

'Because she's a young frightened girl and we don't know if she's got a family, or anywhere to go.' He gave his brother a worried look. 'Father acted too hastily, and I consider that makes us responsible for her safety!'

'You would think that,' Luke said with a shake of his head.

'What does that mean?' he snapped.

'You care too much about other people and what's going on in the world. Look at the way you're always going on about the emerging Nazi Party. Now this R101 airship is really something to get excited about. Just think, Matt, with the kind of aircraft they're now developing it won't be long before we can go anywhere by air.'

'I agree that it is an exciting prospect, but I happen to believe that the Nazis are dangerous. And they're getting far too powerful. They've won almost a hundred seats in this month's German elections.' Matt loved his brother, but Luke couldn't seem to see past his own little world...

Luke continued as if he hadn't spoken. 'And the girl you're getting in a stew about is only a servant–'

'My God!' exploded Matt. 'What an unfeeling beast you are.'

Luke laughed in his usual careless way. 'No, I'm not. I'm a realist. While this girl was under our roof we were responsible for her, but Father has dismissed her. For a very good reason, as far as I can see. Stop worrying, Matt. She'll go back to her family and soon get another job.'

'Suppose she hasn't got anyone who would take her in; have you thought of that?' Matt drove along Oxford Street. 'Keep looking. Some of the buses from our place do come along here. I wish Mrs Douglas had thought to get the number of the bus before it disappeared.'

His brother scanned the pavements. 'She could be anywhere. Why don't you try the Edgware Road?'

Without a word Matt shot down a side road, turned round and headed back the way they'd come.

After another half an hour, Luke had clearly had enough. 'Let's go back. We're never going to find her, and it's nearly dark now.'

With great reluctance Matt had to admit that

110

his brother was right. He'd been driving around aimlessly, without the faintest notion of where the girl might have gone. Concern sat like a heavy weight on him as he drove past Marble Arch Station and headed back home. God keep you safe, he prayed silently.

'Did you find her?' their mother asked as soon as they walked into the drawing room.

'Sorry, Mother.' Matt sat down and picked up one of the newspapers now littering the room. 'Did you find anything?'

'No,' John said. 'Whatever frightened her on the train isn't in any of these newspapers. At least we don't think so, but really, we haven't any idea what or who she's running from.'

Luke poured himself a drink and shrugged. 'It's out of our hands now. We've done all we can.'

'Yes!' Louise glared at her husband. 'We've thrown a young girl out to fend for herself. And I, for one, am very worried about her safety.'

'Ah, my dear, don't upset yourself so,' her husband soothed. 'We've dismissed servants before, and I'm sure this one was lying to us. We couldn't keep her.'

'Maybe not,' she agreed, still looking concerned. 'If she was masquerading as a servant, then we obviously couldn't have kept her. But I would have preferred to know what this was all about, and to see that she had somewhere else to go.'

Matt watched his mother. He had never seen her so concerned, and he felt the same.

'What do you think about all this, Matt?' she

111

asked her youngest son.

'I don't know,' he admitted. 'But I wish I'd been able to bring her back here until we'd got to the bottom of the mystery.'

'There's no mystery,' his father said with an air of exasperation. 'The girl was untrustworthy. You must never take anyone on without proper references again, Louise. It only leads to trouble. Now let us have an end to this. I will not have a thief under my roof! And if those items had really belonged to her, she would have explained, and that would have saved all this unpleasantness.'

'But she didn't steal the snuffboxes, Gilbert, and you had no proof that the dress and pendant were stolen by her.'

'Of course they were! Her silence condemned her.'

Matt glanced at his mother and frowned. They were very alike in temperament. And, it seemed, the only two who were worried about the girl.

'How did you get on today?' his father asked, effectively changing the subject.

Matt explained about his success in stripping down the engine and putting it back together.

'How many bits did you have left over?' Luke laughed.

'Not one,' he told them with a sense of pride.

'Well done,' his father said, happy now the vexing subject of the girl had been dropped.

The conversation turned to general topics and the Stannard family indulged in their usual friendly banter. The unpleasant incidents of the day seemed to have been forgotten.

112

There were people hurrying to and from the trains, and Jenny pretended to be studying the map of the stations on the wall. She was utterly lost and bewildered. Any hope of finding shelter here for the night had vanished. An underground railway station was no place for a young girl by herself. There were already some rather un-savoury-looking characters around, and one was eyeing her in the way that Greaves had. What was she going to do? Could she afford a hotel for one night? That idea was instantly dismissed. What little money she had would have to be used sparingly. But she couldn't wander around London all night. Her insides churned alarmingly. The thought was terrifying!

She touched the pendant round her neck. At least she still had that. She'd have to go to the pawnbroker tomorrow and sell it... Lambeth! Glad and Fred. They'd said she could go to them if she was in trouble – and she certainly was in trouble. Why hadn't she thought of that before? They would take her in for one night, or at least show her somewhere safe to sleep. Then she could decide what to do in the morning.

Galvanized into action, Jenny searched her bag for the address, letting out a ragged sigh when she found it. The paper was torn but still legible. Thank goodness she always carried it with her. Now that she'd made up her mind, she wanted to get there as quickly as possible. In less than an hour it would be dark. She hurried to buy a ticket to Lambeth.

'How do I get there?' she asked nervously.

The man peered over the top of his glasses and leant on the counter. 'You get on a train going to Oxford Circus, change there to the Bakerloo Line and that will take you to Lambeth North.'

'Thank you.' She hurried down the crowded stairs, stopping to see what platform she needed, then rushed to get on the train just thundering into the station.

'Excuse me.' Jenny stopped a woman outside Lambeth North Station. 'Could you tell me where Forest Road is, please?'

'Take a left turn at the bottom of the road opposite you, then left again into Park Street, halfway down there you'll see a road on the right, that's Forest.'

'Thank you.' But Jenny was speaking to herself; the woman was already hurrying away.

She crossed the road and headed in the direction the woman had pointed out. It was quite dark now and she was really frightened about walking along these unfamiliar streets on her own, but she was even more scared of staying out all night, so she kept walking. She found Park Street easily enough, and her pace quickened as she passed groups of men standing outside the houses, smoking and laughing. It was with immense relief that she turned into Forest Road. The house at the top of the road was No. 38; she would have to walk quite a way, because Fred and Glad lived at No. 14.

Whoever had named this street must have had a perverse sense of humour, she decided, as there wasn't a tree in sight. The road was narrow and dingy, with the front doors right on the pavement. The paintwork on the doors and windows was peeling on most of them, revealing rotting wood underneath. Jenny began to shake. These were slum dwellings, and, from what she could see of the men and women standing on the front steps talking to each other, these people were very poor. Her step faltered. How could she ask someone she'd met only once to take her in? But she didn't have anywhere else to go. She would have to throw herself on Fred and Glad's mercy. If they couldn't help her, they might know where she could find shelter until the morning.

No. 20, not far now. She dropped her bag on the pavement outside No. 14 and let out a ragged sigh. Some effort had been made to make the front look presentable. Although a coat of fresh paint was needed, at least it wasn't peeling off, and the step was clean enough to grace the Stannard house. Dismay tore through her when she remembered how they had treated her. They hadn't needed any proof before calling her a thief, and to dismiss her in that way had been brutal. It would have been sensible to ask if she could stay the night and leave in the morning, but, if she'd done that, they might have insisted that she leave the dress and pendant behind. They were all she had left of value and she couldn't risk it. She hoped she never saw any of them again – except Edna, of course. She was going to miss her very much.

A group of men turned into the street, singing at the tops of their voices and reeling about all over the place. Drunk! In panic Jenny hammered on the front door. Oh, please be in, she prayed. The men had seen her and were already calling out; from the remarks they were making, they were obviously intent on having a bit of fun. She picked up her case and glanced around for somewhere to hide, but there wasn't anywhere. It was a narrow street of terraced houses as far as she could see, without even a small gap between them. She was just about to bolt as the door opened. When she saw Fred's kindly face a tear trickled down her cheek in relief.

'I need help, please!'

Fred peered at her in the gloom.

'I'm Jenny.'

'Well, I'll be blowed, so it is.' He stepped back and opened the door wide. 'Come in.'

She practically ran in. The front door opened straight into the living room and Glad was already on her feet.

'My dear child, whatever's happened to you? You're in a right state.'

That was too much for Jenny's frayed nerves. She stood in the middle of the room, head bowed, and sobbed her heart out. Now she was safe, the horror of what had happened this evening was too much to bear. She'd lost her job, been accused of being a thief, and had to leave Edna behind. She tried to pull herself together, being ashamed of carrying on like this in front of people she hardly knew.

Fred took the case out of her hands. 'There, don't take on so. You're all right now. Put the kettle on, Glad.'

'Come and sit down.'

A young woman took her arm and pushed her gently into a chair. It was only then that she looked around and saw that the tiny room was crowded with people. She wiped her eyes, blew her nose and gulped. 'I'm sorry, I shouldn't have come here, but I didn't know what else to do.'

Glad put a cup of tea in her hand. 'We told you to come to us if you was in trouble, didn't we?'

'I know but it's such an imposition.'

Fred grinned. 'Still using those long words, are you? Drink your tea now.'

Her hands were shaking so much it was difficult to bring the cup to her lips, but she managed it without spilling too much. After a couple of mouthfuls she began to feel calmer. Fred and Glad were just as she remembered them. They wouldn't turn her out.

'I was going to try to sleep at Marble Arch Station,' she told them.

Fred tutted. 'You couldn't do that. It's much too dangerous for a young girl.'

'Let's introduce you to everyone.' Glad smiled. 'This is our daughter, Ivy, and her husband, Ron. Their two kids, Alice and baby Bert. And this is Fred's brother, Stan.'

'I'm pleased to meet you all.' She pulled a hanky out of her pocket, blew her nose and gave a watery smile.

'Now,' Fred said, sitting opposite her, 'you tell us what this is all about.'

For the next half an hour she explained what had happened since she'd met them and they'd taken her to the pawnbroker's, and about the Stannards dismissing her because they thought she was a thief.

'But I'm not,' she declared stoutly. 'Those things are mine, honest.'

Glad patted her hand. 'We know that, my dear.'

Of course they would, Jenny thought, but it was wonderful to know that someone believed she wasn't lying. They'd seen the items she'd sold to the pawnbroker. 'I had to leave at once because I was afraid they would find out who I really was.'

'Is that man you told us about still after you?' Fred asked.

'Yes, and he's offering a large reward to anyone who can tell him where I am.' She stood up suddenly, the cup she was still holding rattling in the saucer. That kind of money was probably more than this family had ever seen in their lives. Her situation was hopeless. Why had she ever thought she could get away? But perhaps she could do something good before she condemned herself to a wretched life.

'Sit down, Jen.' Fred relieved her of the cup.

After sinking into the chair again, she gazed at Fred and Glad, feeling bewildered and very lost. 'I don't know how I can survive without a job. I can't go back to the agency, because Mrs Dearing would never find me another place, and I don't stand a chance without references. There's only one thing I can do and that is go home.' She felt like moaning at the thought but managed to keep her anguish inside her. 'But that awful man

118

isn't going to get me unless he pays! If I tell you who I am, then you can claim the reward of a hundred pounds.'

Fred was immediately on his feet, an outraged expression on his face. 'We'll do no such thing! As far as we're concerned, you're a young girl by the name of Jenny who is in trouble. That's all we need to know.'

'Oh, I didn't mean to insult you.' She gazed at each person in the room, wide-eyed with horror that her good intentions had caused such a reaction. Every one had the same disgusted look on their face.

Glad sat beside her and reached for her hand. 'We wouldn't turn you in, not even for the princely sum of one hundred quid.'

'We might not have much,' Stan said, 'but we do have our pride. Fred told us about meeting you and how brave they thought you was.'

'That's right,' Fred told her. 'We don't care who you are. We took a right liking to you when we showed you how to deal with the pawnbroker. Now you've come to us for help and we'll give it willingly.'

'You must be fair worn out,' Glad said with a smile. 'You can bunk down with our grand-daughter Alice tonight. There's room for you two little 'uns in that bed, and in the morning we'll decide what to do, eh? Does you want something to eat?'

Jenny shook her head, tears very close to the surface again, but tears of relief this time. 'No, thank you, I'm not hungry, just very tired.'

'One thing's for sure, my girl.' Fred gave her a

stern look. 'You're not going back to become that man's wife if you don't want to. Is that understood?'

She nodded again, beyond words now for the kindness they were showing to her. Then she stood on legs feeling like pieces of wet rag, and let Ivy lead her up the narrow stairs to where her daughter slept. The room was small and dark with room only for the bed and a cot in the corner, but it looked like heaven to Jenny.

'You have a nice rest now and you'll feel better in the morning.' Ivy handed her the case she'd brought up with her. 'Have you got everything you need?'

'Oh, yes, thank you.' Jenny trembled. 'I thought I was going to have to sleep outside tonight.'

'You did the right thing by coming to us. My mum and dad haven't stopped talking about you and wondering how you was getting on. They're right glad to see you and pleased as punch that you came to them for help.' Then she left and went back downstairs.

I'll never forget this, Jenny vowed as she got in the small bed. One day I'll repay them for their kindness.

10

Exhaustion swamped Jenny as soon as she put her head on the pillow, and the next thing she knew it was morning, with five-year-old Alice sleeping peacefully beside her. She marvelled at the attitude of these people. Alice hadn't seemed at all perturbed about sharing her bed. The cot was already empty, and she could hear the baby crying downstairs. If he had cried in the night, she hadn't heard him, but she'd been exhausted and doubted if anything could have woken her up.

'Ah, you're awake.' Glad bustled into the room. 'Up Alice, or you'll be late for school.'

The little girl tumbled out of bed and ran from the room with a bright smile on her face, then Glad studied Jenny carefully. 'You look better this morning. In bad need of a good night's kip, you was.'

Jenny sat up. 'What time is it?'

'Half past seven. Now why don't you get up, have a bite to eat and we'll talk over what's to be done.'

Jenny swung her legs out of bed. 'Where's the bathroom?'

'We ain't got one of those, Jen. There's a privy and outhouse by the kitchen. I'll boil you up a drop of water so you can have a wash.' Then she bustled out again.

Before going downstairs, Jenny glanced in the other two rooms on this floor. Each contained a double bed and no room for anything else. She wondered where Fred's brother, Stan, slept. There certainly wasn't room up here, so he must sleep downstairs in the front room. The house was very small, she noticed, as she made her way down the steep stairs; you could have fitted the whole of the top floor into the bedroom she'd had at home. And even the attic room she'd shared with Edna had been bigger than these. She was going to miss Edna; they had become good friends. Jenny decided that once she'd sorted things out, she would let Edna know she was all right. It would be wrong to let her worry.

The kitchen consisted of a large white sink with one tap, an ancient gas stove, a small black leaded fire and a well-scrubbed wooden table.

Glad looked up from slicing a loaf of bread. 'There's a kettle of hot water on the fire, and I've put soap and a towel outside for you.'

'Thank you.' Jenny picked up the heavy black cast-iron kettle and went out to the wash-house. The rough brickwork had been given a coat of whitewash, as had the outside toilet. Conditions were primitive in Jenny's eyes, but it was spotlessly clean. She shivered as she stripped down for a wash. Being late September, there was an early-morning nip in the air. It must be freezing out here in the winter, she thought, as she got back into her clothes as quickly as possible.

Picking up the kettle, she went back to the kitchen, a heavy weight of sadness pressing on her. Her quiet moan was laced with fear. What was to become of her?

Her shoulders drooped as she put the kettle back on the draining board. She couldn't stay here. Glad and Fred obviously had enough trouble caring for their own family. They didn't have room for someone who was nothing to do with them.

'Come and sit down,' Glad said, placing an arm around her. 'Fred and Stan will be back for their breakfast soon, and then we'll sort something out for you.'

Jenny didn't know what could be done.

Fred and Stan walked in just then, quickly followed by Ivy. They all sat round the table, and Glad put a thick slice of bread in front of each of them. It was spread with a thin scraping of butter, but it tasted good to Jenny. She was very hungry, and the tea was hot and strong.

'Get some good stuff this morning?' Glad asked the men.

'Not bad, but prices is getting steep,' Fred told her. 'And we've just heard that Talbots Engineering has laid off fifty workers. Things is getting tough.'

'I know, and I reckon it's going to get worse.' Glad's usual cheery expression slipped for a moment, then brightened again. 'At least you and Stan can't get laid off because you work for yourselves.'

'What about Ron?' Stan asked Ivy. 'Is he still all right at his factory?'

'So far, but there's talk about cutting the hours because of falling orders. He's a good carpenter but sales of furniture have dropped off. And that means a cut in pay. I don't know how we're ever going to be able to afford a place of our own, Mum.'

'Don't you worry about that.' Glad dismissed her daughter's worries. 'We're a bit cramped, but we'll manage.'

Fred gave Jenny a wry smile. 'When you told us that your dad had lost everything in the stock market crash, I never thought something that had happened in New York would touch us. I was wrong, though. That disaster is starting to be felt everywhere.'

Jenny was puzzled. It was understandable that as her father had been a member of the New York Stock Exchange, he had lost his money when it collapsed. But how could something like that touch the lives of ordinary people? The Templeton School had been a lovely place, but Jenny was beginning to see how little it taught them about the outside world.

'I hope it doesn't get too bad,' she said.

'Nah, 'course it won't,' Stan laughed. 'As long as we can keep the barrow going, we'll be okay.'

'Barrow?' Jenny looked at Fred for an explanation.

'We're costers, luv,' he told her, and then laughed at her bewildered expression. 'Coster-mongers. We goes along to Covent Garden Market early in the morning, buy up fruit and veg, and sell it from a barrow at the market in The Cut.'

'Oh, I see.'

'Now,' Glad said, 'let's see if we can sort you

124

out, Jen. You got any ideas, Fred?'

He shook his head. 'Bugger if I know.'

'I can't stay here,' Jenny said quickly. 'I'm so grateful you took me in last night, but there isn't room. I'd be a burden to you, and that would make me very unhappy. You must let me pay for my bed and breakfast.'

Glad patted her hand reassuringly. 'We don't want your money, Jen. You're a nice kid and we want to help.'

'What about Ma Adams?' Ivy interrupted. 'Since her old man died she's alone in that house and needs some help.'

'Of course!' Glad beamed at her daughter. 'Ma Adams would love to take her in for a bit of help with the cleaning, shopping and cooking. But Jen will need a job as well.'

'I might be able to get her something with my lot.' Ivy cast a doubtful glance at Jenny. 'Do you mind charring? It's hard graft, but we're free after about ten in the morning.'

Jenny knew that a charwoman cleaned and scrubbed, and she'd been doing that kind of work as under housemaid. 'I don't mind what I do! I'd be very grateful if you could fix it for me.'

Ivy stood up. 'I'm just off to my second job, so I'll see what I can do for you.'

'Thank you.' Jenny began to feel more hopeful. If this Ma Adams gave her a room in her house, and Ivy could get her a job, then she'd be all right. And she wouldn't mind staying with these kind people.

Having finished their bread and tea, the men

also got ready to leave.

'We'll be home at the usual time.' Fred kissed his wife on the cheek. 'Take Jen to see Ma Adams.'

'I'll do that this morning. Do well today.'

'We'll 'oller until we're hoarse,' Stan told them with a grin.

When they'd gone, Jenny gathered up the dishes and began to wash up.

'Thanks,' Glad said. 'I'll just go and get the nipper dressed, and then we'll pop along to Ma Adams; she's only next door.'

The front door was open, so Glad, carrying baby Bert, walked straight in. Jenny followed. The room was identical to Fred and Glad's, except it was badly in need of a good clean. An elderly woman sitting in a battered but comfortable-looking armchair smiled when she saw them.

'Hello, Glad. My, but that kid's growing fast. Here, let me have him while you make us a nice cuppa.'

The baby was handed over, and Ma Adams studied Jenny thoughtfully. Her faded blue eyes alive with intelligence. 'And who's this, then?'

'This is Jenny. She's in a spot of bother and needs help.'

'Ah. Got yourself pregnant, have you?'

'No, I haven't, Mrs Adams!' Jenny was indignant. 'I've lost my job and had nowhere to go.'

The skin crinkled around the alert gaze as Ma grinned. 'Don't get on your high horse, ducky. I was just asking. Stop hovering in the doorway and come and sit where I can see you properly.

126

And the name's Ma.'

As ordered, Jenny sat opposite her just as Glad came back with the tea.

'Bit posh, ain't she?' Ma said, putting the baby over her shoulder and patting his back, giving a satisfied grunt when he burped loudly. 'Where'd you find her?'

'On her way to the pawnbroker's.' Glad took Bert away from her and propped him in an armchair so he could see what was going on.

'I needed some money in a hurry,' Jenny supplied helpfully.

'Folks don't go to those buggers for any other reason.' Ma cackled with mirth and slapped her knee in delight. 'I'd love to have been a fly on the wall then. Who did you go to?'

'Erm...' Jenny hesitated, 'he was called Uncle.'

That produced another rumble of laughter. 'Did you get what you wanted?'

'He finally paid up, with Fred and Glad's help.'

The blue eyes were fairly sparkling now as she turned to Glad. 'I'll bet the crafty old devil thought he was on to a good thing as soon as she opened her mouth. She sounds like one of those posh talkers on the wireless.'

Once away from the pretence of hiding her identity while at the Stannards', Jenny had quickly reverted to her natural way of speaking.

Glad was laughing as well. 'We enjoyed squeezing a bit extra out of him, but Jen was no pushover.'

'No, I don't suppose she was. Now, why have you brought her to me?'

The explanation took no more than five

minutes, and at the end Ma nodded.

'Running away, are you?'

Jenny nodded.

'Good for you. Nice to see a girl with a bit of gumption.'

The praise given with such obvious approval made Jenny square her shoulders, the defeated feeling of earlier completely vanishing.

'I like her,' Ma said to Glad. 'We can do each other a bit of good.'

Then Ma set out her terms to Jenny. 'I can't pay you nothing, but you can have the back bedroom, and in exchange for that I'll expect some help with the house, shopping and cooking. I'm not completely helpless, but I can't stand for long and the shops is impossible for me now. However, my body might be feeble but I've still got all my marbles,' she announced with a flash of pride.

What did that mean? Jenny frowned.

'That means I ain't daft yet,' Ma said, guessing her thoughts.

Jenny's grin spread. That the elderly woman was still in control of her mental faculties was obvious. 'Thank you for giving me a room, and I think we shall get along just fine.'

'You go and get your things, then you can get me a bit of shopping.'

As they left the house, Jenny heard Ma say quietly, 'Thanks, Glad.'

Jenny moved in her few possessions immediately. The back bedroom was tiny, with room for only a bed and a small cupboard, but it seemed like heaven to her. She had been so frightened that she would end up homeless and sleeping anywhere she could find. She knew that some young girls ended up as prostitutes in an effort to get enough money to live on, but nothing on this earth would make her do that. She would rather starve.

After settling in her room, she went to the kitchen and looked through the larder. As there was little food in the house, her first task was to get the shopping. Armed with Ma's list and half a crown, Jenny walked up to the small parade of shops at the top of the street. She watched in fascination as the grocer cut off the required amount of butter from a large slab and patted it into shape with a pair of wooden paddles. She put in another one and sixpence to add to the meagre basket of goods. One lesson she had learnt over the last few months was to be careful with money, so she spent wisely and was quite pleased with her efforts.

She returned to the house and was just putting the purchases on the kitchen table so she could decide how to make the best of them when Ma came in, walking with difficulty and leaning heavily on a cane.

'You never got all that for two and six,' Ma said suspiciously. 'You been spending your own money?'

There was little point denying it with those sharp eyes pricing every item on the table. 'I bought a few extras. After all, you've been kind enough to give me a room and I can't let you pay for my food as well.'

'Humph! Well, if you can't get a job you can stop that.' Ma pulled the wrapping aside on one packet. 'I see you got the butcher's best bangers. We'll have them for our dinner.'

'What time do you have your dinner?' Jenny asked.

'Around twelve will do nicely.'

Jenny was taken aback for a moment until she realized Ma was talking about noon and not midnight. 'Oh, you mean lunch.'

'You're going to have to learn our ways,' Ma told her. 'We has dinner in the middle of the day and tea at five o'clock.'

'And what do you have for tea?' Jenny asked.

'A nice bit of bread and jam.' Ma looked at her with a twinkle in her eyes. 'You gonna make a cake?'

'I thought I'd try.' She had bought what she thought were the right ingredients, though she'd never made a cake in her life. 'I think I've got everything.'

'Try?' The elderly woman chuckled. 'What did they teach you at school?'

'Very little, I'm beginning to find out.' Jenny pulled a face, knowing how ill prepared the girls at the school were for the real world. But most of them were so wealthy they wouldn't have to step outside of their cosy lives.

'You're a bright-enough kid, so you'll soon learn. I've got a good recipe you can follow.' Ma took a torn and greasy sheet of paper out of a nearby cupboard and gave it to Jenny. 'Simple, that recipe, you can't go wrong.' She turned painfully and looked over her shoulder. 'Put the kettle on, ducky, I'm gasping for a cuppa. Did you get any biscuits?'

'Only broken ones. They were cheaper.'

'That'll do fine. I likes a bicky to dunk in my tea.' She tapped her way back to the other room, muttering under her breath, 'The kid might be posh, but she's got a bit of sense.'

Jenny took that as a compliment and set about making the tea.

After enjoying the tea and biscuits, Jenny gave the house a thorough clean. The elderly woman had obviously done her best, but there was a lot she couldn't manage now.

'My, the place looks spick and span. I can see you're no stranger to a bit of spit and polish.'

'I was under housemaid and did this kind of thing every day,' Jenny said.

'Humph. You finished now?' Ma gazed through the open front door.

'Unless there's something else you'd like me to do.'

Ma put on a forlorn expression. 'My step's a right eyesore.'

'I'll soon put that right.' Jenny stood up and smiled, not a bit fooled by the elderly woman's acting. 'You'll have a step to be proud of, Ma. Then I'll get our dinner.'

The step was gleaming when Ivy arrived; she hopped over it so she didn't make it dirty again. 'Crikey, Ma,' she exclaimed, 'that's the best step in the whole street.'

'Not bad, eh?' She was fairly bursting with pride. 'Me and Jen's going to get along just fine.'

Ivy winked at Jenny. 'I've got you a job with me.

Be ready at half past five in the morning and I'll show you the ropes.'

'Oh, Ivy, thank you so much!' Jenny was overjoyed and hugged her in gratitude. It looked as if things were going to be all right after all.

Full of hope and confidence, Jenny set about making the cake, following the instructions in the recipe with great care. She beat the margarine and sugar until fluffy, added the eggs and flour, greased a tin and poured the mixture in. When the oven was hot enough, the cake was put on the top shelf and Jenny stood back with a smile of satisfaction. That was easy.

It was impossible to resist the temptation to have a peek after about twenty minutes. It was rising nicely and she was so proud, but there was one thing she wasn't sure about. She popped into the front room. 'Ma, how do you tell when a cake is cooked?'

'You stick a knife in the middle, ducky. If it comes out clean, then it's done.'

'Thanks.' She returned to the kitchen and hovered by the stove until the cooking time was over. When she opened the oven door, she was disappointed to see that it had collapsed in the middle, but the knife came out clean so it must be cooked.

Using a cloth, Jenny picked up the tin and took it to Ma. 'It's sunk!'

Ma studied the cake and pursed her lips. 'Did you open the oven door too soon?'

'I had a look to see how it was getting on,' she admitted, watching the elderly woman's face carefully. She wasn't sure if she was going to tell her off for making a mess of it, or burst into helpless laughter. It was hard to tell from her guarded expression.

'Ah, that's why. You shouldn't do that.' Ma leant forward and sniffed. 'It smells all right, though. Tip it out and leave it upside down and the hole in the middle won't show so much.'

Jenny eyed it doubtfully. 'Is it going to be edible?'

Ma did chuckle then. 'If you mean can we eat it, well, there's only one way to find out. Put the kettle on and we'll try it.'

As Jenny went back to the kitchen, she heard Ma give a stifled hoot of laughter. When the tea was made, she cut two slices of the hot cake and took them back to the front room. Jenny didn't touch hers but watched Ma eat in silence, gazing into space as she chewed each mouthful and picking up the last of the crumbs with the tip of her finger and popping them in her mouth. After giving the cake her very careful tasting test, Ma grinned at Jenny. 'Don't look very pretty, but it tastes all right. Not bad for a first effort.'

Jenny beamed at the praise.

Ma was still asleep when Jenny looked in her room at five the next morning, and she didn't wake her. She doubted the elderly woman got up early, so she'd get her breakfast when she got back.

Ivy was waiting for her and they went to the first job of the morning: a school about a mile away. Jenny met the boss and was officially taken on as part of the cleaning staff. For the next two

133

hours she scrubbed endless corridors, dusted and polished. She'd thought the work hard as under housemaid, but it had been easy compared to this. She didn't care. She had somewhere to stay and a job. Yesterday she had been on the brink of admitting defeat and returning home to accept her fate. Glad and her lovely family had quickly put that notion out of her head.

The end of the passage was finally reached, and Jenny sat back on her heels to look at the gleaming floor, tired but with a sense of satisfaction. Of course she knew this wasn't going to be easy. Glad and her family lived tough lives, but she would be safe with them for a while. Her life was uncertain, and it would be best to take things a day at a time. What the future held would depend upon the spin of the coin, and one day it would fall as heads, she assured herself firmly. Although she had never been superstitious, she had to cling to some kind of hope or else she would sink into despair, and that would be fruitless. She was young with time on her side!

Jenny was back by eight to get Ma a hurried breakfast of bread and butter. She'd offered to make her toast, but the elderly woman had complained that her teeth wasn't too good now and could she have something she could suck! Highly amused by Ma's dry remarks, she just had time to put the plates in the sink before dashing off to her next job. This was at an engineering factory and even harder work. There were iron filings all over the floor that had to be swept up, then the offices to be polished. The washrooms were a disgrace, the smell making her heave. She followed Ivy's lead, and between them they managed to make them presentable.

'That's it for today, Jen.' Ivy grimaced and rubbed her back. 'Thank goodness we only have to do this place once a week.'

Jenny heartily agreed and was grateful to have had Ivy's bright company on her first morning in the job.

Once back home, Ivy waved goodbye as she hurried off to see to her baby son. 'See you the same time tomorrow, Jen.'

A small sliver of sunlight broke through a cloud and made the dingy street look almost pleasant. Jenny lifted her face and felt the warmth on her tired eyes. She ached from head to toe after scrubbing those endless corridors, but at that moment she felt content. She had somewhere to stay, a job and was among friends. In her situation she couldn't ask for more than that.

When she stepped into Ma's front room she had a smile on her face.

11

Sunday morning was Matt's favourite time. His parents and brothers were all engrossed in the newspapers, and the atmosphere was peaceful. He glanced around the drawing room: there was a fire burning in the grate – so warm, comfortable and safe. His thoughts turned to the young girl who had fled from their house. That had been three weeks ago, and a day never went by without Matt wondering about her...

The butler entered carrying a silver tray with a message for his father.

'What is it, Gilbert?' his wife asked, as he read the card.

He frowned fiercely, obviously displeased about the intrusion on their quiet Sunday morning. 'There's a Mr Albert Greaves and a Mrs Gertrude Osborne asking to see us urgently. Do you know them, Louise?'

'I've never met them, but...' Louise Stannard frowned. 'Greaves? The name sounds familiar.'

'That's the name Gloria mentioned at the New Year dinner party.' Matt put his newspaper down. 'What on earth can they want?'

'Goodness knows,' his mother said, 'but if they are here, we had better find out.'

Her husband sighed. 'Send them up.'

'Do you want us to leave?' John asked.

'No, no.' Their father waved a hand in irritation. 'They won't be staying long.'

From the tone of his father's voice Matt knew that the visitors would be politely, but firmly, ushered out as quickly as possible. Their peaceful Sunday mornings were sacrosanct, and all their friends knew better than to disturb them before lunch.

The visitors were shown in, and the three brothers stood politely while introductions were made; then they all sat down.

'We apologize for calling uninvited like this,'

Mr Greaves said smoothly. 'We are looking for someone and must follow up every lead, however tenuous it might be.'

'Indeed.' Mrs Osborne sniffed in distaste. 'We have even taken to listening to the servants' gossip. That is how we found out that you had dismissed someone for stealing who sounded like my niece.'

Matt was a pretty good judge of character, and there was something about this pair that made him uneasy, especially the man. It was obvious he drank too much and there was a strange, unstable look in his eyes. Not a person to be trusted.

'We are looking for this girl – Eugenie Winford,' Mrs Osborne said, getting to her feet and handing his father a miniature. 'That is a likeness of her when she was twelve. She is seventeen now, but she can't have changed much in appearance.'

His father never said a word but handed the picture to his wife. Matt and his brothers also went over to have a look.

'Charming. And what is your interest in this girl?' Louise asked, after casting a warning glance at her sons.

She was standing right behind her husband and Matt could see that she was gripping his father's shoulder firmly, alerting him not to speak either. It came as a shock, but there was no mistaking that this was a portrait of the girl who had been their under housemaid.

'I'm her aunt.'

'And I'm her intended husband,' Mr Greaves announced.

Matt stared at him, trying to mask his disgust. No wonder the poor girl had fled to scrub floors.

'We understand the girl once in your employ was about the right age and had dark hair and brown eyes.'

'Then you were misinformed, Mrs Osborne.' Louise gave a regretful smile. 'The housemaid who stole from us had fair hair, pale skin and blue eyes. And she was at least twenty.'

'Her mother must be very worried,' Gilbert said, speaking for the first time. 'May we ask why your niece ran away?'

'After her father, Cyrus Winford, lost all his money in the crash and killed himself, Eugenie was distraught and fled. My sister has not coped well, and is incapable of dealing with her own affairs.' Mrs Osborne didn't try to hide her scorn. 'That has left me with the burden of trying to find her wayward daughter.'

Matt turned away and wandered over to the window in order to hide his look of fury. Poor little devil!

'Do you believe that your niece would be working as a servant?' Their mother's face was a picture of disbelief as she handed the picture back to Mrs Osborne.

'We have tried all her friends and anyone she might have gone to, without success,' Mrs Osborne told them. 'She walked out with few possessions and nothing of any great value. So we have come to the conclusion that she would have needed a roof over her head, and one way to do that is to become a servant. We are now reduced to investigating any lead. She is very wilful. After

138

her father's unfortunate demise, Mr Greaves had been willing to give her a good home and a prestigious marriage as soon as she was old enough. Ungrateful girl!'

'She is strong-minded,' Mr Greaves said, 'but she would soon have come in line. The Templeton School has fitted her only for a life of privilege.'

Matt felt like punching his bloated face as he felt John stir beside him. His eldest brother had a very short temper. How he would love to tell this arrogant man that he was quite wrong. Eugenie had indeed been their under housemaid, and had been very capable of hard work. His respect for her grew. What courage the child had.

'Are you certain you haven't seen her?' Mrs Osborne persisted. 'You can't see it in the picture, but she has unusual eyes, inherited from her American father. They are pale brown and in certain lights appear almost amber.'

Gilbert Stannard rose to his feet, clearly intent on bringing this visit to an end. 'As my wife has told you, we do not know the girl. It is a tragedy and I'm sorry we cannot be of assistance to you.'

'If you ever do come across her, I'm offering a handsome reward of one hundred pounds.' Mr Greaves looked proud about that.

'Very generous.' Louise smiled sweetly, then looked across at the butler, who was still standing by the door. 'Show our visitors out, please.'

Matt bowed politely and watched them leave, bursting with fury.

'I hope you've hidden yourself well, little

139

Jenny,' Luke muttered beside him.

There was silence in the room until they knew their visitors had left the house.

'Well!' Louise exclaimed. 'What a disagreeable pair. But that settles the mystery about our under housemaid. Jenny Baker had indeed been Eugenie Winford. No wonder that poor girl ran away.'

'I agree, my dear. However, I didn't like lying to them.'

'But we didn't, Gilbert.' She faced her husband. 'We told them that the girl we had caught stealing was not the one they were looking for.'

'We lied by omission, though,' her husband corrected.

His wife had the grace to look uncomfortable. 'Ah, I know, but what could we have told them? We don't know where Jenny, or Eugenie, is, do we?'

'That's true.' Matt joined in. 'The fact that she attended the Templeton School explains why she rushed out of the dining room during our New Year dinner. Gloria Tremain would have recognized her. In view of what we have learnt, I think we should renew our efforts to find her.'

'John,' their mother said, 'you are looking very thoughtful. What do you make of it?'

'Matt's right – we should try to track her down.' John gazed into space, frowning.

Matt knew his eldest brother well and respected his intelligence. 'What's troubling you?'

'We have been told that Miss Winford's father lost everything in the Wall Street crash, so the family is obviously penniless.' John frowned in concentration. 'That dragon of a woman has given her sister a home. And from the sound of it she has taken over her affairs...'

'And I would think she has no love for her niece,' his father remarked, 'but what is your point, John?'

'As I listened to them, I had the distinct impression that they were quite desperate to find her.'

'That's because that objectionable man, Albert Greaves, wants a young wife.' Louise pulled a face in disgust.

John gave a wry smile. 'I expect you're right. I have a very suspicious mind.'

'Hmm.' Their father pulled the bell rope. When the butler appeared, he ordered coffee for all of them. 'Oh, and would you ask Edna to bring it up, please, and we'd like you and Mrs Douglas to come as well.'

Green bowed and left the room.

'Why do you want to see them?' Luke asked.

'The housemaid was friendly with the girl, and she might have information that wouldn't reach us. And we should tell the staff what's going on, just in case those people start questioning them.'

'I wouldn't put that past them,' Matt said. When they had gathered together Green, Mrs Douglas and Edna, Gilbert explained that Jenny was really Eugenie Winford, and that her aunt and Albert Greaves were doing all they could to find her.

'You would like us to deny that she ever worked here?' Green asked.

141

'We don't like asking you to lie,' John told them, 'but it might be best until we can find out more.'

'Our lips are sealed.' Mrs Douglas looked scandalized. 'That poor dear girl.'

Edna had been standing, head bowed, ever since she'd entered the room.

'If you know anything, Edna, you will tell us, won't you?' Matt spoke gently, for the girl was obviously distressed. 'We will not give her away. She needs help and we would like to see what we can do for her.'

Edna looked up then, tears in her eyes. 'I guessed she was posh, but she didn't mind getting her hands dirty. Never complained neither.'

'She has much courage.' Louise gave the housemaid an encouraging smile. 'You were her friend, so have you any idea where she might be?'

'I don't know where she is, but I did get a letter from her yesterday. She said I wasn't to worry about her 'cos she's all right. Someone's taken her in.'

'Have you still got the letter?' John asked.

Edna pulled it out of her pocket and handed it to him. 'She don't say much. It's no more than a note, really.'

'I don't want to read your personal mail, Edna. We are looking for any clue as to where she has gone.' He studied the envelope carefully. 'This was posted in Kensington. Does she know anyone there?' he asked, handing it back to her.

'I don't think so, sir. The only place she ever mentioned to me was Lambeth.'

'I expect that was just something she conjured

up to throw people off the scent. And she'd be very careful not to post it in the borough she was living in now.' Luke gave Matt an inquiring glance. 'We could go to have a drive around Lambeth, I suppose.'

'We'll do that,' Matt agreed. At least he would feel as if he were doing something. 'But it will be a hopeless task trying to find her. That's if she's even there.'

'You'd have to look in the poor places, 'cos she ain't got no money,' Edna told them helpfully.

'You mean in the slums?' Luke asked.

Edna nodded her head miserably. 'Places like that.'

'Thank you all for your help.' Gilbert dismissed the staff. 'I know we can rely on your discretion.'

Once they left, the family settled down to coffee.

'What are we going to do now?' Luke wanted to know.

'Keep searching for the poor girl.' Louise gave a helpless shrug. 'Though if the determined Mrs Osborne can't find her, we shall have little chance, I think.'

They all agreed that the chances of finding her were slim.

12

'Come and sit down.'

Jenny stopped clearing the table. 'I'll just wash the tea things first, Ma.'

'Leave them, they won't run away.' Ma pointed to the chair opposite her. 'Sit there. I want to talk to you.'

As Jenny sat down, it was hard to stifle a groan of relief. She ached in every limb.

'You look fair worn out, Jen, and you're getting skinny.' Ma studied her with a ferocious glint in her eyes. 'You ain't been born for such hard graft.'

'I'm fine–'

Ma gave a dismissive wave of her hand. 'No, you ain't. You're up at the crack of dawn scrubbing and polishing, and then you comes back here to look after a cantankerous old woman like me. It's slavery, my girl, and don't try to deny it! And I've got a nasty suspicion that you're spending your hard-earned cash on seeing I get some good food. I ain't never ate so good, and I dare you to say that isn't so.'

Jenny couldn't. This was much harder than working as an under housemaid. At least there she had time off and wonderful food. Now it was go from morning to night, with meals of whatever they could afford. She dipped her head, unable to meet the old woman's shrewd gaze.

'You got to have proper food; I know you're not well. And as for the hard work, I'll get used to that.'

'That's as may be. You worry about me too much; I'm as fit as any woman of my age deserves to be.'

'I like you, Ma, and you've been so kind to give me a room with you—'

'Poof!' Ma snorted. 'Kindness ain't got nothing to do with it. You needed a roof over your head and I needed some help. I thought it would be a fair exchange, but I've got the better bargain. Are you sure this is right for you? Couldn't you go home?' she asked gently.

'No, Ma.' Jenny lifted her head. 'No, I would only be replacing one kind of slavery with another. Oh, I know it would be one of silks and satins, but I'd rather scrub floors! Honestly.'

'Want to talk about it? I knows how to keep my mouth shut.'

Without giving away any names, Jenny briefly explained what had driven her to run away. As she finished the story, something occurred to her with such force that it took her breath away in alarm.

'Are you asking me to leave, Ma?'

'God love you, Jen, that's the last thing I want. I've grown right fond of you.' She reached out, took hold of Jenny's hand and squeezed it as hard as her arthritic hands would allow. 'It fair breaks my heart to see a young girl like you working as a skivvy. You should be out having fun, but I'd be terrible sad to lose you.'

'That's a relief!' Jenny's heart stopped thumping. For one dreadful moment she thought she would have to find somewhere else to stay. And she couldn't go through that again. She just couldn't!

'I'd be daft to let you go.' Ma's eyes crinkled at the corners in a smile. 'You've only been here four weeks, but my place has never looked so spruce. And my front step's something to be proud of. Didn't look as good as that even when I could do it myself.'

Jenny stood up and bent over to kiss Ma's leathery cheek. 'Don't you worry about me. I'm happy here – and I feel safe.'

'You are, ducky. That beastly family of yours won't find you here.' She looked over at the table. 'You give me your cup and saucer.'

'But I haven't washed it up yet.'

'I know that. Come on, hand it over.'

Jenny did as ordered, watching with amusement as Ma swished the tea dregs around and then tipped the cup upside down in the saucer. Ma tapped it three times and turned it back the right way again.

'Now let me see...'

Jenny suddenly realized what Ma was up to and she giggled. 'Are you reading the tea leaves?'

'Don't laugh, Jen. I knows what I'm doing, and more often than not I'm right. Uncanny my readings are, that's what people around here say.' The elderly woman gave a superior toss of her head and bent to her task.

'Well, what do you see?' Jenny sat down again, deciding that she would humour Ma.

'Don't rush me! Hmm, now... There's people

146

looking for you–'

'I know that, Ma.' She stifled a giggle again. After the tale she'd just told Ma, that didn't take much working out.

'Don't interrupt! It isn't just two people; it's lots. Some mean you harm; others don't. But you'd do well to stay out of everyone's way for the time being. It's hard to know who to trust.' Ma looked up. 'That don't include anyone in this street. You can trust all of them.'

'I know that, Ma. I hope you're wrong about a lot of people, because I'm having enough trouble staying out of the way of just two.' She went to stand up again but was waved back into her seat.

'I ain't finished yet. This is a real interesting set of leaves. You've got some hard times in front of you, but you ain't gonna be alone all the time...' She grinned broadly. 'You're going to meet a tall, dark, 'andsome man.'

'Oh, Ma,' Jenny laughed, 'you read too many romantic stories.'

The old woman handed her the cup. 'You can make fun all you like, but I feels much happier about you now I've seen your future.'

'Well, I know *your* future.' Jenny collected up the tea things, still chuckling. 'I'm going to wash these up, and tomorrow you'll have a nice apple pie.'

'That would be lovely. Your pastry's getting quite good now.' Then she gave Jenny a suspicious look. 'Where'd you get the apples from?'

'I went scrumping with Ivy this morning.'

Ma roared with laughter and slapped her knee. 'You're learning, my girl. You might be posh, but you're all right.'

With Ma's infectious laugh ringing in her ears she went into the kitchen to cook her ill-gotten gains. They'd had a new job today, cleaning a firm of solicitors' offices. It had been an old house, and the garden had two apple trees in it. The ground had been littered with apples, and Ivy had declared that it was a crying shame to let them rot, so they'd picked up some of the best and shared them out. There was a lot of bruising, but after she'd cut this away she still had enough for the pie.

After it was cooked she put it on the table to cool. Ma would enjoy that tomorrow. Jenny wished she could afford some cream to go with it, but that was out of the question. Ron, Ivy's husband, had been laid off last week, and without his money coming in things were even harder. The number of unemployed was rising every week, and behind the jokes Jenny could see the worry in their eyes as they struggled to feed their families. The most amazing and touching thing was the way they all tried to help each other out. There was genuine concern for everyone in the street. She knew that Fred and Stan were bringing home any veg they hadn't sold, and sharing it out amongst those most in need. She was aware that that act of kindness was depleting their income. They couldn't afford to give produce away, but they still did. She was constantly astounded by their unselfishness.

Jenny bowed her head and struggled to keep the worry at bay. The talk was that this was just the start. The depression was beginning to take hold and touch almost everyone, but it was the working classes who were going to suffer the most. She prayed she would be able to keep her job, because the money was helping to keep food on the table, and like everyone else in the street she did what she could, especially for the old and those with young children. She touched the pendant around her neck and felt comforted. At least she still had that, but she knew she wouldn't hesitate to sell it to help the people she'd come to love.

'Jen,' Ma called, 'you done yet?'

She straightened up, put the smile back on her face and went back to the other room.

'Ah, there you are.' Ma held out a book. 'Read to me. My eyes ain't what they was, and I do love to hear your smashing voice. Quite brings the story to life.'

Jenny opened Jane Austen's *Pride and Prejudice* at the marker she'd put in last night. This was Ma's favourite book, and she never seemed to tire of it. She read until Ma couldn't keep her eyes open, and then helped her up to bed.

This routine became a pattern on Jenny's days. It was a hard life, but there was laughter as well. The residents of Forest Road knew how to throw a party, even if they were *boracic lint* – she had soon learnt that that meant skint, no money. All they needed was a joanna – piano – and a couple of drinks and they were away. She was learning quite a few cockney rhyming-slang words now. There was always a birthday, anniversary or christening. The neighbours would all come with a small donation of food for the table, and troubles would be forgotten for a short time. They didn't have much in the way of worldly goods, but they had something far more precious: friendship and a desire to look after each other. Jenny was certainly seeing the other side of life, and her love and respect for them grew every day.

It was now a year since she had left home. After shedding tears on the anniversary of her father's death, she tried to put it behind her. Her days were too busy to dwell on the past. She had made her decision last November; there was no going back now.

She reached home – for that was how she thought about Ma's now – at the end of another week and was surprised to see the front room crowded. There was Fred, Glad, Stan, Ma and several of the neighbours, all talking very seriously.

'What's happened?' she asked in alarm.

'There's people asking for Jenny Baker or Eugenie Winford,' said a voice from behind her.

She spun round with a whimper of panic to find herself looking straight at Fred. She almost collapsed in relief, expecting to see a policeman there, or someone else in authority. 'Oh, no, they've found me!'

Ma hobbled up to her, taking hold of her hand. 'Now, don't be affrighted, Jen. No one here would tell strangers anything.'

'Who was it?' Her voice wavered as she pictured Greaves's large bulk walking down this humble street.

'Two young men.' Glad made her sit down. 'Don't take on so, ducky. You're shaking some-

150

thing terrible.'

'Right nice they were too.' Ma winked at Jenny. 'Both tall, dark and 'andsome.'

'They were strolling along talking to everyone in this street, and there was plenty around 'cos we all came out to have a look at these toffs.' Stan grinned. 'They had a lot of guts to wander around here, but they was wasting their time. We'd never give up one of our own.'

As Jenny glanced at each face in the room and saw them all nodding in agreement, the panic began to fade. One of their own?

'Don't look so surprised.' Fred's smile was full of affection. 'Since you've been with us, you've mucked in, worked as hard as any of us without a murmur of complaint, and you're looking after Ma real kind like. We've known from the start that you wasn't born to this kind of life, but you're doing good. We're right fond of you for that.'

Jenny gulped back the emotion. 'You've all been so kind, and I don't know what would have happened to me without your help. But you said it was two *young* men looking for me. Did they say who they were?'

'Matthew and Luke Stannard,' Ma announced. 'I asked what they wanted with these girls. They said it was only the one girl, and she could be using either name. She was in trouble and they wanted to help. We told them we didn't know no one by those names. Do you know them?'

Jenny couldn't believe what she was hearing. 'Yes, I do, but that can't be true. Why would they be searching for me? And how did they know my

151

real name?'

'We didn't ask that,' Glad said. 'It would have seemed suspicious if we'd shown too much interest. So you don't think they really wanted to help you?'

'Of course not. They think I'm a thief!' This was too ridiculous! The Stannard brothers had no reason to come looking for her, unless they were after the reward. Jenny was immediately ashamed of that thought. She didn't know them very well, of course, but they were rich enough not to be tempted by one hundred pounds, and she didn't believe Matthew Stannard would do anything so underhand. He had seemed so nice.

'We know you wouldn't take anything that wasn't yours, Jen.' Fred's grin was mischievous. 'If we thought that, we'd never have asked Ma to take you in. You might have nicked all her valuables.'

Ma cackled with mirth. 'If anyone thinks there's valuables in here, I'll help them search. I'd love to see it!'

Everyone in the room was laughing now, and even Jenny managed a smile at the joke.

'So,' said Stan, when they'd quietened down. 'Fred said that there was a reward being offered for you; do you think they're after that?'

'The answer is that I really don't know. I can't imagine the money being a temptation to them.' She frowned in concentration. They'd nearly found her, and this was very worrying.

'How do you think they ended up looking round here for you?' Glad asked.

'When I was working there I made friends with

a girl called Edna. I sent her a letter the other week telling her I was all right, but I posted it in another borough. The only time I ever mentioned Lambeth was in the beginning, when she asked me where I came from. I thought about my meeting with Glad and Fred, so I said Lambeth. It was the first name that came to my mind.'

'You never told her about me and Glad, then?'

'No, Fred.'

'Ah, well, if this is the only place they know of, that's probably why they were here. They might be scouting the whole area.' Fred stood up. 'Don't you worry, Jen. They'll soon see it's hopeless and give up.'

'I do hope you're right,' she said with a sad shake of her head. 'Every time I start to feel safe, something happens.'

Glad squeezed her hand. 'You are safe here. No one's going to say a word.'

They all filed out then, and when they'd gone, Ma said, 'I told you there were lots of people looking for you.'

'Yes, you did, and both are tall, dark and handsome.' Jenny could laugh now, albeit rather shakily.

'I don't think they mean you no harm.' Ma gazed into space.

'I can't take that chance, though.'

'No, with money in the offing you're wise to be wary. Make us a nice cup of tea, duck. I'm fair parched. And I think I'll read your tea leaves again.'

'No, thanks, Ma,' she said, heading for the

kitchen. 'I don't think I want to know what the future holds.'

'I shan't tell you. I never told you all I saw last time.'

'Oh.' Jenny stopped and turned round. 'You saw more than tall, dark and 'andsome?' she teased.

'Lots more.' Ma folded her arms and looked smug. 'Where's that tea?'

13

This was a beauty. Matt, deep in thought, lifted the bonnet of a Rolls-Royce Phantom. He was curious to know more about Jenny's father, Cyrus Winford. What kind of a man had he been? How could he have left his young daughter at the mercy of Gertrude Osborne and Greaves? And why the hell was her mother allowing this to happen? What was the matter with her? He ducked his head to take a closer look at the engine.

'Don't touch that!' Jake Porter called.

Matt grinned at his boss. 'Just looking.'

'Oh, yeah? What's that spanner doing in your hand, then?'

He slipped the tool into his pocket, chuckling.

'Now I feel safer,' Jake grunted. 'I've never met anyone with such an urge to take apart anything mechanical.'

'Are you going to let me work on this with you?'

Matt asked.

'You can watch. Give me ten minutes and I'll be there. In the meantime–'

'I know, don't touch anything.'

'You've got it.' Jake disappeared into the office.

Matt bent over to examine the engine again, whistling to himself, his former concerns dismissed as he contemplated the excitement of working on this beautiful vehicle. He loved it here, and once everyone had seen his enthusiasm and willingness to take orders, he had been accepted without question.

'She's a beauty, isn't she?' Harry said.

Matt straightened up and rubbed his hands in anticipation. He'd made friends with Harry Butler as soon as he'd arrived here. Although their backgrounds were very different, they'd hit it off at once. 'Absolutely wonderful. Who owns her?'

'Used to belong to a bloke called Winford, but it's been booked in this time as Greaves.'

'What the devil is he doing with the Winfords' car?' Matt was astonished to come across that man's name at the garage.

'Said he'd bought it from them.' Harry studied him intently. 'I keep forgetting that you come from a rich family. Do you know him?'

'I've only met him once.'

Someone called out for Harry, and, after giving the car an affectionate pat, he hurried away to see to a customer. Harry was twenty-five and an excellent mechanic – another of Jake's successful apprentices. Matt hoped to be as good one day. In the beginning he'd wondered if, because of his background, there would be hostility towards him, but that hadn't happened. It had added to Matt's pleasure in the job.

He walked round the car and opened the rear door, gazing in and trying to imagine their under housemaid sitting there with a chauffeur to drive her around. A ripple of concern went through him again, as it always did when he thought about her. From a life of wealth and privilege she had plunged into the harsh world of the working classes. The shock must have been terrible, and yet it was what she had chosen to do, rather than fall in with the plans of her obnoxious aunt. Poor thing. She hadn't had any choice, but what courage she must have. The door closed with a soft click, and he shoved his hands in his pockets, lost in thought.

All their efforts to find her had been fruitless, and, to be honest, that was only to be expected. London was a huge place, and it was doubtful if she was even still here. Edna had said that someone had taken her in, so she could be anywhere. The Templeton School was in Kent, and she might know someone in that area. Perhaps he'd drag Luke along there one day. His brother would jump at the chance to visit a girls' school, he thought wryly.

'Take your hands out of your pockets,' Jake ordered as he came and stood beside him.

Matt instantly forgot everything else in his eagerness to work on the Rolls-Royce with his boss.

John was late arriving home that evening, immediately joining them in the drawing room. 'I've been curious about Mr Winford, so I contacted Henry Eddison at the Manhattan Bank, and asked if he'd known him.'

'You shouldn't have done that.' Louise didn't look pleased.

'It's all right, Mother. I made it a very casual inquiry in a chatty letter to Henry.' John took the cup of coffee his mother had poured for him and sat down. 'He didn't know him personally, but, if this is Eugenie's father, then her future could be very difficult.'

'It can't be much worse than it is, surely?' Matt said.

'I'm afraid it can.' John took a letter from his pocket and flicked through it, frowning deeply. 'He said that Cyrus D. Winford was a respected broker. He understood that he had a wife and two children – boys – in America, and his death must have been a terrible shock to them.'

'What!' Their father was clearly shocked. 'Does that mean Eugenie's mother was his mistress?'

'He could be a bigamist and have gone through a ceremony with each of them,' Luke pointed out.

'I do hope not,' their mother said, her eyes full of sadness. 'That poor girl could be illegitimate.'

'I think we ought to redouble our efforts to find her,' Matt said. 'After all we did throw her out, so we do have some responsibility towards her.'

'You shouldn't have let me do that, Louise.' Her husband looked uncomfortable.

'Are you blaming me now?'

'No, my dear, but you know what I'm like. I

was unfair to that poor girl, and Matt's right, we do owe her our support.'

His wife still looked doubtful. 'But we might find out things she would be better off not knowing.'

'Then we won't tell her,' her husband declared.

'Very well,' she sighed. 'I can see you are all set on this. But you must keep everything very confidential, John. The girl has enough trouble in her young life. I would not wish to add to it by meddling in something that is not our affair.'

'We'll be very discreet, Mother.' Luke was serious for a change. 'I'll start by searching for marriage and birth certificates.'

'And I'll continue to look for her.' Matt smiled at his mother. 'Don't worry, we'll be careful not to let word of our interest get back to her family.'

Louise gave each member of her family a stern look. 'Not one of you is to act without first consulting me. And if I say that this must stop, then you will cease immediately. Is that understood?'

Matt recognized his mother's determination and knew she meant every word, as did the rest of his family. They all nodded obediently.

'Good. Now, Gilbert, you will stay out of this. Luke, you will look for certificates, and that is all! Matt, if you can find her you must come and tell me. I will be the one to speak to her.'

No one dared argue with Louise when she was in this forceful mood. Matt knew they would all do as she said, and he also knew that she was right to keep a tight rein on them. Their intentions were good, but they really had no right to interfere in this girl's life, however sorry they might feel for her.

A week later Luke had found a marriage certificate for Elizabeth Sherrington and Cyrus Douglas Winford; she was listed as British and he as American. He had also found a birth certificate for their daughter, Eugenie Elizabeth Winford.

'So they were married,' Gilbert said.

'Well, he went through a ceremony here, but I couldn't say whether it was legal.' Luke's eyes glinted with mischief. 'I could always go to America to find out.'

'You'll do no such thing, Luke.' Their mother's mouth was set in a determined line. 'I want you all to stop this now!'

'But Mother,' Luke protested, 'it's an intriguing mystery. I was thinking of going with Matt to the Templeton School she attended. Someone there might know where she is.'

'Oh, no, you don't, my boy.' His father raised his hands in horror. 'It wouldn't be safe to let you roam around a young ladies' school.'

Matt chuckled quietly as his brother protested.

'Father, you make me sound like a menace to the female sex. They're too young anyway.'

Even John was laughing now. 'But what about the teachers?'

'Ah, well,' Luke said, grinning, 'I'd have had Matt with me, so I couldn't have got into much trouble, could I?'

'You'd have found a way,' his father muttered darkly.

'I forbid this visit anyway.' Louise glared at her two younger sons. 'Where's your common sense? If you go asking questions at her former school, how long do you think it will be before her aunt is told that someone is asking questions about her niece?'

'I do see your point,' Matt admitted. 'Perhaps it would be unwise.'

'It most certainly would!'

'Your mother's right, as usual,' their father said. 'I believe we should drop this whole thing. We have found out all we can, and if we continue we could cause the girl more trouble. I feel badly about it already.'

The discussion that followed was lively and heated at times, with Luke and Matt very reluctant to give up, but in the end it was agreed that they could do no more at the moment. Frustrating as it was, they would have to wait and hope that something came to light about Jenny's whereabouts.

Their mother was clearly relieved at the joint decision. 'It is a distressing story and I am not proud of our part in causing her more anguish, but it is done. She has told Edna she is safe. We must accept that.'

Jenny had soon recovered from the shock of last week. It was hard enough adjusting to this life without also feeling that she had to run and hide.

'Pontoon!' Ma declared.

Jenny, seeing that the cards in her hand added up to twenty-five, gave the elderly woman a suspicious glance. 'I'm bust. Are you cheating, Ma?'

'Who, me?' She was a picture of innocence.

Jenny looked pointedly around the small room. 'I don't see anyone else here.'

'Don't be a sore loser,' Ma cackled, shuffling the cards very expertly for someone with rheumatism and then handing them back to Jenny. 'Your deal. Just one more hand and then I'll have that bottle of stout you've got hidden in the sideboard.'

'You don't miss a thing, do you?' Jenny couldn't help laughing So much for her surprise treat. 'You were asleep when I came in with the shopping today.'

'I was just resting my eyes.' She tapped the table with her cards. 'Twist me one.'

After doing that, Jenny looked at her own. Eighteen – she'd better stick.

'Twenty.' Ma laid her cards face up. 'Can you beat that?'

'You know I can't.'

'Hmm.' Ma winked at her. 'Remind me some time to teach you how to deal from the bottom of the pack.'

'You *were* cheating!' Jenny roared. 'Good job we weren't playing for money.'

Ma stood up, hobbled over to her easy chair and sat down, a deep rumble of amusement coming from her. 'I enjoyed that,' she said. 'Now I'll have that glass of stout.'

Jenny poured Ma her drink, made herself a cup of cocoa and then sat down. 'Do you want me to read to you?' she asked.

'Not tonight.' Ma tipped her head to one side and examined Jenny with deliberate care. 'You

161

shouldn't be spending all your time with me, much as I like your company. Ain't you got no friends?'

With a shake of her head, Jenny looked away from the discerning gaze. She didn't know how old Ma was, and, although she was frail in body, there was nothing wrong with her mind. She was very shrewd and her sharp eyes didn't miss a thing.

'You're lonely, ain't you? Don't you know anyone your own age you could go out with and have a bit of fun?'

'There's only the two girls from No. 20, but they've got their own crowd.' Many times she'd seen them walk by, laughing, and had longed to be invited to join them. 'I had a friend at the house I worked in. Her name was Edna, and we used to go out whenever we could get time off together.'

'Why don't you write and ask her to meet you one day? I'm sure she'd like to see you again.'

Jenny chewed her lip. 'Oh, I'd love to, but I'm not sure...'

'Jen.' Ma leant forward. 'It ain't right, you shutting yourself away like this. You're seventeen now and should be out enjoying yourself a bit. So what if your family finds you? You can refuse to go back with them. No one can make you do something you're set against.' Ma gave her an encouraging smile. 'If they drags you to the altar, all you've got to do is say "I don't", instead of "I do".'

Jenny giggled at the thought. She could just imagine what an uproar that would cause. She got up and kissed Ma. 'You're a wise old devil, even if you do cheat at cards. You're probably right about not hiding any more, but I was so frightened, Ma, and still am.'

'I know, ducky, but take an old woman's advice and get in touch with your friend. You've got this whole street on your side. We'll see you comes to no harm.'

A lump stuck in Jenny's throat as Ma's words made her realize just how fortunate she was to have such stalwart friends. At that moment it felt as if a heavy weight had fallen from her. She would still try to keep out of her scheming Aunt Gertrude's way, but perhaps she could make some discreet inquiries about how her mother was. She had never been outgoing and affectionate towards her, but she was, after all, her mother. Edna might be able to help there.

Her head came up and she gave Ma a gentle smile. 'I'll write the letter tonight.'

'That's the idea, ducky. It'll do you a power of good to have a gossip with your friend.'

As soon as Ma was tucked up in bed and snoring contentedly after her glass of stout, Jenny set about the letter. She knew Edna had a couple of hours off on a Wednesday afternoon, so she told her that she would be in Hyde Park next Wednesday at two o'clock, if Edna could make it.

Then she sealed the envelope and placed it by her bed, ready to post in the morning.

163

14

Would Edna come? Jenny was excited and apprehensive at the same time. She'd left without saying goodbye to her friend and perhaps she might not want to see her again. She'd been tempted to give Edna her address this time, but, for all her brave words to Ma last week, she was still wary of anyone knowing where she was.

Jenny reached Speakers' Corner in Hyde Park, where she'd suggested they meet, and gazed around, worry gnawing away at her insides as she paced up and down. Had Edna received the letter in time? Perhaps this hadn't been such a good idea – she was going to be very disappointed if her friend didn't come.

'Jen.'

She turned round at the sound of the voice behind her. She had come!

'Oh, Jen.' Edna rushed up and hugged her. 'I've been that worried about you.'

They were both laughing with pleasure at seeing each other again.

'I'm sorry I rushed off without seeing you first, Edna, but I panicked.'

'I understand.' Her friend stepped back so she could see her better. 'Oh, my, you're all skin and bones. What have you been doing to yourself? You look as if you've had a rough time.'

'It has been hard,' Jenny admitted.

Edna slipped her hand through Jenny's arm. 'Let's find a café and I'll buy us a pot of tea and some buns.'

They walked arm in arm to Oxford Street, and Jenny listened avidly as Edna gave her all the news about the other servants. It was wonderful to hear her friend's bright chatter and laugh again. It was then that she realized how right Ma had been to urge her to get out.

'This will do.' Edna urged her through the door of the first tea shop they found. 'I've only got a couple of hours and there's such a lot to tell you.'

They were soon settled at a corner table with a large pot of tea in front of them and buns, butter and jam. Jenny's mouth fairly watered at the sight of such luxury.

'Tuck in, Jen.' Edna frowned as she studied her. 'You don't look as if you've had a good meal for ages. Can you tell me what you're doing and where you're living? I won't say nothing to no one without your say so.'

Jenny knew she was going to have to start trusting people again, so she explained about Ma and the work she was doing.

Edna's mouth opened in disbelief. 'Hell, Jen, no wonder you look worn to the bone.'

'It's not too bad. I'm getting used to it now, and I'm very fond of Ma. These are poor people I'm with, Edna, and I've got to do my share. If they hadn't taken me in, I don't know what I would have done. I didn't have anywhere to go.' She took a gulp of tea.

Edna put another bun on her plate. 'Your aunt and Albert Greaves paid the Stannards a visit.'

Jenny's cup clattered back into the saucer. 'Looking for me?'

Her friend nodded and then explained what had happened.

'They denied knowing me?' she asked in disbelief.

'Sent them on their way with nothing.' Edna grinned. 'And we was all told that if anyone came asking questions about Eugenie Winford, we was to say nothing. Which wouldn't have been hard, because we don't know anyone by that name.' She winked to make her point.

'Well, I'll be blowed!' Jenny picked up her knife and spread extra butter on her second bun after that staggering bit of news. 'But how did my aunt find out I'd been working there?'

'She'd picked up on some servants' gossip, I expect. They said that they were following up any lead, however unlikely.'

'It's as well I left when I did, then.'

'The family's dead worried about you, Jen. Would you mind if I told them I've seen you?'

'I'm not sure I want them to know anything. I don't understand why they are concerned. They accused me of being a thief and turned me out.' Jenny shook her head. She still viewed this incident with horror. 'And yet they've protected me from my Aunt Gertrude. Their change of attitude is a complete mystery.'

She looked up at Edna and found her with a wide grin on her face. 'What have I said?'

'It isn't what you've said,' Edna chuckled, 'but the way you said it. What happened to the London accent?'

'Oh, that.' She joined in the laughter. 'I don't need that now. The people I'm with know all about me, and Ma loves me to read to her in my "posh voice", as she calls it.'

'How did you come to know them?' Edna asked.

Jenny told her about Fred and Glad, and her visit to the pawnbroker's. By the time she'd finished, Edna was almost crying with laughter.

'How I wish I'd been there.' Edna mopped her eyes. 'That took some courage.'

'Not really. It was desperation,' Jenny admitted. 'Fred and Glad gave me their address and said I could go to them if I needed help any time. They'd met me only once, but I had nowhere else to go. They've been very kind, Edna. I was terrified I'd have to go home or spend the night in the open, but they took me in without question. I'm grateful and do all I can for them. Unemployment's getting bad, and I was lucky even to get a job scrubbing floors.'

'They sound like good old Londoners. Live in Lambeth, do they?'

Jenny had nodded before she realized that her friend had slipped that crafty question in. 'Did you ever tell the Stannards I might be in Lambeth?'

'Yes.' Edna reached across and patted her hand. 'Do you remember when you first started work at the house and I asked you where you came from?'

'I said the first thing that came into my mind: Lambeth.'

'That's right. You said you'd been to school in

Lambeth.' Edna grinned again. 'What a whopper that was, Jen. It was the only place you'd mentioned, and when I saw how worried the mistress was, I told them. I didn't see no harm in it because I didn't believe you anyway. Neither did they, but the sons, Luke and Matthew, have been scouring the borough for you.'

'I know.'

'What?' Edna sat upright, her eyes wide open. 'Did they find you?'

'Nearly, but everyone in the street told them they didn't know me. Don't tell the brothers, though. I don't want to be found yet.'

'You needn't be afraid of them,' Edna said kindly. 'I'm sure they only want to help. They would probably help you get another place – not as an under housemaid, of course.'

'No!' She gave a firm shake of her head. 'I couldn't leave Ma. She needs me.'

'I understand, but please let me tell them I've seen you and you're all right. I'm sure they'll be relieved to know that.'

'All right,' she agreed. 'But don't tell them anything else.'

'I promise.' Edna then poured the last of the tea from the pot, giving them another half a cup each, talking all the time about the things she'd done since they last met.

The time flew by, and Jenny was sad when it was time for her friend to return to work. It had been really lovely to see Edna again, but it had also made her acutely aware of just how lonely she was. 'Can I ask you a favour, Edna?'

'Of course, anything.'

'My mother's living with Aunt Gertrude in Bloomsbury, and, although she didn't seem to care what happened to me, I'd like to know how she is getting on. Do you think you could find out how she is?'

'Should be easy,' Edna told her. 'I know a girl who works round there and is bound to have heard gossip. You leave it with me; I'll find out how your mum is.'

'Oh, thanks. It would be a relief to know.'

'You're a strange one, Jen.' Edna shook her head. 'Your mum don't deserve to have you worry about her after the way she's treated you. I wouldn't dream of bothering to find out how my mum is. I left for good reasons, and, as far as I'm concerned, that's the end of it.'

'I wish I were more like you, Edna, but I can't just dismiss her like that. She is my mother, and if I knew she was all right, it would put my mind at rest.'

'You leave it with me.' Edna patted her hand and stood up. 'I've got to get back now.'

Once outside the tea shop Edna hugged her. 'Let's meet again. You write when you're free. Perhaps we can go to the pictures next time.'

'I'd like that.' Jenny watched her friend hurrying to catch her bus, then she headed for her own bus stop, already looking forward to their next meeting. She'd have to try to save enough for the pictures.

'Miss Winford?'

Jenny stopped and spun round to face the man who had called her, cursing herself. She should have kept walking as if she didn't know the name.

Too late now. It was their old footman, Gerry.

He hurried up, a big smile on his face. 'You caused a lot of trouble by disappearing like that.'

'Hello, Gerry,' she said politely. 'Have you found another job?'

'Only as a footman again, but it's a nice enough household. What about you? Where are you living?'

Jenny had to think quickly. He would know about the reward, so it wouldn't be wise to tell him anything. 'I'm with friends just around the corner in Great Cumberland Place.'

'I know it. I'll walk you back, shall I?'

'You don't have to go to all that trouble.' Now she was worried about the calculating look in his eyes.

'It's no trouble.' Gerry took hold of her arm and steered her in the right direction, talking amiably about his new job.

She stopped outside one smart-looking house, her heart beating erratically, but she managed a bright smile. 'This is it. It was nice to see you again, Gerry. I hope all goes well for you.'

'And you, Miss Winford.'

She had been hoping he would walk away after that, but he didn't. He just stood on the pavement, smiling down at her.

'In you go, then.'

Now she was really alarmed. He obviously wanted to see her enter the house to confirm that she actually lived there. There was nothing for it but to knock on the door and try to persuade whoever owned it to let her in for a moment.

Her luck was holding. The door was slightly

170

ajar and, without stopping to think, she stepped inside, closing the door behind her. She peered through a small stained-glass window at the side of the door and saw Gerry writing the address on a piece of paper. She had been right to be cautious. He was going to try for the reward!

He seemed to take ages to walk out of sight, and Jenny expected to be discovered at any minute. If the owners found her standing in their hall, they would think she was a thief. Being accused of that once was quite enough! As soon as she thought it safe, she slipped out, leaving the door slightly open as she'd found it, and hurried up the street in the opposite direction. By now she was shaking very badly; that had been a close thing. Too close: she saw a woman come out of a house two doors down and go into the one she had just left. Then she began to grin to herself as she thought how foolish Gerry was going to look when he found out that she didn't live there after all.

That evening the three brothers were having a fierce discussion, with John and Matt trying to convince Luke that the rise of the Nazi Party in Germany was something to be concerned about.

'It won't affect us,' Luke argued. 'All right, I don't agree with the near-hysteria and fanaticism they're causing, but you must admit they're giving the people something to cheer about.'

'Yes, but they're growing too fast,' John said. 'In September the Nazis won about one hundred seats from moderates in the German elections.'

Luke didn't look convinced, but said, 'And you think that makes them a threat?'

Matt leant forward in his chair and spoke with conviction. 'I don't trust this man Hitler. He's already calling for the Treaty of Versailles to be torn up. Once he's got the power and the means, he'll start to regain the territory the Germans lost as the result of the last war. After that he might set his sights on the rest of Europe.'

'Oh, I doubt that, Matt. I'm sure you're being alarmist.' Luke glanced at John. 'Do you think that man would be crazy enough to start a second world war?'

'It's possible. Like Matt, I have grave misgivings about what is happening in Germany. Fanaticism of any kind isn't healthy.' John reached out to pour himself a cup of coffee just as their mother came into the room.

'Coffee?' Luke asked her.

'Yes, please.' She sat down and took the cup from Luke. 'I have some news, but I'm not sure whether to be pleased or even more worried.'

'What is it?' John asked.

'I've just been talking to Mrs Douglas and Edna. It seems Jenny contacted Edna and they met this afternoon.'

'Is she all right?' Matt asked, feeling a surge of relief that Edna had seen the girl.

'It seems so...'

'Well, that's good news, isn't it?' John said.

'I agree it's a relief to know she isn't sleeping on the streets, but–' She stirred her coffee, and then took a deep breath before continuing. 'Edna said she was shocked when she saw her – "all skin and bones" was the way she put it. The poor child is obviously living a hard and frugal life.'

'Where is she?' Matt was on his feet. 'I'll go and bring her back here.'

'Edna doesn't know where she is living.' She smiled sadly at her youngest son. 'And Jenny said she wouldn't leave the elderly woman she's living with because she needs her.'

Matt sat down again, not trying to hide his disappointment. He'd really thought they were about to put right the wrong they had done her. Though why he was so worried about Eugenie Winford, or Jenny Baker, as she now called herself, was a puzzle he hadn't been able to solve. Perhaps it was like the time he had found that emaciated kitten and brought it home for their cook to look after. The poor little thing was so helpless and needed someone to care for it. Jenny Baker had had the same look about her.

The door of the library opened and their father strode in. 'I understand you have some news, Louise.'

His wife went through the story again. 'So you see, Gilbert, there is very little we can do. As she obviously has to work, I would be happy to try to find her a place as a personal maid in some good household, and I've told Edna as much. She has promised to tell Jenny the next time she meets her.'

'It isn't likely she'll agree,' Luke pointed out. 'I think she would find it very hard to trust us after the way we treated her.'

Matt watched his father wince; he was obviously still feeling very uncomfortable about

173

his part in dismissing the girl. 'Edna said she was thin, so what kind of a life is she living?'

'She is out very early every morning scrubbing floors, and the rest of the time she's caring for an elderly woman, whom she seems to be fond of. Jenny told Edna that the people she is with are very poor; she has to earn money because they can't afford to feed her. They took her in and showed kindness when she had nowhere else to go.'

'Oh, God, what a mess!' Gilbert bent and kissed his wife's cheek. 'I'm never going to dismiss a servant again. It's your job anyway, my dear, and I should have left it to you. But I was so furious that someone under our roof had been stealing that I acted without thought.'

'A failing of yours,' his wife said, with a smile of affection on her face. 'However, we cannot change what has happened, and at least we know she is living with kind, if poor, people. In the meantime I have told Edna she is to meet her whenever she can and keep an eye on her. We shall have to be satisfied with that for the time being, and hope that there will be some way to make amends in the future.'

Matt sincerely hoped there would be.

15

It was nearly a month before Jenny was able to meet Edna again: Ivy's two children had gone down with the measles; Fred had been laid up with a nasty bout of influenza; and Ma was growing increasingly frail. And they weren't the only people in the street suffering. Lack of nourishing food was taking its toll. Unemployment was now hitting hard, and each day becoming more of a struggle to survive. Jenny did everything she could: hurrying from one task to another, taking on extra cleaning jobs, spending nearly all her money on food and coal. It was the beginning of December, and with so much sickness around these were essential needs.

Over the last week things had improved: Ron, Ivy's husband, had managed to get a job as a bus conductor; the children were fit once again; and Fred was back on his feet.

Jenny tipped the money out of her purse and counted it. She had been squirrelling away a few pennies each week until she had enough for the pictures and a pot of tea afterwards. She'd written to Edna and suggested that they meet outside the cinema in Hammersmith where they were showing a Laurel and Hardy film, *Big Business*. After the last few weeks a laugh would do her good.

Ma was fast asleep in her chair after a lunch of

stew and dumplings. Jenny put more coal on the fire, kissed Ma gently on the cheek, being careful not to wake her, and stepped outside into the cold biting wind. She hoped Edna was going to be able to come; if she didn't, then she would see the film anyway.

But she need not have worried; her friend was already there. They bought their tickets and hurried into the warmth of the cinema.

'I've got things to tell you,' Edna whispered as they took their seats. 'We'll find a tea shop after the film's over and talk then.'

There wasn't time to say anything else, because the lights dimmed and the programme started. Jenny settled back with a smile on her face. She was going to enjoy this treat.

First there was a 'B' cowboy film and then the main Laurel and Hardy one. It was hilarious, and Jenny couldn't remember when she had laughed so much.

Edna was grinning when they came out. 'Blooming funny pair, ain't they? Now let's get that cuppa. I'm gasping.'

There was a café almost next to the cinema, and they went in there.

'You said you had something to tell me,' Jenny said, when they'd found an empty table and ordered.

'It's about your mum. The girl I know got talking to the housemaid in your aunt's house. She said Mrs Winford was all right and walking out with a very wealthy man. He's old, though.'

'Who?' Jenny asked eagerly.

'She didn't say, but there's talk of a wedding in

the offing. If it's true, then it sounds as if your mum's going to do all right for herself.'

Jenny sat back stunned but pleased with the news. 'An elderly man with pots of money will make her very happy.' She ordered another slice of fruit cake for each of them. After that startling news she was starving! 'Will you let me know if you hear anything else?'

'Of course.' Edna poured them both a second cup of tea. 'Oh, and another thing. Mrs Stannard said that I was to tell you that she would be happy to help you find a job somewhere as a personal maid. She probably knows lots of families who would take you on, Jen.'

'No, I've told you I won't leave Ma.'

'They're really sorry about what's happened to you, and would be only too happy to help you, but I understand how you feel. You've grown right fond of this woman, haven't you?'

'Yes, and I'm happy where I am, Edna.' Jenny smiled at her friend, and while they drank their tea, she took a pencil and piece of paper out of her bag, wrote her address down and gave it to her friend. 'I know you won't tell anyone where I am.'

'I won't utter a word to a soul.' Edna tucked the paper in her purse. 'Thanks, Jen.'

Jenny then told Edna about her meeting with the footman in Oxford Street.

'I'll bet he looked a fool if he did try to claim the reward,' Edna chuckled.

'Probably, but nevertheless I'm quite proud of that deception.'

'So you ought to be.' Edna glanced at the clock

on the wall. 'Whoops, I've got to go.'

Jenny saw her friend on to the bus and caught her own to Lambeth. All the way back to Ma's she pondered the news about her mother. It sounded as if she was making a new life for herself. She wondered who the man was. Perhaps she would write just to let her mother know she was all right, but not give her an address, of course. That idea was immediately dismissed. By allowing Aunt Gertrude to take charge and arrange for her to go to Greaves, her mother obviously hadn't cared what happened to her, so she wouldn't bother to contact her.

She still had tuppence left, and when she got off the bus she went to the baker's and bought two buns for their tea. Ma would enjoy that. It had been a good afternoon, and she sang to herself as she walked home. Now she must think about Christmas, which was only three weeks away. A few coppers put away each week and she should be able to give Ma a special time.

The garage workshop was worryingly empty. There were only two cars in today, and Matt was fully aware of the economic situation; many businesses were struggling and unemployment, if not already a fact of life, was looming. None of them had missed Jake's distracted air of late, and the lack of work told its own story. Matt saw Jake standing at the window of his shop-floor office, gazing at the empty spaces and men hanging around with nothing to do. Some firms in a similar situation were letting the workers in only when there was work, and then sending them home when it was finished. Although the men still officially had jobs, their weekly wage was greatly reduced. Harry was particularly concerned because his wife was expecting their first baby in February.

Matt made his decision, knocked on the office door, then stepped inside, closing it behind him.

'Hello, Matt,' Jake greeted him. 'I was going to have a word with you. We're suffering and I can't afford to go on like this much longer.'

'Are you going to have to lay people off?' he asked.

'I don't want to.' His boss ran a hand through his hair, making it stand up on end. 'I've got a bloody good workforce here and don't want to lose even one of you, but I don't see what else I can do. I'm afraid that as the last in, you'll have to be the first to go. I know how disappointed you're going to be. Young Jim's already leaving to join the army.'

'We're the two lowest paid, so will you be able to survive if you don't have to pay us each week?' Jake was a decent man, and Matt could see how painful this was for him.

'God knows!' Jake sat down heavily. 'I might have to get rid of Harry as well.'

'Don't do that.' Matt spoke quietly – this office was of a very flimsy construction and he didn't want anyone else to hear their conversation. He'd always been able to discuss things with Jake, who chatted to him quite naturally, although he was only his apprentice. 'Let me help, Jake. I'll continue my apprenticeship without pay and invest in the business. Once you're back on your feet

179

again you can pay me back. You've got a first-class reputation and things will pick up again.'

Jake was studying him intently. 'That's more than generous of you, Matt, but you might lose your money.'

'Not a chance,' he stated confidently. 'Let's try to save the business and the jobs. No one need know about my involvement.'

'I know you come from a banking family, but we need to talk this through. My own bank has refused me a further loan, and once you have all the details you might not think it such a good investment.' He gazed out at the shop floor again. 'But we can't do it here; we're already causing a lot of interest.'

'I expect they think you're sacking me,' Matt said, grinning. Jake's eyes now held a gleam of hope.

'No doubt.' His boss snorted in amusement. 'You'd better go out there and put their minds at rest – at least for another day. They know you'd be the first out, and then perhaps some of them. It's a damned worrying time for everyone. Once they've all gone home, we'll thrash out some kind of deal. But there's no way you're going to work for nothing!'

'Right.' Matt left the office whistling to himself, and began to give a car that had just been serviced an extra polish.

'Have you still got a job?' Harry stood beside him, very worried.

'Yes, things are tough, but this is a sound business.' He stood back to admire the shine on the bonnet, and then tossed the duster to Harry.

180

'Jake will survive until things pick up again.'

'Maybe, but will we?' Harry said. 'The chances of getting another job are pretty slim at the moment.'

'You won't need to.' Matt's smile was confident. He was going to make sure his idea worked. 'Everything's going to be all right, you'll see.'

'Wish I could believe that.' Harry chucked the duster back at him. 'Keep polishing. Anyway, I'm glad you're staying. It gives hope to the rest of us.'

It was nine o'clock before Matt arrived home that evening.

'You're late,' his mother scolded. 'Have you eaten?'

'Yes, thanks; I had a pie and a pint in the pub with Jake.' He pulled a wad of papers out of his pocket. 'The garage is in financial trouble, and we've been working out a rescue package.'

John was immediately interested. 'What are you proposing?'

For the next hour Matt, his brothers and father sat around a table, discussing the idea. They all had fine business brains, even Luke; although his brother could appear superficial at times, that was only an act. Matt trusted the judgement of each of them.

'You know you're taking a risk?' John pointed out. 'Things are bad and going to get worse. You are intending to use your inheritance from grandfather, and could be throwing it away.'

'I know that, but I'm prepared to take the chance.'

181

'Do you want a partnership with Jake?' Luke was scribbling figures on the back of Matt's notes.

'No. I just want to try to save the business and the jobs. When things take an upturn, Jake can repay me.'

'Time limit?' his father asked.

'No limit. Jake can have all the time he needs.'

John was carefully checking the figures Matt had brought home with him. 'Well, if you're prepared to risk your money, Matt, then I say go ahead. This is a sound business with an excellent reputation. Even in a depression I still believe he'll get a steady stream of work – perhaps not as much as usual, but enough to keep him ticking over. If he can weather this bad time, then I'm sure the business will recover.'

'That's my feeling.' Matt sat back with a sigh of relief and grinned at his brother. 'Luke, will you draw up a contract? Jake wants all this done legally.'

'I'll do that right away. And if you don't mind, Matt, I'll put in a bit of my own money.'

'Wonderful.' Matt looked hopefully at John and his father. 'Any more offers?'

His father glanced at his eldest son with a wry smile on his face. 'I think we can help Matt out here, don't you?'

John lifted his hand in a resigned gesture. 'Why not?'

Over the next few weeks the business did improve a little, as the garage began to look after the Stannard Bank's cars and those of family and friends. The tuneful whistles of the men could be heard again; the air of worry and tension eased. If anyone suspected that Matt and his influential family were propping up their jobs, they never mentioned it; they were only too grateful to still have work.

They closed at lunchtime on Christmas Eve and headed for the pub across the road. Jake had lost his frown, and the rest were in high spirits. No one would let Matt buy a drink, saying that it was a celebration to mark the finish of the first year of his apprenticeship, but he guessed it was their way of saying thank you for trying to save their jobs. It didn't take a genius to know that Jake's business had been on the edge of collapse, or to guess where the extra money had come from.

By the time he arrived home around four o'clock, Matt was feeling very mellow indeed and a little unsteady on his feet.

'Oh, dear,' his mother said when she saw him, the corners of her mouth twitching in amusement. 'Sit down, Matt, before you fall down.'

He eased himself into a chair, grinning. 'I'm not that drunk, Mother.'

'Really?' She pulled a bell rope and ordered a pot of strong coffee. 'You do remember we're having a party tonight instead of on New Year's Eve, don't you?'

A rumble of laughter came from Luke. 'I don't think Matt will mind Gloria Tremain coming tonight. She might even look attractive through the haze of alcohol.'

'She isn't coming, is she?' he asked his mother

in a horrified tone.

'I can hardly exclude her. Her parents are good friends of ours.'

When the coffee arrived, a cup was poured and handed to Matt. He drank it obediently, muttering under his breath.

His brother helped himself to a coffee, still grinning. 'You'd think she'd have got the message by now that you can't stand her.'

John and their father arrived at that moment.

Gilbert kissed his wife. 'Is that coffee?'

'Yes, dear.' She poured for her husband and son. 'We were just talking about Gloria. She *will* keep pursuing Matt, and he really doesn't care for her.'

Her husband sat down with a weary sigh. 'She's set her heart on becoming part of this family. If she continues to get nowhere with Matt, she'll probably try Luke or John.'

'She'll be wasting her time!' both brothers said at once.

Matt giggled at their vehemence, and his father eyed him suspiciously. 'Are you drunk?'

'Not quite, but I have had a few drinks. Jake and the others insisted on celebrating the end of my first year's apprenticeship.'

'Good Lord, is it a year?' His father shook his head in disbelief. 'Where has the time gone?'

Mercifully, his mother had placed him well away from Gloria, so Matt was able to enjoy the dinner without her constantly claiming his attention. He had never been able to understand why she had set her sights on him. If she were ambitious, John, as the eldest, would be the logical

184

choice. But perhaps she had enough sense to realize that he would be the most difficult one to snare. Luke wouldn't take her seriously, so that had left him.

As soon as the meal was over, Gloria made straight for him.

'When are you going back to university?' she asked, smiling brightly.

'Never,' was his short reply.

That declaration removed the smile from her face, and her eyes opened wide in disbelief. 'But you can't keep working as a mechanic.'

'Why not?'

'My father has always said that you're the cleverest one and will probably be a professor one day.'

'I don't want to be a bloody professor!' he growled. Three glasses of wine during the meal had topped up his alcohol level, and he was in no mood for this. His family had accepted his decision. They knew how much he loved what he was doing and never mentioned his returning to university to take up his studies again.

'You're drunk,' Gloria said haughtily. 'You can't mean to work in greasy overalls for the rest of your life!'

'Oh, but I do.' He glared at her. 'Anyway, I don't see how I spend my life can have anything to do with you.'

'If you are going to be that stupid, then you're not worth bothering with.'

'Good,' he snapped and watched her flounce off, nose in the air. He knew he had been extremely rude, but it was the only way to get rid of her. The subtle approach didn't work with her.

'I see you've upset Gloria.' Luke handed him a drink.

'I do believe I have.' Matt shook with silent laughter. 'She doesn't want anything to do with a lowly car mechanic. Perhaps she'll try John now.'

'Not a chance.' Luke refilled their glasses from a bottle he was holding in his hand. 'Our big brother's too interested in Emma Holdsworth.'

'Is he?' Matt peered across the room at John talking to the elegant girl with fair hair and rather nice turquoise eyes. He was leaning towards her and smiling. 'Good heavens, I do believe you're right. He's kept that quiet. How long has this been going on?'

'About three months.' Luke gave Matt a sad look. 'You're too interested in your messy engines. There is life outside of that garage, you know.'

'Really?' Matt teased. 'I must have a look sometime.'

16

Ma's small front room was packed and even the extra chairs from next door weren't enough. Young Alice was quite happy sitting on the floor with her baby brother, Bert, and everyone else had perched wherever they could. Glad, Ivy and Jenny had pooled their money to give everyone a good Christmas Day. They had a chicken, vegetables and a little fruit from Fred and Stan's

186

market stall, beer for the men, milk stout for the women and lemonade for Ivy's two children. And the crowning glory of this sumptuous meal was a pudding that Edna had brought round as a present from Mrs Peters, the Stannards' cook. Jenny was touched that they should think kindly enough of her to send this gift for Christmas, one she could share with her friends. Fred had produced a small bottle of brandy, which was poured over the pudding and set alight, with cries of delight from everyone.

Jenny had sent a card thanking Mrs Peters and wishing everyone at the house a happy Christmas. She had also sent her mother a card, telling her that she was all right. She realized now just how unhappy she must have been, with her husband having another family in America. To maintain the outward appearance of a stable family home would have been a struggle.

'Come on, Uncle Stan, play for us.'

The shrill voice of Ivy's young daughter caught Jenny's attention as she dragged her uncle to the piano in the corner of the room.

When Stan began to thump out the popular tunes of the day, everyone jumped to their feet and started dancing. Even Ma hauled herself up and with Fred's help joined in. 'Come on, Auntie Jen!' Alice dragged her to her feet, and at six years old made a passable attempt at a waltz. Baby Bert, not quite two, was wriggling and laughing in Glad's arms.

This was the happiest Jenny had been since she'd run away from home. She had great affection and respect for Fred, Glad and their family, but she loved Ma. The bond between them had grown over the months, and now nothing would make her leave this outspoken elderly woman.

'That's enough of that!' Ma said as Fred helped her back to her chair. 'I think that calls for another glass of stout, and then we can give out the presents.'

When everyone had a drink in their hands, Ma told Jenny to do the honours. The presents were, of course, modest and mostly hand-made, but that didn't make any difference to the pleasure they all felt. The children had two toys each, and their cries of delight showed how thrilled they were.

'I want to propose a toast to Jen,' Ma said, claiming everyone's attention. 'This young girl has made my life worth living again. She takes my sharp tongue in her stride, never taking umbrage, and I know she finds the work and poverty hard, but she just gets on with it.' Ma cackled. 'The only time I've ever heard her complain is when she tells me I cheat at cards.'

That made everyone laugh.

'Didn't take her long to suss you out, then, Ma,' Fred remarked.

Ma's face broke into a grin. 'Ah, she's right bright. Anyway, she's real good to me and I wants to thank her properly. Here's to you, ducky, and I hopes and prays that your future will be bright, with lots of love and good friends.'

Jenny gazed at each in turn as they drank her health, and smiled. 'I've already got those things.'

Ma unpinned a small brooch from her dress and handed it to Jenny. It was a circle of tiny pearls, inexpensive but pretty.

'Oh, Ma,' she gasped, 'I can't take this. You ought to give it to one of your own family.' She knew this was much valued by Ma, because she wore it every day.

'Ain't got none, Jen. My hubby and me only had one daughter, and she died of diphtheria when she was three. That was a present from my Tommy when we wed, and now I'm getting near the end of my time I wants you to have it. I got enough insurance to give me a simple funeral so that won't be needed.' Ma gave her a stern look. 'And I don't want no arguing about it. I've given it to you in front of my friends 'cause I want them to know it's yours now.'

Her eyes misted over as she hugged Ma. 'It's the most precious gift I've ever received, but are you sure there isn't anyone else you'd rather give it to?'

Ma shook her head. 'Since my Bessie died you're the nearest to a daughter I've ever had. You've brought a ray of sunshine into my life and it's right you should have it.'

'I'm honoured,' Jenny said huskily, quite overcome by this very special gift. But even more special were the sentiments expressed in the giving. She pinned it to her frock.

'That looks right nice on you.' Ma nodded in approval. 'I've kept it out of the pawnbroker's hands all these years, so I'm going to ask you not to pop it, Jen.'

'I wouldn't dream of parting with it.' She pulled the pendant from under her blouse and held it out for Ma to see. 'My father gave me this and it's my insurance. If I desperately need money any time, this will go to the pawnbroker's.'

'Well, I hope you never have to.' Ma patted her hand and then nodded to her empty glass. 'How about another refill and one of those nice mince pies you've made?'

Ma needed extra help to get to bed that night, because she'd worn herself out, and had a glass or two too many of her favourite stout.

'That was a grand party,' she sighed, closing her eyes. She was asleep before Jenny covered her up.

Jenny crept downstairs and began to clear up the mess. There was wrapping paper everywhere, glasses and plates. She was surprised to see Glad in the kitchen when she staggered in with her arms full of crockery.

'Oh, Glad, don't you bother with that. It won't take me long to wash up.'

'You'll get through it quicker with two pair of hands.' Glad filled the sink with hot water from the kettle she'd boiled up. 'I'm pleased Ma gave you that brooch. She knows how hard you work and is grateful for the care you're showing her. She's right fond of you.'

'And I am of her.' Jenny stacked the plates on the table. 'I didn't like taking the gift, though, but she'd have given me a real telling off if I'd refused.'

Glad swished a glass through the water. 'Ah, she would at that! But she really hasn't got anyone else, Jen, and that's the first time she's mentioned her little daughter for many years.

That was a sad loss to them, and they never had any more kids. She told me the other week that if her daughter had lived she hoped she would have grown to be just like you.'

'I'm touched she thinks of me like that.'

After drying her hands, Glad leant against the sink and faced Jenny. 'Don't you take no notice of her growling; she's very fond of you. She's coming to the end of her time and is more ill than she makes out. I hope you're going to stay with her, Jen.'

'Nothing will make me leave her. I'll stay for as long as she needs me.'

'I thought you'd say that.' Glad kissed Jenny on the cheek. 'Now it's time we both got some kip.'

The next weeks were cold, and the long dark nights were spent huddled around a small coal fire, trying to keep warm. But eventually the evenings began to draw out and there was a hint of warmth in the air at last as spring finally decided to put on a show. It was with a sense of relief that Jenny noted the signs. The three months since the start of 1931 had been worrying. Ma had been taken ill soon after Christmas, and it had seemed once or twice that they were going to lose her. However, Jenny had told her forcefully that she would not allow her to give up, and had stayed by her side, making her eat. All the neighbours had been wonderful. Fred and Stan had kept her supplied with vegetables so she could make nourishing soups; others had brought her wood and coal to keep the fire going. Jenny had insisted on paying them a small amount for each kindly gift, for she was well aware that they were depriving themselves in order to help. She was fortunate to still have the early-morning job, but many others were not so lucky. Unemployment was a great worry now, as she saw every time she walked past the employment exchange. The queues were getting longer each day, and many of the desperate people were resorting to the soup kitchens for something to eat. Her heart ached for them all. She couldn't help wondering how many of her past acquaintances, sitting in their grand, warm houses, were aware of the suffering. Probably not many.

'There.' She tucked a blanket around Ma's legs. 'You'll soon be able to have the front door open so you can see and talk to people again.'

'I hopes you've been doing my step while I've been laid up.' Ma glowered at Jenny.

'It's still the best in the street,' she laughed. That sounded more like Ma!

'Hmm, we'll see. And how long is it since you've been out with your friend?'

'Not for a while.'

'Well, you should have. And stop poking that fire. I'm warm enough.'

Jenny sat back on her heels and gave Ma a suspicious glance. 'Are you spoiling for a fight?'

'Who me?' Ma looked innocent.

Jenny giggled. 'Yes, you.'

'I'm just trying to say that you shouldn't be here wasting your time with a crusty old woman. You ought to go back to that house you worked at ... or even go home.'

Clambering to her feet, she stood in front of

Ma with a determined glint in her eyes. 'Are you trying to get rid of me?'

'The way you're living ain't right. I don't want you to feel beholden to me just because I gives you that brooch at Christmas.'

'I don't feel beholden!' Jenny sighed in exasperation. 'I stay because I want to. And if you think I'm going to leave you, then you're very much mistaken. For some daft reason I've grown to love you–'

'Are you two arguing?' Glad walked into the front room.

'She gets quite shirty,' Ma said, wiping the moisture from her eyes. 'Can't understand it, she was such a timid little thing when she first come. Now look at her. I'm no longer boss in my own house – do this, Ma, do that, Ma, you're not going to die, Ma. Must be the bleeding company she's keeping!'

Ma cackled and Jenny felt like crying for joy. She hadn't heard that wicked laugh for some time.

'I see you're feeling better,' Glad said drily. 'I've brought you a newspaper.'

'Oh, ta. Jen can make me a nice cuppa and then read it to me.'

As Jenny took the paper from Glad, she raised her eyebrows. 'And she thinks she's no longer mistress of her own house?'

Glad winked and left with a huge smile on her face, obviously as relieved as Jenny to see and hear Ma back to her old self.

When the tea was made, Jenny sat opposite Ma and began to read the news out loud. A lot of the reports were about unemployment, quoting a figure of around two million and rising, with no prospect of economic recovery in sight. It was a depressing subject, and she moved on to the more light-hearted stories, stopping at a picture of a tall building.

'What's that?' Ma craned to see the paper.

'It's called the Empire State Building in New York.' Jenny read, 'The concrete and glass building has 102 floors and stands at a height of 1,250 feet. It's going to be officially opened on the first of May.'

'Never!' Ma exclaimed in disbelief. 'How can they build something that tall? It'll fall down!'

'I'm sure it won't.' Jenny tried to picture what it would be like inside. 'It's called a skyscraper.'

'You wouldn't get me in it. It can't be safe!'

'I'd love to see it and go right to the top. I bet the views would be wonderful.'

'Of course you would be interested. I keep forgetting that you're half American.' The corners of Ma's mouth twitched. 'Though with that posh English accent it's not surprising I didn't remember.'

Jenny nodded silently as memories of her father came flooding back.

Ma reached across and took Jenny's hand in her own, obviously sensing her troubled thoughts. 'Your Pa didn't need to kill himself and leave a lovely daughter like you to fend for herself. We ain't got nothing, but we manage, and he'd have recovered in time. Wonder why he did it.'

'I don't know.' She held Ma's hand carefully so as not to hurt her. The rheumatism had got worse over the last few months. 'The more I think about it, the less sense it makes. I'm sure he wouldn't have abandoned his children.'

'Children?' Ma looked up sharply. 'You got brothers and sisters?'

'Two half-brothers in America, my mother told me.'

'Ah, married before, was he?'

'No.' Jenny shifted uncomfortably. 'They must be illegitimate, because from what my mother told me I think they were born after me. My mother and father weren't happy...'

'So he had a mistress in America. Don't look so ashamed, Jen, I've seen plenty of life and knows what goes on.' Ma's face took on a thoughtful expression. 'If he had two families, then it don't make sense he would leave you all.'

'I agree, but that's what happened. When my aunt said she wouldn't take me in, I asked my mother if I could go to my father's family in New York, but she said they wouldn't want me either.' Jenny dipped her head to hide the pain in her eyes. That still hurt so much.

'There, there,' Ma soothed, 'don't you upset yourself, duck. Things have a habit of working out right in the end. You never know, you might meet them one day, and even go to the top of that awful building. And *we* want and love you.'

Gratitude filled Jenny's heart. She was loved here, and that was why she wouldn't leave until Ma no longer needed her.

She was about to put the paper down when a notice caught her attention, making her gasp in surprise. It was an announcement of a wedding.

'What is it?' Ma asked.

'My mother's getting married again in two weeks' time.'

'Who to?'

'Someone called Gordon Frasier.' Jenny looked up excitedly. 'Isn't that the man who owns a chain of gentlemen's outfitters?'

Ma nodded. 'I've heard of him. Well, if it is him, then your mum's doing very nicely for herself. Got pots of money, I've been told.'

'Money has always been important to my mother. The wedding is taking place at St George's Church, quite close to where we used to live.'

'Why don't you go and see her?'

'Not yet.' Jenny chewed her lip in concentration. 'But I'll go and take a peek at the wedding, from a safe distance, of course. I'll send them a congratulations card anyway. I wonder what my new stepfather will be like.'

'If it's the man I'm thinking of, he's getting on a bit.' Ma gave Jenny a crafty wink. 'But your mother might have time enough to work on him and make him leave her all his money, before he pops off.'

Jenny giggled. 'You are wicked, Ma.'

The old lady cackled. 'From what you've told me about her, that's probably what she's hoping for.'

'Yes,' Jenny agreed, fully aware of her mother's love of position and wealth. 'I expect that would suit her very nicely.'

17

'We'll manage.' Jenny slipped her arm around Ivy's shoulder, alarmed by how white she had gone. Only a week ago things had seemed so much better, what with Ma recovering and everyone else back to health. Spring was here and the struggle to keep the sick and young warm was over. But Jenny was beginning to believe that the coin spinning in her life had two tails, as everything had crashed around them again. 'Ron's still got his job as a conductor.'

'But he hasn't.' Ivy looked near to tears, and it took a lot to drag these resilient people down. 'He was laid off yesterday. I can't afford to be out of work, Jen. How am I going to feed my kids?'

Jenny hooked her hand through Ivy's arm as they walked back home. They'd turned up for work this morning only to be told that they weren't wanted any longer. It was something they'd been praying wouldn't happen. She felt as if there were a heavy weight in her stomach, but Ivy must be worried sick. 'What about the dole? Ron will get that, surely?'

'Oh, yeah,' Ivy snorted in disgust. 'He'll get around one pound, five shillings and threepence, and that won't go far with two children. And there's nothing for us women.'

'Mrs Pritchard from No. 30 gets free milk for her children, doesn't she?'

Ivy nodded miserably.

'Can't you try for that?' Jenny was trying to sound positive, but it was hard. Without work, how were any of them going to manage?

'I'll talk to Mum about it, but it's an unpleasant business applying for assistance. You get some busybody from the welfare poking their nose into everything you've got.' Ivy was shaking with worry now.

'What do you mean?' Jenny didn't know anything about things like this.

'When you ask for help, you get caught up in what's called the means test. Everyone hates it. We might be poor but we do have some pride, Jen. This person counts every penny you've got coming in and looks to see if you have anything of value you can pawn. If someone is kind enough to give you a gift of food or coal, the bastards take that off the money they pay you.'

Jenny was appalled.

'They're prying all the time to see you don't get something for nothing. Mrs Gerrard at No. 22 was told to pawn her blankets. And that was in the middle of winter!' Ivy's laugh was humourless. 'Mrs Gerrard's a big woman and she threw the louse out, telling him to bugger off, she'd manage without his rotten help.'

They continued walking in silence. Although it was only seven in the morning, the queue outside the employment exchange was already long. Some men looked as if they'd been there all night in the hope of being first in line for any job that might be going that day.

The two girls stopped and stared. The look of

hopelessness etched on the men's faces tore the heart out of Jenny. How could this happen? The Wall Street crash had been in America and nobody here had thought it could have anything to do with them, but they had been wrong. World trade had slumped, and jobs had been lost at an alarming rate. Jenny had learnt as much as she could about it, watching the depression take hold, not only in Britain but overseas as well. This country now had unemployed of around two million, but America was much worse. There were around eight million over there without work, but it was a much bigger country, of course. However, that didn't mean much to those who were destitute.

'Look at that!' Ivy whispered in despair. 'What chance do those poor devils stand? What chance do any of us stand?'

As Jenny's gaze swept along the line of dejected figures, she gulped back the tears threatening to spill over. Why wasn't the government doing more for the working classes? Suddenly anger raged through her, with an intensity she had never before experienced. At that moment she realized that she was no longer a frightened child. She had grown up.

'Come on, Ivy.' She started to march up the road, dragging Glad's daughter with her. 'We might be out of work, but we ain't down yet! There must be something we can do, and I'm bloody well going to find it.'

'Oh, Jen,' Ivy's spluttered laugh was genuine. 'You sounded just like one of us then.'

Jenny stopped, turned to Ivy and lifted her head

proudly. 'I am one of you. When my father died, I made a choice to become a servant rather than live a miserable life with a man I hated. I've worked my hands raw to survive, and by God I've done it! No more self-pity, no more yearning for the past, no more fear. That's all gone. Now I'm going to roll up my sleeves and fight for us and everyone living on the breadline.'

Ivy threw her arms around Jenny and grinned. 'My mum and dad said you was special. They were right. But what are you going to do?'

'I don't know yet, but I feel like shaking some of those complacent politicians until their teeth rattle.'

'Go get 'em, girl!' Ivy slapped her on the back. 'Pity Ma ain't younger, 'cos she'd be right there with you.'

Despite the worry about losing their jobs, both girls were laughing as they turned into Forest Road.

Once outside Ma's house Jenny stopped and hugged Ivy. 'Try not to worry too much. We'll see your little ones have enough to eat.'

''Course we will.' Ivy's nod was confident, then she became serious again. 'Things are going to get hard around here, Jen. Couldn't you go home?'

'I am home!' Jenny replied in a firm voice.

'Well, in that case,' Ivy said, looking at Jenny with respect, 'we'll make you an honorary cockney.'

Jenny curtsied gracefully. 'I'm touched, ma'am.'

'You must be,' Ivy chortled, 'to want to stay here while there's a depression, for God knows how long it's going to last. Now I'd better go and break the bad news to my hubby and Mum.'

They parted with another hug, trying to make light of their desperate situation. When Jenny stepped inside Ma's front room, she found the elderly woman staring at her from her armchair.

'You're back early. What's happened?' she demanded testily.

Ma was fully dressed and Jenny was concerned because Ma wasn't back to full health yet and needed a lot of help in the mornings. 'Did you get up on your own?'

'Yes.' Ma narrowed her eyes suspiciously.

'You should have waited until I got home,' Jenny scolded. 'What do you want for breakfast?'

'I'm not bloody helpless. And you know we've only got bread and marge in the cupboard until you do some shopping. So stop beating around the bleeding bush and tell me what's happened!'

At that tirade Jenny's placid nature disintegrated and she rounded on Ma. 'Don't you swear at me. If you must know, Ivy and me have lost our *bleeding* jobs. And you're lucky to get bread and margarine because in another week you'll be living on thin air!'

Much to Jenny's annoyance, Ma started to chuckle.

'What's so funny?'

'You are.' Ma's grin spread, her sharp eyes crinkling at the corners. 'Go and put the kettle on, ducky, and we'll talk while we eat our bread and scrape.'

When the frugal meal was ready, Jenny took it into the front room. They ate in silence, and it

201

wasn't until the second cup of tea that Ma spoke.

'I always guessed you had some fire in you, ducky. You ain't scared of that family of yours no more, are you?'

'No.' Jenny lifted her head. 'My so-called family can do what they like. I'll never go back there, and they won't be able to force me to do anything I don't want to now.'

'Bravo!' Ma slapped her hand on the arm of her chair. 'Just let them show their faces round here and I'll give them a piece of my mind. They've treated you real bad, and they don't deserve to have a lovely girl like you. But you're all grown up now and don't need them.'

The thought of Ma laying into her mother and Aunt Gertrude with her colourful vocabulary had Jenny laughing out loud. She had just lost her job, didn't know how they were going to manage – and she didn't care! This was more home to her than the Bloomsbury house had ever been. And Ma, Glad, Fred and Ivy were closer to her than her own flesh and blood.

'So.' Ma held her gaze steadily. 'Are you Eugenie Winford or Jenny Baker?'

'Jenny Baker,' she answered without hesitation.

Ma gave a satisfied smile. 'Well, Jenny Baker, we'd better decide what's to be done, hadn't we?'

An hour later they were no nearer a solution, and Jenny gazed at Ma in disgust. 'I'm useless. I can't sew, can't knit, don't know anything about business.'

'You ain't useless,' Ma corrected sharply, then her eyes twinkled. 'You can scrub a fine step.'

Her gloom disappeared and she grinned at the elderly woman. 'The best one in the street, but that doesn't help us to eat. No one round here's got money to pay me to scrub their steps.' Jenny's hand went to the pendant around her neck.

'You can forget that, my girl. That was a present from your dad and you ought to keep it as a reminder of him. We should be all right for a while. I've got the rent put by for a couple of weeks, and there's a few bob in my purse.'

'And I've got seven and sixpence.' Jenny had been saving to go out with Edna when she had a whole day off, but that would have to wait now. She stood up. 'I'd better get some shopping.'

'Go to Fred and Stan's stall, Jen. They're having a tough time. If people can't buy what they've got, then they can't buy for the next day's trading. They've taken to going late to the Covent Garden Market and buying when the traders reduce their prices to get rid of the stuff. It ain't the top-quality veg they're used to selling, but it's cheap, and that's what the women want.'

'Oh, I didn't know that.' Jenny was even more worried about her friends now. 'Ivy didn't tell me.'

'Ah, well, she wouldn't. They probably haven't said much to her, so as not to worry her. Get some suet and flour for dumplings. That'll fill a corner up.'

Just then Glad came in. 'The whole street's going to get together this evening. Nearly every-one here have lost their jobs, so we're going to band together and see if we can help each other out.'

'Good idea, Glad.' Ma nodded approval. 'Me and Jen's just been racking our brains as well.'

'Where are you going to meet?' Jenny asked. 'I'll try and get Ma there.'

'We've already thought of that. Ma, you can sit in your doorway and we'll all gather outside here.'

'You mind they don't trample on my step.'

'I'll warn them.' Glad was laughing as she left.

'You and your step. You're a saucy old devil, do you know that?' Jenny bent and kissed Ma's cheek.

A wicked chuckle was the only answer to that.

Jenny set off to see how much food she could buy for the least amount of money, feeling ridiculously light-hearted, considering the dire straits they were all in.

She could hear Fred and Stan hollering their produce at the tops of their voices when she was still quite a distance from them. How anyone understood what they were saying was a complete mystery to Jenny. By the time she stopped in front of them she was giggling. Cockney slang was hard enough, but the costermonger's language was even worse.

When Fred saw her, he beckoned her to come behind the stall they were serving from, and Stan, who was dealing with a customer, gave her a cheeky wink.

'Jen, my pet.' Fred hugged her, then held her away from him so he could look into her face. 'Ron's just come and told us you and Ivy have lost your jobs. I'm right sorry. But you're not to fret. Something will turn up.'

'Of course it will.' Jenny gave what she hoped was a confident smile as Stan came over. 'How's trade today?'

'A bit slow,' Stan said. 'But that's only to be expected. People are counting the pennies now, but we're getting by.'

'Good.' Jenny studied the stall, deciding what would be best to buy. 'I'd like two pounds of King Edwards, please. A couple of carrots and onions...'

'You going to make a stew?' Fred asked, as he weighed the potatoes.

'Yes, and I'll put some dumplings in with it. If I make a large pot, then it will do for a couple of days.'

Fred tipped the vegetables in her basket, and then dived in a box under the stall. 'I've got a swede here. It's a bit past its best, but will do nicely in a stew.'

'Thanks, Fred.' Jenny sighed as she looked at the produce. 'Now, what can I have for greens today?'

'How about a bit of spinach?' Stan grinned. 'That'll build up Ma's strength.'

The look Jenny gave him was one of mock horror. 'Do you think that's a good idea? Her language is getting terrible again. And she's told Glad to warn everyone not to mess up her step at the meeting tonight.'

The men roared. 'That sounds more like the Ma Adams we all know,' Fred said, winking at Jenny with affection. 'I don't think she'd have lasted this winter without you.'

'I wasn't going to let her die, because for all her cussed ways I do love her.' Jenny opened her purse. 'How much do I owe you?'

'Nothing.'

As Fred turned away, Jenny caught hold of his arm. 'I won't take the veg unless you let me pay. I've got enough money.'

'All right, Jen, just give us a tanner.'

She gave him a shilling, disappearing into the crowd before he could protest. Her next stop was the butcher, Mr Walters. He also sold fish, and Jenny went to see what he had in today.

'Hello, Jen,' Mr Walters greeted her. 'How's Ma now?'

'Getting stronger every day. I thought I'd buy her a piece of smoked haddock.' She smiled at the shopkeeper, suddenly realizing that the whole community had really accepted her. And it wasn't because of wealth or social position. They had taken Jenny Baker to their hearts because they liked her. It was a wonderful feeling.

He cut off a slice of fish and held it up. 'How's that, or do you want a bit more?'

'No, that's lovely, thanks.'

'I hear you and Ivy have lost your jobs,' he said, as he wrapped the haddock.

'I'm afraid so.' After a quick check of the money she had left in her purse, Jenny said, 'I'll take four of your pork sausages as well, please.'

'I've got a nice ham bone if you'd like it to make a stew with. It's still got a bit of meat on it.'

'Oh, I'd like that. How much?'

'Tuppence to you, Jen.' Mr Walters smiled gently. 'Can't have Ma going downhill again,

206

can we?'

'Dear me, no,' Jenny replied drily as she put the purchases in the basket. After paying Mr Walters, she left with a wave of her hand and headed for the grocer's and baker's. She really was doing very well with the shopping today, and the ham bone was a real treat. She might even be able to make the stew do for three days! They would have some nourishing food for a few days, and that was as far ahead as she was prepared to look at the moment. It would be interesting to see what happened at the meeting tonight.

Everyone in the street turned up, and, with Ma sitting regally in her doorway guarding her sparkling step, ways to survive the crisis were discussed. But there seemed little anyone could do except try to help the most needy amongst them. Ron and another young man, Jimmy, decided they would go out on their bikes with placards hung from the handlebars, offering to do gardening or any odd jobs.

'It'll be better than sitting on our backsides feeling sorry for ourselves,' Ron declared stoutly.

'I've heard there are things called soup kitchens in some places,' Jenny said. 'Couldn't we at least get food for the children from them?'

'There ain't none round here,' the woman from No. 34 told her. 'The nearest one's a bus ride away in Camden, and we can't afford to waste pennies on bus fares.'

'Anyway that's degrading,' her husband muttered. 'That'll be the last straw. We does have our pride.'

'Don't talk rot,' Stan snapped. 'Pride won't fill your bellies.'

'Too right,' Fred said. 'Look at our Jen. Been brought up a lady, but she wasn't too proud to scrub floors when her family lost all their money.'

'And that's the kind of guts that's going to get us through this.' Ma surveyed her neighbours sternly. 'Poverty ain't no stranger to us, but this is a real bad time, and we got to see that the kids don't suffer too much.'

'That's all right for you to talk, Ma.' One man was swaying on his feet, looking belligerent. 'I can't see you doing much about it.'

Ma bristled. 'You come here, Billy Watkins, and I'll show what I can do. And where did you get money to get drunk this early in the evening?'

'None of your bloody business!' He staggered his way back to the pub.

'He ain't gonna be any use while he's in that state,' Glad remarked. 'I'll sort him out to-morrow. Now has anyone got any sensible ideas?'

There was a surge of suggestions. The women would see if they could get any sewing or take in washing; the men would start touting for work – any kind of work.

'What we need is someone with money who'd set up a help centre near here,' Mrs Preston from five doors along said. 'It ain't just us in this street what's suffering. It's the whole blasted country now.'

'We're just going to have to tighten our belts and do the best we can.' Fred took a cigarette packet from his pocket, saw it was empty, screwed it up and tossed it in the air. 'That's one thing I'm gonna have to do without for a start. But things are bound to pick up again.'

With mutters that this couldn't last for ever, they finished the meeting and everyone returned to their homes.

Jenny helped Ma back to her comfy armchair and shut the front door, mulling over the idea of a place where people in dire need could go for help.

'You're quiet, ducky,' Ma said.

'Sorry.' Jenny smiled at her. 'I was just thinking that I'd like to have seen you give that man a clip around the ear.'

'Ah, there was a day when I would have done it too. When things get rough, some men try to escape with drink, but it don't work, Jen. The next day they sober up and the troubles are still there, only worse because they've spent money that should have been used to feed their families. You can't run from these things, but you of all people know that, don't you, pet?'

Jenny nodded.

'Any chance of a cup of cocoa?' Ma yawned.

'I was just going to get it. I've got some biscuits as well. Broken ones, of course.'

'Smashing. Don't matter about them being broken. We chews them up anyway.' Ma caught Jenny's hand as she went to walk by. 'Don't you fret none. Everything's going to be just fine.'

Jenny bent and kissed her cheek. 'Have you been reading the tea leaves again?'

'And right interesting they were too.' Then Ma gave a deep laugh and another yawn.

18

October 1931

'How are we doing, Jake?' Matt perched on the end of his boss's desk when everyone else had left the garage. They had struggled through the summer, and with autumn here the spectre of unemployment was raising its head again.

'We're paying our way – just. But without you propping up the business we'd have gone under weeks ago.' Jake ran a hand through his thinning hair. 'But I'm afraid you're going to lose your money, lad, 'cos I don't know how much longer we can keep going.'

'I've got an idea about that.' Matt stood up. 'Come with me.'

He led his boss to the front of the garage and swept his hand out. There was a large concrete yard where people parked their cars when bringing them in for repair.

When Matt didn't speak, Jake frowned. 'So?'

'We could knock down that low wall and leave a wide-open space so people could wander in, straight off the pavement.'

Jake looked bemused. 'Why would they want to do that?'

'To have a look at the second-hand cars we've got for sale.' Matt shoved his hands into his pockets and hunched his shoulders, hardly able to control his enthusiasm, but he mustn't push too hard. 'People are selling their cars to raise money, and we could pick up quality vehicles cheaply.'

'But who's going to buy them? Everyone's broke, Matt.' Jake spoke as if the boy standing beside him had lost his mind.

'No, they're not. It's only the poor unemployed devils who are on the breadline.' Matt turned to face Jake. 'There's still money around in the more affluent classes. In fact some of them are doing very well and I think we should take advantage of that.'

'I still don't see how selling cars would help us. We might end up with a yard full of vehicles we can't get rid of.' Jake was shaking his head, but was now studying the empty space in front of him intently.

'It would be worth a try.' Matt could sense that his boss was beginning to warm to the idea, so he pressed the point. 'You said yourself that we can't go on like this for much longer, and we don't want to swell the unemployment lines, do we?'

'It's a gamble, but, as you say, it would be worth a try. Dammit, I'd do anything to keep my few remaining men in work!' Jake sighed deeply and ran a hand over his tired eyes. 'But how are we going to buy the cars?'

'My brother Luke is willing to lend us the money to get started.'

Jake gave a dry laugh. 'My God, you Stannard boys are eager to throw your money away, aren't you?'

'We don't look at it that way. I've discussed this

211

with John and my father as well, and they both reckon it has a chance of succeeding.'

'Do they indeed? Well, they're very sharp businessmen...' Jake rocked on the balls of his feet, deep in thought.

Matt said nothing more. He could suggest this to his boss, but in the end it was Jake's decision. If he said no, then that would be the end of it, and probably the end of the garage. It had been a good business for many years, and would be again, if they could only keep it going somehow.

After what seemed an age, Jake spoke. 'Perhaps we should put in a petrol pump as well?'

'That's a great idea!' Matt smiled. 'Is it on, then?'

'Yes!' He slapped Matt on the back and grinned. 'We'll start on the wall tomorrow. Now let's go and have a pint. I'm parched.'

The next morning Jake called a meeting and explained the plan to expand by selling good-quality second-hand cars in an effort to keep the business going. This idea met with approval and enthusiasm from the remaining staff. From a workforce of eight they were now down to only four: Harry, Steve, Alan and Matt as the apprentice. They were all eager to try anything to save their jobs.

'Right.' Jake rubbed his hands in anticipation. 'I want Steve and Alan to demolish that wall out the front, and Harry and Matt to go and buy us some cars.'

Harry grinned at Matt. 'We'll enjoy that, won't we?'

'I thought Matt had lost his senses when he suggested this,' Jake continued, 'but, after sleeping on it, I think it might work. However, lads, if we can't make a go of it, then we'll have a job to survive much longer.'

'Don't worry, boss.' Steve already had a heavy mallet in his hands. 'We'll make it work!'

As Steve and Alan went off to get stuck into their demolition job, Jake turned to Harry and Matt. 'I only want the best vehicles, as we won't be able to sell rubbish in Mayfair. Try for makes like Lagonda, Wolseley, Singer, Daimler, you know, things like that. We don't want cheaper models unless they're in first-class condition.'

'I'll give them a good going-over before we buy,' Harry told him.

'And while you're doing that I'll see if we can have a petrol pump put in.' Jake strode back to his office actually humming a tune.

'Where do we start looking?' Harry asked Matt.

'I've bought a few newspapers, so we can look in those first. And I've got enough money on me to buy at least three cars. My brother Luke is loaning Jake the money to get started.'

'That's good of him.' Harry studied Matt thoughtfully. 'I suspect you and your family are propping us up.'

'No, we're not, Harry. We're investing in a business we believe has a future. Once things pick up, Jake will pay us back.'

'But how long will that be?' Harry turned the page of a newspaper in a distracted way.

'I don't know but we're going to have to come out of the depression and start producing again.

There are things going on in Germany I believe are dangerous.'

'The Nazi movement you mean?' Harry placed his finger over an advert to keep his place, and glanced up.

Matt nodded.

'Well, that is starting here as well,' Harry said. 'This Sir Oswald Mosley is saying that he's going to save the nation.'

Matt's laugh was derisive. 'That's just what Hitler is telling the Germans, but I hope to God we don't believe Mosley.'

'I don't think he's got a chance. We're having a tough time with the depression, but the British people don't like fanatics, and that's what he is. We've got an election at the end of October, and that's only three weeks away, so we'll find out then what the people think of his politics.'

'You two found anything yet?' Jake came up behind them.

'There's a couple of possible cars in the paper.' He smiled at his boss, who was looking quite animated; it was some time since Matt had seen him so hopeful. He just hoped he wasn't steering him in the wrong direction, but he'd discussed this very thoroughly with John. He trusted his elder brother's business acumen. If this idea hadn't stood a chance, John would have told him.

'Well, get on with it, then.' Jake glanced out at the front of the garage. 'Those boys will soon have the wall down, and I want to see at least three cars out there tomorrow.'

Harry and Matt scrambled to their feet as their

boss tossed them a key.

'You can take my car,' he told them. 'Oh, and by the way, the petrol pump will be installed at the end of next week. I'll need some money from sales to pay for it.'

'You'll have it, boss,' Harry called, as they shot out the door, eager to get their new enterprise going.

A week later they had sold enough cars to pay for the installation of the pump, with a little over. And better still, the pump was being well used in this wealthy area, and word had got round that they were buying cars. People were now bringing their vehicles to the garage, hoping to sell them. They did buy the occasional Austin Seven or Tin Lizzy, as they were jokingly referred to, if they were in good condition. Now Jake was always out the front, selling and talking to people, and seemed in his element. The rest of them were working hard all day, repairing and restoring the vehicles to get them ready for sale.

Once again the workshop was alive with tuneful whistles and friendly banter. They all knew it might not last, but it had started well, and for the moment the worry was forgotten.

'What's this?' Ma peered at the plate Jenny had just put in front of her, pulling a face.

'Porridge.'

Ma stuck her spoon in the grey mess and it stood up on its own. She gave Jenny a withering look. 'Is it supposed to be this thick?'

'Erm...' Jenny placed her elbows on the table

and rested her chin in her hands as she studied their breakfast. 'I don't think I've got it quite right yet.'

'You don't think? Jen, girl, you could plaster the walls with that.'

'Perhaps if I put a drop more hot water in it?'

'Don't bother.' Ma tugged the spoon free, dug out a small piece of the porridge and put it cautiously in her mouth. She chewed thoughtfully for a while and then swallowed it. 'Tastes a bit like cement, but I've had worse, and it will fill a corner up.'

Jenny eyed her own plate with misgiving. Porridge had seemed a cheap, filling idea, but now she wasn't so sure. Still, they couldn't afford to waste anything.

'Eat it, ducky. It ain't so bad, and you'll make a better job of it next time.'

They tackled the food in silence, and when it was finished Ma sat back and grimaced. 'Sits a bit heavy in the stomach, don't it?'

There was no arguing with that, and Jenny nodded as she poured two more cups of tea to wash it down.

'What are you going to do today?' Ma drained her cup and put it back on the table.

'My mother's getting married at eleven this morning, so I thought I'd go to the church and see. I'll keep well out of sight, though I doubt if anyone would recognize me now.'

'You're right there.' Ma's expression sobered. 'You've got terrible skinny, pet.'

'In that case I'd better eat some more of that porridge,' Jenny joked.

Ma's deep chuckle made her smile. 'You don't have to worry about me, Ma. I might have lost weight, but I'm healthy enough.'

'I knows that, ducky. It's just that I don't like to see you putting up with such hardship. We've all been born to it, but you ain't.'

Jenny leant over and kissed the elderly woman's cheek. 'You fuss too much about me. I'm young and strong.'

''Course you are.' Ma gave her a cheeky wink. 'Before you go out, do you think I could have another cup of tea and a bicky? That's if we've got any left, of course.'

'I'm sure I can manage that.' Jenny was smiling gently as she took the dishes into the kitchen.

An hour later she left for St George's Church in Bloomsbury, where her mother's wedding was to be held.

The bus dropped her off about a mile from the church, and Jenny strolled along, gazing at the elegant houses. On reaching the one that had been theirs, she stopped for a moment, hoping the people now living there were happier than her parents had been. As she approached the church, she pulled her pudding-basin-shaped hat down to cover more of her face. It was strange, but as she walked past the smart houses, she felt as out of place here as she had the first time she'd gone to Lambeth. She was a different person now. The last two years had changed her, but not for the worse, she thought. In that time she had grown from an unworldly frightened sixteen-year-old to a confident eighteen-year-old. She smiled to herself as she remembered her birthday in August. Glad had bought an iced bun and stuck a candle in it for her to blow out, then it had been carefully shared out amongst them all. Ma's small room had vibrated with laughter. It was the happiest birthday she had ever had!

She reached the church and slid into the middle of a crowd gathered outside. People did love to see a wedding – anyone's wedding. The service was already under way, and Jenny could hear the organ playing the familiar hymn 'Guide Me, O Thou Great Jehovah'. She thought it a strange hymn to choose for a wedding, but it was a popular favourite.

In about fifteen minutes the guests began to file out of the church, and Jenny shrank back as she recognized her Aunt Gertrude. She still had the same sour expression on her face. Then Albert Greaves appeared, talking to a young girl. Jenny gave a quiet snort of amusement. Perhaps he'd found himself another victim! Then her mother walked out, holding the arm of an elderly man – *very elderly*.

Jenny searched her mother's face, trying to find within herself some spark of affection for this woman who had brought her into the world. It came as quite a jolt to realize that there was nothing there. It was as if she were looking at a stranger. But this stranger had abandoned her child when she'd been in need of a kind word, some indication that she loved her. In her selfish horror at being left penniless, Elizabeth Winford had turned away from her child. Jenny didn't think she could ever forgive her for that.

218

With one last look at these people she no longer knew, or wanted to know, Jenny Baker turned away from them for ever.

19

They were managing, but only just, and, with the cold weather nearly on them, Jenny was sick with worry. Ma was extremely frail now, but her tongue was still as sharp, which was a comfort. Ron and Jimmy had been able to find an occasional job of gardening, but there wouldn't be much of that now until the spring. Everyone in the street was gathering together anything they could use to keep a fire going when it got really cold. Any food that wasn't perishable was being carefully hoarded. Everyone joked that they were preparing for a siege, and that's just what it felt like to Jenny. This winter was going to be long and hard, and they all knew it. Fred and Stan were having a tough time keeping the stall going, and more often than not didn't earn enough to buy enough fresh goods for the next day's trading. Unemployment was still growing, and there was no sign of things improving in the near future.

Edna had found herself a young man, and Jenny had seen her only a couple of times lately. Each time they'd met, her friend had brought her a small parcel of food from cook, and she was very grateful for their kindness. Edna had tried to persuade her to get out of Lambeth, but Jenny had firmly refused. In this humble house, in the middle of a depression, she had found kindness, affection and love. She wouldn't leave.

A blast of cold wind whistled through the back door, and Jenny closed it quickly. A centre where people could go for help would be a good thing. Somewhere warm to sit if they couldn't heat their own homes, a bowl of hot soup and perhaps second-hand clothes...

Ma was fast asleep, two cats wailing at each other the only sound from outside. Jenny sat at the kitchen table and closed her eyes. She had visited Lambeth Council's offices to beg for their help, but they had so many people in need that they obviously didn't know which way to turn. The Salvation Army had been next on her list. They had been kind and understanding, but they too were already stretched to breaking point.

Jenny stood up and walked quietly up the narrow stairs to her room. There was one other thing she could do, of course. Pride had kept her back, but in this situation there wasn't room for pride. Tomorrow she'd make that visit!

The house in Bruton Street looked exactly the same as when Jenny had fled from it a year ago. The step was immaculate, and the brass doorknocker gleamed in the watery sun. She wondered whose job it was now.

Slipping round to the servants' entrance, Jenny pushed a note under the door for Edna. It was just to warn her that she was here. She hadn't mentioned this visit to her friend, and she didn't want her to be taken by surprise. Then she went back to the front door, straightened her hat and smoothed the creases from her coat. It was the same one she'd bought at the pawnbroker's with Fred and Glad, and was even shabbier now, but she didn't care.

After knocking on the door she stood tall and lifted her head as she heard footsteps approaching. She didn't quite know when it had happened, but the feeling of being hunted had slowly ebbed away. The one thing on her mind was to try to help those in need. Bold action was needed. If she was coming begging, then she was going to do it openly, through the front door!

For a moment the butler didn't recognize her, and before he had a chance to speak she said, 'Mr Green, please tell Mrs Stannard that Eugenie Winford is here to see her.' As she had come to the front door, it seemed right to use her old name.

'Of course, Miss Winford.' He stepped aside to let her in, obviously struggling to keep his composure, as a butler should.

Jenny walked into the hall, turned and gave Green a sly wink as a way of admitting her cheek in coming to the front of the house like this.

It was too much for him and his face broke into a wide smile. 'Oh, it's good to see you again,' he whispered.

'And you,' she said, as her insides churned. 'Do you think she'll receive me?'

'I'm sure she will. Wait here, I'll tell her at once.' He climbed the stairs in his usual dignified manner.

He was soon back. 'Please follow me, Miss Winford.' His tone was proper for an honoured visitor.

He took her to Mrs Stannard's private sitting room. After opening the door with a flourish, Green stepped inside and announced, 'Miss Eugenie Winford, madam.'

It was with great difficulty that Jenny kept a straight face, her nervousness vanishing as the butler swept past, giving her a wink this time.

'Eugenie!' Mrs Stannard came forward eagerly. 'Please take your hat and coat off. I'll order tea.'

'Please don't bother with tea, Mrs Stannard. I won't take up much of your time.' Jenny was sorry she'd been so abrupt when she saw Mrs Stannard's disappointment. Her former employer really was pleased to see her! But she mustn't worry about these things; she must concentrate on why she was here. 'I've come to ask for your help. And I prefer to be called Jenny.'

'Please sit down, Jenny, and tell me what I can do for you.'

Jenny removed her coat and laid it over the back of a chair, then she sat on a lovely regency chair made of walnut with a deep red satin seat. 'It isn't for me. The people I live with are in desperate need.'

When she looked up, she was shocked to see Mrs Stannard's eyes brimming with tears. Jenny knew how she looked, gaunt and shabbily dressed, so she lifted her head in defiance. She didn't need or want sympathy!

'I must apologize for the way you were dismissed–'

Jenny held up her hand to stop her. 'There is no need for you to do that. It is in the past and forgotten.'

'That is gracious of you.' Mrs Stannard regained her composure. 'How can I help?'

Jenny spent the next fifteen minutes explaining the need for a centre to help the people of Lambeth. When she'd finished Mrs Stannard's expression was grim – she looked angry and Jenny sighed inwardly. This had been a waste of time; her ex-mistress was obviously furious that she'd been approached in this manner. But she'd had to try.

Jenny stood up and put her coat back on. 'Thank you for listening.'

Mrs Stannard was immediately on her feet, holding out a pen and paper she'd snatched from a nearby table. 'Leave me your address, Jenny. I'll talk to my husband and sons tonight.'

'Thank you.' Jenny wrote Ma's address down and handed it over, then she left the room. A short time ago she would have hesitated to tell anyone except Edna where she lived, but, in the light of the suffering the depression was causing, that didn't seem important any more.

Edna was hovering at the end of the passage and beckoned excitedly. 'Come on, Jen, everyone's itching to see you.'

They clattered down the servants' stairs, and once in the kitchen Jenny was greeted with cries of delight and many hugs. Even the housekeeper, Mrs Douglas, kissed her cheek before hurrying away.

'Sit yourself down,' Mrs Peters ordered, 'and

have some lunch with us.'

Jenny eyed the array of mouth-watering food wistfully. 'I wish I could, but I must get back to Ma Adams.'

'In that case you must take it back with you.'

Mrs Peters began to wrap fruit pies, bread and many other things that Jenny now considered luxuries, like cakes; she placed a junket carefully in a basket. How Ma was going to love that, and some for Ivy's two children...

'What about one of those nice meat pies?' Edna had helped fill one basket and was now searching for another in the pantry.

'Whoa!' Jenny laughed as her friend came back with a huge hamper. 'I'll never be able to carry all that, and you'll get the sack if the mistress sees you giving away all her food.'

'No, she won't.' Mrs Douglas came in smiling. 'Madam's just told me to see you go back with plenty, and Edna can help you carry it.'

After finding a smaller shopping basket to use in place of the hamper, Jenny said a tearful goodbye and, with the two baskets and Edna's help, made her way back to Ma's.

'How did your meeting go?' Edna asked as they walked up Forest Road with the heavy bags of food.

'Oh, she was very polite, but I was asking a lot of her. I don't suppose she'll be able to help.'

'She will if she can, Jen. She's a kind woman.'

'I'm sure she is. I've given her my address, so we'll just have to wait and see. Now tell me about this lovely man you've met.'

Edna squeezed her arm. 'His name's David,

and I was rushing through Hyde Park one day when I bumped into him. We sat talking for a while and then he took me for tea. We meet now every time we can wangle it.'

Edna's face shone with happiness and Jenny was so pleased for her.

Much to her husband and sons' surprise, Louise was not in when they arrived home that evening. She'd left a message to say that she may be late and they were to start dinner without her.

Gilbert frowned at the brief note and muttered to himself. 'This is most unlike your mother. She doesn't even say where she's gone!'

'Perhaps she's dining with one of her friends,' John suggested.

'I expect that's it.' Gilbert looked up when the butler came into the drawing room to announce dinner. 'Did my wife say where she was going?'

'No, sir, she left in a hurry after Miss Eugenie Winford called on her.' He appeared to say the name with some relish.

'What!' The four men in the room all spoke at once.

'How did Miss Winford look?' Matt was on his feet, anxious for news of the young girl who still troubled his thoughts.

Green shook his head sadly. 'Very shabby and undernourished.'

'Oh, hell!' That news didn't ease Matt's concerns at all. 'What was her meeting with my mother about?'

'I can't say, Mr Matthew. Mrs Stannard is the only one who knows that.'

It was a silent meal, and by ten o'clock Matt's father was pacing the room, concerned about his wife's continued absence.

At twenty past ten she finally arrived home in a grim and determined mood.

'What is it, my dear?' Gilbert rushed over to his wife. 'What's happened? Where have you been?'

'One question at a time, Gilbert.' Louise sat down with a weary sigh. 'You can pour me a stiff brandy. I need it.'

Matt was nearest to the decanter, so he poured a generous amount in a glass. Now he was dreadfully worried. The only alcohol his mother ever drank was an occasional glass of red wine.

When he handed her the drink, she gave him a wan smile. 'You heard about Jenny coming to see me?'

'Yes.' Matt moved a small table near his mother for her to put her glass on. 'Is she going to come to stay with us?'

'No, she won't leave the people she's living with.' Tears filled her eyes. 'Oh, the poor dear–'

'Louise!' Her husband was now obviously alarmed at her distress. 'Please tell us what this is about.'

'She came to me for help. Not for herself, but for the people living in her area.' Louise finished her brandy, pulled a face at the taste and put the glass on the table. She then told them the whole story.

There was a tense silence when she'd finished, then John cleared his throat. 'So how can we help?'

'I've been with Margaret Hunter and Jane Patterson for most of the day. We've formed a committee and we're going to organize the centre Jenny wants in Lambeth.'

'Well, you've enlisted help from two of the most dedicated charity workers, my dear.' Her husband was still frowning. 'But the whole bloody country is in desperate need. This will be helping only a few people.'

'I know that, Gilbert, but the idea might spread to other areas. Think how many it would help then.'

'I agree with you, Mother.' John joined in the conversation. 'Matt and Luke are trying to save the garage. That's only a few jobs, but to those men it's hellishly important, and worth doing. If you and your friends can get this going, it will help others.' John looked at his father. 'It isn't much in the present climate of unemployment, but at least it's doing something, Father.'

'You're quite right, of course, John.'

'Mother,' Matt said, sitting beside her, 'do you have Jenny's address?'

'Yes, she gave it to me. I promised to let her know if I could do anything.'

'You let me have it and I'll go to see her in my lunch break tomorrow. It'll give me a chance to see what her living conditions are like as well.'

'Thank you, Matt.' She looked exhausted. 'Ask cook for some food to take with you. There are children and elderly there who are the most vulnerable.'

With Ma in bed, Jenny was absorbed in reading

227

yesterday's newspaper, which Fred had given to her. In the election two days ago the Labour Party had been overwhelmed at the polls. Ramsay MacDonald was Prime Minister of a national government with support from all parties. There had been a run on the pound, and last month income tax had been raised to five shillings in the pound and the dole cut by 10 per cent. This had been just another blow for those trying to survive. The voters had obviously shown their anger about the mess the country was in. And Oswald Mosley's New Party had suffered a crushing defeat at the polls.

There was a gentle knock on the back door, and Jenny looked up, wondering who it could be at half past ten at night.

The door opened and Ivy looked in. 'Oh, good, you're still up, Jen. Ted Roper's been taken bad, and Agnes and their son, Jimmy, are frightened.'

Jenny was immediately on her feet. 'I'll come right away.'

Agnes Roper was ashen-faced with worry, and young Jimmy was standing around gazing helplessly at his father. At fifteen he was a gangling youth and, like the rest of them, too thin.

'Oh, thank God you've come!' Agnes clenched her hands into tight fists. 'He's real bad.'

Jenny rushed over to the man lying on the sofa, still fully dressed. He was holding his chest and gasping for breath, clearly in great pain. She pulled off his boots and loosened his tie in an effort to make him more comfortable. It was cold in the small front room.

'Bring me a blanket, Agnes,' Jenny ordered.

'We ain't got none. They've been popped,' Jimmy told her.

A multitude of feelings ran through Jenny – pity, sorrow, worry, fear – but the overriding emotion was anger. What was the government doing when people even had to pawn their blankets so that they could eat? She hoped that now the election was out of the way there would be some improvement.

'I'll get one of ours.' Ivy sped off to their house next door and returned almost immediately with a blanket, and her mother, Glad.

She was a welcome sight, and, as Jenny tucked the blanket around Ted, she said to Glad, 'He needs a doctor.'

'We can't afford no doctors.' Agnes was gazing at her husband and shaking badly. 'They wouldn't come out this time of night anyway. And look, Ted's a bit better now. I think he's asleep. He'll be right as rain in the morning.'

'I'll make us a nice cup of Rosie Lee.' Before Glad disappeared into the kitchen, she gave a sad shake of her head to Jenny.

It was obvious what she was saying. Ted Roper had had a heart attack and probably wouldn't live through the night.

Jenny sat beside Agnes and took her cold hands in her own. 'We'll stay with you.'

'Thanks,' the distraught woman whispered. 'You go to bed, Jimmy.'

The boy shook his head and settled in a chair where he could keep an eye on his dad.

Glad came back with the tea, put the tray on the sideboard and glanced at her daughter. 'Ivy, you go home now. Me and Jen will stay with Agnes and Jimmy.'

'All right, Mum, but you call if you need me.'

As Ivy left, Jenny also settled down. It was going to be a long night, but if Ted did live until morning, she would get him a doctor.

At four o'clock in the morning Ted Roper gave a gasp and died. Jenny wanted to shout in fury at the sheer hopelessness and waste of a life. Ted had been only thirty-eight, but had aged beyond his years with the constant struggle to feed and house his family. The last two years had been the worst, and Jenny was certain that the strain of waiting for hours in a dole queue and chasing around from morning to night looking for any kind of work had been the cause of his early death.

It was seven in the morning before Jenny returned home. Glad had taken charge of the practical details, while Jenny had stayed to comfort Agnes and Jimmy.

Sitting at the kitchen table, she covered her face with her hands. What an awful night that had been. And how was Agnes going to manage without Ted's unemployment money? It was only a little more than a pound a week, and with rent for these small houses at six shillings a week, it had been a struggle to manage anyway. But without even that coming in, Agnes and her son would be in desperate need. Glad was going to the welfare as soon as they opened to see if she could get anything for them, but these things took time. The welfare system was a laborious affair, and many people were not getting the help they needed simply because they didn't understand how to get it.

Because Ma was over seventy, she got what was called the Old Age Pension. Jenny didn't know how much it was, as Glad had always looked after that for Ma, but it was enough to pay the rent and leave a few shillings over for food. But since Jenny had lost her job, by Wednesday each week she was scratching around to get as much as she could as cheaply as possible. She hated to think that Ma had to support her, and she ate very little to make sure the elderly woman had enough to eat.

The food Mrs Peters had given her yesterday had been very welcome. She had shared it with Glad and her family. Now she was going to have to see what she could do for Agnes and Jimmy.

Her sigh was weary. How she wished she could get another job...

'Jen!'

The call from Ma had her rushing to the stairs. The old woman was balancing precariously on the top stair. 'Come and give us a hand getting down these bleeding stairs.'

It was a slow and painful trip down, but eventually Ma was sitting at the kitchen table, muttering irritably under her breath.

'Why don't you let me make you a bed downstairs?' Jenny suggested.

'Not bloody likely! That's the end of the line, girl. I've always gone upstairs to bed and I ain't gonna change that now,' she snapped.

After the night Jenny had just had, she was in no mood to put up with Ma's sharp tongue, but rather than start an argument she turned away to put the kettle on the stove. 'I've got some of that nice home-made bread left. Would you like some?' she asked mildly. 'I'll cut off the crusts and soak them in a little milk, shall I?'

'That'd be nice.' Ma spoke softly. 'Turn round, Jen.'

She did so and suffered the scrutiny of those sharp eyes.

'Sorry I'm such a grump, ducky, but I gets frustrated not being able to do for myself. You look as if you've had a bad night. What's happened?'

'Ted Roper died of a heart attack at four o'clock this morning. Me and Glad have been there all night.'

'Ah, I'm right sad about that.' Ma shook her head. 'He was a good man. It's gonna be hard for Agnes and young Jimmy now.'

Jenny snorted in disgust. 'Even harder than the last couple of years!' She cut the crusts off two slices of bread and dunked them in a dish of milk to soften, then spread some of cook's jam on the bread. She put the dish and plate in front of Ma, and poured her a cup of tea as well.

Ma sat staring at the plates, then lifted her head and glared at Jenny. 'And where's yours?'

'Oh, I'm not hungry.'

'Listen, my girl, if you think I'm going to eat while you sit there with an empty belly, then you're very much mistaken! You'll bloody well eat something!'

That was too much for Jenny's troubled heart

and she erupted. 'Don't you swear at me! I'm doing the best I can. People are dying around me and I can't do a thing about it. I'll have to go and beg to be allowed to scrub some of the fine houses' steps. I'm just a burden on you and everyone else around here. I don't know what else to do, Ma...'

'There, there, ducky, don't take on so.' Ma struggled to her feet, putting an arm around Jenny's shoulders. 'You ain't a burden to me or anyone else. I couldn't manage without you. You're doing just fine and I'm right proud of you.' Ma kissed the top of her head. 'Dry your tears, have a slice of my bread, and go and have a nice kip. You'll feel better then.'

'You're right.' Jenny took a slice of bread from Ma's plate and munched in silence. As she swallowed the last mouthful, she gave a watery smile.

'That's better. Now off you go. I'll clear the table.'

Without another word, Jenny dragged herself upstairs, feeling totally exhausted, mentally and physically.

20

Three hours of sound sleep had helped to ease the tension of Ted Roper's death. But Jenny still hurt inside. It felt as if she were bruised right through. Up until the last two years she had led a sheltered and privileged life; now she was among the harsh realities of the working classes. This was a tough way to learn about real life, though it was a lesson worth learning. She had changed so much, and quite honestly she liked Jenny Baker much more than Eugenie Winford. Eugenie had been a frightened child; Jenny was a mature, strong woman, and gaining in wisdom all the time. She could now see life from both sides of the coin, and her love and respect for all those who lived from day to day in the poorest conditions was enormous.

When she walked into the kitchen, Ma had a pot of tea already made.

'I heard you moving around and thought you'd like a cuppa.' Ma eyed her perceptively. 'Good, you're feeling better.'

'Much, thank you, Ma.' Jenny smiled as Ma poured tea for them both. She was touched by this gesture, for she knew how difficult it was for Ma to do anything now. 'I'll just drink this and then do some shopping.'

'How much money we got left, ducky?'

Jenny took the old Oxo tin from the shelf and opened it. 'Three shillings and tuppence. We'll manage fine on that.'

Ma nodded in approval. 'You've become a real good shopper, Jen.'

'I give the shopkeepers a bright smile and sometimes they slip in something extra.' Jenny laughed at how crafty she was becoming.

'I'm not surprised,' Ma cackled. 'You're turning into a real beauty. A bit skinny, but a lovely girl none the less.'

'My goodness, Ma, first I have tea made for me

and now compliments.' Jenny mopped her brow in mock amazement.

They were both laughing when there was a knock on the front door.

'Come in!' Ma called. Nothing happened.

'Give me a hand to the front room.' Ma got unsteadily to her feet.

Once she was settled in her armchair, the knock came again. 'Better see who that is, Jen. If it's a hawker, then he's wasting his time in this street. No one here's got money to spend on anything but rent and grub.'

Jenny opened the door and the man standing outside came as a shock. Matthew Stannard must be around twenty now, she guessed, and looking every inch the fine man, even in his overalls smeared with grease.

'Hello, Jenny.' He smiled in a friendly manner. 'My mother asked me to call.'

'Come in, young man,' Ma called, craning her neck to get a good look at him.

He stepped inside. 'Thank you, madam.'

She waved a hand dismissively. 'My name's Ma.'

He held out the parcel he'd had tucked under his arm. 'Cook's sent you a few things, Ma.'

'Ah, that's right kind of her. Give it to Jen. The other food she sent us was a real treat. We shared it with the neighbours. It was much enjoyed, young man.'

'The name's Matt.' He stood in the middle of the room, so tall and broad he seemed to dominate the small space.

Ma was scrutinizing him through narrowed

235

eyes, then, as if satisfied, she grinned. 'Sit down, Matt, you're blocking out the light.'

He did as ordered, watching Jenny as she took the food to the kitchen.

She soon returned with a broad smile on her face. 'There's another meat pie there, Ma. I think we ought to give Agnes and Jimmy some for their dinner, don't you?'

'I do. A good meal is just what they need today.'

'I'll take it there in a minute.' Jenny sat next to Ma and looked at Matthew. She was expecting him to say that his mother couldn't help with the centre, but that wouldn't be a surprise; even asking her had been a terrible cheek. Still, she thought cynically, Mrs Stannard had sent the most attractive of her sons to break the news.

As if reading her thoughts, he raised an eyebrow quizzically, then said, 'My mother has gathered together some of the best charity workers around, and they believe they can set up something in this area.'

'Who's going to pay for it?' Ma wanted to know.

'They've already got the backing of two charities who deal with the underprivileged, and they're fairly sure they can get help from the social services.'

''Bout time they bloody well got their fingers out.' Ma folded her arms and glared at Matt. 'My poor Jenny's running herself ragged trying to help, but they won't listen to the likes of us. Don't say nothing to no one around here until your mother's sure she can do this. We don't want folks getting their hopes up for nothing.'

'My mother is a very determined woman, Ma.

236

She'll get some kind of help for this area.'

'We'll see.' Ma still didn't appear convinced. 'The people round here don't really want charity. What they want is jobs. Can you do anything about that?'

'I'm afraid not, Ma.' He lifted his hands in a helpless gesture. 'We're having enough trouble trying to keep the garage in business.'

'Own it, do you?'

'No, I'm just an apprentice there.' Matt leant forward, his expression animated. 'There's going to be a good future in cars, but we've got to survive the depression first.'

'Hmm.' Ma pointed to a patch of grease on his overalls. 'Like working with dirty engines, do you?'

Matt grinned and sat back. 'I love it. Now, about this centre. My mother wants to know if there's a suitable hall around here.'

Just then Glad looked in the door and Ma waved her to come in. Matt scrambled to his feet.

'This is Matt, and he's looking for a hall around here,' Ma told Glad.

'Must have a kitchen of some sort.' Matt continued to stand politely.

'Well.' Glad thought for a moment. 'There's the old community hall in Greenwood Street. Hasn't been used for years, though, so don't know what state it's in. But if I remember rightly it did have a kitchen and some privies.'

'Could someone show me where it is?' Matt asked. 'If it's any good, I can tell my mother this evening and her committee will have a look at it.'

237

'I'll take you now if you like. I've got to go that way.' Then Glad glanced at Ma and Jenny. 'I've made all the arrangements for Ted's funeral. It'll be at St John's Church on Friday at ten thirty. And no one's to waste money on flowers. Agnes said Ted wouldn't like that.'

Glad was already heading for the door, so Matt said a hasty goodbye and strode after her.

'Well, well,' Ma murmured when they'd gone. 'Real polite, ain't he? And not stuck up. Been brung up proper, he has.'

Jenny giggled. 'Been brung up proper?'

'Oh, you and your posh talk,' Ma teased, but she couldn't stop herself from smiling at Jenny's amused expression. 'I've talked this way all my life and you ain't changing me now.'

'I wouldn't want to, Ma,' Jenny said softly. 'You're just lovely the way you are.'

''Course I am.' She chortled. 'Awkward and bloody-minded, what more could you ask for? Now go and give Agnes and Jimmy some of that pie, and we'll have a little bit for our dinner, eh?'

Walking up the road with Glad, Matt was still reeling from the shock of seeing how much Jenny had changed. She had been a robust, if timid, young girl, now she was taller, too thin and obviously very tired. But one thing was abundantly clear: she now had a maturity and confidence that had not been there before.

Matt's heart contracted with pain. She'd had to grow up quickly to survive, he guessed. Dear God, what a way to do it.

'You're very quiet, young man.'

Glad's voice brought him back to the here and now. 'Sorry, I was thinking.' Matt glanced at the woman beside him. 'How did you come to know Jenny?'

She then told him about the visit to the pawn-broker's, and how she and Fred had been impressed with her courage. 'We told her to come to us if she was in need, and that's what she did when your family threw her out. Poor little devil!'

'We're all very sorry about that,' Matt told her. 'My father makes rash decisions at times, and no amount of arguing can change his mind. He's not an unkind man, though. He regrets it now.'

'So he should!' Glad spoke angrily. 'Everyone here loves her, and though she doesn't show it much, Ma adores her. Looks on her as a daughter, she does.'

'Jenny's lucky to have found you–'

Glad stopped suddenly and turned to face Matt. 'You've got that wrong, young man. We're the lucky ones, and if anyone in this world tries to hurt her again they'll have us to deal with.'

'I believe you.' Matt fell into step beside her as she began to walk up the street again. 'Is that why you all denied knowing her when I came round with my brother Luke?'

'Of course. Now, the hall is just around the next corner. Do you think your mother can do something for the people here?'

Matt saw a group of dejected men standing outside a factory gate in the hope of getting work, and gritted his teeth in anger. These poor buggers shouldn't have to beg like this. But what

239

choice did they have? They probably all had families to feed. The gulf between them and the way he lived hit him with such force at that moment that it made him gasp out loud.

Glad gave him a knowing look. 'Not a pleasant sight, is it? You ought to go and see the dole queues, and perhaps stand in line with them for a couple of days, and you might begin to understand the desperation they feel. And you haven't answered my question. Will your mother and her friends be able to help?'

'Yes!' The word hissed out from between his clenched teeth.

'Well, here we are, then.' Glad pushed the door, and, as the lock was broken, it swung open.

It was in a dreadful state, but at first glance the place appeared to be structurally sound. It was large and had a good-sized kitchen with two gas stoves that looked as if they might be all right after a good clean. Matt turned the tap over the sink, and, after a lot of clanging and shuddering, rusty-coloured water poured out. He left it running and it eventually cleared.

'What do you think?' Glad was peering in one of the ovens, and then turned a gas tap. 'Gas has been cut off, so's the electricity.'

'We'll have to get them connected again, but it might do.' Matt shoved his hands in his pockets and spun round on the balls of his feet. 'My mother and her committee will have to look it over first.'

'Right. I'll leave that to you.' Glad was heading for the door. 'You let me know what's decided. You knows where we live.' Then she was gone.

Matt returned to the garage, very subdued. He'd been pleased with his effort to save Jake's business, but this was only a very tiny part of what was happening all over the country. He read the papers, of course, but today was the first time he'd really been in amongst the suffering. Mayfair was not exactly a deprived area!

They were busy that afternoon and sold two cars, but even this failed to lift his spirits. He could see those men outside the factory, feel their hopelessness, and, even worse, Jenny's pinched, tired face kept swimming before his eyes. He felt so angry about everything.

Fortunately Matt calmed down in time for dinner that evening. He explained about the hall and wrote down the address for his mother.

'Sounds like it needs a lot of work before it's fit for use,' his father said. 'You'd better employ a couple of local men to help, Louise.'

'You won't have any trouble getting workers,' Matt said. 'Once word gets round, you'll have them queuing ten deep.'

'I expect we shall, Matt.' His mother gazed at the succulent meal in front of her as if it were an offence. 'How was Jenny?'

'Exhausted, by the look of her. She and a neighbour by the name of Glad had been up all night. The man next door died, evidently.'

His mother's knife and fork clattered on to the plate. 'I've quite lost my appetite.'

A trickle of rain plopped from the brim of Jenny's hat and ran down her nose. The heavy drizzle was

241

the kind that soaked you right through, and it couldn't be a worse day for Ted Roper's funeral. She watched the coffin being lowered into the muddy hole in the ground. It was a bleak, sad occasion, as Agnes stood white-faced with lips clenched together, and young Jimmy sobbed quietly by her side.

Jenny could feel the damp seeping through the worn soles of her shoes, far too thin to keep out the wet. The whole of the street had turned out for Ted, and, as she glanced around at each one, Jenny saw that they all had the same pinched look. The women were showing the strain perhaps more than the men, as it was on them the burden rested most heavily. Not that the men didn't care; they tried every day to get work – any work.

She watched Jimmy place a little bunch of daisies at the foot of the grave, and, stepping back, he gave Jenny a fleeting smile of thanks. She hadn't been able to bear the thought of no flowers at all and had spent a precious tuppence on the simple bouquet of daisies. They gleamed yellow and white on the muddy ground, and seemed to welcome the rain on their dry stalks, the water running like gleaming tears over their bright petals.

The vicar rushed through a prayer, obviously as wet and uncomfortable as the rest of them, but Jenny glared at him. That wasn't right. Ted Roper had been an honest, hard-working man and deserved respect, especially on this day. It was as if her thoughts got through, because the man suddenly slowed to a more dignified pace and began to read from the Bible with a little more feeling.

Then it was over and they filed silently out of the churchyard, to the sound of the thud, thud of earth as the gravediggers filled in the hole.

The men wandered off to wait for the Red Lion to open, so they could raise a glass to Ted's life. No one tried to stop them, and they took young Jimmy with them, at fifteen now the man of the house. Jenny had slipped Jimmy another couple of shillings to buy the men a drink. He wasn't old enough to go in the pub, but she doubted anyone would object today.

She fingered the pendant around her neck and wondered how much longer she was going to be able to keep it.

The pawnbroker's was crowded the next day, as expected. These were the busiest shops around. Women were popping bedding, clothes, saucepans, in fact any kind of household goods. One woman told Jenny ruefully that a saucepan wasn't no good if you had bugger all to put in it.

Jenny waited patiently in line and saw the man in front of her hand over a nice pocket watch, telling Uncle that it had belonged to his father. When the man had the money and turned to walk past her, she saw tears in his eyes. He must have known that the chance of redeeming the watch was very slim.

'And what 'ave you brought me?' The pawnbroker reached for the package she was holding out. She had decided to pawn the lace and beaded dress. It didn't fit now, and she wanted to

243

hang on to the pendant for as long as possible. All the time she had that she felt a little more secure, knowing that it would bring in money when desperately needed. Things were bad and going to get worse – except for the pawnbrokers, who were doing very well for themselves. This one was so happy he was almost smiling!

After much haggling, she managed to get four shillings out of him. It was a scandalous amount for such an exquisite and expensive dress, but it was no use to her now. She pocketed the money and headed for the shops. This would feed her and Ma for a few days, if she shopped carefully.

21

After her visit to the pawnbroker's yesterday, Jenny decided that she was going to make the councillors listen to her this time. But as soon as she walked into the Town Hall, it was obvious that it was hopeless. The place was already packed with people arguing or just standing around looking dejected. The noise was deafening as everyone tried to talk at the same time. Children were hanging on to their mothers and screaming, frightened by the raised voices.

Knowing that she didn't stand a chance of seeing anyone in authority today, she was about to turn around and leave when she recognized a woman coming out of a room with a determined expression on her face.

Jenny pushed towards her. 'Mrs Stannard.'

'Oh, hello, my dear.' She caught hold of Jenny's arm. 'Let's get out of here. It's bedlam.'

After a struggle they finally managed to make their way out of the building.

'Phew! That's better.' Louise grimaced. 'I've spent the last hour shouting at the chairman of the council, and trying to impress him with the name of every influential person on our committee.'

'You're going ahead with the centre?'

'Of course.' Her expression changed from exasperation to triumph. 'We've finally got the go-ahead to use the hall Matt was shown.'

'Oh, that's wonderful!' Jenny's hopes soared. 'When will it be open?'

'We intend to have it running within a week, but it needs a lot of work done on it first. It's in a terrible state.'

At the mention of work, Jenny said, 'You'll need to employ some men, then?'

'About three.' Mrs Stannard looked sad. 'It will only be for a couple of weeks, but there won't be a shortage of applicants, will there?'

Jenny shook her head. 'No, they'll be queuing up once word gets out. Would you give two from Forest Road first chance? There's young Jimmy – his father died recently. Then there's Ron – he's an excellent carpenter.'

'You send them along to the hall at two o'clock tomorrow afternoon.'

'Thank you very much.' Jenny's eyes shone.

Her former employer smiled gently. 'You didn't believe I would bother with this, did you, Jenny?'

'To be honest I thought I was wasting my time appealing to you, but I'll try anything to help my friends. I did think you'd forgotten about it, though.'

'My son Matt wouldn't let me forget,' she laughed.

'Oh?'

'You don't know my boys, Jenny, but they're eager to help in any way they can. They are all fine men.' She looked so proud as she talked about her sons. 'They care. We all care. Even my husband, though you may find that hard to believe after the way he treated you. He still frets about it.'

'He shouldn't do that.' Jenny didn't feel animosity towards any of them now. 'It's all worked out for the best.'

'Has it, Jenny?' Louise said softly.

'Oh, yes, I'm happy where I am.' And she knew that was the truth. The life she was now living had important things her former existence had lacked: friendship, love and a genuine caring for each other. They were all priceless qualities.

Louise glanced at the clock over the Town Hall door. 'My goodness, look at the time. I must hurry, Jenny. There's a great deal to do and not a moment to lose.' Before rushing off, she kissed Jenny's cheek. 'You take care of yourself, my dear.'

Jenny watched her hurry up the road, her stride purposeful. She couldn't believe that show of affection. Louise Stannard had just kissed her former under housemaid! Completely oblivious to the rain now coming down in a torrent, she laughed out loud as she began to run home with

246

the good news for Jimmy and Ron. What a strange world this was.

Breathless, Jenny tumbled into Fred and Glad's front room. 'Oh, good, you're both here,' she gasped, seeing Ron and Jimmy there.

'Stop and catch your breath before you try to talk,' Glad said, grinning. 'Whatever are you so excited about?'

'I've just seen Mrs Stannard at the Town Hall. She's going to open the centre in about a week. She said that if Ron and Jimmy go along to the old community hall at about two o'clock tomorrow, there might be a job for them.' When Jenny saw their faces light up with hope, she added quickly, 'It will only be for a couple of weeks, though.'

'That don't matter!' Ron laughed and kissed her cheek. 'You're soaking wet!'

Jimmy was hopping around in excitement. 'Let's get there early, Ron. When word gets around, there'll be dozens fighting for the jobs. Let's be first in the queue.'

'Ask for Mrs Stannard. Tell her you're from Forest Road and I've sent you.' Jenny was as excited as they were with this bit of good luck.

Jimmy kissed her shyly on the cheek and shot out of the door, red-faced.

'My goodness, everyone's kissing me today.'

'Ah, what it is to be young and beautiful,' Glad teased. 'Thanks for putting them up for the job. They'll be right grateful for anything. Fancy a cup of tea?'

'No, thanks, Glad, I must go and get Ma's dinner.' With a cheery wave, Jenny went next door, to find Ma fidgeting anxiously when she arrived.

'You've been a long time! And what the blazes have you been up to? Where's your 'at?'

Jenny recoiled at the sharpness in Ma's tone, but she answered gently. 'I've been to the council offices. I told you that was where I was going. My hat must have come off as I ran home and I didn't notice.' She edged towards the kitchen. She had expected Ma to laugh at the mess she was in, not react like this.

'You stay where you are, my girl. I ain't finished with you yet!'

Jenny sighed. 'Ma, I'm wet through and gasping for a cup of tea.'

The elderly woman ignored her plea. 'You should have waited until it stopped raining. You'll catch your death of cold, Bessie.'

Nearly at the kitchen door, Jenny stopped and spun round so fast she nearly toppled over. Bessie? Ma's eyes were brimming with tears, and her mouth trembling.

'You could 'ave caught pneumonia,' Ma cried. 'And I couldn't have stood that. You mustn't leave me, Bessie.'

Jenny rushed over and knelt beside Ma, taking her trembling hands in hers. 'I'm only wet. Don't upset yourself, Ma. I'm never going to leave you.'

Ma closed her eyes for a moment and Jenny stayed where she was, terribly alarmed that she had called her Bessie – the name of the little daughter she had lost so long ago.

When Ma opened her eyes again, the tears had gone and she smiled. 'I know you won't leave me.

248

You're a good girl, Jen.'

Relief flooded through Jenny. It had obviously been a momentary lapse. She stood up. 'Would you like a cup of tea first, and I'll clean myself up after?'

Ma nodded, and gave her usual infectious laugh. 'You'd better get in the tin bath with all your clothes on. You've got a hole in your stocking and mud all over your legs.'

Jenny joined in the laughter and went to make the tea. That had been a fright, but Ma seemed all right now.

'Ma,' Ivy said, rushing in. 'Have you heard? Jen might have got Ron and Jimmy a job at the centre!'

The kitchen was only a few steps from the front room, and Jenny could hear them talking quite clearly. Ivy sounded excited. The tea was nearly made when Glad came in as well, so she put two more cups on the tray and a plate of biscuits. Ma always loved a biscuit with her tea.

'Ah, that's grand, Ivy. Jen's in the kitchen and she's in a right state,' Ma said. 'All wet, and lost her 'at.'

Glad walked in and took the tray from her. 'I'll see to this. You go and get out of those wet things.'

'I'll do it when we've had tea.'

'You'll do it now.' Glad gave a look that said don't argue with me. 'Go on, strip off, dry yourself properly and put your other dress on. It won't take a moment and the tea will stay hot.'

Knowing it was useless to argue, Jenny dashed upstairs for her frock and nipped down again to the outhouse. There she peeled off the wet clothes and towelled herself dry until her skin was pink and glowing, put the dry clothes on and returned to the front room. All this had been done quickly and she was now badly in need of a cup of tea.

'Ah, that looks better.' Ma looked her up and down, then smiled. 'We've saved you a bicky.'

'Tell us what Mrs Stannard said about the centre.' Ivy was clearly eager to know about the jobs.

Jenny told them what had happened at the council offices and about her meeting with Mrs Stannard. When she finished, Ma scowled.

'Didn't bother to wait for it to stop raining before running home with the news. Lost her 'at, she has.' This was something that was still bothering Ma.

'Never mind,' Glad laughed. 'We'll find her another one. Now, Jen, where are your clothes?'

'In the outhouse. I'll see to them later. They'll soon dry in front of the fire.'

'Got a hole in her stocking as well.' Ma hadn't finished with the subject.

'I'll darn it for her, Ma.' Ivy was studying the elderly woman, a deep frown on her face. 'You know how neat my darning is.'

Ma nodded. 'That's right, you look after my girl.' Then she inexplicably fell asleep.

Glad, Ivy and Jenny went into the kitchen and closed the door so they could talk without waking Ma.

'She ain't right,' Glad said.

'I know. She called me Bessie.' Jenny chewed her lips in worry. 'Do you think she's getting ...

erm … confused?'

'Looks like it.' Glad glanced back at the room where Ma was sleeping 'She thinks of you as her daughter and she's having trouble keeping you separate from little Bessie.'

'You call if you need us,' Ivy told her.

'And if she calls you Bessie again, don't tell her no different.' Glad patted Jenny's arm. 'It'll make her happy to believe she's still got her daughter. But keep an eye on her.'

'Oh, I shall.' Jenny had been out nearly every day trying to find work, but she would stay close to Ma until she knew she was all right. This muddled thinking was so unlike her, and very worrying.

When Glad and Ivy had left, Jenny went back to the front room and stood gazing at Ma, sleeping peacefully. 'Don't you worry, Ma.' She spoke softly. 'I won't leave you, and if you want to call me Bessie, then you go ahead. I'm honoured to be your daughter.'

Later that evening, when Ma was in bed, Jenny used every kettle and saucepan to boil water. With her clothes steaming nicely in front of the fire, it was time to clean herself up properly. Hoisting the old tin bath from its hook in the outhouse, she dragged it into the kitchen and managed to fill it enough to have a decent soak in warm water. She settled in with a sigh of bliss.

Leaning back, she closed her eyes, letting her mind drift, thinking of nothing in particular. Only when she realized that the water was nearly cold did she spur herself to wash her body and her hair. She then used one kettle of warm water to rinse away the soap, stepped out of the bath and dried herself.

It was a laborious task emptying the tin bath, but she'd done it a few times and had got the hang of it now. Once most of the water had been bailed out, she dragged it into the yard and tipped it up to remove the rest. By the time the bath was back on its hook, Jenny was tired – but clean.

Hoping she hadn't woken Ma, she crept upstairs and listened at her door, pushing it open just a little. The gentle snoring told her that Ma was fast asleep, so she went to her own room, leaving her door slightly open as well. Tonight she wanted to make sure Ma was all right. She had obviously been upset, and for a while had become confused.

Once in bed, Jenny gazed up at the ceiling, eyes wide open, deep in thought. She was weary, but doubted if she'd get much sleep – her mind was in a whirl. She felt so helpless being out of work and not being able to contribute to the everyday expenses. She could only guess at the anguish mothers must be feeling as they struggled to feed the children. That thought brought her mind back to the centre. Thank God something was going to be done!

22

A good night's sleep had obviously restored Ma, and, apart from a couple of times when she seemed to lose the thread of what she was saying, everything appeared fine. Jenny was relieved and sang to herself as she wiped the dishes and put them away. She had given Ma her favourite sausages for dinner and every scrap had been eaten.

She was just about to put the kettle on the stove to make their tea when she heard Ma's voice, raised and angry. Jenny dashed into the front room and saw Ma standing up and waving her stick at two people. Concerned about Ma, Jenny took little notice of them until she had hold of the elderly woman and steadied her. Then she looked up to see who was causing the commotion.

The breath caught in her throat when she saw her Aunt Gertrude and Greaves with looks of distaste on their faces. Jenny's first reaction was fury that these people should dare to turn up their noses at Ma's front room. The furniture might be shabby and well worn, but the place was spotlessly clean.

'There you are!' Aunt Gertrude stepped forward as if to take hold of Jenny, but Ma fended her off with her stick.

'You keep your hands off my girl, you evil old hag!' Ma brandished the stick menacingly, leaving no one in any doubt that she would love to give the glowering woman in front of her a good whack. 'I've heard all about you. You're a right nasty pair, and that's for sure!'

Gertrude Osborne stepped back. 'Get your things, Eugenie, you are coming with us.'

'No, I'm not!' Jenny coaxed Ma back to her chair, but held her hand all the time. She wasn't going to let them upset Ma like this.

'How did you find me?'

'You were seen outside the Town Hall yesterday by someone who knows you. They followed you to be sure of where you lived, and then they came to me,' Greaves said with some satisfaction.

Jenny could guess who that was and gave a snort of disgust. 'That must have been Gerry, mother's old footman. Still after the reward, is he?'

'Of course.' Greaves had a smug look on his face. 'One hundred pounds is a temptation to any young man. I'm surprised it's taken this long.'

'Well, you've wasted your time coming here, because I'm not leaving. And I've certainly no intention of coming to live with you!' The expression on her face must have shown her distaste, for she saw him clench his fists in anger. It wouldn't take much to make him lash out, she realized. This was the confrontation she had dreaded – and yet, now it had happened, she wasn't frightened of them. The only emotion she felt was loathing.

'Has her mother asked her to return home and live with her?' Ma spoke to the aunt again, calmly this time.

'Of course not! She's far too content with her

new life to be bothered with a wilful daughter.' Mrs Osborne glared at Ma. 'Though I can't see what business it is of yours.'

Ma ignored that last remark and winked at Jenny. 'If her mother don't want her, then unless you've got something written on paper to say you can take her away, you can get out of my house. But we'll let Jen say what she wants to do, shall we?'

'I'm staying here. If my mother wants to talk to me, then I'll listen, but you're only my aunt and can't force me to do anything against my will.'

Albert Greaves went red in the face with anger. 'Be quiet, and do as you are told!'

As he grabbed at Jenny, Ma rapped three times on the floor with her stick. Glad and Ivy immediately appeared.

'You having a spot of bother, Ma?' Glad asked.

'Me and Jen want this pair chucked out, please, Glad.'

'I'll go and get the men, shall I, Mum?' Ivy suggested.

'No, don't bother.' Glad eyed the two inter-lopers. 'I'm sure we can manage them between us.'

'Eugenie's not staying in this hovel.' Greaves was now shouting loud enough to alert some of the neighbours, and the pavement outside was becoming quite crowded.

Jenny almost laughed out loud. Her aunt and Greaves didn't stand a chance. If they didn't leave soon, they would be marched away. She rounded on Greaves. 'Stop calling me by that ridiculous name. I'm called Jenny, and I'm not coming with you – ever!'

Ma hauled herself out of her chair again, glaring at Gertrude Osborne. 'You've heard her. Get out, and take that blob of lard with you.'

'You haven't heard the last of this,' her aunt called, as they left.

There was silence in the small room for a few moments, then Glad, chuckled. 'The neighbours are following them to make sure they leave the street.'

Jenny gave Ma a cheeky glance. 'I didn't know you knew anything about the law.'

The familiar cackle was a welcome sound. 'I don't, but I figured those two don't know much about it either.'

Jenny laughed in delight and immense relief. 'That's the last I shall see of them. They won't risk coming here again.'

Glad pursed her lips and frowned. 'Don't be too sure, Jen. Those two must be desperate to get you back.'

'But why?' Jenny knew they had been pursuing her for the last two years, but they couldn't force her back now. She was certain Glad was mistaken. It was probably their pride that had kept them searching. There wasn't any other reason. 'There isn't anything they can do, Glad, I'm eighteen, and I hope, wiser. They can't touch me now.'

Glad didn't look too convinced, but she had to agree. 'I suppose you're right. Still, I should keep an eye out for them.'

'I will,' Jenny said, not feeling at all concerned. They'd found her and she'd sent them away. That was the end of it, now perhaps she could get on with her life!

'And I'll watch out for them as well.' Ma scowled. 'If they take one step inside my door again, I'll clout them good and proper next time.'

They all laughed as the tension eased.

'Now, where's my cuppa?' Ma looked around expectantly. 'You make it for us, Ivy. And I think we might have a few biscuits left to celebrate chasing off that nasty pair, eh?'

Glad, Ivy and Ma were enjoying their tea when Ron and Jimmy erupted into the room, flushed with excitement.

'We've got a job!' Jimmy danced up and down.

Ron hugged Ivy. 'We was first in the queue, but when others saw us they twigged that something was going on. By the time the women turned up, there was a couple of dozen men waiting.'

Glad had found another two cups and poured tea for the happy men.

'But Mrs Stannard came out and asked for us.' Jimmy was too excited to sit down. 'They took us on, and two more. We start tomorrow!'

'Of course it might not be for long,' Ron said, obviously trying to calm Jimmy down. 'Mrs Stannard warned us that it could only be for a couple of weeks.'

'There's always a chance they'll keep us.' Jimmy gulped down his tea, not allowing anything to dim his joy. 'They're going to pay me fifteen bob a week, and Ron and the others are getting eighteen bob. Isn't that great!'

'That's wonderful news.' Ivy was nearly in tears.

'Do you know what their plans are?' Glad asked Ron.

'They're going to serve hot food Monday to Friday, free for those unemployed, and a small charge for the women and children of them in work.'

Glad nodded in approval. 'That makes sense. If they can make a bit of money from them as can afford it, then they can help them as can't.'

'That's right.' Ron continued. 'We're going to make one room comfortable with a warm fire, so it can be used during the day by anyone who can't afford to heat their own home. They're going to keep the place open from eleven to four. The mums with little ones will be pleased with that.'

'It sounds wonderful.' Ivy was holding her husband's hand and smiling with relief now.

Ron gazed at her affectionately. 'Don't get too excited, darling. It's a job, but in a couple of weeks we could be back where we started.'

'I know' Ivy sighed. 'But even two weeks will help.'

'Of course it will.' Ron winked at Jimmy. 'We've got another surprise for everyone, haven't we?'

The young boy's grin spread as his mother came to join them. 'One of the women gave everyone in the queue two bob each, but me and Ron got another two bob from Mrs Stannard.' He jingled the coins in his pocket. 'So me and Ron are going to get fish and chips for all of us.'

'You ought to save that money,' Jenny told him.

'Nah, I've already told Mum and she agrees. Don't you, Mum?' When Agnes smiled and nodded, he said, 'Mum said it's a fitting way to thank you and Glad for what you did for us when my dad died. And if it wasn't for you, Jen, we wouldn't have got this job.'

Ma touched Jenny's hand. 'Let them do it. They want to celebrate this bit of good luck.'

'All right, but you must get only one portion of fish for Ma and me. We'll share it.'

'Oh, Jen,' Ron said suddenly, 'I nearly forgot, Mrs Stannard said would you pop in the hall some time. She'd like to see you.'

'She might have a job for you as well.' Jimmy couldn't stop smiling.

'I'll go there tomorrow, and you'd better come with me, Ivy, just in case there's work available.' She saw the happy faces and marvelled at what a difference the chance to earn some money had made. Just for a little while they could enjoy the luxury of knowing they had a job and could share their good fortune with friends.

As soon as Fred and Stan were home, Ron and Jimmy went to the fish shop in the next road, returning loaded with packets wrapped in newspaper. There was a glorious smell of crisp batter, and salt and vinegar on the piles of chips.

There was much laughter as they gathered in Ma's front room to eat their special treat, using fingers to pop the lovely morsels of fish and piping hot chips into their mouths. Ron had even bought a couple of bottles of beer, which he shared out between them, and milk stout for Ma.

Jenny listened to the chatter and thought what a good couple of days it had been. Ma seemed her normal self again, and she had faced her aunt and Greaves, but this time surrounded by friends. They had left knowing they couldn't control her now. Then had come the wonderful news that the centre was going to be open soon and that there were short-term jobs for Ron and Jimmy.

It had been *very* good!

23

'I've just sold another car. That beautiful Lagonda you picked up the other day, Matt.' Jake slapped him so hard on the back it nearly knocked him off his feet. 'When you suggested this I thought you were crazy. But it's working. Not only are we selling, but the people who buy are bringing them back for servicing and repairs.'

'Ah, well.' Harry wiped his greasy hands on a rag. 'Your family know all about business, and if they were prepared to risk money in the venture, then it had a good chance of succeeding. And it looks like you've got another customer, Jake.'

Their boss hurried off and began talking to a man inspecting the few cars they had in stock. In about fifteen minutes he was back, rubbing his hands and smiling broadly. Matt couldn't help noticing how much younger he looked now the worry had lifted from him.

'He wants a second-hand Rolls-Royce!

Doesn't care about the age, so long as it's in first-class condition.' Jake pushed Harry. 'You and Matt get cleaned up and go out and find one. I told him we'd have one for him by tomorrow afternoon.'

'What!' Matt stared at his boss in astonishment. 'It'll probably take longer than that just to track one down.'

'It had better not. I gave the man my word.' Jake chuckled and handed Harry an envelope with cash in it. 'By the way, that was Lord Rollinton's chauffeur. His lordship wants it as a twenty-first birthday present for his son. Don't stand there with your mouths open, get moving, and don't come back without one!'

Matt and Harry collided as they both made a dash for the sink in the corner of the workshop.

'Where the hell are we going to find a Rolls by tomorrow?' Harry muttered as he scrubbed away at his hands.

'God knows.' Matt was trying to clean his hands in the same water as Harry. It was so black that the grease was clinging in a sticky mess all around the waterline.

Harry pulled out the plug, ignoring the mess, and wiped his hands, throwing the towel to Matt. 'Come on, you must know someone who wants to sell their Rolls-Royce.'

Matt inspected his fingernails, his mind working furiously. Now who would want to part with their car? An idea burst into his head and he almost laughed out loud. 'What about the Greaves car?'

'Ah, that would be perfect.' Harry slipped his

jacket on. 'Do you think he'd sell?'

'Let's go and see. Get his address from Jake's workbook.'

Harry dived for the book, riffling through the pages. 'Here it is – he lives in Bloomsbury.'

They both headed for the door as Jake bellowed, 'Are you two still here?'

'By the way, if we do get to see him, I'll have to keep out of the way. He saw me once when he came to my home, but I don't think he'll recognize me in these working clothes.'

'That could be tricky.' Harry was obviously curious. 'I get the impression you don't like him, so what was he doing at your place?'

'It's a long story, but if he recognizes me we'll never be able to make him part with the car.'

'In that case don't say a word, pull your cap down over your eyes and keep behind me. I'll do the talking. But what do you think are the chances of buying it from him?'

Matt shrugged. 'I've no idea. Depends on how hard up he is, I suppose.'

'Blast!' Harry stared gloomily ahead. 'He's loaded, I'm told.'

'Afraid so.' Matt clenched his jaw in determination. 'But I'll get the car off him if I can. A man like that doesn't deserve to own such a beautiful vehicle!' And he certainly doesn't deserve to own such a lovely and courageous girl as Jenny, he thought. Fury burnt through him every time he thought of the terrible life her aunt and this man had planned for her. If there was the slightest truth in the tales they'd heard about Greaves, then the man was a brute. The more he learnt

262

about Jenny the more he admired her.

Matt pulled up outside an impressive four-storey house, gleaming white in the pale sunshine.

'Phew!' Harry whistled softly through his teeth. 'We could be wasting our time here.'

'You could be right, but it's worth a try. Jake hasn't given us much time to find a decent Rolls, and we know this one is superb.' Matt got out of the car and began to stride towards the flight of steps leading up to the front door.

Harry caught hold of his sleeve and raised his eyebrows in query. 'Don't you think we ought to go round the back to the servants' entrance?'

'Whoops, I forgot. Force, of habit.'

Placing a firm hand on Matt's shoulder, Harry guided him to the side entrance. 'You're a common working man now. It's the servants' entrance for the likes of us.'

They were both laughing as Matt knocked on the door and stepped back. 'I'll keep out of the way because if I see that man I might tell him just what I think of him.'

'Oh, you really must tell me what he's done to you.'

'He hasn't done anything to me, but he has to someone I know.'

There wasn't time to say more as the door opened to reveal a footman in dark blue and gold livery. Pretentious, Matt thought, as he considered the simple uniforms his mother insisted her footmen wore.

'Yes?'

'We're from Mayfair Automobiles and we'd like

to see Mr Greaves, please.' Harry spoke politely.

'What's it about?'

'We'd like to talk to him about his Rolls-Royce. We service it for him.'

Matt stayed in the background, just like an apprentice should. He was happy to let Harry deal with this, but he wanted to get the Winford car off Greaves so badly he could almost taste it.

'I'll call the chauffeur. You can talk to him and he will relay the information to Mr Greaves.' The footman gave a haughty toss of his head and disappeared, leaving Matt and Harry standing outside. He even had the damned cheek to close the door on them.

Harry's muttered comments about the footman had Matt chortling. 'My, my, Harry. I didn't know you knew such words.'

Another man appeared, obviously the chauffeur. 'There's some worry with the car?'

'No, it's in good condition,' Harry said. 'Mayfair Automobiles wondered if Mr Greaves would consider selling.'

'I doubt there's any chance he would be prepared to part with it.'

There was something in the chauffeur's tone that made Matt's hopes rise. He hadn't intended to speak but changed his mind. 'Would you ask Mr Greaves? We'll pay a fair price for it – in cash.'

'I'll ask the master.' The chauffeur stood aside. 'You'd better come in.'

They were shown to a small room on the first floor and told to wait. Matt roamed around the room, inspecting the furniture, and then he stopped and gazed at a wall devoid of mirrors or paintings. He reached out and ran his fingers over some marks.

'What you looking at?' Harry stood beside him.

'See these marks? It looks as if something used to hang here and the wall has been cleaned to remove the marks. Paintings, I should think.'

'So?'

Matt spun round, his eyes taking in every detail of the room as he headed for the door.

'Where are you going?' Harry was alarmed that Matt might start to wander around this elegant house.

'I've got to have a quick look at another room.' He stepped out of the door, nipped across the passage to the room opposite. It was a dining room and sumptuous. Or was it? It didn't take him long to make up his mind. The signs were obvious.

He shot back to Harry, who was now agitated. 'What the bloody hell are you doing? Suppose they'd come for us and you weren't here? They would have thought we were thieves.'

Matt tipped his head back and laughed with glee. 'Don't be too generous with your offer for the car.'

'Why not? If we're going to get it, we'll have to pay top price for it.' Harry eyed him with interest. 'What makes you think he'll sell?'

'Because the man's in financial trouble.'

'How can you tell?'

'There are empty spaces on the walls; marks on the carpets where furniture had stood for many years.' Matt couldn't control his excitement.

'He's selling possessions!'

'But he's reputed to be a very, very rich man.' Harry looked perplexed.

'If that's true, then why is he selling?' Matt rubbed his hands in anticipation. 'The man's struggling, I'm sure, but he's obviously managed to keep it quiet.'

Harry's expression was thoughtful. 'That puts a different picture on things.'

'It certainly does. Bargain hard, because I believe he's desperate and will sell.'

They stopped talking suddenly as the door opened and the chauffeur looked in. 'Mr Greaves will see you. He'll meet us round the back of the house.'

They followed, and when they saw the Rolls standing outside its garage Matt drew in a breath of appreciation. It really was a beauty. The dark blue bodywork and chrome fittings gleamed in the pale sunlight. He began to walk around it, drinking in the sheer elegance of the vehicle.

'Here comes Greaves,' Harry whispered. 'For God's sake, Matt, stay out of the way and don't give him a chance to recognize you.'

Matt pulled his cap further over his eyes to cover more of his face and walked to the rear of the car, pretending to examine the tyres.

'You won't find anything wrong with the car.' The chauffeur was following Matt. 'But you know that already, as your garage has looked after her.' The man smoothed his hand over the paintwork with an expression in his eyes that said it was going to break his heart to part with this, and he hoped his master wouldn't sell.

'Can't be too careful.' Matt kept his voice low so it didn't reach the two men now in the process of negotiating a deal. 'You might have had an accident since we last saw the vehicle.'

The chauffeur looked highly offended. 'I'm an excellent driver. I do not have accidents!'

'That is insulting!' Greaves exclaimed loudly. 'It's worth double that.'

Matt dipped his head to hide his smile. He couldn't hear what Harry was saying, but it was obvious he was bargaining hard to get the Rolls as cheaply as possible. He would have loved to join in, but he had to keep out of the way, for if Greaves recognized him they would be thrown out. His father had treated Greaves and Mrs Osborne abruptly when they'd visited his parents in search of Jenny, making it very clear they were unwelcome. Their father never could hide his feelings. He spoke first and thought about it after. He was inclined to upset some people, and Matt hadn't missed their visitors' expressions when they were dismissed without even being offered refreshments.

'Can I have a look in the boot?' he asked the chauffeur. Harry and Greaves were still haggling over the price, and, as the discussion continued, he knew that he had been right. Greaves was desperate for money. If he hadn't been, he would have walked away from Harry by now. He was still poking around in the boot when Harry tapped him on the shoulder.

'We've got it, and at a very reasonable price. You go back in our car, and I'll drive this one back to the garage.' Before Harry put the envelope of money Jake had given them back in his pocket, he held it open for Matt to see: there was still quite a lot left.

'My God,' Matt muttered, 'the man must be in a mess financially.'

Harry winked, closed the boot carefully and gave Matt a shove. 'Wait for me down the road.'

Matt was off like a hare. A few minutes later he burst out laughing. He couldn't wait to tell his family about this. Everyone believed Greaves to be immensely wealthy. Well, he wasn't.

On reaching the car, he got in and drove to the end of the road to wait for Harry. He began to tap the steering wheel, turning things round in his mind. If Greaves was in trouble, why didn't he find himself a wealthy wife? Why bother to pursue a penniless young girl? It just didn't make sense.

Harry pulled up beside him, grinning in delight. 'Jake's going to be well pleased with this deal. Thanks for spotting the man was in trouble, Matt. That gave me the advantage, and when I offered him cash he wasn't able to resist.'

'Well done,' Matt complimented him. Harry was an excellent mechanic, but he was also showing signs of becoming a good salesman, with a sharp appreciation of the business side of things. 'Do you think Jake will mind if I sneak an hour off? I'd like to pop along to Lambeth and see how my mother's getting on with the soup kitchen she's setting up.'

'Once he sees the Rolls he won't mind what you do for the rest of the day.' Harry was laughing as he pulled away, heading back to the garage.

It was bedlam as Matt walked into the old community hall. One man was ripping out old cupboards that reached from floor to ceiling. Another was swinging a sledgehammer at a fireplace that had been bricked up. There were others elsewhere making a heck of a racket. The air was full of dust, and it was settling in a thick carpet everywhere. He went into what was eventually going to be the kitchen and found his mother and two members of her committee poring over some drawings, obviously done by the tall man who was explaining something to them.

His mother smiled when she saw him. 'Hello, Matt. What are you doing here at this time of day?'

'I've been out with Harry buying a car.' He wasn't going into details now; he would wait until they were all together this evening before he said anything. 'I thought I'd see how you're getting on.'

'As you can see' – his mother brushed brick dust from her jacket – 'we're in a mess, but we will open next week.' She turned to the man beside her. 'Ron, this is my son, Matt.'

After shaking hands, Matt said, 'Do you think my mother's being too optimistic about getting all this work done in such a short time?'

'We'll make it, even if we have to work all night.' Ron sounded very positive.

A young boy came by, staggering under the weight of a large piece of concrete.

'My goodness, Jimmy,' Mrs Stannard exclaimed. 'Where did you find that?'

'It was at the back of the fireplace, ma'am.' He puffed with the effort of holding the heavy weight. 'Just going to dump it out the back.' He tottered off.

Diving for the door, Matt held it open and Jimmy weaved his way into the yard, jumping back quickly as he let go of the block of concrete, letting it crash to the ground. He turned and grinned at Matt. 'Wouldn't have been able to light a fire with that wedged in the grate.'

Going back to his mother, Matt said, 'If you need more help, Luke and I could do some work in the evenings.'

'No, my dear.' His mother lowered her voice. 'These men need the jobs. They're so grateful to have something useful to do instead of standing in the dole queues every day.'

'How long can you keep them?'

'We've told them about two weeks, but I'll see what I can do about Ron and Jimmy after that. They're friends of Jenny.'

Just then a burst of girlish laughter came from a room at the end of the corridor.

'That's Jenny and her friend Ivy,' his mother said. 'They're scrubbing out the toilets.'

'Mother,' Matt said, shocked, 'you haven't roped Jenny in to scrub, have you?'

'We are paying her and she's only too happy to do any kind of work.' She gave her son a sad look. 'You must forget how she started life. She's one of the unemployed now, with an elderly woman to care for. All she asks for is the chance to earn some honest money.'

'I guess so.' He walked to the end of the passage

270

and opened the cloakroom door. Jenny was kneeling down, scrubbing away at a particularly nasty stain on the wall.

'Wouldn't it be easier to slap a coat of white-wash on that?' he suggested.

Jenny looked up, blowing a strand of dark hair out of her eyes. 'We've got to save as much money as possible. It'll look fine when we've finished.'

The other girl was giving him an uncertain look and fiddling with the brush she was holding in her hands, allowing the soapy water to drip unnoticed down her skirt.

'Ivy, this is Matthew.'

'Pleased to meet you, sir.'

Matt looked at the pair with a smile on his face. They were wearing clothes so old they were torn and threadbare in places, their hair was in disarray and their faces pink with exertion, but they appeared to be perfectly happy with their task. He realized his mother was right, they were grateful for any job, and didn't give a damn what it was as long as they could earn a little money. Some girls were turning to prostitution, but he knew instinctively that these two would rather starve than sink to that level. Since her father's death, Jenny had joined the working classes, and, like her friends, she still had standards and a certain amount of pride. In common with the vast majority caught up in this terrible depression, they were honest, hard-working people...

'Matt!' his mother called.

He smiled apologetically at having to leave suddenly, though in truth he would have loved to stay longer and talk to them. 'I mustn't keep you from your work.' Closing the door, he returned to the kitchen.

'Ah, there you are. Will you tell your father I might be late? Ask cook to delay our dinner for one hour, please.'

'All right.' He kissed her cheek. 'I can see you have everything under control, so I'd better get back to work.'

When Matt arrived at the garage, everyone was clustered around the Rolls-Royce, now sitting proudly on their forecourt.

Jake slapped him on the back and beamed. 'Well done, lad. Harry told me you'd sussed out the situation with Greaves. We're going to make a fine profit on this deal.'

'Harry's a tough negotiator.' Matt winked at his friend. 'It's a talent he's kept well hidden.'

'Once we've sold the Rolls, you two can find us a couple more cars to sell.' Jake was rubbing his hands together in anticipation. 'This was a damned good idea of yours, Matt. If it goes on like this, I'll soon be able to pay your brother back the money he lent us to get started.'

Matt nodded, noticing the happy faces at the garage now. His family were making a small contribution to a few lives in these difficult times. It wasn't enough, though. What was unemployment now – over two million? Too many – too much suffering.

24

'Matthew's handsome, ain't he?' Ivy cast an amused glance at Jenny as they walked home at four o'clock that afternoon. 'And so tall.'

'They're all tall, and a good-looking family.'

'What are the other sons like?' Ivy was obviously intrigued.

Jenny cast her mind back to when she'd seen them together that first Christmas. But in truth, the only one she'd taken much notice of was the youngest. Strange that. 'John's the eldest. He's serious and a fine businessman. Luke comes next. He's easy-going and over-fond of the girls. Matthew's the youngest and, I believe, the nicest of the three.'

Ivy nodded. 'I can see that. He's got such lovely, kind blue eyes.'

'You didn't miss much,' Jenny laughed, 'and remember you're married.'

'Oh, I wouldn't change my Ron for anything.' Ivy slipped her hand through Jenny's arm as they turned into Forest Road. 'Anyway, men like that make me feel awkward.'

'What on earth for?'

'Well, he's posh. Don't laugh, Jen.' Ivy thumped her arm playfully. 'You act so natural around him and his mother because you was brought up like them, but you also fit right in with us.'

'I'm glad you think that,' Jenny remarked drily,

'because this is where I belong now.'

'Your life's like one of those books, but you've come from riches to poverty.' Ivy grinned. 'It's the wrong way round. You're supposed to rise from the slums to the gentry.'

Jenny laughed, highly amused. She knew how much Ivy loved the romantic stories of the day. 'In my case it would take a miracle for that to happen.'

'I suppose so.' Ivy sighed wistfully. 'It must be terrible hard for you, Jen. You knowing what it's like to have so much, and now you've got nothing. It's all right for us – we was born in poverty and are used to it. Though with all this unemployment, it's the hardest I've ever known it.'

After pondering this statement for a while, Jenny said, 'It isn't true that I've got nothing now. I might not have any worldly goods, but I've got something far more precious. I've got Ma, you, your mum and dad, and all the people in Forest Road.'

Ivy glanced up at her admiringly. 'You could have turned out bitter and nasty after what's happened to you, but you ain't.'

'That kind of attitude wouldn't have got me far. I could have gone along with my aunt's plans for me, but I wouldn't. I had to make a new life for myself, and I've done that.' Jenny squeezed Ivy's arm. 'And I'm so glad I did.'

They walked the rest of the way in silence, and Jenny let her thoughts wander over Ivy's statement that she seemed at ease with people like the Stannards, but still fitted in with her friends in this humble street. She was lucky, she realized: not many people had that opportunity to see the heads and tails of life. Matthew was doing it to some extent by working in the garage as an apprentice, but at the end of each day he went back to his life of luxury. So it wasn't the same for him; but Jenny had the feeling that he understood her position more than many others.

The girls parted at their doors, promising to meet at ten the next morning to go to the hall to see if there was another day's work to be had. The ladies were employing them only on a day-to-day basis.

When she stepped inside, eager to tell Ma about her day and show her the money she'd earned, she was surprised to see the chair empty.

'Ma!' she called, running to the kitchen and then to the outhouse. No sign of her. She must be upstairs, but why would she go there? Ma never slept during the day, except for a nap in her chair.

Jenny was halfway up the stairs when Glad appeared at the top, her finger to her lips. 'What's happened?' she asked in alarm.

'Ma's had a bad turn. She's asleep now, though.'

Jenny rushed to Ma's bedroom and knelt beside the bed, taking the frail woman's hand in hers. What she saw made her heart miss several beats. Ma's face was white, and the left side of her mouth was pulled down slightly.

'We think she's had a stroke,' Glad whispered. 'She's lost the use of the left side of her body.'

'I must get a doctor.' Jenny was on her feet, eyes

brimming with tears. 'I've earned enough today to pay for one.'

'I think that would be best. I'll stay with her while you go for him.' Glad settled herself in a chair she'd brought up from the kitchen.

Jenny was in the street in a moment and running for all she was worth. The doctor's house was about half a mile away, by a small parade of shops. With each gasping breath she prayed that he was there.

Dr Rayner was just getting out of his car when she hurtled up to him. 'You must come, please.' She bent over, trying to catch her breath. 'Ma Adams is bad. I can afford to pay you.'

'Forest Road?' he asked, opening the car door for her to get in when she nodded. 'I know her house.'

They arrived in no time, and the doctor hurried up the stairs, having a quick word with Glad before examining Ma.

It was an anxious wait and Jenny thought her heart was going to break when Ma woke up and gave everyone a bewildered look. But she never said anything. Ma had always been tough and determined, but how was she going to recover from this? She would hate being completely helpless.

Dr Rayner straightened up after replacing the covers and patted Ma's hand. Then he signalled that they should go downstairs.

'It's bad, isn't it?' Jenny thought what a daft question that was, when any fool could see that Ma was very ill.

'I'm afraid so. Mrs Adams has had a stroke.' He

had a sympathetic look in his eyes. 'She is very frail, and you must prepare yourself for the worst.'

Those words cut through Jenny, but she gulped back the emotion threatening to engulf her and straightened up. She had to know the truth. 'You mean she's going to die?'

'Would she stand more chance in a hospital?' Glad asked. 'If so, we'll get the money somehow.'

The doctor shook his head. 'There isn't anything we can do for her. She would probably be happier in her own home. She will take a lot of looking after, though.'

'That's all right.' Jenny was determined that Ma should stay here. 'I'll look after her.'

'And we'll all help.' Glad shook hands with the doctor. 'Thank you for coming.'

'Yes, thank you.' Jenny took the few shillings she earned today out of her pocket. 'How much do I owe you?'

The doctor glanced around the shabby room, giving a quiet, weary sigh. 'I wasn't able to do anything, and there isn't any medicine that will help, so I won't charge you.'

'But we must pay for your visit,' Jenny insisted. He picked up his bag, ignoring the money she was holding out to him. 'Use that to buy some nourishing food. You look as if you can both do with it.'

'Would you like me to stay?' Glad asked when the doctor had gone.

'No, I'll be fine. I'll get us something to eat and then I expect Ma will sleep for a while.'

'You call if you need us, Jen. I'll come round in the morning with Fred and Stan so we can turn Ma. She'll get sores if we don't move her a couple of times a day.'

'Thanks, Glad.'

She kissed Jenny on the cheek. 'Try not to be too upset. We'll all pitch in to make Ma's last days as comfortable as possible.'

After Glad had left, Jenny went to the kitchen. There was still a nice bit of soup left, so she heated that up and took it upstairs. Before entering the room she pinned a bright smile on her face. 'Who's being spoilt with supper in bed, then?'

Ma watched her intently. 'Sit me up.' Her speech was slurred.

Jenny nipped into her own room and pinched a pillow from her bed, placed it behind Ma and hauled her to a sitting position. She fed Ma, wiping her chin as the soup trickled down from her stiff lips. All the time she chatted away brightly, telling her about the work she and Ivy had been doing today. She got little response, but at least Ma was eating.

After the last mouthful, Ma leant back on the pillows and startled Jenny with a string of swear words, slurred but nevertheless clearly audible.

'Ma!' she laughed, but in truth she felt like crying. It was clear that there wasn't anything wrong with her mind, and she knew that this was going to be frustrating for Ma. 'Do you want a cup of tea?'

Ma nodded, grabbing hold of Jenny with her right hand. The left was lying useless on the blanket. 'What's the doc say?'

'You've had a slight stroke, but you'll be as right as ninepence in a couple of weeks.'

There was a humph of disgust. 'Bloody liar!'

Sitting on the edge of the bed, Jenny schooled her expression carefully. The last thing she was going to do was tell Ma what he'd really said. She didn't want to admit that Ma was dying, even to herself. Doctors had been wrong before. 'You're going to be fine, and I'll be with you all the time. Now, I'll just pop downstairs and make our tea. I've got a few biscuits left.'

As soon as Ma finished her tea, she fell into a sound sleep. Jenny hauled a more comfortable chair up the stairs, and settled herself beside the bed for a long night's vigil.

It wasn't until they'd had dinner and were all settled in the sitting room that Matt told his family about Greaves and the Rolls-Royce.

'Are you sure he's in financial difficulty, Matt?' John asked. 'I haven't heard a whisper about that.'

'The signs were all there – blank spaces on the walls and furniture missing. But when he took Harry's offer of cash for the car I was certain. He could have got more for the Rolls if he'd held out.' Matt could practically hear John's mind working. 'He's desperate. I'm sure of it.'

'If that's the case, why is he so intent on finding Jenny?' Their father was frowning fiercely. 'He would need to marry for money, surely?'

'That's what has been bothering me ever since I saw the house.' Matt stared at John, who was

279

deep in thought and stirring his coffee aimlessly.

Putting the spoon in the saucer, John looked up. 'I'd better look into this. If Greaves is in trouble, I should be able to find out.'

Luke took an apple from the fruit bowl and tossed it in the air. 'The plot thickens,' he said. 'I do love a mystery.'

'It's all very odd.' Their mother seemed bewildered. 'An under housemaid who turns out to have come from a wealthy family – now living in the slums of London. And a man reputed to be extremely wealthy – now short of money.'

Luke chortled. 'It would make a good pantomime.'

'Except it isn't funny, Luke.' Matt knew his brother just couldn't help being flippant, and it grated at times, but Luke wasn't uncaring.

Luke raised his hands in surrender. 'Sorry, Matt, I don't mean anything by it. It must be wretched for the poor girl, but you must admit that it has all the ingredients of a good suspense story.'

'Damned strange business, if you ask me.' Their father poured himself an after-dinner brandy. 'See what you can find out, John. He doesn't bank with us, but it's best to have the whole picture in case he comes asking for a loan.'

'Yes. Some who are in difficulties have been going from bank to bank, trying to raise money. I'll make a few inquiries tomorrow.'

'Good.' Their father nodded in approval. 'If anyone can find out what the situation is, it's you, John.'

The Rolls was sold the next morning at a good profit. In fact it was enough to repay Luke almost half the money he had lent Jake to get started, and to buy two more cars to sell. They weren't quite so fussy now, and if a car needed work, they had the expertise to make it look as good as new. They found that there was more money in doing this than in just buying quality cars, and they made sure they had a good selection at all prices. The petrol pump was still well used. The garage was once again busy and they were all in high spirits. With the economic depression really gripping the country, it was nothing short of a miracle that they were doing so well. Their Mayfair location had a lot to do with their success, though.

In his lunch break, Matt decided to go to see how his mother and her committee were getting on at the hall.

When he arrived, he found his mother in the kitchen, looking rather harassed. 'Hello, Matt. I'm glad you've come. Have you got some spare time?'

'I can spare an hour. Why?'

'I wondered if you'd go to see if Jenny needs anything. She hasn't been able to come today because Mrs Adams has had a stroke.'

'I'll go round there straight away.'

It was only a short distance, but he drove to save time. He knocked on the front door, and when there was no reply he turned the handle and found it unlocked. He walked in. The house seemed uncannily quiet, and he remembered the last time he'd been here and seen Ma Adams

281

sitting in her chair, studying him with shrewd eyes. The room was empty now.

'Jenny,' he called softly.

'Oh, hello.' She came down the stairs carrying a tray.

He was shocked by her appearance. Her dress was badly creased, her hair untidy, and she looked exhausted, with great dark shadows under her eyes. 'Mum told me about Ma. Is there anything we can do for you?'

The cups on the tray rattled as her hands shook. He took it from her and placed it on the sideboard. 'How bad is she?'

'She's got worse during the night.' Her voice wavered and she looked at him with tortured eyes. 'Ma's dying... What am I going to do without her?'

Matt stepped forward and gathered Jenny into his arms. He stroked her hair as she laid her head on his shoulder and sobbed. He felt like doing the same. Not for the elderly woman upstairs, whom he'd only met once, but for this lovely girl.

How much more sorrow and hardship must she endure? A father who had killed himself; a mother who didn't want her; the Stannards who had branded her a thief, and turned her out; and her aunt who had tried to marry her off to that obnoxious man Greaves.

At that moment he was so furious at the cards of life this gentle girl had been dealt that he could have killed someone!

25

For the next week Jenny never left Ma's side. With the help of Glad and occasionally Fred and Stan when Ma needed lifting, she kept Ma clean, fed and as comfortable as possible. But each day the elderly woman deteriorated, until she hardly seemed aware of anything or anyone. In the beginning Jenny had clung to the belief that she would recover, but it was hard to fool herself any longer. Ma was dying. It could only be a matter of days now, Glad had told her gently.

Jenny and Glad had just given Ma a nice wash, and changed her nightdress and sheets. When she was settled back in bed, propped up on the pillows, Jenny kissed her cheek. 'There, Ma, that's more comfy, isn't it?'

In a rare moment of recognition, Ma's eyes lingered on Jenny, then she sighed and fell asleep.

Glad put her hand on Jenny's shoulder. 'You go and get yourself something to eat. You look fair washed out. I'll stay here for a while.'

With a nod of thanks she wandered downstairs, made herself a cup of tea and gazed at it listlessly, too tired and distressed even to drink it. Ma had become a grandmother and mother to Jenny since she'd been here. They'd laughed, joked, argued and teased each other, and a deep bond had been formed. To lose her now was going to be so hard, but she was determined to do everything she could to keep her alive, or at least as happy as possible in the circumstances before the end came.

'Jen.' Edna appeared in the doorway.

'Oh, how lovely to see you!' Jenny got up and threw her arms around her friend. 'I'm sorry I haven't been able to meet you, but I've had so much to do. Can you stay a while? Would you like a cup of tea?'

'I've got half an hour.' Edna sat down at the kitchen table. 'Where's Ma?'

Jenny shook her head, her mouth trembling. 'She's had a stroke.'

'Ah, I'm sorry, Jen.'

'What are you doing here at eleven in the morning?' Jenny hastily changed the subject. Her emotions were too raw to talk about Ma's illness at the moment.

'I've left my job.' Edna held out her left hand to show off the half-hoop diamond engagement ring. 'I'm getting married next week to David Hughes. He's asked me to marry him and I've agreed.'

'That's wonderful!' Jenny jumped up and hugged her friend, so excited for her. She knew Edna had had a tough life and deserved some happiness. 'I'm so pleased for you. Where are you getting married?'

Edna laughed at her friend's obvious delight and playfully pushed her back in her chair. 'If you'll stop hopping about, I'll tell you. David comes from Wales, so we're going to be married there in a week's time. He's got a job to go to – something to do with accounts. He's well educated,' she said proudly. 'And his family have found us a house to rent.'

'Wales?' Jenny's pleasure seeped away as she realized what this meant, but she kept smiling somehow. She was going to lose Edna. But she mustn't be selfish and let her dismay show, because this was absolutely wonderful for her friend. 'That sounds exciting.'

'It is, and I've had a lovely letter from David's mother. She sounds ever so kind and very pleased about the wedding.'

With cups of tea and a couple of biscuits in front of them, they settled down. It had been some time since they had been out together, so this was a chance to catch up on all the news.

'Tell me all about it,' Jenny urged.

Edna waved her hand, laughing. 'It's been a proper whirlwind romance, but he's so nice and we love each other.' She became serious. 'I've got a chance of a new life and I'm taking it, though I'd have married him even if he'd been a chimney sweep.'

'That's real love, then,' Jenny teased.

'We'd like you to come to the wedding. I know it's a long way, but David's mum said you could stay with them for a couple of days.'

The disappointment was intense, but not even for such a special occasion would she go away for several days. 'I can't leave Ma.'

'I was afraid you was going to say that, but I do understand. I wanted to bring David round to meet you, but he's had to go back to Wales to arrange the wedding and sort out his new job. I'm going on the train tomorrow.'

285

'You must write and tell me all about it, and send me a photo if you can.' Jenny kept her tone cheerful. Edna was happy and she wouldn't want to dim her joy.

'I'll do that.' Edna stood up to leave. 'And one day you must come and visit us.'

'That will be something to look forward to.' She kissed Edna and waved brightly as her friend walked up the street.

As soon as she was out of sight, Jenny returned to the kitchen, sat down and bowed her head in sorrow. Now she'd lost her friend.

That blasted coin definitely had two tails!

The next morning Jenny was wondering how she could go out for some shopping, with Glad out and Ivy working at the hall. She would never leave the house unless there was someone here with Ma. She emptied the tin they kept their money in, counted it and began making a list. It was essential to decide exactly what she was going to buy. Careful planning was the key to providing a decent meal each day, and Jenny was quite proud of her shopping skills these days. It didn't matter how tempting something might be: if it wasn't on her list, she didn't buy it, unless it was cheaper than the item she had originally planned.

The list when finished was depressingly short, but it was all wholesome food. Apart from a few biscuits that Ma loved, luxuries were out of the question. Her mouth fairly watered when she remembered the lovely puddings and cakes she'd had in the past, but they weren't essential. And

286

the day would come when they would be able to buy them again: the depression couldn't go on for ever. With that positive thought, she placed the coins on top of the list next to her shopping basket. As soon as someone came, she would pop out.

While Ma slept, Jenny could snatch a few quiet moments for herself, and she sat down to think. Edna would be on her way to Wales now, and a new life. It had come as a shock to have her friend move away, but she couldn't be more pleased for her. Edna deserved this chance of happiness, and it was a ray of hope that lives could change for the better.

A knock on the front door brought her out of her musing. When she opened the door and saw Matthew standing there, she felt a blush creeping up her face. She had cried on his shoulder. What must he think of her?

'Hello, Jen.' He studied her face intently. 'How's Ma?'

'Much the same.' She stepped aside. 'Would you like to come in?'

'Thanks.' He strode straight into the kitchen and, seeing the money and list on the table, said, 'Are you going shopping?'

'Yes, as soon as I can find someone to sit with Ma, but everyone's out at the moment.'

'I've got half an hour to spare. I'll get this for you.' He scooped up the list, coins and the basket, then headed for the door before she had time to object. 'Do you go to the shops at the top of the road?'

'Yes, but only buy what is on the list. I've put

the price beside each item.'

He was already striding towards the shops, and she wasn't sure he'd heard a word she'd said. Jenny fumed. If he wasted their precious money on unsuitable purchases, she would be very angry. Watching his tall figure disappear with her shopping basket on his arm, she shook her head in disbelief. Who the hell did he think he was, sweeping in here and taking over?

Suddenly she saw the funny side of it and began to giggle. What were the shopkeepers going to think when a strapping young man turned up carrying her shopping basket? Well, it was too late to stop him now. If he wanted to make a fool of himself, that was up to him. He obviously didn't care what other people thought of him. She could admire him for that attitude.

Nipping upstairs to check on Ma and finding her asleep, Jenny went back to the kitchen to put the kettle on. The least she could do was offer him a cup of tea when he returned.

He was back in less than twenty minutes, and Jenny gaped at the overflowing basket. 'You never got all that with the money I gave you.'

'No, I bought a few extras.' He began putting the packets on the table.

Jenny watched open-mouthed, becoming angrier by the second. There was butter, bread, jam, bacon, eggs, sausages, tea, milk, biscuits – whole ones – fruit, veg and even a small chicken. *A few extras?*

'I can't afford all that. You'll have to take it back.'

'Don't be so bloody proud, Jen.' Matthew was

clearly exasperated by her attitude. 'You and Ma have got to eat. Look at you, you're starving.'

'We are not! And who the hell gave you permission to call me Jen?'

'Don't change the subject.' Matt raised his voice. 'All I've done is buy you a little extra food. If it upsets you so much, you can pay me back when you've got the money.'

'Don't be ridiculous,' she snorted. 'Where do you think I'm going to get that much money from? And stop shouting!'

There were three sharp taps from the room above.

'Now look what you've done, you've woken Ma up.' Jenny headed for the stairs at a run, with Matt right on her heels.

Ma was propped up and holding her stick in her good hand.

'Hello, Ma,' Matt said cheerfully. 'Sorry we woke you, but your Jen needed a good talking to.'

Jenny couldn't believe her eyes when Ma winked at him.

'Ah, I see you approve.' He sat down on the edge of the bed and removed the stick from her hand, laying it on the blanket where she could still reach it. 'Now, I don't want you to worry about her, because I'm going to be around. All right?'

Ma winked again and Matt leant forward and kissed her forehead. 'Good, that's settled, then.'

What's settled? What the devil was he on about? Jenny had thought that Ma couldn't understand, but she was obviously communicating with Matthew.

'I've bought you a nice little chicken for Jen to cook and make soup with the bones. And a pound of your favourite sausages, because the butcher told me you're real partial to them.'

Ma winked again.

'Now I'll leave you to get some sleep while Jen cooks you a lovely meal.' He patted Ma's hand. 'You keep her in line now. Her language is something shocking!'

Jenny could hear Ma's cackle in her head as she watched Matthew stand up and give Ma a wink; then he clattered down the stairs and out the front door.

'Well,' was all Jenny could say as she stood motionless, absolutely amazed at the scene she had just witnessed. 'Do you know what he was on about?'

Ma gave a crooked smile. She actually smiled! Jenny did the same in relief. It was as if Matthew had woken Ma out of the stupor she had been in since the stroke. Hope flooded through her. Perhaps her dear Ma was going to survive against all the odds. 'Terrible bossy, isn't he?' she joked, feeling light-hearted.

The smile came again, and Ma lifted her hand to shoo Jenny away.

'I see, you want your chicken, do you?'

Ma actually nodded this time. Jenny sang to herself as she went downstairs and set about the meal.

'My, something smells good,' Glad said, as she looked in the kitchen an hour later.

'It's a chicken!' Jenny beamed. 'You'll never guess what happened today.'

Glad sat down while Jenny told her about the argument with Matthew because he'd bought extra shopping, and his conversation with Ma.

'She's so much better, Glad,' Jenny told her excitedly. 'She actually smiled. Isn't that marvellous? Perhaps she's turned the corner and is going to pull through.'

'Don't raise your hopes too much,' Glad warned. 'I've seen folks rally for a while and then sink back again.'

'I know that can happen.' Jenny's smile faded. 'But I can hope, can't I?'

'Of course you can.'

Fred came in. 'I'll just pop up and see her.'

Fred was with Ma for almost half an hour. When he came down, he handed Glad a piece of paper with spidery writing on it. 'Ma wants you to sign this, Glad.' He gave his wife a pen and when she'd put her signature on the bottom, Fred tucked it in his pocket.

Fred and Glad had always looked after Ma's affairs, and Jenny thought this was another good sign. Ma was obviously feeling bright enough to give them instructions to deal with something. 'She's much better, isn't she, Fred?'

'She's quite perky and looking forward to the chicken.' He laughed. 'She's fairly drooling at the mouth, and I've given her a pencil and pad so she can write messages while she's still thinking straight.'

'That's a good idea.' Jenny approved. It would be lovely to be on the receiving end of Ma's caustic remarks again, even if they were only written ones.

291

The chicken was beautifully tender, and Jenny was delighted when Ma ate every morsel. She cut herself off a small amount; the rest she sliced up and took next door to Ivy for the children. The carcass with vegetables was made into a large saucepan of soup for the next day.

As the gorgeous smell of cooking filled the tiny kitchen, Jenny felt rather ashamed of the way she had reacted to Matthew's shopping trip. He was only being kind, but she didn't want him to feel he owed her something.

Giving the soup another stir, Jenny pondered why that should worry her. After a taste she added a little more salt. The spoon was halfway to her mouth again when she realized why she had exploded at him. She liked Matthew, had done from the moment she had seen him that first Christmas, and she wanted his friendship. Wanted to know he liked her for herself.

The spoon dropped with a clatter. Oh, dear, that wouldn't do at all! He was from a wealthy family, and even though she had once been in the same situation, she was now penniless. It was ridiculous, but these things still mattered to society. She ought to know, because she'd been brought up with these prejudices. If she became too friendly with him, his family would believe she was trying to edge her way back up, through him. She gave a snort of disgust, imagining what his father would have to say about that! No, she must forget the whole thing. Anyway, he was probably only helping because he felt sorry for her, and she didn't want or need anyone's pity.

Things were difficult at the moment, but it wouldn't always be like this. The fact that Ma was so much better was a hopeful sign.

She turned the gas down to simmer the soup, shaking her head in disbelief. How stupid to have her first crush on one of the Stannard family.

26

That evening Matt arrived home still highly amused by the argument he'd had with Jenny about the extra shopping he'd bought for her and Ma. Where had that timid frightened under housemaid gone? The girl who had turned on him with such fire was so different. Now eighteen, she had grown in stature and confidence. He doubted if she was afraid of anyone or anything now. The last two years must have been unbelievably hard for her, but, instead of becoming cowed by the experience, she had come through it magnificently. He liked this new, mature girl. Although too thin, she was absolutely beautiful.

He grinned to himself as he remembered the old woman winking saucily at him. It wasn't any surprise that Jenny loved her so much, because even in sickness there was still a hint of her feisty nature. He'd understood the plea in those sharp eyes – you look after my girl, lad, it had said. When Ma died, and she knew she was going to soon, he would make sure Jenny was all right. That should cause a fight or two, but when that day came he was well aware that she was going to be distraught. She would have the support of her friends, of course, but he would also be there, whether she wanted him to be or not!

John walked in just in time for dinner. 'I've got some news.'

'Tell us before we sit down to eat,' his mother suggested.

'Greaves *is* in trouble.' John sat down and stretched out his long legs. 'He's a gambler.'

'The stock market?' Luke sat forward, interested.

'No,' John said, shaking his head. 'He's always boasted that he didn't lose anything in the crash, but he has on the horses. He invested a lot in four steeple-chasers, and bet heavily on them whenever they raced. None of them ever won, and he had to sell them at a huge loss. By this time he was in debt and continued gambling to try to recoup his losses, with disastrous results.'

'That's a fool's way to try to make money.' Their mother was clearly disgusted. 'He doesn't sound very bright, and from what I saw of him he is too fond of the drink.'

'Well spotted, Mother,' John grinned. 'That's another of his problems.'

'So he's selling the family silver to pay his gambling debts.' Matt grimaced. 'The damned idiot. If he doesn't pull himself together, he'll lose everything.'

'From what I can gather he's quite close to that now.' John stood up as the dinner gong sounded. 'He needs an injection of cash very quickly.'

'Good thing you found this out, John.' Gilbert

helped his wife up. 'He needn't bother coming to us for a loan.'

Luke slapped Matt on the back. 'Well, he won't be bothering Jenny again. She hasn't got a dime.'

'If he does, she'll really give him what for!' A deep chuckle of amusement rumbled through Matt; it also contained relief. That was one problem she wouldn't have to deal with again. 'She's changed beyond belief.'

'She's had to change to survive,' his mother said gently. 'Some might have crumbled under it, but it has made her strong.'

'Yes, it has.' He had to agree with that. She wouldn't let anyone push her around now, but that strength must have been there in the beginning or she would never have had the courage to run away in the first place. The harshness of her life since then had brought her true character to the surface. He had thought he was being courageous by leaving university to become a car mechanic, but that was nothing compared to what Jenny had achieved. His admiration for this plucky girl just grew and grew.

During the next two days Jenny's hopes soared as Ma began to order her around again with the aid of the pencil and paper. She still couldn't speak, but was obviously in control of her faculties and aware of everything going on around her. Her frustration at being helpless also showed quite often, when she threw the pencil across the room with fury gleaming in her eyes. Jenny understood how difficult it must be for her and patiently ignored the outbursts.

Ma was in this kind of mood when she and Glad struggled to move the fuming woman and change the sheets.

'Don't be so difficult, Ma,' Glad scolded when she was pushed away while trying to brush Ma's hair. 'You'll feel much better when you're clean and tidy.'

Grabbing her pencil, Ma scribbled, 'Won't. Bugger off.'

Jenny laughed, enjoying these flashes of spirit from Ma. If she continued to improve, she would soon be shouting at them. Everyone kept telling her that there was no hope of recovery, but she didn't believe that. She wouldn't believe it. While Ma still had fight in her, anything was possible.

Ma was writing again, and she thrust the notebook at Jenny. It said, 'Get Matt. Want see. Now!'

'What do you want to see him for?' Jenny was perplexed by the demand.

The word 'now' was underlined with such a heavy stroke that the pencil lead snapped. Ma tossed it away in disgust and then waved Jenny towards the door.

'You'd better do as she says.' Glad sighed, picking up the pencil and sharpening it. She glanced up at Jenny, giving a wry grimace. 'She's certainly making good use of the one arm she can move. I'll stay with her while you find him.'

'I'll go to the hall and ask his mother to give him a message.'

The pencil was snatched out of Glad's hand and the word 'garage' written down.

'Now look here, Ma, I'm not going to Mayfair where he works,' she protested. 'I'll tell his mother that you want to see him, and that's all!' She left quickly as a scowl darkened Ma's face.

There was a spring in her step as she approached the hall. The thing that struck her was the difference in the place. The outside had been cleared of rubbish and given a coat of whitewash. It had brightened the building beyond recognition. A large notice on the outside said that all unemployed were welcome to a free hot meal. The front door wasn't open, so she went round to the side door and let herself in.

'Hello, Jen.' Jimmy called as she walked into the main hall. 'What do you think of the old place now?'

'My goodness, what a difference.'

The main hall was filled with wooden tables and chairs; there was new lino on the floors; and every wall and ceiling had been painted. The kitchen had been opened up with a serving hatch that went along the entire wall, so food could be served straight into the dining area. Jenny could see Ron's carpentry skills had been put to good use here. There was a smaller room just off the hall, and she looked round with a gasp of pleasure. There was a good fire burning in the grate, bathing the room in a warm glow. Again the lino was new, and there were plenty of comfortable chairs to sit on. These were all second-hand, but they were in good condition.

'Nice, eh, Jen?' Ron came and stood next to her, gazing at the room proudly. 'The mums can bring their kids here, and in that cupboard in the corner there are books and toys for them to play with.'

Mrs Stannard joined them. 'Hello, Jenny. Everyone has worked so hard, and we're ready to open tomorrow. Our committee's made Ron the manager, so he'll look after the place for us, with Jimmy's help. Unfortunately we can't afford to pay much.'

'It's better than the dole,' Ron said. 'Me and Jimmy are right grateful for the chance to do something useful.'

'Does that mean a permanent job for both of you?' Jenny grabbed Ron's arm and knew it was when she saw his smiling face.

'For as long as the place is needed,' Ron said.

'That's just wonderful!' Jenny was so pleased. 'Does Ivy know?'

'Not yet. I'll tell her tonight.'

Jimmy tumbled into the room. 'Have you heard about our jobs?'

'Yes.' Jenny held out her arms and the three of them hugged each other in delight. Then she turned to Mrs Stannard, who was watching with a smile on her face. 'Thank you so much for doing this for them.'

'They are the best men for the job. I only wish we could employ more.' She looked downcast for a moment.

Seeing how much she cared, Jenny leant forward and kissed her briefly on the cheek. 'Every man who is given a job makes one less for the dole queue, and to employ two is doing much. That's two families who don't have to worry where the next meal is coming from.'

'Of course you're right. Now we can probably find you something as well.'

'That's very kind of you, Mrs Stannard, but Ma takes a lot of looking after at the moment.'

'I'm sure she does. How is she now?'

'Getting bossy. That's why I'm here. She wants to see your son Matthew, so could you please let him know?'

'Of course I will. He often comes along in his lunch break. I'll let him know as soon as I see him.'

'Thanks. Now I must get back.' She ran home buoyed up by the good news about Ron and Jimmy, but she mustn't say anything until their families had been told.

'Did you find his mother?' Glad asked when she arrived.

'Yes, she said she'd tell him, though I can't understand why Ma's set on seeing him.'

Giving a shrug, Glad picked up her bag. 'Goodness knows what's going through her head at the moment. I'm off, then.'

Jenny set about heating up the vegetable stew and popped in a few dumplings. Ma wasn't eating as much as usual, but Jenny was determined to see that the meals were as inviting as possible.

As soon as she walked into the bedroom, Ma held up her pad: 'Is he coming?'

'I've left a message.' Jenny sat down on the edge of the bed and began to feed Ma. 'He'll come as soon as he can. He does have a job and can't leave when he likes.'

Ma seemed to accept that and chewed thoughtfully on a fluffy dumpling. I do wish you could talk, Jenny thought, as she put the empty bowl back on the tray. She'd dearly love to know what this sudden urge was to see Matthew. And why the hurry?

She was pondering this question, wiping Ma's mouth with a cloth, when there came the sound of someone running up the stairs.

Matthew appeared, all smiles. 'Hello, Jen, hello, Ma, how are you today?'

She waved her right hand for him to come closer, giving a crooked grin of pleasure.

He bent over and kissed her on top of her head, then turned to Jenny, who was watching the scene in bemusement. Anyone would think these two had known each other for years. When he also kissed her cheek, she was sure she heard Ma laugh.

'Now, Ma, I received your message.' He turned his full attention to the woman in the bed, and sat on the edge. 'What can I do for you?'

The word 'tea' was scribbled down and held up for Jenny to see. She was then told to go away with a wave at the door.

Picking up the tray, Jenny went downstairs and washed up before making the tea. Ma clearly wanted to see Matthew on his own, but it was a puzzle why she was acting like this with someone she hardly knew.

Feeling she'd given them quite enough time, Jenny made a pot of tea, sorted out a few biscuits and put three cups on the tray. This she took up to the bedroom.

Ma was settled back on the pillows, eyes closed

and holding Matthew's hand. Jenny put the tray down with a crash on the small bedside table. 'You've tired her out!'

Ma's eyes shot open and she shook her head slightly.

'I don't think so.' Matthew slipped a sheet of paper into his pocket. 'Ah, tea. We're both gasping, aren't we, Ma?'

He proceeded to pour them all a cup, popping a piece of biscuit in his mouth as he did so.

'Have you had any lunch yet?' Jenny guessed he was on his break.

'Haven't had time. I'll grab something on my way back.'

'I can make you some toast.' Jenny was on her feet, but he put out a hand to stop her.

'I'm all right.' He handed her a cup. 'Sit down for a while.'

She did, feeling tired, which was normal since Ma had had her stroke. It wasn't the extra work she minded – nothing was too much trouble if it made Ma comfortable. No, it was the constant worry and sadness she felt knowing that she could lose the woman she had come to love dearly. Ma was her family now.

'They've made a wonderful job of the centre, haven't they?' Jenny said, still delighted with what she had seen.

Matt nodded, taking a mouthful of tea. 'Mother believes it's going to be a boon to those with young children, as well as providing a hot meal for the unemployed.'

Jenny dunked a biscuit in the tea for Ma and, after she'd eaten it, held the cup to her mouth so

301

that she could drink. 'I must go there when it opens and see how they cope.'

'You do that, Jen. I'm sure there would be a part-time job for you.'

'Not until Ma's better.' Jenny wiped Ma's mouth with a cloth and sat down to drink her own tea, watching as the elderly woman drifted into a peaceful sleep. She seemed to spend most of her time asleep, but at least when she was awake now she was more alert.

'I think you ought to know, Jen, that Greaves is in financial trouble.' Matt finished his tea and put the cup back on the tray. 'Our garage bought a Rolls-Royce from him. I believe it used to be your father's.'

'Really? I suppose mother sold it to him.' Jenny sat up straight and began to laugh quietly. 'Aunt Gertrude told me he was rich and I would be wearing the finest jewels.'

'Well, either she didn't know or they were both telling lies.' Matthew raised an eyebrow at her obvious amusement. 'You don't seem bothered about it.'

'I'm not. Don't you see, this is the best news I could have had? I'm much too poor for him to bother with now, and I'm free of them at last. I'm so glad I ran away.'

'It looks as if you certainly did the right thing.' Matthew stood up and said, 'I must be getting back to the garage now.'

'Thank you for coming.' Jenny picked up the tray, only to have it taken out of her hands by Matthew. She followed him downstairs. 'Ma does like to see you.'

He put the tray on the kitchen table and paused, watching her put the dishes in the sink. 'And are you pleased to see me, Jen?'

She was startled by the softly spoken question. 'Of course I am.'

'Good. I did wonder, after the way you ticked me off last time.'

Now she felt awful. 'I'm sorry about that. The chicken was lovely, thank you.'

A mischievous gleam shone in his eyes as he tried to control a grin from spreading across his face. 'I accept your apology.' Then he turned on his heel and left.

You're a difficult man to understand, she thought. What was so amusing about my apology?

When she opened the larder, she understood. Sitting on the marble cold slab was a joint of beef and an array of other food items. He must have brought them with him and packed them away before coming upstairs. She groaned in frustration. You squeezed an apology out of me, knowing all the time I was going to find this! Well, I take it back. You are not responsible for me, but how on earth do I make you see that?

The next day the beef was cooked. After she'd cut off enough for her and Ma, Jenny sliced the rest thinly and made a pile of beef sandwiches. These were shared amongst Fred and Glad's family, with a couple left over for Jimmy and his mother. She felt better about giving so many a treat from the gift, but she really was going to have to have a serious word with Matthew. The feeling persisted that he was doing this only because he felt sorry for her, and it rankled. It wasn't that she didn't appreciate his kindness, but she would prefer him not to do it. She was going to end up beholden to him, and she didn't want that.

Jenny frowned, feeling she was stupid to let it worry her so much. But it did.

27

Over the next week there wasn't a sign of Matthew and Jenny couldn't decide whether she was pleased or sorry. He was probably keeping out of her way in case she told him off again. Which she had every intention of doing.

Ma was continuing to improve and was even attempting a word now and again. It was hard to understand, but at least she was trying to talk.

'Why don't you pop along and see the centre now it's open?' Glad said, as she came into the kitchen. 'I'll keep an eye on Ma for an hour.'

'I'd love to, thanks, Glad.'

'Off you go. A short break will do you good.'

Jenny grabbed her coat and hurried up the road. It was the beginning of December now and there was a cutting north wind blowing. This winter was going to be hard for so many people. But this area now had the centre, and she was longing to see it. She'd been told that people were coming from all over the borough, and there were long queues every day.

The front door wasn't open yet, so Jenny went to the side entrance. There were already people gathering, hunched up and trying to shelter in the porch from the wind.

'Ask them to open the door, luv,' one man called. 'It's bloody taters out here.'

Jenny knew enough rhyming slang now to know that meant cold. She waved. 'I'll see what I can do.'

'Jenny!' Mrs Stannard greeted her with obvious pleasure. 'How lovely to see you.'

'I'm sorry I haven't been before, but I don't like to leave Ma alone.'

'Of course you don't. I quite understand. You go and have a look round. We've put a few finishing touches to it since you were last here.'

'How long before you open?' she asked. 'Only there are people waiting and there's a bitter wind blowing.'

'We're almost ready to serve the food, and then they can stay all afternoon if they like.'

'That will be a blessing for them.' Jenny started to explore and was more than thrilled. The kitchen was bustling with activity, and there was a wonderful aroma of cooking wafting through the dining hall. Someone had even put bits of greenery in jam jars for the centre of each table. Jenny smiled, immediately guessing that that was Jimmy's handiwork. He must have pinched them from a park, because there wasn't much in the way of plants in their back-to-back houses. She gasped in pleasure when she walked into the next room. There was a lovely fire burning in the grate, and chairs set around it. On a small table were newspapers to read, something the men would really enjoy. This place had been almost derelict. What an achievement! The doors were due to open in fifteen minutes, and then those poor frozen people could have a hot meal and linger by the fire to talk or just sleep. One small room was full of second-hand clothes for those who needed warm clothing.

'This is lovely.' Jenny walked back into the dining hall and smiled her pleasure.

'Yes, it is.' Louise gazed around with satisfaction. 'We really feel as if we are doing something to help those who are finding it difficult to feed their families. Can you stay for a while, my dear? We are about to serve lunch.'

'I'm sorry, Mrs Stannard, I must get back to Ma. She'll be wanting her dinner, and Glad can only stay for an hour.'

'Would you like to take some food back with you for Ma and yourself?'

'No, thank you, we're all right for today.' With a wave to Ron and Jimmy and all the other helpers, Jenny went to the side exit as the people began to pour in through the front door. She turned back to Mrs Stannard. 'My goodness, can you feed all these?'

'We never turn anyone away. Fortunately we are getting funding from the council, and also generous donations from people we know.'

The tone of devilment in Mrs Stannard's voice reminded her of Matthew. She grinned. 'You mean you're putting pressure on them?'

'Of course, my dear. They can afford it.' She gave a quiet laugh.

Jenny headed for home, chuckling to herself. She crossed the road and was almost in her street when she became aware of men walking on each side of her, and much too closely. They were burly, rough-looking men, and she felt uncomfortable. She stopped. 'Can I help you?'

One gave a harsh laugh as they both grabbed hold of her arms, lifting her off her feet. Thoroughly alarmed now, Jenny lashed out with her feet, kicking wildly to make them put her down so she could get away. 'Let me go!' she shouted.

'You're coming with us,' one of them growled, his voice deep and menacing.

With her feet still not touching the ground, she kicked for all she was worth, catching one of them a good crack on the shin. He grunted and used his free hand to give her a hard slap across the face. Her struggles became frantic now, and she bellowed at the top of her voice. 'Help me! Help!' But the street was quite empty, as most people were at the centre.

'Shut up or we'll hurt you bad. That bloke don't care what state you're in, just so long as he gets you.'

It was the same man who spoke; the other one remained silent and seemed to be enjoying himself. Jenny was terrified and intent on doing as much damage as she could. When they released their grip on her slightly and her feet touched the ground, she managed to pull them for a few yards back to the top of Forest Road, where she felt sure someone would help her. There must be someone around. She was just about to shout again when a car screeched to a halt beside them and Matthew leapt out. He began to throw punches at the two men, but two to one were not good odds, and he was soon receiving the worst of the punishment.

The man who had spoken still held her arm in a cruel grip and was hitting out at Matthew with his other hand. The silent man now had a knife in his hand, and an evil look on his face.

'No!' Jenny screamed. 'Run, Matthew, run!'

What happened next was a blur to her. The man was stabbing at Matthew, people were running up the street, there was shouting and screaming – or was that her? The grip on her arm was suddenly relaxed, and she fell to the pavement with a bruising crash. She dragged herself away from them and stood up, using the wall of a house for support, sobbing in terror.

'Get the coppers, Jimmy,' someone shouted. 'We've got them now.'

Apart from some cursing, the fight was over.

'Are you all right, Jen?'

Still feeling disorientated and stunned, Jenny gazed up at Stan and nodded. It was only then she took in the scene. The two men were pushed against the wall, hands tied behind their backs with belts and surrounded by her friends and neighbours. And Matt? Oh, dear God! He was being supported by Fred, blood spreading in a dark stain down his sleeve and across his chest. He was a terrible grey colour.

'Oh, you shouldn't have tried to rescue me on your own.' She stumbled over to him, but he didn't seem to know what was going on. 'Please get him to a hospital!'

'We'll take him to St Thomas's.' Stan got in the front of Matt's car and Fred in the back with the badly injured man.

Jenny tried to get in the car as well, but Fred shook his head. 'No, Jen, you stay here. The coppers might want to talk to you.'

Glad appeared and put her arm around Jenny. 'Ma's asking for you. She's heard the commotion.'

Jenny was torn between Ma and Matthew. Who should she be with? Both, but that wasn't possible. She turned in circles, agitated because she didn't know what to do. The decision was made for her as Stan drove away.

She watched them disappear up the street, relieved that they had been around to help Matthew. 'Why aren't Fred and Stan at the market?' she asked Glad.

'Business was slow this morning, so they popped home for a bite to eat. And a good job they did.' Glad put her arm around Jenny, who was now shaking.

Jimmy arrived back, gasping for breath after running. 'The coppers are on their way, and I've told Mrs Stannard.'

Before the police arrived, Jenny wanted some answers. She walked over and faced her attackers, anger out of control. The two men had taken a beating, she saw, and that was no more than they deserved. They had stabbed Matt. He might die. There wasn't an ounce of compassion in her for these villains. 'What did you want with me?' When they didn't answer she raised her fist

309

and the man who had spoken flinched. The last thing he obviously wanted was another punch in the face. His lip was cut, one eye was closed, and it looked as if his nose was broken. Even a woman could add to his pain now. 'Tell me!'

'A bloke called Greaves gave us twenty quid to take you to him.'

Greaves? Her hand dropped to her side in surprise. 'What on earth for?'

'Dunno.'

A car pulled up with Luke driving and Mrs Stannard sitting beside him, deathly pale. 'Where have they taken Matt?' she asked, her voice trembling.

'St Thomas's.' Ron leant on the window and explained briefly, then stepped back as the car sped off.

'Jen.' Glad touched her arm. 'Come on, Ma's worried.'

'You go,' Ron said. 'The coppers are just arriving and we'll deal with this lot.'

'Thanks.' Jenny began to run home, anxious to let Ma see she was all right.

Ma held out her hand as soon as she entered the bedroom. 'Tell me,' she croaked.

She knelt by the bed and cradled Ma's hand in her own, explaining what had happened. By the time she'd told her about Matthew being stabbed, the tears were flowing down Ma's cheeks. 'You go see. Now!'

Ivy came up the stairs at that moment. 'I'll stay with Ma, Jen. Go to the hospital.'

Without a moment's hesitation Jenny was off and running for the bus stop. She was lucky as one was just arriving. It would have been agony if she'd had to wait.

Arriving at St Thomas's, she rushed to Accident and Emergency, guessing that was where they would have taken him first. The sight that met her brought her flying feet to a sudden halt, and she whimpered in panic. Mr and Mrs Stannard, Luke and John were all there, grim-faced with anxiety. The three men were standing, shoulders drooping. Mrs Stannard was sitting, head bowed, obviously trying to hold back the tears.

Jenny forced herself to move and fell to her knees in front of Mrs Stannard, quite expecting to be told to get out of their sight. But she had to know. 'I'm so sorry,' she gasped. 'How is he?'

'He's lost a lot of blood and they're working on him now.' John made her stand up and then sat her beside his mother.

She brought Mrs Stannard's cold hand to her cheek and held it there, desperate to give some kind of comfort if she could. 'You must regret the day I came into your life. I'm so sorry, so sorry.' How inadequate that sounded, but she couldn't think of anything else to say. If they lost their fine son because of her, they would never forgive her.

'None of this is your fault,' Mr Stannard said gruffly. John and his father appeared to be the only ones capable of speech. Luke and his mother were lost in silent misery.

'Will you tell us what happened?' John stood in front of her, but spoke gently and didn't appear to be angry with her.

Jenny explained as much as she could remember, but she faltered when she got to the part she still viewed with horror. 'When Matthew tried to rescue me, I told him to run. I did! Those men were really nasty. I saw one of them pull a knife out of his pocket and I was frantic. I fought as hard as I could, but...' She shook her head in despair. 'He shouldn't have risked his life for me. I yelled at him to run. He should have run!'

'Matt wouldn't have left you at the mercy of those thugs.' Mrs Stannard spoke for the first time. 'You mustn't blame yourself. We've brought up the boys to oppose wrongdoing of any kind.'

Jenny gazed at each face in turn and saw only kindness towards her. They should hate her.

'Do you know why those men attacked you?' Luke had now found his voice.

'One of them told me that Greaves had paid them to catch me.'

'Greaves again!' John was obviously furious. 'What is that bloody man playing at?'

'I don't know but I'm certainly going to find out!' Jenny was on her feet now with fists clenched. 'As soon as we know how Matthew is, I'm going round there.'

'You mustn't do that!' John and Luke spoke together.

'The boys are right,' Mrs Stannard said sternly. 'For some strange reason Greaves will do anything to get hold of you. If you go to his house, you might not leave it again.'

That was sensible, of course, but she wanted answers from that obnoxious man. For some in-

explicable reason, Greaves was going to dangerous lengths to catch her. The question 'why?'
thundered through her mind. 'I can get a couple
of the men from my street to come with me.' Her
gaze was pleading. 'They're tough and used to
trouble, and they won't let anything happen to
me.'

Mr Stannard sighed, shaking his head. 'You
mustn't go anywhere near him.'

A doctor strode towards them and everyone
leapt to their feet.

'I'm Dr Sterling, Mr and Mrs Stannard. We've
managed to stop the bleeding and no vital organs
were damaged, but your son is very weak. We've
had him transferred to a private room, where
he'll have round the clock nursing.'

'Is he going to be all right?' Matthew's father
asked gruffly.

The doctor smiled. 'With plenty of rest he will
make a full recovery.'

The sighs of relief all round were audible, and
Jenny felt tears gather in her eyes. She sent a
silent prayer of gratitude upwards.

'We'd like to see him.' Mr Stannard looked as if
a weight had been lifted from him as he
straightened up.

'Of course.' The doctor cast Jenny a glance.
'Family only, of course.'

The disappointment was crushing, because
Jenny knew that unless she could actually see
Matthew it would be hard to believe he was going
to be all right. There had been so much blood...
Of course she knew why the doctor had given her
such a strange look. This scruffy dishevelled girl

could not be one of the family. She bowed her head mournfully and stepped back. The doctor had said he was going to recover, and she would just have to cling to that.

Then Mr Stannard took her completely by surprise by saying, 'This is the young lady my son was trying to save. I think it would make him rest easier if he could see she was unharmed.'

'Very well. Please come with me.' Dr Sterling led the way. 'He has been taken to a room on the next floor.'

Jenny hesitated, still uncertain what she should do. The doctor had clearly agreed with reluctance to let her see Matthew.

'Come on, my dear.' Mrs Stannard took hold of her arm, and they all made their way up the stairs.

Matthew was obviously exhausted after his ordeal and having great difficulty keeping his eyes open, but he did manage a brief smile that quickly turned into a grimace.

'Don't worry,' he assured his family. 'There's no great harm done.'

'The doctor told us.' Louise kissed her son on the forehead. 'We won't stay long. We just wanted to see you for a moment, then we'll let you sleep.'

Jenny hung back by the door while the rest of his family greeted him. He was still terribly pale, but a slightly better colour than immediately after the attack. Her relief was overwhelming. He would be taken good care of here. She started to leave the room.

'Jen?'

At the sound of Matthew's voice she stepped towards the bed, her whole body trembling with emotion.

'Are you unhurt?'

'Yes,' she whispered, 'thanks to you. I'm so sorry...'

'That's all she keeps saying,' Luke teased, appearing to be back to something like normal now that he knew his brother was going to survive.

'You don't need to apologize,' Matthew said firmly. 'Tell Ma I'll be along to see her as soon as I'm on my feet again.'

The doctor checked his patient. 'You must all leave now. Come back tomorrow when he's more rested.'

After taking their leave, they filed out of the room. Jenny glanced back and saw that Matthew was already fast asleep.

'I'll drive you back,' John said, when they were outside the hospital.

'I can catch a bus.' Now that Jenny had seen Matthew, the anger was building inside her against Greaves. How dare he send thugs after her armed with a knife!

John's eyes narrowed. 'I'll take you home because I want to be certain that you don't charge off to confront Greaves on your own.'

How had he guessed that's just what she was planning to do? He held her arm, and she allowed him to lead her to the car without further protest. This eldest brother was not someone you argued with. His strength of character and determined nature were clear to see. Each son was different in character, but all were fine men. Their

315

parents must be so proud of all three.'

'I'll come with you.' Luke held open the passenger door of the car. 'Dad can take Mum home in my car.'

After saying goodbye to Mr and Mrs Stannard, Jenny was made to sit in the front, with Luke in the back.

As they drove away from the hospital, John said, 'Have you any idea why Greaves wants you so badly?'

'None at all.' She was completely bewildered by what was happening. It just didn't make sense after two years. Surely he couldn't still want to marry her?

Luke leant forward until he was looking through the two front seats. 'You'll have to do some more digging, John.'

'I intend to,' was the curt reply, 'but it might just turn out that having set his mind on Jenny, he's not prepared to give up.'

'I must admit that it does seem the only logical answer.' Luke rested his hands on the back of John's seat. 'But sending murderous villains after her is rather desperate, isn't it?'

The conversation came to an end as they pulled up outside Ma's house. The street was immediately alive with people wanting to know how Matthew was. There were smiles all round when told that he would make a full recovery.

Fred hugged Jenny. 'And what about you, dear, are you all right?'

'I'm fine, but I'm so angry...'

Luke gave his easy laugh. 'Jenny's fuming and wants to go to tell Greaves just what she thinks of

316

him, but she mustn't do that. It's far too dangerous.'

'I'd like to give that devil the thrashing he deserves,' Ron growled. 'It was bloody lucky no one was killed today.'

'I understand how you feel' – John gave a grim smile – 'but I should hold off on that, if I were you. While we were waiting for Matt to be patched up, the police arrived. If it can be proved that Greaves is behind this attack, the law will deal with him.'

'And if they don't, then we'll give him something to think about!' Jimmy looked around for approval and smiled when Fred, Stan and Ron nodded.

Jenny was alarmed; her friends could end up in serious trouble. 'I don't want this turning into another fight and you all ending up in prison. I've caused enough trouble for everyone.'

'Let the police handle this,' John admonished.

'We will.' Fred shook hands with John and Luke. 'We're right glad to know Matt's going to be all right. Nice lad. Thanks for bringing our Jen back home. We'll look after her, don't you worry.'

With that assurance, the brothers got back in the car and drove off.

'Go and see Ma, Jen,' Fred said. 'She's fretting bad.'

Jenny ran up the stairs and found Glad sitting beside the bed, holding Ma's hand. She stood up to make room for Jenny.

'Matthew is going to be just fine.' Jenny was alarmed at how ill Ma looked.

Grabbing hold of Jenny's hand, she croaked,

'Tell me.'

'He's weak, but the doctor said that with lots of rest he'll make a complete recovery.'

After giving a ragged sigh, Ma slumped back on the pillows and closed her eyes, still holding Jenny's hand. Soon the grip relaxed as she fell into a weary sleep.

Anger boiled up again in Jenny. This had clearly been a setback for Ma. At that moment she hated Greaves and her family for all the anguish they were causing; she was sure that her Aunt Gertrude and her mother were also involved. How could he act without their permission?

She bowed her head, exhausted beyond belief. Her problems had all started with the Wall Street crash just over two years ago. The place her father had talked about with such pride had reached out and disrupted not only her life but also the lives of millions. And now violence was touching those she cared about. And she *did* care about Matthew very deeply, she admitted. That had been clear from the moment she had seen the man attacking him with a knife. If he had died trying to rescue her, she would never have been able to forgive herself. His life was very precious to her.

Ivy came into the room and put her hand on Jenny's shoulder. 'Mum's gone back home, so I'll take over while you get some sleep, Jen.'

'Oh, I don't know.' She cast an anxious look at Ma.

'I'll call you if there's any change.'

Jenny stood up, swaying with reaction and fatigue.

'If she wakes and wants me–'

'I'll let you know.' Ivy gave her a gentle push.

'Promise?'

'I promise.'

28

'Good, you're awake,' said Dr Sterling, bending over the bed.

Matthew dragged his eyes open and pain shot through him when he tried to move, so he abandoned that idea.

'You're going to be sore for a few days.' The doctor smiled benevolently. 'But by the end of the week you'll be up and about again. Fortunately the knife didn't cut anything vital.'

Amen to that, Matthew thought, pulling a face. 'I'll have to take your word for that. I hurt all over.'

'Let's see if we can make you more comfortable.' He pulled back the sheets, and a nurse came to assist with a tray of instruments and dressings. 'The police want to talk to you, but I told them to come back this afternoon.' He was silent while he examined the wounds after the nurse had removed the dressings.

Matt clenched his teeth to stifle a groan. God, but that hurt!

'The wounds are looking fine. Nurse will put fresh dressings on, give you a shave and then you'll feel better.'

'How many times did that ba–' Matt remembered just in time that there was a woman present and moderated his language. 'How many times was I stabbed?'

'Three, but you're a healthy young man and should heal quickly.'

'I'm glad to hear it,' Matt said, relieved when they had both finished their probing.

He did feel much better after they had finished, and being allowed to sit propped up was a relief.

'Your family are waiting to see you. I'll send them in.' The doctor strode out of the room.

The door opened again almost immediately, and he was astonished to see not only his parents but also John and Luke. 'Good heavens, who's looking after the bank?' he joked.

'It can function without us for a couple of hours.' John pulled up enough chairs for them to sit down.

'You gave us all a scare yesterday,' his father said.

'I gave myself a scare. I never expected one of them to come at me with a knife.'

'The doctor says you're going to be fine.' His mother smiled affectionately at him, but the worry was still visible in her eyes.

'I'll be up in no time,' he assured her. 'How's Jen?'

'She's all right.' Luke gave a disbelieving shake of his head. 'John and I took her home because she was ready to go to give Greaves a piece of her mind.'

Matt moved in alarm and felt perspiration

break out on his forehead as the pain ripped through him.

Luke held up his hand. 'We talked her out of it and warned her friends. They agreed with us that she mustn't go anywhere near him.'

'Thank God for that!' Matt sighed in relief. 'They're a rough crowd she's living with, but they do love her and I'm sure they won't let her do anything silly.'

'They're not the only ones who love her, are they?' Luke pretended to straighten Matt's pillows and spoke softly so that only his brother could hear. He winked knowingly and sat back again.

Ignoring the remark, Matt turned to his father. 'The police are coming to see me this afternoon, but do you have any idea what those men wanted with Jen?'

'It was obvious they were trying to abduct her, and evidently one of the men said that Greaves had paid them to take her to him.' His father frowned, puzzled.

'What the bloody hell is that man up to? Sorry, Mother.'

'I'm just relieved to see you lively enough to cuss.' The worry began to fade from her face.

'I know you've always been against our inter-fering in Jenny's life, Mother, but we have been drawn right into it now. We must find out why Greaves is so obsessed that he will condone attempted murder, for that is what the attack on me was. That man wasn't playing; he intended to kill, and I think we should try to find out if that's what he intended for Jen. If he wants her dead for some bizarre reason, then we'd better find out quickly.'

'We came to the same conclusion last night,' John told him. 'We feel the answer is in America, so I've already sent a message to Henry Eddison in Manhattan, explaining that we've found Eugenie Winford, and asking if he has any further information about the father.'

Matt suddenly felt drained. His family were dealing with everything, so he must try to relax. It was obvious that Jen was in danger, and he wanted to get back on his feet as soon as possible.

'We'll leave you to rest, son.' His father stood up. 'If we find out anything of importance, you will be told at once.'

'Thanks.' Matt managed to rouse himself enough to say goodbye. When he was alone again, his mind began to whirl. Was that monster Greaves trying to kill Jen because she had rejected him? It was impossible to believe that he would go to such violent lengths. Only someone who wasn't right in the head would do that.

He drifted off into a troubled sleep.

Hearing a sharp knock on the front door, Jenny went to answer it and found two policemen on the step, their bikes propped up against the house.

'Miss Baker?'

She nodded.

'We'd like to take your statement about the attack on you yesterday. I'm Sergeant Pegg and this is Constable Wilkins.'

'You'd better come in.' They were both big men and seemed to fill the small front room. 'Please sit down. Would you like a cup of tea?'

'No, thanks, miss.' The sergeant took a note-book and pencil out of his pocket. 'We'd like you to tell us exactly what happened.'

She told them all she could remember, though her recollection of some of it was rather hazy. But the terror was still vivid in her mind and she was shaking by the time she had finished. 'What about Greaves? He should be punished as well.'

'Ah, well, we was told by other witnesses that you said he was involved, but we do have a problem with that.' The sergeant licked the end of his pencil, then wrote a few more words. 'We've been to see the gentleman and he denies having anything to do with it.'

Jenny snorted in disgust. 'He would, but one of the men told me they'd been paid by Greaves to attack me.'

'They've changed their tune now,' the constable said. 'Did anyone else hear that?'

She tried to picture the scene. Who was standing near her? 'I really don't know. The man's mouth was cut and he wasn't speaking clearly, but he *did* say it. I'm certain.'

'We'll have another word with everyone, of course.' The sergeant licked his pencil again. 'But without proof, we can't charge Mr Greaves with anything.'

'But that's scandalous!' Jenny was appalled.

'That's the law, miss.' The notebook and pencil were tucked back in the sergeant's top pocket. 'But we can put those two ruffians away for a long stretch. Attempted murder of Mr Stannard and the attack on you.'

'That's something, I suppose.' It made her angry to know that Greaves was probably going to get away with this.

The policemen stood up and the young constable gave her a sympathetic smile. 'It ain't right, miss, but it would only be your word against his.'

'I know,' she sighed, 'and he would be believed, not me. Will I have to go to court when these men are tried?'

'Unlikely. The prisoners have admitted trying to harm you and attacking Mr Stannard.' The sergeant gave a wry shake of his head. 'They couldn't hardly do nothing else with half of this street as witnesses, and every one of them eager to talk. Makes a change. Usually we can't get people to open their mouth around here, but we've more witnesses than we can handle.'

As the men went outside again, the constable looked back at Jenny. 'We're going to see Mr Stannard now, but if we do turn up anything we can use against Greaves, we'll let you know.'

Jenny watched them ride off, then closed the door. It was time to get Ma her dinner, and then she'd try to snatch an hour to go to see Matthew.

The sausages sizzled and spat in the pan, and she kept turning them until they were golden brown all over. She then put two on a plate with a large spoonful of fluffy mashed potato; a dribble of gravy was poured over the meal. This was Ma's favourite, and Jenny knew she would be waiting impatiently as the tantalizing smell wafted up to her bedroom.

She was surprised to see Ma asleep. She smiled affectionately. How peaceful she looked; it was a

324

shame to wake her, but the dinner would get cold. She would be in for an even bigger telling-off if she allowed that to happen.

Placing the tray beside the bed, Jenny leant over and gave Ma a gentle shake. Nothing happened, so she shook her a little harder this time. Still no response!

Her heart began to thud in her chest. Ma didn't look right. 'Ma, wake up!' Plucking Ma's hand off the blanket, she held it to her cheek. It was still warm. Was she breathing? It looked as if there was a slight movement. She placed her hand on Ma's chest and watched carefully, but panic was taking hold. There didn't seem to be any sign of breathing now.

'Ma!' she shouted. After a couple of seconds she turned and fled down the stairs, out the front door and into Glad's place.

Glad was on her own and jumped to her feet as soon as Jenny crashed into the room. 'Whatever is it, Jen?'

'Ma,' she gasped. It felt as if all the air had been drained out of her lungs.

Without asking questions, Glad rushed next door, with Jenny right on her heels.

'I can't wake her!' Jenny watched Glad bend over the motionless form of the elderly woman, searching for signs of life.

'I'll get the doctor!'

Glad caught her arm as she was set to run off. 'There's no rush, Jen. She's gone, I'm afraid.'

'But she was breathing. I'm sure she was breathing,' she cried in anguish. 'I cooked her favourite dinner. Are you sure?'

'I've seen enough death to know.' Glad guided Jenny back downstairs. 'You make a nice pot of Rosie Lee. I'll lay Ma out and take care of the necessary.'

Jenny was dry-eyed with shock as she set about making the tea. Ma had been doing so well. At least she had until Greaves had set those two murderous villains on her, and Matthew had been stabbed. And the police didn't think they could touch him. He ought to hang! Suddenly she cried out in fury. The worry and shock had just killed Ma...

The tears began to flow. She had planned to see Matthew this afternoon, but she couldn't do that now. They had liked each other, and she couldn't tell Matthew about Ma's passing until he was stronger. Ma's death had to be reported, and all sorts of things done. She couldn't leave everything to Glad.

The next few days passed in a blur of pain and loss for Jenny, and she was grateful to have Fred and Glad with her. The funeral was only two days away, and she knew it was going to be a distressing time. But at least she would be able to say a proper goodbye to Ma, something she had not been able to do with her father. She would use this service as an opportunity to put that right. In her mind it would be a dual burial for the two people she had loved so much: Ma and her father. The shock of learning that he'd had another family in America had soon gone. He had been such a kind man, and she hoped he had been happy with them.

It was raining again. Matt stared out of the hospital window and brooded. He was going home today and should be elated. His recovery had been excellent, and in another week he would be back at work, getting his hands greasy again.

The door opened, and his mother and Luke walked in, smiling brightly.

'All ready?' Luke picked up his brother's bag, stopping suddenly when he saw Matt scowl. 'What's the matter? Are they keeping you in after all?'

'Why hasn't Jenny been to see me or sent a message? Is she all right?'

'Ah.' Luke put the bag down again and glanced at his mother.

'What does that mean?' Matt glared at Luke. 'What's happened to her?'

'She's all right, Matt.' Louise made her son sit on the bed. 'But Ma died the day after you were injured, and Jenny didn't want to upset you.'

'Oh, dear God!' Matt now understood. 'She'll be devastated.'

'She is, my dear. She loved the elderly woman very much.' She smiled encouragingly at her youngest son. 'Now, I expect you'll be glad to get out of this place.'

'I certainly shall.' Matt stood up. His heart ached for Jenny. This was another terrible blow for her. 'When's the funeral?'

'Today at ten thirty at a church in Short Street, near The Cut.'

Matt glanced at his watch. 'If we hurry we can just make it.'

'Oh, but Matt,' his mother protested, 'Jenny wouldn't expect you to go, and I'm not sure you're strong enough–'

'I'm fine,' he said, stopping her. 'I liked Ma and I'm going to her funeral!'

'We'd better get a move on, then.' Luke had obviously picked up the note of determination in his brother's voice. 'It's a good thing we brought raincoats and an umbrella.'

After saying goodbye to the staff who had nursed him so carefully, they got in the car and Luke headed for the church without delay.

The service was under way by the time they arrived. Matt, Luke and their mother slipped into the back pew. The church was crowded, but Matt could just see Jenny in the front row, head bowed. He wanted to rush over to comfort her, to tell her that Ma had asked him to watch over her, and that he had every intention of keeping that promise.

Fortunately it stopped raining by the time they gathered around the graveside. It was while they were standing there that Matt became aware of how weak he still was. He swayed slightly and Luke caught hold of his arm, holding him up. Taking several deep breaths, he glanced quickly at his mother, but she didn't seem to have noticed. He planted his feet slightly apart to steady himself; he was determined to see it through to the end of the service.

Finally it was over, and, as the coffin was lowered, he gave a silent assurance to Ma that he would do as she had wanted; it was also what he wanted.

'Matthew.' Jenny was beside him, her eyes swollen from crying. 'Thank you all for coming.' She gave them a tremulous smile. 'Ma would have been pleased.'

Matt bent and kissed her cheek. 'I'm so sorry, Jen, but you should have told me.'

'You had enough to deal with without more bad news. When did you get out of hospital?'

'An hour ago,' Luke said. 'He thinks he's stronger than he is.'

'Oh, you must take him home at once, Mrs Stannard.' Jenny looked anxious. 'You shouldn't have come.'

'I wouldn't have missed the chance to say good-bye to Ma. What are you going to do now?' Matt was hoping to persuade her to live with them until she sorted her life out, but he knew this wasn't the time to say that.

'I haven't given it much thought but I'll stay at Ma's house for a week or two. After that...' She gave a helpless shrug.

'I'll come to see you as soon as I can.' Matt watched her expression, expecting a refusal, but she merely nodded.

There wasn't a chance to say anything else as Fred, Glad and the rest of the family came up to ask how he was. It was another ten minutes before he was back in the car and heading for home.

29

Friends and neighbours crowded into the small house, each bringing some item of food or drink so they could hold a proper wake for Ma. The day before, Jenny had made two cakes and had cried when they'd both risen beautifully, remembering her first effort that had collapsed in the middle. It was such a bitter-sweet memory.

'That was good of Matt and his family to come.' Glad was filling half-pint glasses with beer. 'Ma would have liked that.'

Jenny stopped slicing the cake and put the knife down. 'Do you believe there's anything after this life, Glad?'

'I don't rightly know, but Ma was sure there was. She always said she'd be with her old man and Bessie again one day.'

'Oh, I do hope she's right.' Jenny wiped the moisture from her eyes. 'I would like to think I'll meet Ma and my father again. My dad was such a gentle man, and I did love him so.'

'I don't see it does no harm to believe life goes on, especially if it gives folks comfort.'

'You're right, Glad. I expect it gave Ma comfort to believe she would see her little girl again.'

'I think it did.' Glad picked up the tray and winked at Jenny. 'If it is true, then she'll be waiting for you, asking where the hell you think you've been.'

Jenny laughed for the first time in a week.

An hour later everyone had gone except Fred and Glad.

'Now, Jen' – Fred leant on the mantelpiece, looking all businesslike – 'have you decided what you're going to do?'

This was something she had been avoiding, but it was now a decision she would have to make. The thought of moving on again was enough to make her heart sink. 'I suppose I'll have to find somewhere else to live.'

'I think you ought to take over the rent of this place and stay here.'

Jenny gave Fred a startled look. 'I wish I could, but how would I pay the rent? I couldn't possibly afford to furnish a place of my own.'

'I'm sure you could get a job at the centre, even if it's only part time, and you could always get something to eat there.' Glad smiled encouragingly. 'It's worth a try.'

How she wished she could stay in the house she had been so happy in with Ma...

'It's what Ma wanted you to do.' Fred took a sheet of paper out of his pocket. 'This is properly signed and Ma wrote it while she was in her right mind. She leaves the entire contents of this house to you, Jen. Ma's even put your real name – Eugenie Winford – so there's no mistaking who she means.'

'This is all mine?' Jenny's mouth dropped open in astonishment. 'But why me? There must be someone else it should go to, surely? She must have relatives somewhere.'

'She ain't got no one else, and she loved you, Jen,' Glad said. 'She wanted you to have a home after she'd gone. It ain't much, but if you can manage the rent, it'll be a place of your own and you won't have to move on again.'

Jenny clasped her hands together tightly in relief, as it dawned on her that she needn't move, providing she could find the rent each week. A place she could call home! Gratitude welled up inside her at Ma's thoughtfulness. The idea that she could be homeless again had been scary. Now she wouldn't have to face that ordeal. 'I'll get the rent somehow and stay here, just like Ma wanted.'

The night had been surprisingly restful for Jenny. She had slept only in snatches since the attack and Ma's death, but seeing Matt at the funeral, and knowing that he cared enough to come straight from the hospital, had made her spirits soar. He had looked so tall, and, although still rather drawn, she could see he would soon be back to full health again. The relief had been immense, and when he'd smiled at her it had seemed as if a bond had been formed between them because of their shared experience.

She swung her legs out of bed and stood up, shivering in the cold early morning. Getting up at five had become a habit, one she couldn't seem to break. Slipping her coat over the winceyette night-dress, she began to wander around the house, still hardly able to believe that this was now hers. By leaving her few possessions to Jenny, Ma had made it clear that she wanted her to have a place of her own amongst the people who had taken a frightened, homeless girl to their hearts.

Standing in the middle of the front room, she gazed around. When she had moved in with Ma more than a year ago, she'd had no idea how much they were going to love each other. How she missed her – but she knew that Ma's illness had frustrated her and made her miserable. Her suffering was over now, and perhaps she was with her husband and daughter once again.

With a sad smile she ran her hand over the back of Ma's favourite chair as she passed it on the way to the kitchen.

First she lit the old black leaded fire, and then put the kettle on to make a pot of tea. Once that was done she sat at the kitchen table. There were plans to make. Through Ma's generosity she had the chance to make a life for herself here, and that was just what she intended to do!

A job was essential – not an easy task in these days of horrendous unemployment – but she was determined to find some way of earning money. She was sure Mrs Stannard would find her a job at the centre, but she didn't want to do that if it could be avoided. She had caused that family enough trouble, and she would feel awful begging them for work. No, she must find something without their help, and she would start the search today. This might be the time to sell the pendant and that, hopefully, would give her a few weeks' rent, and a breathing space to find work. Ma had always been against her selling the last reminder she had of her father, but Jenny didn't think she would have objected in these circumstances.

She had been so lost in her plans that the tea she had poured was now cold; it was tipped away and another cup poured. This one she drank immediately. She wasn't hungry yet and would get herself something to eat later.

Whatever Greaves had planned for her had gone disastrously wrong. Because the police had questioned him, she didn't believe he would attempt anything else again. Nevertheless, it was terrifying to see what he was capable of. After his visit to Ma's with her aunt she had been sure she wouldn't see him again; it had been unwise to dismiss him so lightly. But he was probably a coward at heart, and having nearly been caught must have frightened him. She sincerely hoped it had scared the wits out of him!

Now that the kitchen was warmer, Jenny got washed and dressed, then cleared out the fire in the front room and laid it ready for lighting later in the day. She wouldn't waste the coal, as she intended to be out most of the day.

There was a sharp rap on the front door, then it was pushed open and Fred looked in. 'Morning, Jen. I thought you'd be up.'

'Come in, Fred.' Jenny stood up, wiping her dirty hands on her pinafore. She grinned when she saw how muffled he was: only his eyes and nose showed. There was a woollen scarf tied around his head and then wrapped around his neck, with his cap perched on the top of it. Woollen gloves and several layers of coats completed the picture. 'You sure you're going to be warm enough?'

He rubbed his hands together. 'It's bloody cold

at Covent Garden this early in the morning. It's more like February than the middle of December. Wouldn't be surprised if it didn't snow for Christmas.'

'Let's hope it doesn't.' The thought of families living in icy rooms because they couldn't afford to heat them worried Jenny.

'I might have found you a job.' Fred rubbed his nose, looking uncertain. 'Only thing is, it's out in the open, and if you ain't used to it–'

'I don't care what it is, Fred.' She led him into the kitchen, where it was warmer, eager to hear more about it. 'I'll take anything.'

'I thought you'd say that. Go along to The Cut Market about eight and see Bet Hawkins. She's got a stall six down from ours. Her old man fell down the pub step last night and broke his ankle, silly sod.' Fred held his hands over the stove. 'Anyway, she needs help for a while, so I told her about you. She said she'd keep the job for you if you want it.'

'Want it? Of course I do!' She grinned in delight. 'What does she sell?'

'Anything she can lay her hands on like, pots, pans, china, linen and baby clothes.' Fred chuckled at her obvious excitement. 'Wrap up well. How loud can you holler?'

'They'll hear me five miles away.' She hugged Fred. 'Thank you. This means I can really make my home here.' Jenny sniffed as tears threatened. 'I'm so lucky.'

'Ah, Jen.' Fred shook his head. 'You're a wonder. You talk as if this house was a palace.'

'It is to me, and it's full of happy memories.'

'Fred, you here?' Stan walked in. 'There you are. We must get moving. Morning, Jen, you gonna see old Bet?'

'I'll be there on the dot of eight.'

The men started to walk out when Fred looked back. 'This won't be permanent, Jen. As soon as Bet's old man's on his feet again he'll be back.'

'I understand that.' Jenny gave a cheeky grin. 'Perhaps he'll fall over the pub cat next time and take some more time off.'

Fred and Stan left, their laughter echoing up the street.

There was a bitter wind blowing and Jenny was glad of the red scarf and gloves the Stannards had given her the first Christmas she had been with them. How long ago that seemed. She made her way up Lower Marsh Street, across Waterloo Road, and into The Cut. It was hard to imagine that it had really been a marsh and had been drained a long time ago. The Cut was bustling, with the stallholders setting up for another day's trading and already shouting to attract customers.

She gave a cheery wave to Fred and Stan as she went by. Ah, this must be it, she thought, as soon as she saw a woman around sixty struggling to open a large box.

'Mrs Hawkins?'

The woman looked up, puffing from her exertions with the box. 'Yes.'

'I'm Jenny, and I was told you need help for a while.'

'Did Fred send you?'

Jenny nodded, desperately hoping the woman would take her on.

'You must be Ma Adams's girl, then.'

'I am,' Jenny acknowledged with some pride.

'Good, come and help me get this bloody china unpacked. Christmas only two weeks away and my old man has to fall over. Says he didn't see the pub step.' Bet Hawkins let out a howl of laughter. 'He steps over the bleeding thing every night, you'd think he'd know it was there by now!'

'I expect he's sorry now.' Jenny fought back a grin, not sure if she should show she was amused.

That produced another bellow. 'He'll be even sorrier 'cos I'm gonna make him pay your wages.'

Jenny joined in the laughter then. She'd got the job!

'Let's get this lot on the stall.'

Without wasting time, Jenny pitched in, setting out china as instructed. There were also loads of boxes of tea cloths, and she couldn't believe her eyes. 'Can you sell all these?'

'I don't buy nothing I can't shift.' Bet separated them into bundles of ten. 'All we gotta do is get a crowd round us and they'll go.'

'How much are you going to charge?'

Bet's ample frame began to shake with laughter. 'My God, they said you had a posh way of talking. My customers are gonna love you.' She held up a cup, crooked her little finger and tried to imitate Jenny's accent. 'Roll up, roll up.'

It was such a sorry attempt that they both ended up with tears running down their faces.

'Oh,' Bet said, wiping her eyes, 'I ain't laughed so much for years.'

Neither had she, Jenny realized.

'People are coming to see what we're up to. Just follow my lead and talk posh. That'll get their attention.'

The next two hours were hilarious as she watched Bet at work. The pile of tea cloths was already much smaller. They were concentrating on selling those first.

'How much?' a newcomer in the crowd shouted.

'You have a go,' Bet said. 'I'm right parched after all that shouting.'

'Two and sixpence to you, sir.' Jenny used her best Templeton School accent, and the crowd erupted into laughter.

'Bloody hell!' the man yelled. 'Where'd you find her, Bet?'

'Good, ain't she?'

The crowd had grown in size, attracted by the laughter, and they had everyone's attention.

'She is that, but I still ain't paying half a crown. That's robbery.'

'Two shillings, then, sir.' Jenny was thoroughly enjoying herself.

'One and threepence for a dozen and I'll take a ton.'

'One and fivepence and it's a deal.' Jenny was confident because she knew this was above what Bet was prepared to accept.

'All right.' The man pushed forward, rolling his eyes and joking with the crowd. 'Who can resist such a fine lady?'

'Well done,' Bet murmured, busy packing a box full of tea cloths. 'He's got a shop in the next street and often buys from me, but you got a better price out of him than I could have done.'

'Er, how many is a ton?'

'A hundred.'

'What!'

Bet winked at her. 'Take the man's money afore he changes his mind.'

They concentrated on the china after that, and Jenny was amazed by how much business they were doing. Where she lived people didn't have money to buy such items. Over lunch of a hot pie and a dollop of mushy peas from the shop behind them, Bet explained that it was only the unemployed who were suffering so much. Anyone with a little bit of money always came to the market because they could get things cheap.

There was a lull in the middle of the afternoon, and Bet thrust a couple of mugs at her, telling her to get them filled at the café. As they sat drinking the welcome hot tea, Jenny felt very happy. She was enjoying this so much that she hadn't even noticed the cold. Fred and Stan were still making a small profit from their stall, Ron and Jimmy had full-time jobs at the centre, Ivy was occasionally picking up work there, and now she had been taken on by Bet. Oh, Ma, she thought, if you could only see how well we're doing now. But perhaps she could.

Trade picked up again in the afternoon. Jenny was surprised when she realized that it had grown dark and that everyone had started to pack up – the day had just flown by. Bet had an old car near by, and Jenny helped her to pack everything away.

'Now, let me see.' Bet dived into the pouch she wore around her waist. 'We've done real good today, and I'll pay you each day.' She handed Jenny five shillings. 'It might not be that much every day, depends how much we sell, but you've earned that today.'

Jenny was almost speechless. 'Thank you so much.'

'My pleasure, Jen, you've been a right laugh to work with. See you tomorrow, make it half past seven.'

'I'll be here.'

'Right, I'm off. Better get my old man a couple of pints or he'll sink into the miseries.' Her laugh was almost as loud as the roar from her old Austin Seven as she drove away.

'Ah, there you are.' Fred walked towards her. 'This is handy – you can come home with me and Stan every evening.'

She fell into step beside him and held out the coins. 'Look, I got five shillings for one day's work, and Bet paid for my pie at lunch.'

'Nice going.' Fred smiled kindly. 'Keep that up and you'll be able to pay the rent easily.'

'I will, won't I?' She almost skipped along beside him as they walked to the van, oblivious of the cold weather. She had a place to call home, a job, and yesterday she'd had a long letter from Edna telling her all about the wedding and enclosing a beautiful photograph. And, most important of all, Matthew had recovered after the stabbing. Jenny felt that things couldn't get much better.

30

It was three days before Matt felt strong enough to go out. Going to Ma's funeral had drained him, but he was glad he'd made the effort. After doing nothing but sleeping, eating and talking to his family, he could feel his energy increasing, and he was eager to get back to the garage and his beloved cars.

'Don't overtire yourself today,' his mother admonished, seeing him put on his coat. 'Where are you going this morning?'

'I thought I'd pop along to the garage and see how they're getting on. Jake and Harry visited me in hospital a couple of times, but they wouldn't let me talk business.'

'Quite right too. Remember that the doctor said you must take it easy for a week.' She cast a worried glance at her son. 'Christmas is only two weeks away, so couldn't you go back to work after the New Year?'

'No. I want to get back as soon as possible,' he said gently. He knew how upset his mother had been and he wouldn't do anything to worry her, but he must start doing something or he would go crazy. He'd never been one to sit around and idle his time away. 'And I promise that if I get tired today I'll come right back.'

His mother pulled a face. 'I keep forgetting that you are a grown man now.'

'I am. I'll be twenty-one next March.' He bent and kissed her cheek.

'Where have the years gone?' Her eyes clouded. 'I was so afraid you weren't going to see your next birthday.'

'It looked worse than it was.' Matt fished in his pocket for his gloves and put them on. 'After I've seen Jake and the others, I might call on Jenny and find out what she intends to do now Ma is dead.'

'I've been worrying about her as well. I shall be at the centre this afternoon,' she told him. 'If she needs anything, ask her to come and see me.'

'All right.' Matt whistled as he went out to his car. He'd hated being confined, but he'd be careful today because he didn't want to put back his recovery. Stan had driven Matt's lovely Singer back here after taking him to the hospital; he couldn't wait to drive it again. He'd restored this vehicle himself, and it was his pride and joy. He breathed in the cold air, glad to be alive. That attack had been a nasty business. Dr Sterling had told him that if one of the stab wounds had been two inches further to the left, he would have died instantly. It was certainly going to make him look at life differently, and he was determined to make the most of every minute.

When he arrived, there wasn't room for another car in the front, so Matt went round the back and into the workshop that way. He stopped in amazement: it was just as crowded inside.

'Matt!' Jake came towards him with a huge smile on his face. 'How marvellous to see you up and about. When will you be able to start work again?'

'In a week, maybe sooner.' He gazed around – there were cars taking up every bit of space in the workshop. Some were expensive models, but there were also a couple of Austin Sevens in a bad state of repair. 'What's going on?'

Harry, Steve and Alan came over, and brought another young man with them. His name was Andy, and he had just been taken on.

Harry laughed at Matt's puzzled expression. 'Unbelievable, isn't it? What's happening is that people are buying cars from us and we're taking their old ones in part payment.'

'It's working well, Matt.' Jake's face fairly glowed as he spoke. 'We then do up the old cars and sell them. There's been so much work that we've had to take on Andy here, and we'll be pleased to have you back. When you're fit, of course.'

'Nearly there, Jake.' Matt rotated his right shoulder. 'It's just a bit sore, but that will soon go.'

'Well, when you start work again you can hold the spanners and make the tea if you get tired.'

Matt tipped his head back and laughed. 'Not a chance, Jake, I can't wait to get my hands greasy again.'

'Don't suppose you can.' His boss chuckled, then glanced at the clock. 'Come over to the Duke of Wellington with Harry and me. We'd like to buy you a beer and a bite to eat.'

'Thanks.' It had taken Matt a while to get going this morning and it was already lunchtime.

'Steve, look after things for an hour. We'll only

be across the road if you need us.'

It was lovely to sit with a beer in front of him again and talk about the business to Jake and Harry, wonderful to see their smiling faces. They chatted away with enthusiasm, joking all the time. Matt leant back, sipping his beer, and just revelled in being with them. He had nearly lost his life and that put a different perspective on things. It was as if everything were in sharper focus, making each moment precious.

After promising to see them again soon, Matt headed for Lambeth. He couldn't get any reply from Ma's old house, and he was worried in case Jenny had had to move out at once.

'She ain't in.'

'Do you know where she is?' Matt recognized Glad, who was standing on her step with a young child in her arms.

'I'm right pleased to see you looking better, lad.' Glad gave a nod of approval. 'Jen's got a job up The Cut, at the market.'

'What time does she finish?'

'Hard to say. They packs up when there ain't no more customers. Why don't you pop along there? I'm sure she'd like to see you.'

'I think I will.' Matt hesitated for a moment. 'Does she still live here?'

''Course, this is her home now. Ma left all her bits and pieces to Jen. Do you want a cup of tea before you go up there?'

'No, thanks, Glad.'

She nodded. 'We're all right grateful to you for what you did for our girl. She's a fine lass.'

'Yes, she is, and I'd do anything to help her,' he

344

said, knowing this was absolutely true. When he'd seen her in danger he hadn't given a thought for his own safety; all that had concerned him was Jenny.

'Thought so.' Glad smiled. 'She's had a rough time, but she don't ask for no favours in life. She deserves better than this, though. From the moment we met her, my Fred said she was special, and she is.'

'I know she is, Glad. Where is she working at the market?'

'Just ask for Bet Hawkins's stall. You'll find her there.' The baby began to grizzle. 'Oops, he wants his dinner and changing by the feel of him.' With a grimace she disappeared back into the house.

Matt got in his car and drove to the market. Leaving his car in the next street, he began to wander along The Cut, gazing at all the stalls. He had never been down here before, but it looked as if you could buy just about anything, and from the shouting it was obvious that each stallholder was determined to outdo the others. Hearing his name called, he stopped and saw Fred and Stan waving to him. He walked over to their colourful vegetable stall and shook hands with them.

'Matt, it's good to see you about again.' Stan smiled broadly. 'How are you feeling now?'

'Stronger, thanks. I didn't have time at Ma's funeral, but I'd like to thank you both for getting me to the hospital so quickly.'

'Think nothing of it.' Fred gave a dismissive wave of his hand. 'We've already had a note from you and a letter from your pa. Anyway, it's us who should be thanking you for saving our Jen from hurt.'

Matt was struck by the way everyone from Forest Road referred to her as 'our Jen'. She had adapted to their life so well that you would almost believe she had been born there – until you heard her speak, of course. 'I've just been round to your place and Glad told me Jen was working here.'

'That's right.' Fred came from behind the stall, put his hand on Matt's shoulder and pointed further down. 'See that crowd?'

He nodded.

'You'll find her there with old Bet.'

He could hear the laughter as he got near. When he reached the stall, he stood at the back of the group of people, watching with amusement. Like everyone else in the market, Jenny was swathed in just about every bit of clothing she possessed. Her nose was nearly as red as the scarf she was wearing, but she was laughing as she joked and cajoled people into buying from them. There wasn't any attempt to hide her cultured accent, and Matt's breath caught in his throat as he realized exactly how much she had changed. She was who she was, no pretence, no hiding her identity. This was Eugenie, who preferred to be called Jenny. She was secure in her new life, confident and loved. He didn't know much about her father, but the rest of her family seemed to care little for her, except as an object to be manipulated. Though why that should be was still a mystery.

346

'Come on, one and six for ten tea cloths. It's a bargain! You won't get an offer like that again – they're going up to one and nine tomorrow.'

Jenny's voice brought Matt out of his musing.

'A tanner for six,' someone shouted.

'Now, now, sir.' Jenny placed her hands on her hips. 'That's rather mean, isn't it?'

'It's worse than that!' Bet joined in and glared at the man in question. 'You're a tight old git, Jack. Surely you can spend a bit more than that on your lovely wife?'

The crowd roared in glee. 'You tell 'im Bet.'

Matt couldn't resist joining in. 'I'll give you two shillings for six!' A hush fell on the crowd as they turned to stare at him. 'And a kiss.'

'Who from?' Bet chortled. 'My lovely young helper or me?'

'Both of you, of course. I want value for my money.'

There were cheers and whistles coming from everyone now. 'Come on, Bet. It ain't everyday you get an offer like that.'

The outrageous offer had been made on the spur of the moment, and Matt wondered if he'd gone too far and embarrassed Jen, but she was laughing along with everyone else. He walked towards her with the two shillings in his hand.

He got a quick peck from Bet, and, much to the crowd's delight, she pretended to be so overcome she had to sit down and fan herself with a tea cloth. Still laughing, Jenny came from behind the stall, stood on tiptoe and brushed her lips over his cheek. It was only a brief, gentle touch, but Matt felt it right through him.

347

'Thank you for everything,' she whispered. Then she took the two shillings and gave him fifteen tea cloths. Holding up the two shillings, she grinned at everyone. 'We've given him fifteen for the money. The kisses were free for a friend.'

Now in a thoroughly good humour, the crowd surged forward to buy various items. Bet had a wicked gleam in her eyes and gave him a wink of thanks.

Seeing he wasn't going to get a chance to speak to Jen, Matt asked, 'Can I come to visit you?'

She nodded, smiled and went back to serving customers.

It was about four o'clock when Matt arrived home, tired but content after seeing Jenny so happy. He could still feel the touch of her lips and grinned to himself. That had done more for his recovery than all the doctors.

His mother had just returned from working at the centre, and she was in the sitting room with a tray of tea and cakes in front of her.

He kissed her cheek and tossed the tea cloths in her lap. 'Present for you.'

Her mouth twitched at the corners. 'Very nice.'

'I thought you'd like them,' he joked. 'Jen's got a job at the market and I bought them from her.'

As they relaxed, he told his mother about Ma leaving Jenny her furniture and the fun she seemed to be having working on the market stall. By the time he'd finished, she was nodding with pleasure.

'I'm relieved she now has a secure home and a job at last.'

Matt helped himself to a cake. 'She was enjoying herself today. I've never seen her so happy.'

His mother studied him with a thoughtful expression on her face, and then changed the subject. 'Tell me how things are at the garage.'

This took about another twenty minutes, and then he yawned, tiredness suddenly swamping him.

'Why don't you have a rest before dinner, Matt?'

'I think I will.' His legs felt heavy and his whole body ached as he went to his room. Kicking off his shoes, he flopped on the bed and was instantly asleep.

The first dinner gong woke him and he scrambled to his feet with a groan. He had felt all right when he'd been out, but now he was aware that he'd overdone his first day. He had always been fit and healthy, and it was hard to make himself take it easy. Still, the doctor had said the weariness would fade as he began to move around more.

All he had time for was a quick wash and change into a suit. They didn't *dress* for dinner unless they had guests, but his father did insist on a jacket and tie.

He arrived in the dining room just as they were sitting down.

'Your mother told us about your day out,' his father said. 'How did you feel?'

'Rather tired when I got back, but the doctor said I'd feel stronger each day.'

'Is Jenny now going to stay at the same house?' John asked. 'You remember I mentioned Winford a while ago to Henry Eddison – well, he asked if we knew where Winford's daughter could be found. I said we did, so we don't want to lose track of her now.'

When his brother paused, Matt leant forward. 'And?'

'He said he'd spoken to some people who had known Cyrus Winford, and it seems there's a lawyer by the name of Dwight Roberts who's on his way here to see her.'

Matt frowned. 'Did he say why?'

'No.' John was obviously as puzzled as everyone else. 'But I don't like the sound of it. This lawyer booked a passage as soon as he heard we knew where she was. I hope it doesn't mean more trouble for the girl.'

'Why do you think it might?' their mother asked.

Gilbert poured himself another glass of red wine. 'Well, my dear, this man Greaves has been desperate to get his hands on her, and now Mr Roberts is coming all the way from New York, saying that he has been searching for her.'

Matt felt his insides tighten as he pictured Jenny's smiling face. Was there more trouble heading her way? Luke had found a marriage certificate for the Winfords, but was it a bigamous marriage? If so, that would mean Jen was illegitimate. His mind began to search for another reason, any reason, for the lawyer's visit, but everything he came up with was bad. 'We mustn't leave her alone with him!'

'We don't intend to,' his father said, his mouth set in a determined line. 'He's coming on the

Mauretania and arrives at Southampton the day after tomorrow. Luke and I will be there to meet him when he docks, and we'll bring him back to stay with us.'

'Don't worry, Matt, we won't tell him where she is if it means more trouble for her,' Luke assured him. 'But it must be important for him to dash over here so quickly.'

'That's what worries me.' Matt stared grimly at his plate of succulent beef, his appetite gone. 'From what we've heard, her father was destitute after the crash. We also know he had another family in New York, so perhaps they're going to question her legitimacy.'

'But what would be the point in that?' Louise frowned.

Matt shrugged helplessly.

'We could go on speculating all night,' their father declared, 'but we shall soon find out. Damned strange business, though.'

They all agreed with that statement.

The end of her first week at the market saw Jenny buoyant with hope. Bet's husband wouldn't be able to work before Christmas, so the job would give her enough to pay the rent for a few weeks if she was careful.

After lighting the fire and making herself toast and tea, Jenny tipped her money on to the table and counted it. She had earned a guinea, which was a fortune to her, and on top of that Bet had paid for her lunch each day. It had been such fun, and she had surprised herself at the way she shouted and joked with the customers. Bet said

351

she was a natural, but it was a talent she hadn't known she possessed.

She counted the money again, just to be sure, then surged to her feet to tell Ma how lucky she was, and what a special Christmas they would have this year. The pain hit her when she reached the front room and saw the empty chair. Was she ever going to get used to Ma no longer being here? 'Oh, Ma, I miss you so much,' she murmured. 'I long to tell you how well things are going.'

She went back to the table, put nineteen shillings in the tin and two in her purse, and finished her tea as she gazed at the wedding photograph Edna had sent her. They were a happy pair, and it gave Jenny huge pleasure to look at it. It had pride of place on the mantelpiece.

'Hello, Jen!' Ivy called, poking her head round the kitchen door. 'Dad tells me you've been selling kisses. It's the talk of the market.'

Jenny roared – she could just imagine the gossip flying around The Cut. 'Do you want some tea?'

Ivy took another cup off the shelf and sat down. 'So tell me all about it.'

Jenny related the story of Matthew's visit to the stall. They both ended up giggling.

'Weren't you embarrassed?'

'No.' Jenny shook her head. 'Matthew started it, and the crowd enjoyed the fun. Anyway, joining in was my way of thanking him for what he did. He'd asked for a kiss, so I gave him one.'

'He's nice and so brave.' Ivy gave her a studied look. 'You could marry him – you come from the same background.'

'Eugenie Winford did, but I'm no longer that person. I'm Jenny Baker who comes from Lambeth and scrubs floors or works at the market to make a living.' She smiled wryly. 'I'm happier at the moment than I can ever remember being. I'm sad about my father and I miss Ma dreadfully, but I've got lovely memories of them. I don't look ahead too far or yearn for things I can't have.'

Ivy nodded. 'We takes each day as it comes as well. Mum always says that it's the best way. Her favourite saying is that it's no use trying to cross your bridges before you get to them.'

'Very wise. That's something I've learnt over the last couple of years.'

'Yes, Mum's got good sense.' Ivy finished her tea. 'We wondered if you'd like to come in tonight for a chat instead of sitting by yourself.'

'I'd love to, thanks.'

31

The car sped towards Southampton, his father driving, Luke in the front seat and himself in the back. Matt had insisted on going, as he was eager to see the American lawyer and find out what he wanted with Jenny.

They got lost trying to find the right dock, but, much to Matt's delight, they arrived just as the *Mauretania* was approaching her berth. Although launched in 1906, she was still a magnificent sight. She had been painted white for her part-time cruises to exotic places like Bermuda, and, with the pale winter sun glinting on the four funnels, she was breathtaking.

There was a great deal of activity and shouting as the liner was eased into the berth, and the excitement was catching. Even Luke, who was laconic at the best of times, was chatting and pointing out what was happening as the huge ropes secured the liner in place.

John had sent a telegraph to the ship yesterday to let Mr Roberts know they would be meeting him. However, once the passengers began to disembark, Matt realized just how easy it would be to miss him, as they didn't have any idea what he looked like. He turned to his father. 'How are we going to find him in this crush?'

'Leave it to me.' Their father strode towards the liner and up the steps, pushing his way through the passengers coming down.

Luke grinned and shrugged his shoulders as their father disappeared from sight.

After no more than fifteen minutes he re-appeared, talking to a spare-looking man of around fifty with a shock of white hair.

'These are two of my sons, Luke and Matthew.'

'I'm sure glad to meet you.' His smile was warm and his handshake firm.

'Shall we collect your luggage for you, sir?' Luke asked.

'I have it here.' Dwight Roberts held up a small suitcase. 'I always travel light, and, because you know where Miss Winford is, my business here shouldn't take more than a couple of days. I want to get back home in time for Christmas.'

'Well, as you have all your luggage, we can get back to London straight away.' Gilbert Stannard led them towards the car.

Much to Matt's disappointment, the lawyer wouldn't discuss his business during the journey. This was understandable, of course – they were not related to Jenny – but he had hoped to find out if it was good news or bad.

'Did you have a pleasant journey?' Louise said, when she greeted their guest on arrival.

'A bit on the choppy side, ma'am; this isn't the best time of year for a transatlantic crossing.' Dwight Roberts's chuckle was full of amusement. 'But I'm a good sailor and didn't miss any meals. I hardly saw some people the whole way across.'

'We were about to have afternoon tea, Mr Roberts. Will you join us or would you prefer to go to your room to rest before dinner?'

'I would enjoy your English tea. And please call me Dwight.' He waited until Louise was seated before sitting down. 'It's kind of you to put me up while I'm here.'

Matt was impatient listening to the social pleasantries; it was obvious they weren't going to be told a thing. All Dwight talked about was how beautiful the ship had been, with her exquisite wood panelling and the large domed skylight in the library. As interesting as this was, it was not what Matt was eager to hear about.

'We thought you would be more comfortable here than in an hotel,' Louise said, handing him a cup of tea.

'Indeed.' Dwight gazed around the room in appreciation. 'This is a lovely house.'

'It has been in the family for nearly a hundred years,' Luke told him.

Matt couldn't stand it any longer. 'We understand you've been trying to trace Miss Winford.'

'Yes, indeed.' Dwight put his empty cup on the table. 'Is she here? Would it be possible to see her now?'

'She doesn't live here and will still be at work,' Matt said rather too hastily. 'Can you tell us why you need to see her?'

'I'm afraid I can disclose my business only to Miss Winford.'

'We understand that.' Gilbert stood up and walked over to the fire, resting his hand on the marble surround. 'But you must understand that we have all become fond of the girl, and we would not wish to see her upset.'

Matt was staggered by his father's announcement, but grateful he had said what they were all feeling.

Dwight frowned. 'It is imperative that I see her. That's all I can say.'

'We will bring her here to meet you.' Louise offered Dwight some small cakes, and when he shook his head she replaced the plate on the table. 'As you can see, we have become protective where Eugenie, or Jenny, as she prefers to be called now, is concerned. Would you object to my being present when you talk to her?'

'And me,' Matt said.

She nodded. 'And my son Matthew, who has

recently come out of hospital after being injured saving Jenny from a violent attack.'

Dwight was appalled. 'Attacked? That's terrible! Would you tell me what happened?'

Matt explained about the violent incident and who was responsible.

'Nasty things have been going on.' Dwight shook his head in concern. 'I now understand Miss Winford's need to get away from her aunt, but if she had contacted me, then none of this would have been necessary.'

'She couldn't if she didn't know anything about you,' Matt pointed out.

'As soon as her father died, I sent her a telegram asking her to get in touch with me.' Anger blazed in the lawyer's eyes. 'It looks as if her aunt never gave her the message. You say they were trying to make her marry this older man?'

'Yes, she has had a very difficult time.' Louise refilled his cup. 'But you haven't said whether we may be present.'

'I can see that Cyrus's daughter has been badly treated and that makes me very angry. As you obviously care for her, I will agree if you promise that you will remain in the background and not interfere with the meeting in any way. And only if she tells me that she wishes you to be present.'

'She will,' Matt stated with confidence. 'It's Sunday tomorrow and I don't think she's working in the afternoon, so I'll bring her to you then.'

'Thank you.' Dwight appeared satisfied with the arrangements and settled back to enjoy his tea.

Matt studied him carefully: outwardly he was

calm, but the expression in his eyes was one of fury. Dwight Roberts was a very angry man indeed.

The moment Sunday lunch was over, Matt drove to Lambeth. Dwight had pressed them for her address over dinner last night, but they had refused to give it. At first he had been annoyed by their intransigence, but after listening to more of what had happened to her over the last two years, he had understood.

Matt was apprehensive as he knocked on Jenny's door. He desperately wanted to protect her, but the lawyer had come over as soon as he'd heard that someone knew where she was. They had no right to stop that meeting. He believed she was strong enough to face almost anything now, but, if not, he would be there to support her.

'Come in,' Jenny called at his second knock.

She was sitting by the fire with a book on her lap. 'Hello, Jen.'

'Oh, hello. Come and sit by the fire. It's cold out there.'

'Thanks.' He sat down and held his hands out to the warmth. He had been rehearsing what to say all the way here, but now he was reluctant to speak. She looked so relaxed and content; he didn't like to think that they might now be about to throw her life into turmoil again.

'Would you like a cup of tea?'

He shook his head. 'I've got something to tell you. There's a Mr Dwight Roberts staying with us. He's a lawyer from America who's come over especially to see you.'

'America? Did he know my father?' Jenny frowned. 'But why has he come to see me and not my mother? Or does he want to see both of us?' The colour drained from her face. 'Are there more debts we don't know about?'

'I'm sorry, Jen. He won't say more than that he's been looking for you ever since your father died. You, not your mother.' Matt reached out and took hold of her hands as they twisted with anxiety. 'We wouldn't let him come here, but I said I'd come to tell you he's waiting for you.'

She dipped her head, obviously trying to control her emotions, and when she didn't speak, Matt said, 'You don't have to see him if you don't want to.'

Taking a deep breath, she raised her head, wide-eyed with worry. 'I must know what this is all about. Are you sure he never said anything?'

Matt shrugged helplessly. If only he could answer her question. 'It must be something to do with your father.'

'I can't imagine what would bring him all this way. My father lost all his money in the crash and killed himself. End of story.' She removed her hands from his and stood up. 'However, I'd better see what he wants. If it's more bad news, then I'd better face it. I'll get my coat.'

Matt helped her on with her coat, wondering what Dwight Roberts was expecting to see when he met Cyrus Winford's daughter. He doubted it was this shabbily dressed girl with calloused working hands.

The journey was made in silence and Matt

didn't try to talk, knowing that she was concerned about the meeting and probably wanted to stay quiet.

When they arrived at the house, Mrs Stannard was waiting for them in the hall. 'My dear.' She kissed Jenny's cheek. 'We've put Mr Roberts in the library. He has agreed to let Matthew and I be with you, but if you'd rather see him on your own...'

Jenny was relieved someone would be with her, for she was very concerned, and couldn't think why a man should come from America just to see her. 'I'd like you both there, please.'

Matthew took her coat, hung it up and smiled. 'Let's see what this is all about, shall we? We'll sit the other side of the library, but we'll be there if you need us.'

Glad of his strong presence and his mother's quiet calm, she walked up the stairs to the library.

The man who greeted her was not as stern as she'd imagined he would be. He had very kind pale blue eyes, and when he smiled she felt a little better. He looked genuinely pleased to see her.

'Ah, Miss Winford. I'm so pleased to meet you at last. Your father spoke of you all the time.'

'You knew him?' His accent sounded just like her father's and a lump lodged in her throat. 'Did you see him after the crash? Was he so unhappy?'

'The only thing that made him unhappy was the fact that he couldn't see you more often. Please sit down. He was a dear friend, and I was his lawyer for many years.' Dwight Roberts had papers spread across a desk. 'Before we start,

360

your father's second wife asked me to give you this letter from her. She has also enclosed photographs of her two sons – your half-brothers.'

She took the envelope, her hand trembling, and stuffed it into the pocket of her dress. What was he talking about? How could her father have felt anything other than despair? Nothing less than that would have made him take his own life. And why was the lawyer talking about another family? Half-brothers? 'His *second* wife?'

Dwight frowned. 'I thought you knew. He divorced your mother seven years ago.'

Jenny felt as if a tram had hit her as she stared at the lawyer in horror. 'I was never told.' She sat up straight; whatever the rest of the news was, it couldn't be worse than this! 'You said my father divorced my mother. On what grounds?'

'Infidelity.'

Her laugh was harsh. 'You must be joking.'

The lawyer shook his head. 'These are the papers. See for yourself.'

What she saw on that legal document was almost too much for her, and she began to shake in reaction. It was true! Her mother had committed adultery with a man she had never heard of. 'Why didn't my mother marry this man after the divorce?'

'I believe he was already married and managed to patch up his marriage after the scandal.'

'He must have been very rich for my mother to have taken such a chance.' She grimaced in disgust, lifting her head defiantly, drawing on every ounce of courage she could find to face these revelations. 'It seems my family have kept a great deal from me, Mr Roberts. You had better tell me the whole story.'

'Your father believed you had been told on your sixteenth birthday, but I can see that isn't so.' He leant back in the chair. 'Well, after the divorce your father married again in New York. She's a charming woman who gave him two sons. They were very happy together, and she understood the love your father had for you. He tried to get custody of you so he could take you to America to be a part of his new family, but your mother refused. To avoid a nasty court battle that would have hurt you, he gave way. It nearly broke his heart to leave you. He came here two or three times a year to spend time with you.'

The shock was receding, and Jenny could feel rage bubbling up inside her. She had known that her mother was selfish, but this was unbelievable! Gathering her thoughts with great effort, she said, 'I'm pleased my father was happy with his new family, but it makes it even more puzzling that he should have killed himself.'

Dwight Roberts was on his feet so suddenly that the chair he'd been sitting in went flying. 'Who told you that?'

Jenny was shocked by his reaction. 'My aunt, Gertrude Osborne.'

'What the hell is that woman up to?' Dwight raged. Matt came over, poured the agitated lawyer a brandy, righted his chair and made him sit down again.

He downed the drink in one gulp. 'I'm so sorry, Miss Winford, you've been told a pack of lies!'

She half stood up and then collapsed back.

362

'Lies? What do you mean? Oh, God, please tell me what's going on!'

'Your father did lose nearly everything in the crash, but he was a good businessman and would have bounced back, in time. Only he wasn't given time.' Dwight looked sad. 'He was shot by a crazed man who had lost everything and blamed your father.'

'He was murdered?' The words came out in an anguished whisper. How could her aunt have told her he had committed suicide when he hadn't? It was unbelievable.

'Yes. After killing your father, the man turned the gun on himself.'

She was going to be sick! Her darling father hadn't killed himself; he had been cruelly murdered. She touched the pendant round her neck. Thank heavens she'd never sold that. It was the only reminder of him she had left – apart from the memories, of course. But it was all too much! She turned round, seeking support. 'Matthew!'

He came over immediately, sat beside her and placed his hand over her tightly clenched fist. She uncurled her fingers, holding on, trying to draw some of his strength into her shocked body.

'Soon after your father's death,' Dwight continued, 'I contacted your mother with the full story. I received a reply from Mrs Osborne, saying that she would be handling your affairs.'

'But why lie? And why try to make me marry Greaves?' Jenny wanted the whole story now. For two years she had believed her father had chosen death rather than face poverty, and deep down she had harboured the belief that that was a coward's way out. And that was something she had found impossible to believe about her father.

'*Money!*' Dwight ground out.

'But I haven't any.' She indicated her worn dress. 'As you can see.'

'That isn't true. Your father made substantial provisions for his children in case anything happened to him. There are insurance policies in your names, and these are unaffected by his losses. I was also able to save the house in America for his wife, but everything else had to go, including the London house. The sum of $25,000 was to come to you at the age of eighteen, or if he died before you reached that age. It was to be controlled by a parent or guardian until you were eighteen. And–'

'They knew!' Jenny was on her feet immediately, not giving him a chance to say anything else. She was incandescent with rage. 'They knew!'

She spun on her heel and charged for the door, only to be stopped by Matthew, who caught her arm. 'Where are you going?'

'Going?' She glared at him in disbelief. 'I'm going to face those callous, manipulative, selfish bastards. That's where I'm going!'

Dwight Roberts was on the other side of her, holding her other arm, and she tried to shake herself free. 'Let go of me!'

'You're not going anywhere on your own,' Matthew threatened.

'Come if you want, but you're not going to stop me.' Freeing herself, she shot out of the room and hurtled down the stairs, with Matthew and Dwight charging after her.

'Jenny, stop!' Louise called, but the girl ignored

her plea with an expression on her face akin to murder.

Matt grabbed Jenny's coat and brushed aside the rest of his family, who had gathered in the hall, wanting to know what was going on. Dwight, for all his extra years, was fitter than Matthew and was right on Jenny's heels.

Jenny was aware of the commotion she was causing, but she had only one thought in her mind: to tell her family what she thought of them. A car drew up beside her and the passenger door was thrown open.

'Get in,' Matthew demanded.

Dwight pushed her into the car, slammed the door and clambered in the back. 'We're coming with you, whether you like it or not.'

She cast a mutinous glare at the men, and then folded her arms, shivering slightly.

'Your coat is in the back. Give it to her, Dwight.' Once Jenny had struggled into her coat, Matthew turned in his seat to face her.

'Now, tell me where you're going.'

'Russell Square, and I'll direct you from there.'

Matthew put the car in gear and headed for Bloomsbury.

32

Never in her life had Jenny been so angry. She wanted answers only her family could give her. Her face was contorted with disgust. Family? She was going to finish this business once and for all, and the only way to do that was to confront each of them in turn. They weren't going to get away with this. Oh, no! Her hands clenched into tight fists. They would be dealing with a very different girl from the one they had tried to swindle.

The fact that she now had some money of her own didn't interest her. What was making the red mist rise before her eyes was the way they had lied about her father. She beat her fists on her knees. How could they do that? How could they be so cruel?

'Where to now?'

Matthew's voice penetrated her seething mind, and she managed to spit out the directions to her aunt's house. She would go there first.

As soon as they were parked, she opened the car door, got out, ran up the steps and banged on the front door with all her might.

The door opened almost at once, and she pushed the butler aside. He caught her arm and she tried to rush past him.

'Let her go!' she heard Dwight drawl in his lovely American accent, so reminiscent of her father's.

'Where's Mrs Osborne?' Matthew demanded.

'In the drawing room,' the man spluttered, glaring at Matthew and Dwight. 'But who are you? And how dare you burst in like this!'

'I'll announce myself.' Jenny ran up the stairs and erupted into the room, throwing the door open with such force that it crashed against the wall.

The occupants rose in alarm.

Jenny glared at her mother, aunt and Greaves. 'How kind of you all to be here at the same time,' she snarled.

'Eugenie!' Her mother was the first to recover, and eyed her daughter up and down with a look of distaste. 'What disgusting clothes you are wearing.'

'I've got holes in my shoes as well.' Jenny couldn't resist taunting her mother, who was always so immaculate.

'What is the meaning of this sudden appearance,' her aunt demanded, 'and who are these two?' She waved a hand at Matthew and Dwight, who had closed the drawing-room door and were leaning against it with their arms folded. 'If you don't all leave at once, I shall call the police.'

'Oh, please do.' Jenny smiled evilly and glanced at Dwight. 'Do you think we can have them arrested for attempted embezzlement?'

'It would be fun to try,' he drawled, hooking his thumbs in his belt and looking every inch the gunslinger from the movies.

'What are you talking about?' her mother demanded. 'What's all this nonsense about embezzlement?'

Jenny gave her a long contemptuous stare, just managing to control a humourless laugh. 'So they didn't even tell you about the money.' Her gaze swept over the three of them. 'I know all about the way you've lied to me. Now I want to know why! I'll start with you, *mother!* Father divorced you for adultery. He wanted custody of me. You never cared for me, so why didn't you agree?'

'If I'd done that, he would have taken you to America, but while you were with me he had to support us both. What did you expect me to do? He was wealthy. I wasn't going to live in poverty!' She looked outraged at the very idea.

Jenny turned away in disgust and dismissed the avaricious woman from her thoughts. She was no longer her daughter.

'And now you, *aunt*. Why did you tell me that my father had committed suicide when you knew it wasn't true?' Her voice trembled. In her view, this was the most heinous crime. 'You never liked him, always running him down, but why try to demean him even in death?'

'I don't have to explain myself to you,' her aunt said haughtily. 'You look as if you have just come out of the slums.'

'I have, and it's a whole lot more savoury than here, I can tell you. The people I live with might be poor, but they are honest!' She stepped forward menacingly until she was face to face with this hated woman, pleased to see that she was now taller than her aunt. Jenny spoke through clenched teeth. 'You will answer my questions or I'll give you the thrashing you deserve.'

'Albert!'

Jenny laughed and cast a quick glance at Greaves. He looked as if he wanted to run, but he wasn't going to be able to get past Matthew and Dwight. 'It's no use calling for that coward. I'll ask you just one more time. Why did you hate him so much, and why did you lie to me?'

A look of sheer malice crossed her aunt's face. 'Yes, I hated him! He should have married me. Instead he chose my stupid sister and I never forgave him for that. When Osborne proposed I married him, only to find out he was nearly penniless. I got my revenge on Cyrus in the end by telling everyone he'd shot himself.' Her laugh was ugly. 'That made him look like a weak man. And with Albert's help I was determined to get my hands on some of the money he'd left you.'

The temptation to hit the cruel woman was great, but Jenny managed to resist – just. She stayed toe to toe with her. 'And you thought you could take control?'

'Of course. You were too young to handle your own affairs.'

'Why were you so determined to marry me to him?' She nodded in Greaves's direction. 'As my husband he would have had control of the money, surely.'

'We'd drawn up a written agreement to share it. We were both in financial difficulties.' Gertrude Osborne was speaking quite freely now, obviously realizing that it would be useless to refuse to speak.

Jenny raised her eyebrows at Dwight. 'A legal agreement between thieves. What do you think of that?'

'Despicable, Jenny,' he drawled, 'but they'd forgotten one thing. Your father appointed me your guardian and left me in control of the purse strings.' He gave an apologetic shrug. 'But, do you know, I do believe I forgot to mention that to them.'

She tutted in a parody of censure. 'How very remiss of you.'

He grinned.

Now Jenny turned her attention to Greaves. 'You are the most evil of the pathetic trio. When I wouldn't come to you willingly, you sent two thugs after me. They stabbed Matthew and nearly killed him. I'll never forgive you for that, and if there is ever a way to have you charged with attempted murder, I'll see you stand trial.' She had the satisfaction of seeing him blanch at the threat. 'Would $25,000 split between the two of you have cleared your debts?'

'Not quite, but there was more to come when you were twenty-one,' Greaves mumbled, now with a very unhealthy-looking flush to his skin. 'A lot more, and as your husband I'd have had it all.'

She turned slowly to face Dwight. 'More?'

He raised his hands in surrender. 'You rushed out before I got to that part.'

'How much?'

He grinned again. 'About $50,000.'

'Really?' Jenny fought to control a hysterical laugh from bursting out as she heard her mother gasp. This was becoming more ridiculous by the minute.

Her mother stepped forward imploringly. 'I

370

didn't know about the money until now. If I had known, I would never have allowed you to go to Albert. All I knew was that my allowance stopped immediately and that I was penniless. You can come home with me, Eugenie. My husband is old and sick, but I've got a lovely house–'

'Dear Lord,' Jenny gasped. 'Your greed has clouded your sense of reality. No, more than that – it has completely destroyed your ability to tell right from wrong. You are beneath contempt. You may not have known about the money, but you must have known my father didn't kill himself. and yet you let your sister lie to me.'

'Well, Gertrude thought it would be for the best. And I needed her then.'

'Best!' Jenny exploded. 'I never thought you were very bright, with your single-minded urge to climb the social ladder, but you really are stupid, aren't you?'

'Don't talk to me like that!'

'Shut up!' Jenny swept a ferocious gaze over each one of them. 'I don't want to see or hear from any of you – *ever again*. I hope you rot in hell for the anguish you have put me through!'

With that parting shot she turned and walked out, head held high, as the two men opened the door for her. Matthew and Dwight fell in behind her as she left the house.

It was over! She was free of them, with lovely memories of her father filling her mind. The doubt was gone. He hadn't killed himself. He had loved her. Now as far as she was concerned, Ma had been her mother, and Fred and Glad her uncle and aunt. She couldn't wish for a lovelier family. She was going to give them the best damned Christmas they had ever had.

'Take me home, Matthew, please,' she said when they reached the car.

'To Lambeth?' He opened the door for her.

'Of course. Where else would I go?'

He ignored her sharp tone. 'You could come and stay with us until–'

Her emotions were still in turmoil and she gave him a withering look. 'What, now I've got money?'

'Don't insult me, Jen. When have I ever cared if you were rich or poor?'

She was instantly contrite. That had been unkind and she'd hurt him. He'd only ever shown her kindness; he didn't deserve to be spoken to like that. She touched his arm, her eyes full of remorse. 'I'm so sorry. Please forgive me. I don't know what I'm saying.'

He gathered her in his arms and held her gently for a moment, then kissed the top of her head. 'I know, it's all too much at the moment, isn't it?'

She nodded and got in the car, not speaking all the way back to Lambeth as she struggled to come to terms with everything.

It was dark by the time they arrived, and both men followed her indoors. She put more coal on the fire and poked it until it burst into life.

'Would you like tea?' she asked politely, but secretly wishing they would go away so she could be on her own. It had been a traumatic day.

They shook their heads, and she sat in Ma's chair – something she had never done before, but it gave her comfort now.

'Cosy place you've got here.' Dwight gazed around the small room, then smiled at her. 'Real quaint.'

'Yes, it is. When will I be able to have the money?'

'I'll deposit it in a bank of your choice tomorrow.'

'Thank you. Will you put it in the Stannard Bank, please?'

'Sure.' Dwight studied her intently. 'You're a real plucky girl and your father would have been proud of you today. And for the way you've survived the last two years.'

Her eyes clouded with tears and she bit her lip, determined not to break down. It was hard, because now that the anger had vanished she felt drained and emotional.

'I'll collect you at about ten tomorrow and we'll go to the bank together, shall we?' Dwight asked.

'Yes, thank you.' She blinked rapidly until she could see clearly again, and said, 'I need to be alone now. I've got a lot of thinking to do.'

As they left, Matthew stopped at the door and stared at her, his expression troubled. She smiled to assure him she was all right, and with a slight nod he left with Dwight.

Matt hesitated and slapped his hand on the top of his car, bowing his head, because it felt as if his heart was going to shatter. The picture of Jenny sitting in Ma's chair, small and frail, was imprinted on his mind. She had seemed numb, not even bothering to take off her coat. It was a complete contrast to the girl who had faced her family with such ferocity. He couldn't leave her alone like this.

'She'll be all right, Matt.' Dwight placed a hand on his shoulder. 'She's had one hell of a shock, and now reaction has set in. She needs to be alone.'

'I don't like to think of her being by herself,' he murmured, then spun on his heel and strode to Fred and Glad's house, knocking firmly.

Stan opened the door. 'Hello, Matt, come in, and your friend.'

'Glad,' he said, as soon as they set foot inside the room, 'would you keep an eye on Jenny this evening?'

'Of course.' Glad studied Dwight. 'What's happened?'

It was Dwight who spoke. 'I'm a lawyer from New York and I've brought her news of her father. Things she didn't know.'

'She's in shock.' Matt explained. 'She said she needs to be alone, but I'm not happy about that.'

'Don't you worry, lad.' Fred stood up and shook hands with Dwight. 'Thanks for letting us know. We'll watch out for her.'

Matt breathed a sigh of relief. They would be able to help her more than he could at the moment. 'We'll be back tomorrow morning.'

After taking their leave, Matt drove home as quickly as possible. After the way Jenny had stormed from their house, they must be worried sick, wondering what was going on.

He was right.

'What's been happening?' his father demanded as soon as they arrived.

'We've just seen a display of controlled fury my old friend Cyrus would have been proud of.' Dwight was still grinning, obviously having enjoyed himself.

'Controlled?' Matt laughed. 'Dwight, Jenny really let rip at that disgusting family of hers.'

'She sure did.' The lawyer sat down and stretched his legs out, still grinning.

'I think we'd all better have a whisky while you tell us about it.'

'I'll get it.' John poured one for everyone, including his mother.

'Is Jenny all right?' Louise asked Matt anxiously.

He nodded. 'She wants to be by herself, but I've asked Fred and Glad to keep an eye on her this evening.'

'That was sensible.' She looked at the lawyer. 'Now, Dwight, we have been kept in suspense long enough.'

For the next half an hour the Stannards listened to the incredible story, and heard about Jenny's reaction and her confrontation with her family.

Luke leant forward, hands on knees, and listened intently to every word. 'Damn, it never entered my head to check for divorce papers. That was careless of me.' He grinned. 'I'd love to have seen her,' he declared.

'It sure was something to behold, wasn't it, Matt?'

'Yes, she was magnificent.' Matt got up and refilled everyone's glass. 'She stood in that opulent room in her shabby clothes, proud and unashamed. It was her mother, aunt and Greaves

375

who appeared shabby as their greedy deeds were uncovered.'

'I'm so relieved she's found out the truth and will now have money of her own.' Louise dabbed her eyes.

'You don't have to worry about her any more.' Dwight smiled. 'Matt and I will be keeping an eye on her from now on.'

'She might need some financial advice.' Gilbert slipped into his banker's role. 'From what we've seen of her affection for the people she's living with, she's liable to give it all away.'

'She's asked that the money be deposited with your bank,' Dwight said, 'and we shall be doing that in the morning. As for wasting the money, I doubt that. She's the image of her father, and we can only hope that she's inherited his fine business sense. But, whatever she decides, the money is hers to do with as she wishes.'

33

How long she'd been sitting motionless in Ma's chair, Jenny didn't know. Time seemed to have lost all meaning as the enormity of what had happened today dawned on her. The room was lovely and warm now, so she roused herself enough to stand up and remove her coat. She needed a cup of tea.

Every move seemed an effort as she dragged herself to the kitchen and put the kettle on. She stood watching it boil and slipped her hand into her pocket, pulling out the letter Dwight had given to her. She had forgotten all about that.

After making the tea, she took it back to the front room and sat in Ma's chair again. When she opened the envelope, two photographs fell out with the names 'Hal' and 'Rob' written on the back. Two young dark-haired boys, each clutching a brightly coloured ball, stared out at her, and a petite woman with a bright smile on her face had her hands on their shoulders to hold them in line. Standing behind them, looking so proud, was her father.

She clutched the pictures to her to protect them from the tears that had suddenly burst from her like a torrent. It was caused by a mixture of delayed mourning for her father and joy that he had, for a few years, found happiness with his new family. She didn't try to stop the tears. And she sobbed for the cruel death her father had suffered, and the sadness of all those who had loved him.

When there were no more tears to be shed, she wiped her eyes, blew her nose and settled down to read the letter from her father's wife. Gracie was her name, and she wrote about the boys and how much like their father they were. At the end of the letter she told Jenny that there would always be a home for her with them if she wanted to come over to the United States.

Jenny sipped her tea. She had decisions to make about her future, but she felt too exhausted to think straight. The idea of going to America was appealing. After all, there was very little to keep her here...

'Oh, but there is.' It was as if Ma were speaking in her mind. 'What about Matt?'

'What about him?' she replied out loud.

'You're in love with him, ducky.'

'Am I?' She frowned as the conversation ran around in her head.

''Course you are. Stop denying it.'

'But he doesn't love me.'

'Don't be daft, Jen. Would he risk his life for someone he didn't care for?'

Jenny took a deep breath and sat up straight. The attraction between herself and Matthew had been strong right from the beginning, but she hadn't dared admit her true feelings. He just felt sorry for her, that's what she'd always told herself. But she did love him! And had done for some time. As she admitted that, she could almost hear Ma's amused cackle.

There was a knock on the door, and Fred and Glad came in. Fred sat beside her. 'Matt asked us to look in and make sure you're all right. Are you?'

She nodded. 'It's been quite a day.'

'So we gathered,' Glad said. 'That lad was right worried.'

Jenny gave a wry smile. There he was again, concerned about her as always. It gave her a warm feeling to have someone care so much for her. If it hadn't been for Edna, Glad, Fred, Ma and Matthew, she would have been absolutely lost since she ran away from home. The coin had certainly landed as heads when she'd met these wonderful people – and she hadn't even realized it.

'You look fair worn out.' Glad picked up the tea things. 'You pop off to bed and I'll clear this up for you.'

'I want to tell you what has happened.' Jenny yawned. Fred patted her hand. 'It'll keep, Jen. You go and get some kip.'

'No, it won't, I'm bursting to tell you.' Then she explained about this extraordinary day, making Fred and Glad laugh when she told them about her confrontation with her family.

'Good for you, lass,' Fred exclaimed. 'Bloody criminal what they've done to you.'

'That's wonderful news!' Glad looked ecstatic. 'Now you won't have to work your fingers to the bone. What you gonna do now?'

'I'm staying here, Glad. Ma left me her furniture and this is my home now.'

'We're right pleased about that.' Fred beamed at her, and then became serious. 'But I think it'd be better to keep this news to ourselves. You don't want people pestering you, do you?'

'No, I need time to sort myself out before anyone knows.' Jenny yawned again.

'Off you go, up the apples and pears.' Fred hauled her out of the chair. 'You need a good night's sleep. We'll talk some more when you're rested.'

Glad kissed her on the cheek. 'We're so happy for you, Jen. It's a relief to know you're gonna be all right now.'

It was the early hours of the morning before Jenny slipped into a sleep of utter exhaustion. Her mind had been whirring like a top. What

379

should she do? Go to America or stay here? In a few short hours her life had completely changed. It was only after forcing her skittering thoughts to quieten that she had finally slept.

She was awake at her usual time of five o'clock. In the comfort of her old feather bed, she mulled over her thoughts of late last night. One thing she had learnt was to take each day as it came, and, although there would be changes to her life, she wasn't going to act in haste or do anything drastic. This was her home, and, for the moment, this is where she would stay. Christmas was only ten days away, and the New Year would be time enough to make big decisions.

The first faint glimmer of dawn began to lighten the sky from black to dark grey. Jenny stretched, then jumped out of bed, shivering as her feet hit the cold lino. She was too excited to stay in bed any longer. There was a lot to do this morning. Dwight and Matthew were coming for her at half past ten, and before that she must go to tell Bet she would need a couple of hours off. She had no intention of letting the stallholder down, as this was a busy time of the year, and Bet's husband wouldn't be fit for work until after Christmas.

Jenny washed and dressed in the kitchen, where it was warmer. As she put on her shoes, she noted what a dreadful state they were in. Not only did they have holes, but one was splitting where the upper joined the sole. While at the market today she would see if she could get a cheap pair, and perhaps even a warmer coat.

What luxury!

Before getting breakfast, she sat down and wrote a letter to Gracie, thanking her for the photographs and invitation to stay. She explained that she couldn't come at the moment, but would visit when she could.

With that done, she sang to herself and made some porridge, chuckling when she recalled Ma's comments about her first effort. But she'd got it right after a few goes and Ma had come to like it, especially on a cold morning such as this. 'Lines the stomach a treat,' she used to say.

Oh, how she wished she were still here to share in this good fortune.

Just before eight Jenny started for The Cut; she had decided that she'd be able to help Bet for a couple of hours, and then go back as soon as her visit to the bank was done with.

The car was already outside her house when she returned, and she ran towards them. 'Morning. Sorry I'm late,' she gasped, as Matthew got out and held the door open for her. 'The market was so busy. Will this take long? I promised I'd get back as soon as I could.'

'An hour or two at the most,' Dwight said from the back seat.

'Don't worry, Jen.' Matthew smiled as he got back in the car and started the engine. 'I'll drive you straight back to the market when your business is finished.'

'Thank you.' She turned to Dwight and was surprised to see Luke there as well.

'Hello, Jen, hope you don't mind my coming along. Dwight has asked me to represent him here in London and briefed me on the legal position of your inheritance. If you need any professional advice, I can help. I'll be keeping in close contact with him.'

She smiled her approval of this arrangement. 'I will appreciate your help, because there is something I want to do, but don't know how to go about it.'

'What's that?' Dwight asked.

'I want to buy the house I'm living in.'

'Good idea. That's a nice solid little place, from what I saw of it.' Dwight glanced at Luke. 'Your first job will be to look into that for Jenny.'

'I'll get on to it today. Who do you pay your rent to, Jen?'

She told him the name of the collection agency – Greenways – and watched him make notes in a small book.

A deep rumble of laughter came from Matt, and when Jenny glanced at him he winked at her. 'Only recently passed his exams, and already he's the efficient lawyer.'

They were soon at the imposing Stannard Bank in the City. Even the soot-stained façade couldn't diminish the effect of the elegant pillared entrance and marble steps. Luke didn't stay with them but dashed off, saying he had people to see.

'I'll wait in the car for you.' Matthew helped her out.

'Aren't you coming in with us?' She was rather nervous and wanted him with her. She had never had anything to do with banks before, and he was such a sensible man. It would be a comfort to have him to turn to if she was confused. 'Please stay with me.'

He nodded and looked pleased that she had asked.

They were shown into a spacious office dominated by the largest oak desk she had ever seen. John stood up as soon as they entered and pulled forward another chair when he saw that his brother was with them.

They were soon settled, and she watched in fascination as John and Dwight dealt with the business side of the transfer of funds. It was difficult to believe this was happening to her, and she sat with her hands tightly clasped in her lap, leaning forward, drinking in every word. Matthew didn't speak, and each time she glanced at him he smiled; she knew he was supporting her in his quiet way.

Finally John pushed some papers towards her and held out a pen. 'We need your signature in the places I've marked with a cross. I realize you've been using the name Jenny Baker, but the money is in the name of Eugenie Winford, and you'll need to sign in that way, please.'

She had become so used to the name she had used since she'd run away that it was strange to sign her proper name. When the four documents were signed, she put the pen down and pushed them back across the desk.

John immediately stood up and went over to her with his hand out, smiling broadly. 'Welcome to the Stannard Bank, Miss Winford. We are delighted you have chosen us, and I assure you that we shall look after your affairs diligently.'

They all laughed at the formal greeting, even

John, who perched himself on the edge of the desk. 'I expect you have questions?'

'Erm ... well, yes. How much is $25,000?'

'It will depend on the exchange rate, but it should be in excess of £7,000.'

Her mouth dropped open and she drew in a shaky breath. 'That much?'

John nodded. 'It would have been more, but in September the gold standard was abandoned and the pound devalued from $4.86 to $3.49. We've set up an account that will earn you interest as well.'

She looked at Matthew and wiggled her shoulders in delight. If she'd been standing, she would have done a little jig. It sounded exciting! After living on the bread-line she now had money of her own. He grinned, joining in her pleasure.

'What are your plans?' John asked, claiming her attention again.

'Well,' she spoke eagerly, 'I want to see if I can buy the house I'm living in. Luke is already looking into this for me.'

'You could afford something better,' Matthew pointed out gently.

'No,' she said, shaking her head, 'that's my home for the moment. I'm not going to go mad. I need time to let this sink in.'

'Very wise.' John nodded in approval. 'From what Matt has told me about the house, it should be a sound investment.'

'There is an alternative, Jen,' Dwight said. 'You know you can come back with me to New York. Gracie told me she would love to have you stay, for always if that's what you wanted.'

Jenny didn't miss Matthew's sudden movement beside her, and his sharp intake of breath. 'I can't make a decision that big at the moment, Dwight.' She dived into her pocket and took out an envelope. 'I wrote a letter to Gracie this morning; could you please deliver it for me?'

'I'll do that.' Dwight put the letter in his case. 'You would have loved Christmas in New York. The whole place is ablaze with coloured lights, with a Father Christmas on every sidewalk and in every store.'

She laughed. It was so lovely to hear him talk just like her father. 'Perhaps I'll come next year.' She turned her attention back to business and said to John, 'When will I be able to use some of the money?'

'It will take a few days, but you can have any-thing you want straight away. How much would you like?'

'Erm...' Jenny did a calculation in her head. New shoes and a coat were a necessity. Then there was a chicken for all her friends in Forest Road, so they could have a decent Christmas dinner, and she was sure Glad would help her make loads of puddings to share out. Some decorations... 'Could I have five pounds, please?'

'That isn't much.' John smiled kindly. 'Let's make it ten guineas, shall we?'

'Yes, please, if that's all right.' It sounded an awful lot to her, but she would be able to buy the children presents as well, and perhaps herself a new frock. She picked at the threadbare skirt over her knees. Yes, definitely a new frock!

John called in a cashier and she soon had ten

one pound notes and ten shillings, which she put carefully in her purse. She'd be able to do such a lot with this.

'Any time you need more, just come in and see a cashier or ask for me.' John stood up.

She did the same and shook his hand enthusiastically. She had always believed John was lacking in humour and kindness, but this wasn't true. In their own ways, all the brothers were kind.

They said goodbye to John and returned to the car. On their way to the market, Jenny twisted round to look at Dwight. 'When are you returning to New York?'

'I have a passage booked for tomorrow. I sail at three o'clock from Southampton. I shall only just make it back in time for Christmas with my family.'

'Oh, I'm sorry you can't stay longer. Would you take a present back for the boys Hal and Rob – my half-brothers?' she added proudly. 'There's a man in the market who sells wonderful hand-made toys. I'm sure we could find something there they'd like.'

'Sure thing. I'd love to have a walk round to see if I can find something cute for my wife.'

Jenny turned back, felt the money in her purse and grinned at Matthew, who winked at her.

'What else are you going to buy?' he asked.

'Shoes, coat, perhaps a frock. I can get them at the market quite cheap.'

Dwight chuckled. 'I thought you'd be dashing off to the fashionable stores.'

She gave him a horrified look. 'Certainly not!

Where would I wear such creations?'

'One smart dress might be a good idea, Jen.' Matthew concentrated on the road ahead as he spoke. 'Someone might ask you out to dinner and a show.'

'Who on earth would want to do that?'

'I would.' Matthew stopped the car near The Cut. 'Would you come out with me if I asked?'

Jenny had never been taken out by a young man before, though she had often listened to Edna telling her what fun it was. The last two years had been a struggle just to survive. Going out and enjoying herself had never been things she had thought about. But now her life was different. She smiled at him shyly. 'I'd like that – if you care to ask me, of course.'

'I'm asking. So when would you like to go?'

'Let me see ... I have so many appointments.' She placed a finger on her chin and pretended to be thinking hard, teasing him. 'I think I'm free any evening between now and Christmas.'

Matthew gave her an affectionate glance and then laughed. 'I'm glad you can fit me into your busy social life.' He got out of the car, came round and opened her door, helping her out and bowing graciously over her hand. 'As soon as I've made the arrangements, I'll call on you, Miss Winford.'

'Why, thank you, sir,' she simpered, and they both burst into gales of laughter. She felt almost drunk with happiness.

'When you two have finished fooling around,' Dwight scolded, his grin firmly in place, 'we have toys to buy.'

Jenny slipped between the two men and tucked her hands in their arms, leading them straight to the toys. 'What do you think they'd like, Dwight?'

He inspected the array of wooden toys. 'These are excellent. Something English, I think.'

'What about these?' Matt held up two London buses.

'Perfect. The boys will love those.'

'How much?' she asked Ted, the stallholder.

'Half a crown each to you, Jen.'

She handed over the five shillings, and when the toys were wrapped she gave them to Dwight. 'With my love, and tell Gracie I'll keep in touch. I won't be able to see you again before you leave, Dwight, because I can't let Bet down, but have a safe journey home. And thank you for coming all this way to see me and tell me the truth about my father's death.'

Dwight hugged her. 'It's been a pleasure to meet Cyrus's daughter at last. You're everything your father said you were – and more. I shall expect a letter every month to let me know how you're getting on.'

'I promise. Now I must get to work.' She hugged Dwight again, having become fond of him in the short time she'd known him. Then, so as not to leave him out, she gave Matthew a quick hug as well before tearing off to Beth's stall.

34

'What do you think?' Jenny twirled round to show off her new clothes to Glad and Fred.

'You look a proper picture.' Fred nodded in approval. 'Where's Matt taking you?'

'A new restaurant that opened earlier this year in Piccadilly; it's called the Monseigneur.' She fiddled nervously with the frock. It had come from the market, but looked quite good really. The material swirled easily around her legs as she moved, although it wasn't silk, of course. The dark red suited her colouring beautifully, and there was embroidery around the neck in a brighter red. Her shoes were black with a fashionable strap across the instep; Ivy had cut her hair in the latest short style; and to complete the ensemble she wore the pendant her father had given her and Ma's brooch. After two years of being so short of money, she was finding it hard to spend on what she now considered luxuries.

A car pulled up outside and Jenny grabbed her coat, also new from the market. This was black with an imitation-fur collar; she found it so warm after the threadbare one she had been wearing. 'He's here!'

'You look like an excited kid,' Glad said, laughing.

'Well, this is my first date!'

There was a knock on the door and Fred

opened it. 'Come in, Matt. She's all ready.'

Matthew took one look at Jenny and stopped dead. When he didn't speak, her spirits plummeted. Perhaps she should have bought a better frock.

'She's a pretty sight, ain't she?' Fred looked proud.

'I'll say.' Matthew recovered. 'You look beautiful, Jen. And you've had your hair cut.'

Her hand reached up and touched her shining dark hair. 'Ivy did it for me.'

'It really suits you.' He bent and kissed her cheek. 'All the other men are going to envy me tonight. Shall we go?'

She was relieved. For a moment she had thought that he wouldn't want to take her out.

'Just a minute.' Fred looked pointedly at Matt. What time you gonna be back?'

'I'll have Jen back by twelve o'clock. Will that be all right?'

Fred agreed and must have noticed Jenny's surprised expression. 'Someone's got to look out for you. You ain't got no dad to keep an eye on the young men.'

'I won't keep her out too late, sir,' Matt said politely, making everyone laugh.

'That's the first time I've ever been called sir.' Fred slapped Matthew on the back. 'Off you go, have a good time and take good care of our Jen.'

'I won't let her out of my sight.' Matthew led Jenny to the car, still smiling.

'What's this place like?' she asked, as they drove up Forest Road.

'It's a luxurious restaurant, very popular. So

390

popular in fact I had to get Dad to book a table for us. The Roy Fox Band is there, though Lew Stone is leading it because Fox is ill. But Lew Stone is very good.'

'That sounds lovely.' This was so exciting. She loved the dance bands and the beautiful music they played.

Matthew gave her a quick glance as he was driving. 'The vocalist is Al Bowlly.'

Jenny gave a squeal of delight. 'Is he really? He's got the most wonderful voice. Don't you think so?'

'Yes.' Matt chuckled at her enthusiasm. 'I had no idea you liked him so much.'

'I do, I do!' Jenny could hardly control herself.

'We'll park here and walk round the corner.' Matthew stopped the car and came round to help her out. 'It will be crowded by the restaurant.'

It was no more than a couple of minutes' walk, and Jenny found herself looking up at the name MONSEIGNEUR GRILL in large letters right across the entrance. They went in and, once her coat was taken from her, they were shown to their table. It was obvious that this was a very fashionable place, the clientele smart and well-to-do, but the affluent surroundings didn't intimidate her. This was the kind of place to which her father had taken her. It was now clear why her mother had never accompanied them on these outings. They were divorced, and her father's visits here were solely to spend time with his daughter. The pang of sadness was instantly dismissed. It was all in the past, and she was glad she now knew the whole story.

The waiter held her chair for her and she sat down. Their table was right next to the band and only a couple of steps away from the dance floor. Jenny felt her feet wanting to tap in anticipation. Edna had said that she was lucky because she could fit in with either the working classes or the wealthy. And she realized, looking at Matthew, that he was the same. He came from a wealthy family but was happy working as an apprentice mechanic. After what they had been through together, often it wasn't necessary to speak – just a look or smile was enough to know what the other was thinking. They had become very close lately.

Since receiving the money she'd had a sense of confusion. One minute she had been scrimping to find enough money for food, and the next she had money in the bank. But, as she gazed around the restaurant, the feeling melted away. Rich or poor, she was who she was, and her experiences had moulded her into a stronger, more secure person. She was a girl who knew she could survive whatever life threw at her.

'Jen.' Matthew touched her hand. 'You were miles away. What would you like to drink?'

She came out of her musing and smiled brightly. She was being rude, and this was no time for sombre thoughts; she was here to enjoy the evening and Matthew's company. 'I'd like some wine, please.'

'Not champagne?' he asked. 'I think our first proper date should be special, don't you?'

She laughed. 'I'll leave it to you. In fact, you

can even choose what we shall eat.'

He beckoned the waiter over and ordered champagne, then studied the menu.

The rest of the evening was one of pure delight: the food was excellent, the band terrific and Al Bowlly a dream. They danced the evening away. All too soon it was time to leave.

As they made their way back to the car, Jenny slipped her hand through Matthew's arm and smiled happily up at him. 'Thank you for a really lovely evening.'

He bent and kissed her nose. 'It was my pleasure. Will you come out with me again – to the pictures perhaps?'

'I'd love to, but it will have to be after Christmas. On Christmas Eve we're giving the children a party at the centre, and with only three days to go there's a lot to do.'

'I know. Mother's roped us all in to help, even Father!'

They reached the car and were soon on their way back to Lambeth. The moment they arrived, Fred opened his front door. 'Had a good time?'

'Lovely, thanks.' Matthew whispered to Jenny, 'He's checking up on me.' Then he looked at his watch under the light of the street lamp and said, 'It's five to twelve.'

Fred grinned. 'If you're going indoors with Jen, I'll expect you out sharpish – no more than five minutes.'

'Fred,' Jenny giggled, feeling quite light-headed from the champagne. 'Or should I call you Dad?'

Glad's head appeared in the doorway. 'Leave

them alone, Fred. We can trust Matt to act like a gent.'

'I was a young man myself once.' He leered at his wife. 'I knows what's going on in his head.'

Glad couldn't stop her smile spreading. 'But you was never a gent! Come inside, you daft old fool.'

'Not so much of the old, woman! Come on, I'll show you just how *old* I am.'

Matthew and Jenny doubled over with laughter as Fred and Glad disappeared from the doorway.

'Don't worry, sir,' Matthew called, 'I'll stay only five minutes, I promise.'

Fred's head appeared briefly, and he winked. 'I'll be watching. And you'd better not make it longer 'cos at this time of night you'll come out and find all your wheels gone. There's a lot of tea leafs round here.' He jerked and disappeared, after obviously having been pulled indoors again.

'What's a tea leaf?' Matthew asked.

'A thief.' Jenny opened the front door. 'Are you coming in for a minute?'

'Five minutes!' he protested. 'I've been given five minutes.'

They were laughing as Matthew closed the door behind them, but, gazing around the empty room, he became serious once again. 'I don't like the thought of you living here on your own, Jen.'

'I've been thinking about that, and if I can manage to buy this house, I'm going to ask Ivy and her family to move in. It's much too crowded next door, but Fred and Glad took them in when they got chucked out of their place by a greedy landlord. They couldn't possibly have afforded the rent he was asking.'

The frown left his face and he drew her into his arms. 'That's a great idea. I'll get Luke moving.' Then he dipped his head and kissed her very gently. 'Thanks for a lovely evening.'

Jenny was flustered by the kiss and didn't know what to say. That was the first grown-up kiss she'd had, and it had quite made her head spin. At eighteen she was a late starter at this dating lark. It was exciting, though. 'I've enjoyed myself,' she managed to say. 'Would you like a cup of tea?'

He shook his head, stepping away and glancing at his watch. 'I've had my five minutes, and if I don't leave now Fred will charge in here and throw me out!'

Jenny gurgled. 'I think he's taken on the role of my father.'

'I'm pleased he has. You are so lovely, and if some of the men around here find out you've now got money, they might start pestering you.'

He thought she was lovely! 'Fred and Glad were afraid of the same thing when I told them, so we've decided to keep it just between ourselves.'

'Very wise. Now I really must go. I'll see you at the children's party, and after Christmas we'll go out again.'

'I'd like that.'

He gave her another kiss and left. Before driving away, he stopped outside Fred's and tooted his horn to let him know he was leaving – on time.

As Matt drove home, he couldn't help smiling. Jenny was financially secure now; they'd had their first real date, which had been a great success; he was fully recovered and already back at work. The future looked good for both of them.

The next day at the market was busy, and Bet was well pleased with the takings, so she gave Jenny six shillings. Jenny didn't feel guilty about taking the money because she'd worked hard for it, and she was going to put it to good use. She ran along to the toy stall and caught Ted as he was packing up; she spent her earnings for the day on toys. Ted promised to have them wrapped and delivered to the centre in time for the party. She would do the same tomorrow and the next day until she had bought enough presents for all the children.

On arriving home, she found the three brothers waiting for her, stamping their feet trying to keep warm.

'Come in, please.' The fire was ready to light, and she put a match to it straight away. 'I'm sorry it's cold in here, but it will soon warm up.'

Matthew smiled. 'Don't worry about that, Jen. Luke and John have some business to discuss with you. I'll put the kettle on, shall I?'

'Please. I'm gasping for a cup of tea.'

Luke settled in Ma's chair. 'I've managed to track down the owner of these houses. I've had a real tussle with him, and he refused to sell.'

Jenny was disappointed and it must have shown on her face, because Luke leant forward. 'Don't worry. I could see he wasn't as disinterested as he made out, and we settled down for some hard bargaining. I pointed out that the house was badly in need of repair. I had a strong feeling that he would like to sell the whole street, but he finally began to give way when I suggested that we might be interested in two houses, and no more.'

'Two?' she gasped. 'How much is that going to cost?'

'He gave the price of £300 for your house and next door, Fred and Glad's. But that's just a starting price; we should be able to get them for less than that.'

She pushed a strand of hair away from her eyes and looked at John, who hadn't said a word up to now. 'What do you think?'

'The houses might not be in a desirable area, but they are sturdy places, and would be a sound investment.'

Jenny's mind was racing, and she dipped her head as she thought this through. She had only considered buying this house, but to own Fred and Glad's as well sounded like a wonderful idea. However, she had better be honest with John. The businessman in him would naturally think of any purchase as being an investment, but that wasn't what she was planning. It wasn't a huge amount out of her money. 'I would like to buy both houses, but I'm not thinking of this as a way to make money. I owe Fred and his family a great debt of gratitude, and I wouldn't collect rent from them.'

It was clear that John didn't agree with this, but he stifled his objections and nodded. 'That would be entirely up to you. The houses are freehold, and I suggest you make an offer of £250 and be prepared to go up to £270 or £280 at the most.'

'Do you think the owner will accept that?' she asked Luke.

'I'm sure he will. Do you want me to go ahead with the purchase?'

'Yes, please. As John thinks it's a good idea, make the offer.'

'Tea's up!' Matthew came back carrying a tray of tea and a plate of biscuits.

They sat chatting for a while about the Christmas party for the children, and then they left, leaving Jenny excited and praying that her offer would be accepted. She nibbled on a biscuit, revelling in the idea that she might soon be the owner of not one but two houses!

The noise was ear splitting as Father Christmas came in the hall with a sack over his shoulder. The children screamed and hurled themselves at him, almost knocking him off his feet.

Matthew and Luke were doubled over with laughter.

'Don't just stand there,' Jenny scolded, 'let's go and help the poor man.' She waded in until she reached the beleaguered Father Christmas. 'Get over in the corner by the presents,' she yelled above the din, 'I'll try to get this rabble into some kind of order.'

'Thanks, Jen.'

As he fought his way through the mass of children, Jenny watched in disbelief. She hadn't known who was going to be Father Christmas, but the voice was familiar. He wouldn't do this, surely? But if it was him, then she now understood Matthew and Luke's hilarity.

The two brothers joined in the task of trying to bring order, and they eventually managed to get the children sitting in front of the figure in red with an enormous white beard. Each child received a present: pink wrapping for the girls and blue for the boys. Father Christmas hammed it up with far too many ho, ho, ho's, but the kids loved it.

Jenny shook her head in amazement. 'Is that really John?'

Luke howled with glee as one scruffy little boy with the seat hanging out of his pants clambered on to John's lap and refused to move.

Matthew mopped his eyes and nodded, speechless with laughter. Everyone else – Mrs Stannard and her committee, Fred, Glad, Ivy, Ron and Stan – was in the same state. Mr Stannard had turned up as well. Jimmy and Agnes were pitching in and seemed to be enjoying themselves as much as the others.

Jenny was glad she had bought extra presents, as they had far more children than anticipated. They were all from unemployed or very poor families. No one had been turned away.

The cries of joy from the little ones as they tore open their parcels brought tears to Jenny's eyes. This was probably the only present they would get.

'Just wait until they see all that food,' Luke gurgled. 'My God, there will be jelly everywhere.'

'We've got plenty of helpers.' Matthew slipped his arm around Jenny's shoulder and smiled down at her. 'Have you told Fred and his family about the houses yet?'

'No. Now that our offer has been accepted, I'm going to talk to them after dinner tomorrow.' She was bursting to tell them but had waited until it had all been settled. They'd had to go up to £280. That had been accepted, and the deposit paid. Luke would deal with the paperwork in the New Year.

'Children!' Louise Stannard clapped her hands. 'I want you all to make an orderly queue. Tea is waiting for you in the hall.'

That was asking the impossible, and there was a stampede for the food. Toys were clutched firmly in one hand, with the other used to demolish the sandwiches, cakes, jellies and biscuits.

All the helpers were fully occupied, and at one point Jenny dragged a small boy off the floor as he tried to suck up some jelly that had fallen. She spooned some more in his dish and was rewarded with a brilliant smile, minus two front teeth.

By the time the parents collected their children, each was stuffed full of food and was hugging the precious toy and a bag containing an apple, orange and a few sweets. In the eerie quiet after they had gone, the exhausted helpers gulped strong cups of tea. No one spoke, but every so often someone chuckled as they remembered the party. It had been a joyous time.

Christmas Day was special. Jenny had made sure that each family in the street with the man un-employed had a proper meal. Gifts of a chicken, pudding and vegetables were made by Fred and said to come from an anonymous friend. Everyone had assumed the food came from the centre, and it had been accepted with much gratitude.

Jenny's house was crowded with Fred, Glad and their family. The place rang with laughter as the children opened their presents, and as a special treat Jenny had bought a turkey. There had been a moment of panic when she had thought it might not fit in the small oven, but it had – just. The gorgeous smell of good food cooking made their mouths water.

There were murmurs of approval as they tucked in, savouring each mouthful of the wonderful feast. Jenny waited until they were all sprawled out, replete after the huge meal, before telling them her news.

She began cautiously. These were proud independent people and she didn't want to offend them. 'Have you managed to find anywhere to live yet, Ivy?'

'Afraid not. We've been trying to find something close to Mum and Dad, but the rents is too steep.'

'Why don't you, Ron and the children move in here with me?'

Ivy's mouth dropped open and she sat up straight. 'Would you mind? How much rent? Oh, but you'd have to ask the landlord first.'

Jenny grinned. 'I am the landlord, and the rent is nothing.'

Pandemonium broke out as everyone began to ask questions at the same time.

'You've bought this house, Jen?' Fred was astonished.

She nodded. 'And your house as well. From the 15th of January your rent will also be nothing.'

'Jen!' Glad exploded. 'That's too generous; you must take rent from us.'

'Why?' Jenny went and knelt on the floor in front of Fred and Glad. 'That night you took me in I vowed that if ever the time came when I could repay you, then I would. That time has come. Please let me do this for you.'

There was silence as they digested this staggering turn of events.

It was broken by Stan. 'Good Lord. Does that mean I'll be able to sleep in a bed instead of on the settee?'

Glad squeezed Fred's hand and gave a slight nod of her head. Ivy was mopping up her tears.

'Do you agree?' Jenny prompted.

The entire family nodded, too overcome to speak.

'Good.' Jenny rose to her feet and opened the sideboard. It was full of bottles of whisky and beer. 'Let's drink to our good fortune, shall we?'

Ron and Stan poured the drinks and handed the glasses round, not forgetting the children, who had a glass of lemonade each. They were too interested in their toys to take much notice of the grown-ups.

Fred raised his glass. 'I always said you was special, Jen. The day we met that frightened child on her way to a pawnbroker's was the luckiest day of our lives. I think 1932 will be an easier year for all of us – and all because of you.'

And you deserve it, Jenny thought. It is only a small payment for your kindness to me.

35

'Can I ask Jenny to our New Year dinner?' Matt said, as he watched his mother working on the seating plan.

'Of course, Matt. That would be lovely.'

'And can I ask Emma Holdsworth?' John asked.

'Indeed you can, John.' His father nodded approval. 'Charming girl. So that's who you've been seeing on the quiet.'

Louise gazed at each of her sons in turn, and then settled on Luke. 'And have you found a girlfriend you would like to bring?'

'Not me,' he laughed.

'Ah, well.' She looked down at her pad, a smile hovering on her lips. 'That will leave you free to deal with Gloria Tremain.'

There was a collective groan from the brothers.

'Do you think Jenny will come if Gloria's here?' Louise looked doubtful. 'She knows her, doesn't she?'

'It won't bother her,' Matt said confidently. 'She was only frightened of meeting her when she was hiding her identity. That doesn't matter now.'

'I'm so pleased everything has worked out well for her at last.' Their father poured himself a brandy. 'Fine girl – great courage and good sense.'

Matt relaxed, satisfied. It was clear he had his parents' approval; now all he had to do was convince Jen that he was the man for her.

'I don't know, Ivy.' Jenny pulled a face. She was wearing the same red dress. Things had been so hectic since Christmas Day, with Ivy and her family moving in, that she hadn't thought to buy a better dress for the Stannards' New Year celebration.

'You look smashing, Jen. That's a real pretty frock and Matt likes it.'

'Yes, he does.' Jenny told herself to stop fussing; she looked perfectly respectable. She still wasn't used to having money again, but it wouldn't take too long, she thought wryly. She was already beginning to cast a critical eye over the quality of her clothes, and that was something she hadn't done for a long time. It was only because of Matt, though. She wouldn't want to let him down in company.

Ivy scooped up little Bert as he tottered up to Jenny. 'No sticky fingers on Auntie Jen's frock,' she scolded gently. 'She's going to a posh do, as a guest this time instead of a servant.'

'What a turn around.' Jenny couldn't stop smiling. 'I must write and tell Edna all about it. She'll curl up with laughing.'

'Will it seem strange to you?' Ivy asked.

'Probably, but as long as I don't start clearing away the dishes, I should be all right.'

They were both giggling at the thought when Matthew arrived.

'You look lovely, Jen.' He walked in smiling. 'That colour suits you so well.'

Ivy winked at Jenny as they left.

'Eugenie,' Gloria Tremain exclaimed when they arrived at the house. 'Where have you been hiding?'

Jenny had never liked Gloria at school, as she had a sharp tongue and thought herself better than anyone else. Smiling sweetly, she said, 'Somewhere I couldn't be found.'

Gloria's gaze swept over her in derision. 'Your dress is ... unusual.'

'I think Jen looks beautiful,' Matt said stoutly.

That produced a trill of amused laughter as Gloria touched his arm. 'Oh, Matthew, you are funny. You said that as if you meant it. Still, I expect you find it such fun to bring a market girl to the party. Don't you, darling?'

He shook her hand free and turned his back on the taunting girl. 'Ignore her, Jen. Come and meet John's girlfriend, Emma; you'll like her.'

She did like Emma and was pleased to see John standing proudly beside her. He was the most serious of the brothers, but she had been privileged to see the softer side of him when he'd acted as Father Christmas. He was a man you could rely on, and the pretty blonde girl beside him seemed just the person to give him the loving support he needed.

When they went in to dinner, Green gave Jenny a sly wink, causing an amused rumble of laughter to come from Matt.

'You must go down and see them later,' Matt whispered in her ear when they were seated.

'Oh, I shall. Do you think Gloria would like to wish the servants a happy New Year?' she asked, and they both dissolved into laughter at the thought of the snooty girl talking to the hired help.

The meal was wonderful and she enjoyed each dish, admiring the smooth way the meal was presented, knowing the frantic activity there would be downstairs. The conversation was lively and she joined in quite naturally, easily slipping back to the social training she had received at the Templeton School. Gloria Tremain kept giving her withering looks from the other end of the table, but Jenny was enjoying herself far too much to let that bother her.

After dinner they gathered in the large drawing room to welcome in the New Year. On the stroke of twelve Jenny received a kiss from each of the Stannards, even Matt's father. It was done with such genuine warmth that she knew they liked and accepted her. Once she had said to Edna that there was no way back to the life she had known, but thanks to her father's love and concern for her future, the last two years had been only a slight pause. It had been a finishing school of life, and the best education she could have received.

At just past twelve she and Matt went downstairs, and they spent a lively half hour with the staff before he took her home.

A party was in full swing at Glad and Fred's when they arrived, so they were dragged in; it was three in the morning before Jenny crawled into bed, tired but so happy. Matt had given her a long, lingering kiss tonight, and her heart was still skipping.

'Happy New Year, Matt.' Jake slapped him on the

back and then handed him a cheque.

'What's this?' he asked, puzzled.

'That's the money you lent me plus interest.'

He gazed at his boss in astonishment. 'Can you afford to do this now?'

'I certainly can.' Jake grinned in delight. 'Once again the business is doing nicely, and it's all thanks to you and Luke. You were both prepared to risk your money to keep us going, and your confidence has turned things around very quickly.'

'This is wonderful news!' Matt had realized they were doing well, but not this well. 'Thanks, Jake. If you ever need help in the future, you come straight to me.'

'I will, lad, and I'm grateful for your brilliant idea about selling second-hand cars. Without that, I would have gone bankrupt for sure.'

'I couldn't have let that happen,' Matt said with a shake of his head. 'I would never have been able to finish my apprenticeship.'

Jake threw his head back and laughed. 'Well, you'd better get back to work because you've still got a way to go yet.'

'Yes, boss.' Matt grinned, tucked the cheque into his top pocket and went back to the work-shop, a spanner already in his eager hands. He knew just what he was going to do with the money: buy a house for himself and Jen, because he intended to marry her before the year was out.

The daily need for Jenny to earn enough money for the rent and food had gone, and it was a liberating thought. Bet's husband had hobbled back to work, so she could now choose what she wanted to do, and decided that it would be good to help out at the centre for a while. The local people had come to rely on it, and word had spread, bringing others who were walking as far as five miles to get a hot meal. Poor devils! And there seemed no end to the depression.

Louise Stannard was already in the kitchen when Jenny arrived. She smiled. 'You're up early.'

'Habit, I'm afraid. I wondered if there was anything I could do to help here.'

'That would be most welcome. There's a sack of potatoes for peeling.'

Jenny removed her coat and set to work. 'Ron and Jimmy told me that some men and women are walking miles to get here.'

'They are, and what worries us is that they might have young children who can't walk this far. I've seen some of them eat a couple of mouthfuls and then slip the rest of the meal into a bag to take away with them. We make sure their plates are filled again.'

'Why don't we make pies that they can take home and heat up for the children?' Jenny stopped peeling the potatoes and frowned. 'The trouble is, we could be besieged and wouldn't know if the food was going where it was most needed.'

'The committee have already considered something like that, but it would be undignified for people to have to show proof of their need.'

'Where is the dignity in starvation, Mrs Stannard?'

At that stark question, Louise sat down and bowed her head. 'Ah, you would know all about that, wouldn't you, my dear?' Then she looked up, a determined glint in her eyes. 'Let's try it! The only question they need to answer is how far they have walked to get here.'

'Is there enough money for such a scheme?' Jenny wanted to know.

'We'll find the money!'

'I'd be happy to make a donation.'

'No, that won't be necessary.' Louise gave a small laugh. 'Many of our acquaintances have deep pockets, and I'm sure the committee can prise some more out of them.'

Ron, Ivy and Jimmy arrived then, followed immediately by two more of the committee. The idea was discussed and agreed on. Everyone went to work to provide the extra food.

By the end of the day Jenny was delighted with the way things had gone. The gratitude in people's eyes was reward enough.

36

Spring! Jenny walked along the dingy narrow street of terraced houses. Everything looked grey – bricks, road, pavements and even the sky – yet she was smiling with happiness. There wasn't a splash of green anywhere, but she could picture the oak-lined drive leading to the Templeton School, the young leaves on the trees bursting out of sticky buds and shimmering in a light breeze. She took a deep breath and could almost smell the carpet of bluebells clustered underneath outstretched branches, and yellow primroses dotted here and there in the bright green grass.

She sighed. It had been a beautiful sight and something she had looked forward to each year – the eagerness of new growth. Perhaps she would make time today to wander through one of London's parks and enjoy the exhilaration of life bursting forth. Glancing up, she saw a small patch of blue sky. Yes, that's what she would do.

Jenny hummed a tune as she practically danced up Forest Road. Since Christmas she had gone out with Matt at least twice a week, and had Sunday lunch with his family now and again. And last night he had told her that he loved her! She loved him too and was bursting with happiness.

'So this is where you've been hiding yourself. What a disgusting place!'

Jenny stopped in mid stride and looked into the scornful eyes of Gloria Tremain. What on earth was she doing here?

'No wonder Matthew laughs about the hovel you live in. He's told me so much about it, I thought I'd better see for myself. What a laugh we had about the evening he took you to the Monseigneur and you went into raptures about that singer, Al Bowlly.'

Jenny was stunned. What was Matt doing talking to Gloria about her? He couldn't stand the girl.

'You poor fool,' Gloria sneered. 'Couldn't you see he was only amusing himself with you? He's

410

going to marry me – and soon.' She pulled her coat open. 'See, I'm pregnant and Matthew is the father.'

Jenny stared at the slight bulge in Gloria's stomach and felt all the air leave her lungs. She tried to breathe, only managing to take in small gulps of air. The hated girl's harsh laugh cut through her confusion, and she stood straight, head up. 'You're lying!'

'Do you really think Matthew would be satisfied with you? He's a passionate man and needs a *real* woman.'

Jenny couldn't ever remember hurting like this. The pain was almost making her cry out. But she wouldn't give Gloria that satisfaction!

'I know he's been playing around with you, but, knowing we were going to be married soon, I let him have his fun.'

Fun!

'But that's all over now. Go back to your slum friends and leave him alone.' Then, with a look of triumph on her face, she walked to her car, which was parked on the other side of the road.

As Gloria drove away, Jenny couldn't move. She had lost all control over her legs. In a few short minutes she had plunged from joy to despair. Matthew – the love of her life – had deceived her. Gloria had been far too confident for it not to be true, and he must have told her about their date at the restaurant. She also remembered Gloria calling him 'darling' at the Stannards' party. She hadn't thought anything of it at the time, but now…

Somehow she must have turned round and

gone back home, because she found herself standing in the front room, staring down at Ma's chair. She collapsed on to it and wrapped her arms around herself, too shocked to cry.

She sat like that for some time, and slowly anger replaced the pain. Far too many people had deceived her – her mother, aunt and Greaves – but Matt's cruelty was the hardest to bear. The only people who had been completely honest with her were Fred and his family, and she had counted Matt amongst them.

Laying her head back on the chair, she closed her eyes. She was stunned. She couldn't think straight; couldn't tell fact from fiction. She would confront Matt as soon as she could, but in the meantime she had to think about herself.

'There's nothing here for me now, Ma,' she murmured. 'I'll go to America and see what it's like. I couldn't bear the pain of knowing that he was married to someone else. I made a new life for myself once, and I'm sure I can do it again if I have to.'

Never being one to waste time when her mind was made up, Jenny hauled herself out of the chair, went to the kitchen and splashed water on her face; then she picked up her bag and left the house, not fully aware of what she was doing or where she was going. The feeling driving her was the same as the one she'd had when her father had died. The need to do something!

She arrived at the bank and strode in. 'My name is Eugenie Winford,' she declared as soon as she arrived, 'and I would like to see Mr John Stannard, please.'

The teller had been gone only a minute when John appeared, smiling. 'Hello, Jenny. Please come into my office.'

When they were both seated, he asked, 'What can I do for you?'

'I want enough money to buy a ticket to New York.'

'Ah, going to visit your father's family.' John nodded. 'They will be pleased to see you.'

'Yes, and I might stay there if I like it.'

John looked up sharply in astonishment. 'You mean you might not come back?'

'That's right. If I do decide to stay, I'll ask you to transfer my money.'

'I don't understand.' John sat back and studied her intently. 'My brother Matt is going to be upset. What's happened?'

'I don't think your brother will be at all upset, because I have just been told that he has found someone else and they are to be married soon.' She got to her feet, not wishing to discuss the painful subject any more. 'Will you instruct the young man at the desk to give me one hundred pounds? I think that should suffice for the moment.'

'Just a minute, Jenny.' John came from behind the desk and barred her way to the door. 'This is absolute nonsense. Who is the person Matt is supposed to be marrying?'

'You must ask him that. I intend to demand an explanation when I see him!' Not giving him the chance to ask more questions, Jenny pushed past him and waited at the counter for her money.

John joined her and counted out the money

himself. She put it in her purse, thanked him politely and left.

On arriving home, not being able to sit still, she began to pack her battered old suitcase with her few belongings. She needed to get away, give herself time and space to think clearly. She had fallen headlong in love with Matt, believing he was perfect. That had been foolish; everyone had their faults, including her. She knew she was acting rashly, but it hurt so much.

'What are you doing, Jen?' Ivy was standing in the doorway, watching her.

'I'm leaving for America tomorrow. I'm going to Southampton and I'll get the first ship going to New York.' She continued to stuff things into her case.

'Tell me what's happened,' Ivy pleaded. 'You were so happy this morning and never said a word about going away.'

Jenny stopped what she was doing and gulped, looking at Ivy with tortured eyes. Finally the tears came, in great wrenching sobs.

'Oh, no.' Ivy put her arm around Jenny. 'Don't leave like this. Whatever's wrong, we can sort it out between us.'

'I can't stay – I just can't!' She sobbed on Ivy's shoulder. 'I love him so much.'

'What's going on?' Glad came in, carrying little Bert.

'I'm so glad you're here, Mum.' Ivy made Jenny sit on the bed, and then went to her mother, whispering urgently.

Jenny didn't care what they were saying; she was so unhappy and tired. She stretched out on the bed and was instantly asleep.

'I wanna see Matt. It's urgent like.'

On hearing Fred's voice, Matt stood up so suddenly he hit his head on the open bonnet of the car he was working on. 'Ouch!' Wiping the grease from his hands, he went over to Fred, worried about the grim expression on his face. 'What's happened, Fred?'

'We don't rightly know.' He glared at Matt. 'Our Jen's breaking her heart and it seems to be about you. If you've hurt her, I'm gonna break your bloody neck!'

'I haven't done anything to upset her.'

'Then why's she going to America tomorrow?'

'What! She can't do that.' Matt couldn't understand this. They had been getting on so well and even declared their love for each other. Now he was really alarmed.

'Don't you say what she can or can't do!' Fred was shouting now. 'She's got her case packed already.'

'And she's withdrawn enough money for her fare and expenses.' John strode into the workshop. 'She told me some ludicrous tale about you having found someone else and would be marrying her soon. What have you been up to, Matt?'

'Nothing. Oh, God, what's going on?'

Jake came over. 'You'd better go and find out, lad.'

Matt didn't bother to change out of his overalls, but instantly hurtled towards his car, calling over his shoulder, 'Are you coming, Fred?'

Lambeth was reached at breakneck speed and

Matt screeched to a halt outside Jenny's house, disgorging a white-faced Fred.

The front door was shut and Matt hammered on it. 'Open the bloody door, Jen.'

Glad opened it and glowered at him. 'You ain't coming in here in that temper.'

Realizing this wasn't the way to deal with the crisis, he stepped back and took a deep breath to calm his racing heart. Then he said softly, 'Sorry, Glad. I don't know what this is all about, but I must see her.'

'She's upstairs.' Glad moved aside, allowing Matt and Fred to come in. 'But you ain't seeing her on your own.'

'All right. Just as long as I can talk to her.' He ran up the stairs, taking them three at a time, with Fred and Glad right behind him.

The commotion had woken Jenny up, and when he saw her sitting up looking confused, her face tear stained, it tore him apart. He sat on the bed and tried to take her hand in his, but she pulled away. 'What have I done, my darling? Please tell me.'

She stared at him for a few moments, as if she were looking at a stranger. 'You've got some explaining to do. Your future wife paid me a visit this morning.'

'My what?' Matt jumped to his feet, his face like thunder. John had said something about this.

'The girl you're going to marry soon – the one who is expecting your child.'

'What?' This was unbelievable. Where had this ridiculous tale come from?

'Is that the only word you know?' Jenny ex-

416

ploded. 'She said you were going to marry her because she was having your baby. I want to know if it's true!'

'You're talking rubbish, Jen.' Matt ran a hand through his hair in agitation. If he didn't sort this out quickly, he would lose Jenny – if he hadn't already. 'The only girl I want to marry is you, and I certainly haven't made you pregnant!'

'You better hadn't, mate.' Fred stepped forward threateningly and Glad pulled him back.

Jenny shuffled to the edge of the bed and frowned. 'Why would she tell me such things if they weren't true? And she was definitely pregnant.'

'She? She?' Matt raged. 'Who the hell is she?'

'Gloria Tremain.'

There was silence as this penetrated Matt's mind; then he erupted. 'That bloody woman! I'll kill her. It's a pack of lies, Jen. I swear she's trying to make trouble between us. I've rejected her and she's obviously trying to get her own back by breaking us up. If she is pregnant, it's nothing to do with me. I've never touched her – or wanted to.'

'But if that's true–'

'It is!' Matt gazed at Jenny's strained, unhappy face, and felt his future with her slipping away. She had been told so many lies in the last two years that it must be hard for her to know what was the truth. He grabbed her hand and pulled her off the bed. 'Come on, we're going to sort this out right now.'

She tried to pull away.

'You believed Gloria, so you're accusing me of

417

playing games with your affections. Well, I'm not going to have my integrity questioned in this way. We're going to face her together, and if you still want to go to America then, I'll put you on the boat myself.'

He pushed Fred out of the way and started down the stairs, making Jenny go before him.

The Tremains lived in Kensington and in a house not nearly as grand as Jenny had imagined from the girl's airs and graces. She now had grave doubts that Gloria had been telling the truth, which made her even unhappier. Matt wasn't going to stand for this – she had lost him for sure. He was furious, and if he had been going to marry Gloria, then he would just have shrugged it off and walked away. But that would have been very callous, which didn't fit with his character at all. She should have faced him before deciding to run away again. But she had acted in panic because it had hurt so much.

'Matthew–'

'Don't, Jen!' Matt was grim-faced as he led her to the front door. 'Let's get this cleared up; then we'll talk.'

Mrs Tremain opened the door. 'Hello, Matthew.'

'We've come to see Gloria. Is she in?' Matt gripped Jenny's hand tightly, making sure she didn't run away.

'Yes, she is. Please come in.'

Gloria and her father were in the sitting room reading when they came in. She looked up and a moment of uncertainty flashed in her eyes – then it was gone.

Matt stood in front of her, furious and still holding tightly to Jenny's hand. 'That was a nasty trick you played on Jen.'

'Who is Jen?'

'You know who I'm talking about, Gloria. Now we will have the truth. Are you and I engaged to be married?'

Gloria gave her parents a nervous glance, then shook her head.

'Say it,' Matt demanded.

'No, we are not!'

'And am I the father of the child you are expecting?'

Jenny flinched when she saw the colour drain from Gloria's face, and the alarm of Mr and Mrs Tremain. Oh, Lord, she thought, they don't know. Their daughter must have been hiding this from them.

'What is this nonsense?' Gloria's father asked Matt.

'Ask your daughter, sir.' Matt faced the parents. 'Gloria has been trying to make trouble by telling Jen a pack of lies. I'm sorry to upset you, but I want the truth – and now!'

Mr Tremain nodded and glared at his daughter. 'I don't know what you've been up to, my girl, but you will answer Matthew.'

Gloria stood up and lifted her head defiantly. 'I am not engaged to him, but I am pregnant. He is not the father, though.'

Jenny sagged in relief and cursed herself for being so gullible.

Gloria rounded on Matt, now out of control and shouting. 'What do you want with her? Look at her, in her shabby clothes. How can you prefer her to me?'

'Gloria!' Her father caught her arm. 'Sit down. If you really are with child, then you must marry the man who is responsible.'

'I can't!' She sat as ordered and folded her arms. 'He's already married.'

Mrs Tremain was crying quietly as her husband turned to Matt and Jenny. 'I can only apologize for our daughter's conduct. We will deal with her.'

Matt nodded grimly. 'I'm sorry you've had to find out like this, but I couldn't let Jen be upset by Gloria's lies.'

Without saying another word they left the house. Jenny couldn't help but feel sorry for the parents. They now had a great problem on their hands. And so did she. Matt wouldn't want anything else to do with a girl who had believed such malicious lies about him.

What a damned fool she was!

37

Matt didn't take Jenny home; instead he headed for his own house in Mayfair. She didn't argue or speak, because she was feeling too ashamed of herself for having doubted him. And she had probably done irreparable damage to their relationship. She couldn't blame him if he wanted to find somewhere private to have this out with her.

Once inside, he led her up to the library and, finding it empty, took her in. He closed the door behind him, leant against it and folded his arms across his chest, His gaze raked over Jenny, who was standing silently in the middle of the room. The silence was unnerving, and she wished he would get this over with so she could go home and wallow in the misery of losing him. She had no one to blame but herself. How could she have been so foolish as to have allowed a seed of doubt to be planted in her mind? Why hadn't she waited until she had seen him, before rushing off with the mad idea to go to America?

When he did speak, his words startled her.

'Don't go to America, Jen.'

'But, but...' she stammered, trying to gather her thoughts. This was a time to be honest. 'Without you there's nothing here for me.'

'Do you love me, then?'

'Of course I do!' She was getting rattled now, and in no mood to let him torture her like this. He only had to say they were finished, and she would walk out of here and out of his life. It would be agony, but she wouldn't make a nuisance of herself if he no longer wanted to see her. Closing the distance between them in three steps, she looked up at his face. 'I love you so much that Gloria's lies tore me apart. I didn't know what I was doing! My heart was telling me it wasn't true, but my mind reasoned that Gloria had nothing to gain by deception.'

A single tear trickled down her cheek and she swiped it away. 'It hurt so badly that I just had to do something. I hardly remember going to the bank and asking John for money...' She ground to a halt. 'Say something, damn you!'

'I love you.' Ignoring her startled gasp, he reached out and drew her into his arms.

The tears came in earnest as she snuggled against him. 'How can you say that after I doubted you?'

'Jen.' He kissed her nose and smoothed his hand over her hair in a gentle movement. 'I admit that at first I was dreadfully upset that you should believe those lies about me. I'm sure Gloria was very convincing, but I never told her anything about us. I didn't make a secret of it, so all my family knew I'd taken you to the Monseigneur Grill. My parents might have mentioned it to Gloria's family, and she found out that way. You've been hurt so much, and your doubt is understandable.'

'I wish I understood.' She sniffed and gazed up at him, hardly daring to believe this was happening. 'But you were so angry.'

'Not at you. I was damned if I was going to let Gloria destroy what we have.'

'I don't deserve you,' she murmured.

'Well, I'm afraid you are stuck with me for the rest of our lives. Will you marry me, my darling?'

'Yes, please!' She sighed as his lips claimed hers. When he finally broke off the embrace, he held her away, looking into her eyes. 'Come on, let's go and tell the family.'

Jenny was nervous. Suppose they didn't approve of their youngest son marrying her?

But she need not have worried. They were all delighted.

When all the excitement had settled, Louise Stannard picked up a pad and pen, looking expectantly at Jenny. 'Now, what kind of wedding do you want?'

Matt laughed and sat beside Jenny, holding her hand. 'We're being organized, Jen. Tell mother exactly what you want and she'll be in her element arranging it.'

'Would you mind doing it?' she asked his mother. 'Only I don't want my family involved.'

'I understand that, my dear, and I shall love planning the wedding.'

'Well...' She hesitated and looked at Matt, wondering what he would like.

He squeezed her hand. 'Go ahead, Jen. Whatever you want will be fine with me.'

After smiling her thanks, she turned back to his mother. 'I would like a quiet wedding with only the immediate family present at the ceremony. I'll ask Fred to give me away, as he's been like a father to me.'

'Excellent idea.' Louise began to make the first notes. 'A white dress, of course. And what about bridesmaids?'

'I'll ask Ivy's young daughter.' Jenny smiled happily. 'Oh, she'll just love that! And I'll ask Edna and David to come as well. I'm sure my friend would love to be a bridesmaid, and we'll dress them in pink, I think.'

'Lovely' Louise scribbled away. 'Where shall we hold the reception?'

'What about the community centre?' Matt suggested. 'We can then invite all of Forest Road and everyone from the garage.'

'That's just the thing,' Matt's father agreed. 'Plenty of room there, and you can get in caterers for the wedding breakfast, my dear.'

Louise nodded. 'I know the very people.'

Jenny felt a pang of concern. 'Can we have plain, wholesome food, Mrs Stannard? My friends aren't used to haute cuisine. But you know that by working at the centre, don't you?'

'I do indeed, and I shall make sure that there is something for everyone.'

'Erm...' Jenny still had one doubt. 'Will you want a separate celebration, for your family and friends?'

'Certainly not!' John declared, and the rest of the family firmly agreed.

'That's all settled, then.' Gilbert had ordered champagne while they had been talking, and he now handed round glasses. 'Let's drink to Jenny and Matt. May you have a long and happy life together.'

After the toast, Louise looked at her list. 'This will take a while to arrange. When do you intend to get married?'

Matt looked at Jenny and raised his eyebrows. 'We hadn't got around to that. What do you think, Jen?'

'What about my birthday in August? Will that give you enough time?'

'Yes, four months should be plenty.' Louise pursed her lips as she studied her son. 'Where are you going to live, Matt?'

'I thought we'd look for a house somewhere near the river. Perhaps Barnes or in that area.'

'Sounds good.' John drained his glass and, ever

424

practical, said, 'You'd better get moving with that, Matt. It might take a while to find something suitable.'

The next three months were hectic for Jenny and Matt, as they searched for a house. They eventually found a lovely four-bedroom house near Kew with a long garden leading straight to the river. It was in good order, and they fell in love with it immediately. Then they worked every spare moment to get it ready and furnished in time for their wedding. Matt was taking Jenny to America for the honeymoon, so she could meet her father's wife and boys. It was a trip she was looking forward to, and Gracie had written saying that they were all very excited about the visit. They would go to the top of the Empire State Building together. It would be a wonderful adventure, and all the more enjoyable because she would have Matt with her.

Finally the big day arrived. Jenny's dress was exquisite: flowing lace, with a filmy veil held in place with a circlet of white roses. She wore the pendant her father had given her and Ma's brooch in memory of them. She wished they could have been here for this happy occasion, but they had been included in her thoughts. Her bouquet was of white and pink roses. As the wedding was starting from the Stannards' house in Bruton Street, they had settled on St George's Church. Alice and Edna looked very pretty in their long pink dresses. Alice was so excited she could hardly keep still, but Edna kept a sharp eye on her, and the little girl quietened down when they reached the church, taking her duties very seriously.

'Here we go, Jen.' Fred looked as if he were about to burst with pride as he led her towards the altar.

The smile Matt gave her when she reached him was enough to bring tears to her eyes with happiness.

'You look breathtaking, my darling,' he whispered.

The ceremony was over far too soon for Jenny, but it had been really lovely. The small party then headed for the community centre at Lambeth, which was already packed with family and friends all awaiting the arrival of the bride and groom.

The reception was a resounding success, with everyone joining in together and having a thoroughly good time.

'Ah, this is a grand do,' Fred declared. 'Matt's family and friends aren't stuck up, are they? They likes a drink as much as us.'

Jenny agreed as she gathered together Fred, Glad, Ron and Ivy. She had a special gift for them and hoped they would accept without too much fuss. 'I want to give you the houses you're living in.' She handed over envelopes with the deeds to the two houses. 'This is with my love and gratitude for all you've done for me.'

They were stunned for a moment, and then Fred glanced around for Matt. 'Hey, lad, come here. Do you know what your wife's doing?'

'I do, and I agree with her decision.'

Jenny and Matt were enveloped in hugs, with

426

Glad staring in disbelief at the documents. 'Oh, my Gawd, we're property owners!'

That called for more drinks all round, and Jenny was so happy she had been able to do this for them.

An hour later Matt and Jenny managed to leave the party, which looked as if it was going to continue for many hours to come. They were going to their own house for the night and then catching a liner to New York the next day.

There was one more thing to do, and, still clutching her bouquet, they drove to the churchyard where Ma had been buried. There she placed the roses on the grave, and stood in silence for a moment remembering the woman she had loved so much. She could almost hear her infectious laugh as she said, 'Tall dark and 'andsome. Told you so!'

As Jenny turned away, walking arm in arm with her husband, she had a clear picture of a coin. But it was no longer spinning – it had settled, heads at last.

The publishers hope that this book has given you enjoyable reading. Large Print Books are especially designed to be as easy to see and hold as possible. If you wish a complete list of our books please ask at your local library or write directly to:

Magna Large Print Books
Magna House, Long Preston,
Skipton, North Yorkshire.
BD23 4ND

This Large Print Book for the partially
sighted, who cannot read normal print, is
published under the auspices of

THE ULVERSCROFT FOUNDATION